In praise of Susan Emshw

Susan Emshwiller's *Thar She* .... a whale watching trip on its head. This quirky dry-witted account of one woman's search for her son swallowed by a whale, blossoms into a search for herself. The story's descriptive details struck that sweet spot of believability that readers will never doubt the possibility of life inside a whale. Funny, tender, and uplifting, this journey of discovery is a nonstop, cover-to-cover read, flipping one page after the other hoping, cheering, and breathlessly wondering about the final outcome for mother and son in this suspenseful tale of rescue.

ANNE ANTHONY, author of
A Blue Moon & Other Murmurs of the Heart

If you are holding this book in your hand, congratulations. If you have chosen to buy this book, chosen from all the books you could have chosen to buy, HUGE CONGRATULATIONS. You are in for a wild and heartfelt ride. What can I say about Susan Emshwiller's writing, except that there is no one like her. She is truly an original.

NANCY PEACOCK, Piedmont Laureate, author of
The Life and Times of Persimmon Wilson

Susan Emshwiller wears all her hats in this remarkable and satisfying novel. A page-turner adventure, well-researched and exciting, *Thar She Blows* is equally as strong for its human drama of a mother and son searching for each other and also themselves. Characters so genuine, flawed, funny and true, they win you over to this improbable premise from the first pages. Enjoy the ride!

GREGG CUSICK, author of
My Father Moves Through Time Like a Dirigible

Remember when you used to get lost in a book, and forget to stop to eat? THAR SHE BLOWS is that book. Susan Emshwiller has crafted a romp of a tale about Ann, a woman defined by the color beige, and her 19-year-old, screen-addicted son Brian. When Brian is swallowed by a whale, Ann escapes both her suburban home and her senses in a valiant and delightful journey to rescue him. Make your meals in advance, because once you start reading THAR SHE BLOWS, you're going to want to keep going straight to the end!

MIMI HERMAN, Piedmont Laureate, author of
The Kudzu Queen

THAR SHE BLOWS

Also by Susan Emshwiller

Dominoes - a play
(Dramatists Play Service)

Defrosting Popsicles - a play
(Playscripts)

THAR SHE BLOWS

a novel by
Susan Emshwiller

PINEHEAD PRESS

Thar She Blows
© 2023 by Susan Emshwiller
Santa Fe, NM

www.susanemshwiller.com

PINEHEAD PRESS
www.pineheadpress.com
ISBN-13: 978-0-9894236-3-2 (paperback)
ISBN-13: 978-0-9894236-8-7 (ePub)
Library of Congress Control Number: 2023903648

Cover design and interior illustrations
© 2023 by Susan Emshwiller

Cover images used under license from Shutterstock.com.

Author photo by Chris Coulson

for Chris,
who keeps me laughing

THAR SHE BLOWS

— BRIAN'S LATE —

SIX O'CLOCK. *Fine.*

You had your chance, Brian. Now I'm mad. But hell, never mind ol' Mom. Take a few more hours. Catch a movie, hang with your low-life friends, play computer games, do whatever.

I won't call. I'm not going to check up on you. *You* need to call *me.*

I stare at the phone. The phone stares back.

Now what?

I'll do a load of laundry. Collect the beige towels from the upstairs bathroom.

Pass Brian's room. Maybe he has something that needs washing.

The doorknob is slimy and his room is dark. I flick the switch but no lights go on. Great. My son the handyman. Can't even change a bulb. Try the mini blinds. The rod to turn them is gone. The string to pull—cut. You don't want any light in here? What don't you want to see, Brian?

Tap the computer keyboard. The screen lights up on the figure of a grotesque, muscle-bound cartoon man. Must be my son's avatar or whatever they call that. I turn away, trying not to judge. I guess Brian'd rather be a superhero than what he is—a schlubby, overweight nineteen-year-old boy with pasty skin from living in this darkness.

Lit by the computer screen, the room is a mess. Clothes everywhere. There's an energy here that creeps me out. Maybe it's knowing he's always online with some game, killing people. Maybe it's that he graduated but is still at home. Maybe it's that he's never had a girlfriend and at the rate he's trying, never will.

1

Look. His underwear is stretched. I'll have to order him a larger size. Again. This isn't a growth spurt like when he was thirteen. He's fat. He's nearly six feet tall, but all blubber. Rolls 'round the middle. Pringles and Cokes. I've got to stop having that crap delivered. If he gets diabetes it'll be my fault.

I gather clothes. Why am I doing this? He should do his own laundry. I don't even like touching his things. They're all sticky from god knows what. But, I'm doing a load so might as well. He's not going to. I can ask and plead 'til I'm blue in the face. Nothing works.

He wants to move into the garage. Maybe I should let him. Except then I'd be all alone in this beige carcass of a dream house.

Every house in this development is a dream house. And every dream house is beige. Dan wanted everything inside to match the beige stucco outside. Step into a sea of beige walls, pull the beige vertical blinds, turn on beige lamps… Dan even chose beige handles for the kitchen cabinets. I hate this place and I'm the one living here.

I pick up the clothes from the floor. Brian's carpet needs cleaning. It's not beige anymore. Close the door to my son's dungeon, and head downstairs to the beige washing machine.

Dump in the soap. Set dial to Extra-Dirty-Stinky-Teenager-Wash. Slam the lid, push start, turn, and there I am. Why Dan wanted mirrors all over, I don't know. Well, I guess I do. He loved his "physique" as he called it. Paid more attention to his body than he did to his wife and son.

I'm getting as pasty-faced as Brian. This indoor skin needs some sort of spa treatment, but I can't face going to those places. Not that I can face going anywhere. I'd step in and people would stare and snicker. Not tall enough. Not buff enough. Not anorexic enough. My beige hair, blow-dried with an under-curl, is undoubtedly out of fashion with today's Mom-requirements. Probably need violet contacts to liven up these dull grey eyes.

Years ago, I tried to be a Southern California woman. I ate salads. Converted to soy milk and gluten-free for a while. Dabbled with yoga and grunted through one session of Pilates. Nothing stuck. Maybe that's why I don't go out anymore. Everyone's more *put together* than I am. Everyone looks like they're on television. My face could be a police drawing. Generic. Reporters asking the neighbors about me would get, "Her? Couldn't say. Haven't seen her in forever. She stopped going out. What I remember is—she was kinda unmemorable. Kinda beige."

Six-twenty. Still no call.

I dial. The phone rings and then his voice, "This is Brian. Leave a message."

"Damn it, Brian. You promised to call if you were going to be late! You'll miss dinner. Let's just see how you manage on your own. I'm not going to lift a finger to put something on the table—"

I hang up.

No. I *will* put something on the table. Something with vegetables. Some broccoli, cauliflower, spinach monstrosity he'll hate. The later he is, the more pungent the overcooked slop will be.

What can I make? Not much left in the fridge. 'Bout time to go shopping.

—*GO shopping? Ha! You don't leave the house.*

—*It's more convenient to order delivery.*

—*You're terrified of the world. Haven't made it past the front door for two years.*

—*Not true.*

—*You even looked up agoraphobic!*

The doorbell rings.

Now what? It's too late for FedEx or UPS with any of my orders. Maybe it's a disadvantaged youth selling magazines.

The badge tells me otherwise.

"Mrs. Ketchum? I'm afraid there's been an accident. Your son Brian—"

Knees turn to liquid.

The bronze-skinned officer catches my elbow and steers me inside. He fits right in with his beige uniform. "Mrs. Ketchum, we don't know anything for sure yet."

His mouth continues to move, making sounds, and his eyes are trying to be concerned, but he's cut off from emotion. Is he tired of bringing bad news to parents? Do his eyes warm up when he gets home, or are they always dead? No, not dead. Not dead. Brian's not dead.

I interrupt the moving mouth. "Is he dead? Is my boy dead?"

"Ma'am, we're still gathering information. We don't have a lot to go on. It seems your son fell overboard and the Coast Guard is conducting a thorough aquatic search for him. We're interviewing the participants aboard the vessel that witnessed the event."

Where do they teach these people to talk!?

The room is darkening. Am I fainting? No, someone's in the doorway. A Ken-doll with a badge. Ken looks uncomfortable, like he and his partner are wanted elsewhere.

I wave at Ken to go. It comes out as more of a *get the fuck away* gesture.

Ken disappears into the evening glare.

Brian fell overboard. But he can swim. He'll be okay.

"He fell overboard. No one pulled him out?"

"Ma'am, I'm sorry, there isn't more I can tell you." The officer's lips flatten to a thin scar across the bronze skin. I try to understand what that means.

"Is your husband home?"

I can't believe he's asking that. Like everyone's got a big happy family.

"Is your wife home?" I ask.

"Ma'am?"

"Don't like the question? Maybe you're divorced? Some of us are."

Bronze-man glances to the door, hoping for Ken-doll backup. No such luck. He returns to me, mentally flipping through his emotional playbook and settling on compassion. "Ma'am, do you have someone I can call? A friend or neighbor?"

"Who's in charge?"

"Ma'am?"

"Who the hell do I call to find out what happened?"

The officer drops the fake concern from his eyes. He pulls a pad from his perfectly pressed breast pocket, writes a number down, and

4

hands it to me. "This is the officer that will be your liaison on this case. He'll have the most current information about your son."

My son.

I think I may throw up.

The officer talks into his shoulder. "Carswell, find me a neighbor."

My eyes fog. The carpet needs cleaning.

That Ken-doll must have darkened the doorway again or I'm...

My eyes open. I'm on my couch looking up at the cottage-cheese ceiling. What happened?

"Ann? Are you okay?" a voice whispers.

I turn to look at the perfectly coiffed woman. From what I remember the last time I went out, she's the one that lives at the end of the block with the yapping dogs. She's groomed like she's heading for a celebrity brunch. Gold earrings, long fake eyelashes. I can't remember her name. P something Pamela? Prudence?

"It's me, Ann. Pat."

Pat. Patty cake. Pat on the back. Pat of butter.

The lights are on in the living room. Dark outside. What happened?

Oh.

"Pat, did they say more about Brian?"

Pat pats my hand. She's hot. Or I'm very cold.

She purses her lips to express her unease with the subject. "Ann, I'm sure—I'm sure it will work out. Don't worry. He'll be found."

Something's in my hand. I unclench, exposing the crumpled piece of paper. A number for the liaison officer whoever.

I sit up slowly, hoping the blood will stay in my head. "I need to call this number, Pa—" What was her name? Something about butter?

"Pat," she reminds me and pushes my phone across the coffee table with a long pink nail.

I dial the number. When the officer answers, I interrupt him. "This is Ann Ketchum. Your officer said my son Brian fell overboard in a boating accident. I need you to tell me what happened and how he is."

"I'm sorry, Mrs. Ketchum. We're assessing the situation, and we'll keep you informed when we know more."

"Where is Brian? Is he alive? You need to tell me."

"Mrs. Ketchum, we will get in touch with you the moment we have any—"

I hang up on him. This is completely unacceptable.

They'd tell me if he was alive. They'd want to share that. That must mean Brian's dead.

I need to do something.

"Pat, can you go?"

Pat sputters a bit, "They said I should stay."

"Until I was okay. I'm okay now."

Relief spreads across her tight, tan forehead. She searches her purse and hands me a business card. She's a realtor. It has a picture of her smiling with perfect teeth and perfect hair. She gives me the identical smile. "If you're sure. Buttons and Bows will be needing their dinner. I can come back later if you—"

"I'm fine. You go feed Bows and—the other one. Thanks for coming."

Pat steps backwards to the front door, nodding and fluttering her hand in apologies and explanations.

When the door clicks shut I get up, lock it, and start vacuuming.

The vacuuming will take a while. The house is large. Too large for two people, especially if one spends all his time in his room. I vacuum the family room (stupid name), the living room (no one does that here), the dining room (we eat everywhere else), the master bedroom (without the Master), and the guest room (Ha!). Every few minutes I'm positive I hear the phone ring and turn off the roaring machine and listen to the silence of no one calling. When I get the hall done, I pull the vacuum into Brian's room, but I can't turn it on.

Tears come up hot and fast.

If Brian's dead—why did I wash his clothes!?

MOM'S GOING to kill me.

She'll think I forgot to call. She'll be worried first and then she'll be mad and by now she'll be back to worried.

I didn't forget, Mom! Honest. I've been trying!

I can't see. My eyes are open, but there's nothing but blackness. Ears pop again. Are we going down? Please don't. I scream and it goes nowhere, muffled by the spongy cavern. I puke salt water in the black void. Who knows where it lands.

Shaking uncontrollably, my legs are cramping. All my body's cramping. Panic bubbles up again. Hand to chest. My phone's still on the cord around my neck, safe and dry. Thank you, Mom! I lift it and the blue light shines in the darkness. I'm in a narrow, slimy place— *yuck!*—can't look.

I turn the camera and FLASH! A selfie. Wide-eyed and grimacing—I look terrified. *What a dork!* Delete. Try again. FLASH! Worse. A little half-smile. Not cool.

I dial Mom again. No service.

A moan blasts all around me, so loud it hurts! A low vibrating note that won't stop. Now a high one, like a squeaky door. Like someone making Halloween noises.

Shit! The air is leaving again. I suck in a breath and get nothing. There is no oxygen!

I'm knocked backward in a rush. Like I'm in a rocket launching into space. The momentum presses me flat against the hot, moist walls and I vomit again and gasp for any air but get nothing. The rocket slows and I'm almost floating and there's dim light above me, dusk light from a hole the size of my head, the mushy walls widen out and cold fresh air rushes in and the hole closes. Blackness. I breathe deep as we descend.

Try Mom again. Nothing. I shouldn't keep trying. I'll use up the battery. I should shut off the power, but—I want to keep the light on.

—*Lard Ass is scared of the dark.*

—I am not!

—Scaredy cat. Scaredy cat.

—I'm not listening to you. I'm thinking of something else.

—I know what you're thinking. I'm in your head.

—I'm not scared. You don't know me.

—I know you better than anyone. I know you better than you. You can't ignore me now. You're stuck with me and no one else ''til we die in here.

—I won't die in here. I'll be found. Billy and Toke will tell.

—Yeah, the stoner tells what he saw. Everyone's gonna believe Toke.

—— TOKE TALKS ——

THE RINGING SOUNDS far away.

Please be Brian. I race to the phone and, "Hello?"

"Mrs. Ketchum? Ann? It's Roger, Kevin's father."

"Kevin?"

"Your son's friend."

Kevin? "Oh, you mean Toke?"

A cough and pause and then the father's voice continues, "Kevin was with Brian on the boat. I thought you'd like to know what he saw."

Twenty minutes later, I've had two cups of coffee and father and son stand awkwardly in my perfectly vacuumed living room.

Toke bobs his head as if it's priming the pump to talk. It works. "Mrs. Ketchum, me and Lard Ass—"

"Lard Ass?"

"I mean Brian."

"You call my son Lard Ass?"

Toke shrugs. "Everyone does."

"Everyone?"

The twit sticks out his chin, like that's an answer.

Without meaning to, I slap his face.

8

Toke's father dives between us, grabbing my wrists. He looms over me, sympathy and anger tangling across his features. "Easy, Ann. No call for that." *When was the last time a man looked in my eyes? When was the last time a man touched me?* These aren't thoughts for now.

I don't hit people. The boy's face is pink on one side. "I'm sorry, Toke."

His face reddens on both sides now.

"Kevin," I correct. "Tell me what happened."

"Um, so me and La—Brian—and Billy and some girls were on the boat and it was all cool and shit—sorry."

I wave to let the boy know I've heard the word shit before and for him to keep going.

"We saw the spout and the spray flew up and Brian was at the end of the boat on that part, you know, like in Titanic, the tip? And then there was a gigantic crash like we got torpedoed and we all got off balance and Brian tried to stay on, but he fell off."

"Into the water? Didn't you try to pull him up? Throw a life jacket? A rope?"

"We couldn't pull him up. He was gone. The whale swallowed him."

Cartoon images fly into my head. Someone sitting around a campfire in the ribbed cavern of a whale. That's a Disney movie. Make believe.

After a lot of yelling and wrist grabbing, I'm staring at Toke's phone, watching the shaky video of Brian falling into a monstrous mouth and vanishing. I play it over and over and I'm sure I'll see the edits or the strings or something to show it's fake.

Only Toke doesn't act like it's fake.

Toke's father shifts his weight. "Ann, can we send the video to you? You can see it on your computer. Bigger. Play it slower maybe. I don't know how to do that, but—"

Handing the phone back to Toke, I tell him, "Send it to me."

Toke gets my phone number and sends it to my cell. I want them gone now.

"Sorry I hit you, Toke. Kevin."

"Sorry about Lard As—Brian, Mrs. Ketchum."

Roger leads his son out solemnly. When they close the door, I watch the video again, then send it to Brian's email. Up in his room, I click on his computer to watch it big. Now I'll see all their tricks.

The camera shot bobs and jiggles. The sun is shining. Waves are glittering. Brian's at the tip of the boat, alone as usual. He's got that hang-dog look. A spout of water shoots high. Girls squeal. A jolt to the boat and Toke's voice "Shit" and shots of the deck and bare feet and then up and Brian's tipping off and the water rises as a huge mountain and it splits open on black and Brian falls in and the black closes, dropping down under the waves with screaming and Toke yelling "shit, what the fuck, shit, did you see that, fuckin' what the fuck—!"

I watch again and pause on my pale, pudgy boy falling into the mouth of a black beast.

Brian's been eaten by a whale.

There are no fairytales.

Brian's dead.

My knees land hard and my coffee lurches up and stains Brian's stained carpet.

This can't be happening. This can't be how life goes.

Wake me up.

Rewind.

Let me go back, please. Let me go back.

I stare at the frozen image on the computer. Brian's eyes are wide. He's scared. My son's last moments were of terror as he was eaten by a whale.

My gut heaves and sobs burst out.

How did this happen!?

— ON DECK —

HOW DID IT HAPPEN? Probably my fault.

10

It started okay. Three guys. Three girls. A boat. Beers. The California sun gleaming off the waves, somewhere off Catalina Island. I was having an okay time, considering.

The names of the girls? One was something that starts with a T. Something that has to do with jewels or money. Tiffany? Tiara? Topaz? She was the hottie, but my best bud Billy had dibs on her. The other two were a 5 or 6 at most. "Passable" in our lingo, but neither Toke or me was doing much in the way of moves. Toke might do okay with the ladies if he wasn't so blotto. Which he always is. I'm not way into the trying-to-impress thing. Do most of my action with my eyes—when the girls aren't looking. I'm not sure I'm even a 4. Too much blubber. That's why I was the only one on deck in a T-shirt.

A horn blast made me jump and jiggle fat, which the girls seemed to get a kick out of. A Coast Guard ship slowed near us. Toke slipped me his Ziploc of weed like I was supposed to get caught with it instead of him. "Hell, Toke, I ain't legal age either."

"Stash it, dude. I can't see any more of the chick."

"The chick?" I asked, shoving the baggie into the back pocket of my shorts.

"Miss Demeanor." Toke punched my shoulder.

The punch hurt. It was supposed to show I was a righteous guy, but I knew I was only a schmuck to him and the others. Comic relief.

The Coast Guard man lifted a megaphone. "You kids don't go chasing anything. One boat already got rammed. Stay smart and stay safe."

We waved like we got the message. The Coast Guard ship moved on.

I took my phone from my pocket and pretended to send an email.

Glancing up, I saw one of the girls looking at me. A woody sprang. Fuck. I turned from her and set my phone on the bench cushion so I could put my hands in my pockets and hide the bulge. An awesome wave rolled under us and the girls went *oooo* and I had to pull a hand out to hold on and the phone fell and slid as we tilted, sliding toward the open back of the boat. FUCK! I dove and scrambled after it, probably looking like a white flabby crab, sneakers squeaking on the slippery deck, reached for the phone as it hit the edge and my hand grabbed it right before it fell into the waves.

"BOIN-OIN-oin-oin," Billy sang.

"Nice one!" Toke said, bobbing his head for emphasis.

I pulled Mom's dorky waterproof case from my shorts, shoved the saved phone into it, and slipped the cord over my head.

"Lookin' super cool!" Billy yelled across the boat.

I gave him the finger.

Billy grinned. "Toss me a brewski, Lard Ass!"

The girls all giggled, repeating "Lard Ass" to each other. Thanks, Billy. Thanks for that.

"Don't mind if I do, Bro," Toke said, holding out his hand for a beer.

I froze my fingers in the Igloo, pretending everything was fine, and tossed Coronas to Toke and Billy.

"Hell-lo-ooow," lilted one of the girls, her head tilted just so with the unmistakable *aren't you forgetting something?* The three girls did synchronized long-lash blinks at me.

I don't know why I did it, but I got them all beers.

"Thanks, Lard Ass," said the pretty one, and everyone laughed including me, and I got a beer and walked to the bow or stern or starboard-whatever—the pointy front of the boat—and glared at the flat line where blue sky meets blue sea and pretended I was alright.

The water and sky were pretty boring, so I checked for messages on my phone and, 'cept for Mom reminding me to wear sunscreen, there was nada. It was clumsy to use the phone through the clear plastic. I wanted to take it from the stupid waterproof case with the dumb neck strap, only everyone would've figured I was taking it off so I wouldn't look dorky, which would've made me look more dorky, so I left it on. Now, I'm glad I did.

"There, there, lookit!" a girl screamed.

A little squirt of spray spouted near our boat. The back of a grayish thing spread the surface of the water and dove back down.

"Awww! Come back!" yelled another girl.

"It's a dolphin. Too small for a whale," Billy, the expert, explained.

The girls cheered when it rose again. Another mini geyser.

"Watch," Billy yelled and pitched his beer bottle hard. The Corona hit the blow-hole. "Bullseye!" The grey back jerked and vanished underwater.

"Don't do that, Billy, you're littering!" the best-looking girl said.

A huge spray blew, skyscrapers high, showering us all and *ooo-* and *ahh-* and everyone had their cell phones, trying to get selfies with the monstrous monster. Being at the tip, I got the best shot and started making a video. Only I didn't get a chance to say *ahoy matey* or *thar she blows* before the boat was rammed. The girls screamed and another SLAM and my video took shots of the sky and spray and my arm and I was going over the side. Over the skimpy railing, ready to belly-flop, be a laughingstock, in free-fall, I took a breath, and WHAM! I landed somewhere—not exactly water, looked at sky above, and black closed over everything.

I remember thinking, *Shit, I'm in the whale.*

I was rushed with the torrent in underwater blackness, bounced off soft walls in a tunnel, warm and undulating, faster, sliding backwards, hit squishy wall, sharp turn, and dropped to a stop.

—I need to breathe!

—Don't do it, Lard Ass!

Unable to see, I felt thick muck, bits of bones, flesh, goop—all over and around me.

In the blackness, sounds of fish flopping.

A powerful force pressed the slimy walls, crushing in from everywhere. Rhythmically, again and again. Massive muscles pulverizing me. This was the ultimate tenderizer, and I was the meat. My ankle bent sideways. I couldn't scream or I'd fill with sludge.

I thought—*I'm not dead yet, but I will be in a second.*

—Pull your fat ass outta here!

I pushed off with my good ankle and wriggled up, clawing at anything, battered by the slick walls. Still holding the same breath, arms shaking with effort, I climbed the throbbing walls, digging my fingers into unseen flesh, wrenched out of that torture chamber and back in the tube. Another rush of water and fishy things surged past. I heaved against the tide, feet on either side, pressing for leverage, clawing up, hit by hundreds of thrashing things. Fighting to hold the breath. A small blue light swirled closer fast, a glowing wriggling creature headed for my face and *Fuck!* whirled past. Let me outta here! A jog in the tunnel. Sharp turn. That had to be it. There should be a flap. A trap door. A secret passageway. I pressed and pulled and felt the edge of something. A rim or ridge. Got fingers under. Got them in—*I need air!*—forced the flap open, squiggling, wriggling my way in, and dropped inside—

Whoooosh. I gasped and sucked in—air. Hot air engulfed me. I'd made it to the lungs.

And here I am. Alive, for now.

—*Yeah, but not for long.*

—*I survived getting swallowed by a whale.*

—*Only a duffus gets swallowed by a whale! Billy didn't. The girls didn't. Not even stoned-out-of-his-mind Toke.*

—*I guess I shouldn't have been alone at the end of the boat.*

—*If you weren't such a Loser, you wouldn't have to be alone at the end of the boat. You brought this on yourself, as usual. It's all your fault, Lard Ass.*

— FAULT —

I SHOULDN'T HAVE let Brian go whale watching. I shouldn't have said yes. A little firm mothering and he'd still be here.

I should have kept quiet about my boy's endless video gaming. If I hadn't nagged, he might have stayed home today and he'd be alive.

I shouldn't have gotten divorced three years ago. Or is it four now? It changed Brian. He withdrew and got unhappy. I should have stayed with Dan. I should have tried harder. I should have accepted things more. If I had worked on the marriage, we would be a family still. Dan would be here and we might all have done something fun today. Maybe we'd have gone to Disneyland. Brian only went twice. His twelfth birthday and that time with the kids at school when he got scared and had the man stop the ride and everyone teased him. But today would have been different. Fun in Disneyland as a family! My boy would have had a great time and he'd be asleep in his bed, breathing softly, having dreams. Instead, he's dead! I should have done things differently! I should have changed! But I didn't and now my son is dead and it's my fault.

And what about everyone calling him Lard Ass? What kind of mother lets people do that to her son? What kind of mother lets her son *become* a Lard Ass?

— LOGISTICS —

THIS PLACE SUCKS. It's pitch-black, sticky, smelly, and cramped. And the non-stop heartbeat thump, thump, thumping below me is getting on my nerves.

It's a muggy, sauna-hot, hundred-degree goo-fest in here. Drippy slime everywhere.

I lift the dorky waterproof case around my neck, turn on my phone, and light up this hell. The inside of a whale looks like curving walls of slime and super gross throbbing blood vessels. It's hard to tell the color. Grayish blueish pink? The space is like a huge Redwood tree crashed down and bugs ate out the middle and made a mushy hollow trunk that forks out to smaller mushy dark branches. Opposite the branching end is a long narrow tunnel that goes up to the blowhole at the top of the whale's head. My spot in the trunk area stretches wide or compresses tight depending on if the whale is sucking in or pushing out air. Not high enough to stand in—well, I can almost stand, but it's squishy and always moving so it's easier to lie down or stay on my butt as this whale keeps rising and diving and turning and leaping, and I'm always tumbling one way or another. When I tumble, I try not to clog the branches. Last thing I need is this whale not breathing.

I turn the phone away from the grossness and pull up a game.

—*Turn off the phone.*

—*Just one game.*

15

—Don't be stupid, Lard Ass.

—I need distraction!

—You're wasting the battery! Turn off the fucking phone!

I turn off the fucking phone. The afterimage of that wonderful rectangle glows in my eyes. Maybe I can imagine the game.

The whale lurches up again—a supersonic elevator. I vomit more salt water. This is like riding a wicked-bad roller-coaster that runs constantly and you're blindfolded and sometimes it slows so much you think it's stopped, then you drop fast and your stomach flies up and you roll and smash the slimy sides, and it isn't like a roller-coaster at all because you can't signal the man to stop even if all the other kids laugh and the name *Wuss* spreads everywhere like a taco fart in the car and you'll never live that one down.

I gotta pee. Where do you pee in a whale?

—Don't pee in the lungs, Lard Ass.

—I can't hold it 'til I'm rescued—

—Rescued? You're never getting out.

—I have got to pee!

—So do I! Find that flap you came through and stick your Johnson out.

Find the flap. How do I find the flap? There's the tube that goes up to the blowhole and somewhere along this—Maybe I can listen for the rush of food heading to the stomach. Crawling over the blackness, I lay my ear against wet sponge. The slow booming heart throbs louder.

I risk the phone battery and move the light along the tube. There's the edge of the flap. Lying over the seam, I unzip and push a bit and slide Johnson through. *Ooo.* That was something.

—Don't even think about it.

—I'm not doing anything!

—I know you. You will not jerk off with a whale's lung flap, Lard Ass. Even I couldn't live that down.

I let go and pee. What a relief.

The whale twists and I pull out fast. We're moving again. We're rushing upward. Up for another breath? Please, cough me up on land.

— THE WHALE —

THE WHALE'S HUGE HEAD breaches the surface and spray blasts into the night air. A curve of the back—black, scarred, flecked with barnacles—rolls with the dark waves until the tail rises to cover the moon and smashes water, fragmenting lunar reflections and pulling them below.

Descent. Moving past a flickering mass of silvery fish. The rage the whale felt earlier is gone. Now only a dull sickness fills the beast. Something is wrong inside.

The whale dives. Hoping this shortness of breath won't last.

— LAST STUPID MOMENT —

IT'S DARK. I'm in Brian's room, lying on the bed, looking at the ceiling. A few dust-covered model spaceships hover over me. Scattered across the desk and bureau are computer game disks. Is that all he did in life? Play games of killing? Didn't he want more?

Maybe I was a bad example. I've done nothing since Dan left. I should have taken up computer games. At least I could have connected with Brian as we wasted our lives. We might have been a team. We might have talked about our scores or dramatic kills. We might not have argued. Constantly.

Yesterday we argued. That stupid moment has become the last memory of him.

How did it happen?

He was alive. He stood downstairs about to leave. His shirt was on inside-out. What was the last thing we said to each other?

GETTING READY for my boat trip. Trying to pick out a T-shirt to cover my fat rolls. Why do I have such jerky shirts? This one with the snake and devil—they'll think I'm trying to be cool and that is so uncool. This one with the faux faded hometown sports team. Everyone knows that comes from Target.

That boy is driving me mad. Look at this. In the middle of the living room for god's sake!

"Brian! What's with the bowl of cereal in the living room? Are you done with it?"

I call down, "I'm done!"

It'd be so cool to have that be the end of it, but I know better. Mom can't have any "discussion" that doesn't last forever and she's always yelling.

He's always yelling. I should just give up. Walk away like Dan did.

"It's got half a bottle of milk in it."

"Sorry."

"What if I want milk?"

"I said I was sorry!"

"You ever think of anyone else?"

"All the time, Mom." If she only knew. I can't do shit without second-guessing what people think.

"At least eat it if you're going to waste all this milk!"

"The milk's gone bad!"

I suppose he thinks that's my fault. Is it?

Toke's shiny jeep drives up. What kind of father buys his stoner son a new jeep? My car is over eight years old. Who's going to buy me a new car? Brian expects me to buy him a car, but he's not getting shit. Look at that entitled brat out there, fixing his ragged hair to look worse. That kid better not be smoking weed and driving.

"Toke's here!"

I grab the plain T-shirt and take a whiff. Stinks bad. Better to look like a dork than smell homeless. The Simpsons T smells passable but it's got burrs from when Billy and Toke and me were walking in the arroyo and for no reason Billy shoved me and I fell in that mess of brambles and Billy goes, "BOIN-OIN-oin-oin." Fuck him. If I put this T-shirt on inside-out maybe people will think I'm making a statement and assume it's ironic but it'll be scratchy on the inside with these stupid burrs. Better scratchy and ironic than a homeless stinker. I put it on.

Toke honks outside. I grab my phone. Shoulda charged it. Downstairs. One-dollar bill in my wallet. I'll borrow a twenty from Mom. I know she has it 'cause she makes me get cash for her from the ATM. Don't know why she wants cash since she never goes out. Maybe she wants it so I will steal it so she can yell at me.

Her purse is where it always is. It never moves. Slide the zipper silently.

I heard you come downstairs. I'm not deaf, you know. You're as predictable as the endless sunny weather. I'll give you a moment and then spring.

She pops her head around the corner. "What the hell are you doing?"

"Can I borrow a five, Mom?" I know there's nothing in here but twenties.

Mom shakes her head, not with a *no* look, but with a *I'm-disappointed-in-you* look. Same ol' same old.

"Is this the type of person you want to be?" she asks. "The type of person who steals from purses?"

He's got to get a job. Who would hire him? You can't get a job looking like a slob.

"I'll pay you back."

Same ol' same old.

Mom sneers, "I've heard that before."

I give her the mournful look. "Gotta have something—for emergencies."

Look at him. He's got his worried-boy face on like it will soften me. Still, I guess he'd better have cash for emergencies.

19

She takes the purse from me and, after pretending to look for something smaller, hands me a twenty.

"Thanks. See you later."

He better call. Better not drop that cell phone in the ocean.

"Hold up. Take that waterproof phone thing I bought you."

"It's dorky, Mom."

You are a dork!

"Fine. Drop the phone in the ocean. You will not get another. Not even if you pay for it. I'll cancel the plan. And you won't have another until you realize its value. Put the phone in the dorky waterproof thing or don't. Your choice."

I grunt and stomp upstairs—

"Don't grunt at me. Have the decency to use words."

—grab the dorky waterproof thing, stomp down, put my phone in it and dramatically slide the cord over my head. "Happy?"

"You can thank me later," Mom snarls and turns away.

Toke honks again.

"Be home by five." *Better not be late and make me worry.* "If not, call me. I'm serious!"

"Whatever," I mumble and step out.

Silence. I've got peace for a whole day. Now what?

The minute I get into Toke's car, I take that dorky phone cord off.

— THE FIRST MORNING —

WHAT DO YOU CALL someone whose son is dead? Your husband dies and you're a widow. Your parents die and you're an orphan. Your son dies and—maybe they even take away the name mother. Am I still a mother?

I empty the pockets of all his clothes. I line up everything on his desk in front of the smudgy keyboard and PlayStation controls. Something has got to be a clue. Something here has got to explain why my son is dead. A quarter, movie ticket stub, Chapstick, ATM receipt. None of it makes sense.

Maybe he left a note with an explanation, premonition, apology, anything. Open his desk drawer. There aren't any pens or pencils or even paper. No kid uses such old-timey things. Push around the contents. Seven chargers. A Snickers bar. Three thumb drives. Pocket knife. Game disks. Broken headphones. Tangle of computer wires. Used Band-aid. Crumpled Doritos bag. Lots of crumbs of all sorts. A business card from a computer shop. A picture of Brian as a kid sitting between me and Dan.

I need to call Dan. Tell him his son is dead.

I dial my brother, instead. As it rings I imagine Tobey in his colorful San Francisco Victorian, padding barefoot from the airy kitchen past the provocative Buddha statue in the hall, calling to his husband, *Arthur, where's my phone?* He answers on the sixth ring.

"Tobey, Brian's dead!" I sob.

"No! What happened!?"

I tell him all about it.

"That's unbelievable. Horrible! What did the police say? Is the Coast Guard—"

"You need to call Dan for me. Tell him Brian's dead."

"Oh, no. I—"

"If you don't, he won't know."

"Ann, it's not right. Dan has to be told, and it should come from you. Brian's his son, too and—"

"You tell him. You do that for me. I can't," and I'm sobbing again.

"Okay, sis. Okay. I'll call him. And I'll get the first flight down I can."

"—"

My inability to speak must translate over the phone because Tobey responds, "I'll be there soon. Right now, eat something. Lie down. Cry. I love you."

He hangs up.

I picture my brother telling Arthur. Being held in a tight hug. I picture him dialing the phone and Dan being annoyed as his cell jangles. I picture the vein on Dan's head pressing out and his face turning red. Last time I saw him was Brian's graduation almost two years ago. Was that the last time I left the house? We sat beside each other in the crowd of parents. Dan's fastidiously clipped brown hair was blond. As usual, he was wearing beige khakis, a beige shirt, and raw-canvas tennis shoes. Still the body of an athlete. Could be a male-model, but it'd have to be for something suburban. An advertisement with him grinning by a golf cart or barbecue grill. Something where he could show those perfect teeth and exude: Dependable. Steady. A man's man.

The doorbell stops me picturing more.

I run, stumbling downstairs. What am I wearing? Doesn't matter, it'll be about Brian. Someone found Brian. The whale spat him out unharmed and he treaded water and the Coast Guard rescued him and they're at the door.

I open to lenses and microphones. Words fly at me, "Your son—whale—swallowed."

I blink.

A reporter pushes his microphone closer. There are hairs caught in the black spongy cover. "Mrs. Ketchum, eyewitness reports all suggest that your son was swallowed by a whale. How do you respond—?"

I slam the door on the shouts.

Vultures. Feeding off the dead.

The bell rings again. I'm not going to answer. I back away—

A key in the lock! Could that be Brian!? They got it wrong! He's not dead!

My ex-husband Dan opens the door. He marches across the carpet, puts his arms around me, and the two of us sob on each other.

We cry for quite a while until my foot cramps from being on tiptoes, so we break apart and I head for the kitchen to make him a cup of coffee. Dan follows, asking questions. He wants to know how it all happened. The milk smells bad, so I add artificial powder to make his coffee beige and tell him what happened to his son.

"What were you thinking!?" Dan yells. "Alone on a boat with no adults?"

"These aren't children, Dan. Brian's nineteen."

"Don't tell me he's nineteen. I know my son's age!"

"Do you know they call your son Lard Ass?"

"What?"

"Never mind."

Dan sips the coffee, staring at the photos on the fridge door: Brian sneering in the backyard, Brian sulking in his cap and gown, Brian sucking in his pudgy middle.

A shudder rolls over Dan's shoulders. "I've got to go tell the family about Brian."

The family. The new one. I'm not part of that word anymore.

He turns to me, eyes glassy, working to keep back tears. "You shouldn't have let him go, Ann."

"I didn't expect he'd be swallowed by a whale."

Dan hands me his coffee and steps toward the front door. "You should have expected the worse! You know how he is. Of course, something bad would happen! He's just like you!"

I throw the mug to shatter it against Dan's perfect hair, but it doesn't even cross the living room. Beige liquid flies to land on beige carpet as the cup bounces on thick pile, hits the couch leg, and cracks in half. Dan shakes his head and walks out to the circling reporters.

— FREAK OUT IN THE BEAST —

TRYING THE PHONE AGAIN. No connection. The battery is getting super low. Turn it off.

Fuck, it's hot in here. I gotta strip.

—Where you gonna put your clothes, Lard Ass? The hamper? Fold them nice and neat in the bureau? You don't keep them on, they'll scatter in the dark.

Ahh! The oxygen is leaving again! Shit, I hate this! Please go up for air. The whale makes sounds like a grumble-warble, squeaky wagon-wheel, clicking, ending with a gong.

"Up, you bastard!" I yell in the dark.

I'm slammed back and pressed against the slime and there's rushing all around and my ears pop and the lung walls heave in and whale mucus flies up into daylight blow-hole open and the lung walls drop and widen, spreading, pulling in such delicious cold air—smell of fresh clean—-the caw of a gull!—-and BLACK.

We dive.

"I want to get out! Let me out!" I kick the sides of this damn place. Pound the lungs with my fists. "LET ME OUT!"

The whale lurches and spasms, torquing to the side and slamming me against squishy wall.

—*Stop it, Lard Ass! You want to get us killed?*

—*I want to get out!*

—*I want to get out, too, but out isn't a fucking good idea right now.*

—*I'm getting out!*

—*Why not slip out the flap, go into the stomach, get turned into mash, slide through the intestines, and out the big butt hole, Whale Shit?*

—*I'll go out the mouth!*

—*Try it. Hold your fucking breath and swim upstream and make it to the mouth and somehow pry the enormous jaws open and keep holding your breath and swim up, up, up, who knows how far, to the surface and you're out. Free. But out where?*

—*Out! Out is where!*

—*Out in the middle of the cold fucking ocean with sharks and no boat. Got your floaties? You get out of this whale and you're dead.*

I punch the squishy walls again. "LET ME OUT!!!"

The whale dives and we're pointed down and I fall toward the tunnel to the blowhole.

—*I'll crawl out the blowhole!*

—*You're too fat, Lard Ass!*

I stick my head down and squiggle my shoulders into the black tube. It's super tight. Press farther. Folds of fat squeeze.

—*You'll get jammed. Go back!*

My arms are pinned. My belly is mashed.

—*I can't back up! I'm stuck!*

—*You'll suffocate the whale! Get out!*

"HELP! HEELLLLLPPP!"

The whale spins wildly. It's gotta feel something's wrong. It twists, arches, and plunges down. The dropping elevator. All the blood goes to my head.

—*Not down! Don't send me in farther!*

In a lurching move, the whale reverses, elevator to the penthouse and—I drop out, splatting against wet blackness.

"I HATE YOU!" I pound the spongy walls.

The whale roars low and high at the same time and twists in pain.

—*FUCK HEAD! YOU PUNCH THIS WHALE ONE MORE TIME AND WE DIE!*

I collapse sobbing. He's right. I'm right. I'll poke a hole in these lungs and the whale will die. If it stops breathing, I stop breathing.

"I'm so scared, Mom."

My inside voice doesn't have a thing to say to that. He just lets me sob in the dark.

— SOMETHING IS CRYING INSIDE —

THE WHALE HOVERS near the surface, unsure whether to dive, in case the pain starts again. The thrashing inside has stopped, but the lungs feel battered and bruised. Something is hurting from within and whatever it is, the whale can hear noises from it. Deep under the black scarred flesh, past the thick blubber, just above the slow heart, something is crying and making the whale sick.

— ANOTHER ARRIVAL —

THE DOORBELL RINGS and I squint through the peephole. Dark arched eyebrows. Black hair groomed to perfection. Immaculately trimmed beard. The mole on his cheek he hates and I love. My brother.

Opening the door a crack, Tobey slides in as The Press yells questions.

Slam and lock and his arms are around me.

"I'm so sorry, Ann. This is horrible."

I tell him everything and show him the video and he cries with me. After a while, he finds out I haven't eaten and vows to rectify that. The fridge has nothing viable.

"I'm going to get you groceries. Come with me."

I shake my head. He doesn't know I don't go out anymore.

"Okay. Rest. Take a nap. I'll get every kind of comfort food. You need to eat. Keep your strength up."

He declines my car keys. "Being from San Francisco, I doubt I remember how to drive. I'll call for a ride. Promise me you'll take a nap."

I promise and he leaves and I open the fridge to clean out the decayed food. Pour the sour milk down the drain. Smell rises and it smells like Brian when he hasn't showered and gets me crying. Veggies in the trash. The bread is moldy, but it was touched by Brian, so I have to keep it. The furry cheese as well. This ketchup is almost out and I never use the stuff, but it was his, so has to stay. This is impossible. I should take a nap.

Lying down on the couch, the tears come again. I close my eyes to stop the blurring of the world. Can I possibly sleep?

The home phone rings.

My heart leaps.

"Hello?"

"Mrs. Ketchum, I'm from KMOB news. Please come outside. We have a few questions to ask—"

I slam the phone down. Bastards.

My cell phone rings. Fucking assholes don't get the message. Or maybe this is Tobey.

I pick it up to check and see *Incoming Call: Brian.*

"Brian! Is that you?"

Clicking. Muffled sounds—

"Brian, talk to me."

A high tone and scratchings.

"Brian? Brian?"

A muffled something. The phone goes dead.

"NOOOOOO!"

— PHONE HOME —

MY PHONE WORKED!

I dial Mom again. She'll figure something out. Find a way to save me.

The phone beeps. NO SERVICE.

—*Damn it! You just worked!*

—*You're wasting your battery. We're in a whale, Lard Ass. Do you see any cell towers in here?*

—*I'll try until the battery's dead. I need her to know where I am!*

—*She doesn't even know you're missing. She probably thinks you're hanging out with Toke. You call her and she'll think you're in his basement.*

Dial again.

It rings. *Fuck, it's ringing!*

There is a click and garbled sound. Is that Mom?

"Mom! I'm in a whale! Can you hear me? I'm in a whale!"

Garbled sounds and a click.

—*I got through. She heard me and will find a way to get me. I'll be saved.*

—*She didn't hear you and she wouldn't believe you if she did. You're not getting out of this, Lard Ass.*

— DANCING —

I DANCE across the floor, spinning on the coffee-stained carpet.

He's alive! Brian's alive. I heard him. He's in the whale and he's alive.

I dial his phone. It rings.

And rings.

Please pick up.

And rings.

Please.

His sweet voice comes on. Trying to sound so grown up. "This is Brian. Leave a message."

I can't help but leave a message. "Hi, honey. I heard you. I thought you were dead. But you're alive. Everything will be okay. Call me when you get this."

I hang up. Shoot. I forgot to say I love you.

I dial again and remember to say it this time. "Didn't want you to think I forgot that. I love you so much, honey. Hurry home." I don't want to hang up but I do.

I'll make tacos tonight. His favorite.

Soon he'll be home and he'll tell me all about it.

Now what? I should let Tobey know that Brian's alive.

Just as I reach for the phone, it rings. I grab it, "Brian?"

"Mrs. Ketchum. It's Lieutenant Whettig from the Los Angeles Police Department, calling regarding your son Brian."

"Yes! You found him?"

"I'm afraid we're calling off the search. Brian's body hasn't been recovered—"

"It hasn't been recovered because he's in the whale. He called me. Find the whale and get him out."

There is a pause and the Lieutenant sounds serious when he starts in again. "What's your son's cell phone number? We're going to investigate and if your son called, and this is a hoax, he will be prosecuted to the full extent of the law—"

I happily give him Brian's number, suggesting, "You can track people with their phones like in the movies, right? Get a helicopter and fly over the ocean and find him and put a homing device on the whale and—

"Ma'am, ma'am, ma'am," he repeats until I stop talking. "I'm going to give you the number of a person to talk to in Social Services. She can help you sort out your feelings—"

I hang up as the doorbell rings.

Peeking out, I see the top of someone's head in front of the waiting reporters. Pam the Neighbor.

She slides in the room as I open the door a crack. Pam flutters her hand toward the front yard. "These reporter people won't leave. Vans everywhere. It's making a mess of the street. We can't park."

It's all about her.

"I'll talk to them now, Pam."

"Pat," she corrects. "Don't you want to—freshen up first?"

I glance in the entryway mirror. Wow. I'm a mess. I haven't blown my hair since yesterday morning and it's going every-which-way, the chastened curls reasserting themselves. My eyes are bloodshot with brown mascara smeared around them. There's a stain down the front of my blouse. Coffee vomit?

Pat gives me public speaking pointers as I spray down my hair and redo my makeup. Talk naturally. Be sincere. Look at the camera. Don't fidget.

"You look good, Ann. Don't want to look too good under the circumstances. How do you feel?"

"Fantastic."

Pat puts a hand on my arm. "Fantastic? I'm not sure that will go over well—"

"I didn't tell you? He's alive! My boy's alive!"

Smile lines tickle the edges of Pat's eyes. "They found him?! That's wonderful! A happy ending!"

"We still have to get him out. But he called from his cell. He's alive in the whale."

The smile lines vanish. Pat repeats my words back to me and I nod happily.

"He called. I heard it. Not clearly, but I'm sure it was him."

As I start toward the door, Pat stops me. "Don't go out there. You'll make a fool of yourself."

"The Press can help. Publicity. People will know to look for this whale. The news will help find Brian."

Pat's mouth twitches and I can see she's holding back a torrent of words. "Dear, that wouldn't be a good idea. If you tell the Press, people will find you—crazy," she finally says.

I want to slap her, the busybody bitch. That would be the second person I've slapped. Maybe something's wrong with me. Stress? Am

29

I acting crazy? Part of me thinks she might be right. The other part gives her an apologetic shrug.

Pat's perturbed. "Don't say I didn't warn you. I want nothing to do with it. Give me a minute to get home before you go out."

Pat disappears outside. I don't give her even two seconds before I open the door. Pat glares at me and slips to the side, running over the lawn to her own beige house. The cameras turn to me, microphones pressing close.

"Mrs. Ketchum, can you describe what happened to your son. What do you know?"

"I only know that he went boating with friends. A whale struck the boat and he fell overboard into the mouth of the whale. He was swallowed. But I heard from him. He just called. He's alive in the whale."

The reporters call out questions. I pick: "Ma'am, how can that be?"

"I don't know. But it is."

"Are you saying it's a miracle? Like Jonah from the Bible?"

"I don't know. I just know Brian is fine. He's good with animals."

"Did you call him back?"

"Yes. But there was no connection. Maybe the whale dove."

"Ma'am, is your son the type that does pranks? Could he be scamming the world?"

I shake my head. "He wouldn't know how."

"How can a person live in a whale? Is he like Geppetto in the Pinocchio story?"

Who's Geppetto? I guess I don't know that story, but I know they're trying to bait me. I've got to make this about Brian. "Please tell your viewers to watch for the whale. If they see it, let someone know. If everyone looks, we can find him."

"How will they know which whale?"

"I—don't know." I wave my hand, signaling the interview is over.

A voice calls out, "Mrs. Ketchum, do you have a message for your son?"

"A message?"

"If you could tell him something on the evening news, what would you say?"

"He's in a whale. He can't get television."

"If he could. What would you like him to know?"

This is one of those questions the news loves. I know what I'm supposed to say. I know what they want. I hate to do it, but if I don't, I'll be a pariah. I take a deep breath. The words come easily because we all know them. "I'd tell him Mommy's doing everything she can to see he's released. I'd tell him to hold on."

The Press press closer. We all know the last line.

"I'd tell him I love him."

My tears form on cue. They're real, but feel fake. I wave and go back inside.

— DEAD —

I WANT TO HEAR Mom's voice again. My scared, stupid face is reflected on the phone screen. Ignoring it, I dial. Please go through. No ringing. No service.

I dial again. No service.

Again. No service.

I need to know that Mom heard me! I need to know. Connect, damn it!

The phone goes black. I push power, but nothing happens. Seriously? Dead battery?

—*Only a loser would do such a stupid thing! You suck, Lard Ass.*

I'm in complete darkness. Alone in this horrible place.

But Mom knows. She'll get me out.

— A DREAM? —

I WANT TO HEAR his voice, so I call Brian's phone again. It rings and rings and then that sweet voice. My boy.

31

"This is Brian. Leave a message."

I wait for the beep. A machine-voice surprises me. "Mailbox full."

When he gets all these messages, he's going to think I'm hovering.

The doorbell rings. I peek out the hole. Tobey's back, surrounded by even more Press. When I unlock the door, he slips into the room.

"Tobey, Brian's alive in the whale!"

My brother freezes, staring at me.

"He called. He's in the whale!"

Tobey carries the groceries into the kitchen, ignoring me. He doesn't know how to react to the good news. I trot behind him. "Really, Tobey. He called. We have to figure out how to find him, get him out of the whale, and bring him home."

"Ann," Tobey sighs, "you've gone through a shock. It's understandable you'd want to grab at anything that would make it untrue."

"It happened. He's alive and called me."

"Sometimes in grief we—"

"I heard him."

"You didn't." My brother unpacks the groceries, sure that he ended the argument. Eggs. Milk. Roasted chicken. My stomach does a little flip when the oily, warm smell hits. I am hungry! I open the plastic container and dig my fingers into the hot carcass, pulling off a chunk of breast and stuffing it in my mouth.

Tobey gets his little satisfied smile, like he won because I'm eating. "You want a napkin?" he asks benignly.

I wipe my greasy hand across the front of my blouse in answer.

Tobey gets himself a plate and napkin and cuts a bit of chicken from the side I haven't mangled. "You say Brian called. I'm going to remind you that Brian was swallowed by a whale. That means he was in the water. From one who has dropped a phone in a toilet, I can tell you, phones don't work in the water."

I've got him now. "For your information—" I pause to lick my fingers, "—I bought my son a waterproof cover for his phone and it was around his neck. The phone didn't get wet. It works. He called."

32

"Did you take that nap you promised? Maybe you were dreaming."

Fear grips me. What really happened? I lay down and closed my eyes, but I didn't sleep. Did I? *Did* I dream this? No, please no.

Tobey touches my arm. "What *exactly* do you think you heard?"

I recognize that tone. It's the older brother tone, waiting for little sister to make an ass of herself. I hate him for that.

"I heard some clicks and scratching and then a voice, a little broken up, said 'Mom.'"

"A voice, or clicking and scratching?"

"Brian's voice, Tobey. Brian's voice. He said he was in a whale."

Tobey mumbles something. Probably telling himself I've gone cuckoo. He pulls out his phone and taps in something. "Let's find out what happens to something swallowed by a whale." Swish. Swish. He clears his throat, sounding just like Dad when he was going to give us a lecture. "The digestive system of the whale has compartments similar to ruminants, like the cow or hippo. The first stomach does not break down the food with gastric juices, but uses muscular walls to crush the food."

"Fuck you, Tobey. Brian didn't get crushed." I grab a chicken leg, rip it from the body, and chomp into the bulbous muscle.

"You said he had a waterproof cover for his phone. So he got swallowed, went into the first stomach and the muscles started working. Brian's cell phone got 'pocket dialed' by the stomach muscles."

"You don't have to believe me. *I* believe me. I thought you'd be happy!"

"Ann, honey, you're grieving. It's called denial. Makes a person crazy—"

I fling the chicken leg at my brother. He dodges but it hits his shirt sleeve, leaving a greasy stain. Tobey glares at me. We're kids again. Seven and nine.

"An—nn!"

"Get out of here. Go back to Arthur!"

"Be reasonable—"

I grab what's left of the chicken and raise it high, its juices dripping down my arm. It's burning my hand but I don't care.

"GET OUT!!!"

Tobey leaves. I lock the door with slimy fingers.

—*What if Brian didn't call? What if I dreamed it? I remember I closed my eyes. The phone rang.*

The phone! I grab my cell phone and push the call log and incoming and there it is!—2:16 incoming from Brian's phone! It happened and this is proof! I have proof!!!

I open the door to show Tobey, but he's marching fast, already past the news vans, and he probably would still say it was a pocket dial.

Stomping back to the kitchen, I bend to pick up the drumstick and a wave of nausea rushes over me. Did Brian get ripped apart like this chicken? Did the stomach muscles pulverize him?

I imagine him screaming, crushed, leg bent backwards, fins of fish stabbing him, and in that mess, his phone lights up, a bone fragment presses the screen and I'm called as his horrified mouth fills with pulped creatures...

—*Don't think that way! He called. He's alive.*

—*He's mash. He's sludge moving through the stomach and intestines, where he becomes whale shit and is dumped into the dark sea.*

The chicken heaves up from my belly and I rush to the sink.

— HUNGER —

MY STOMACH RUMBLES. I can't believe it. All this time and I haven't thought of food once. I'm starving! I could go for a hamburger and coke and super-size fries. Or pizza. Or tacos and nachos and a shake.

—*Keep dreaming, Mr. On-The-Way-To-Diabetes.*

—*That's not what the doctor said.*

—*She said you were overweight and pre-diabetic.*

—*It's not my fault.*

—Nothing is.

—I'm HUNGRY! I want something to eat!

I wonder if I could reach out through the flap and snag a fish on its way to the stomach.

—Try, Lard Ass. One slip and you slither out, down to be whale-snack.

—I can hang on.

—Sure you can. And you could do a sit-up in Phys Ed.

—I can't just not eat. I'll starve to death.

—You got so much lard you'll last for weeks.

The tears bubble up and I'm blubbering, crying like a kid, only I can't stop and there's no one here to kiss-an'-make-it-better. I lie in the darkness and howl my chunky heart out in the lungs of the whale.

And my whale sings back.

— DAN SAW THE NEWS —

SEVERAL CHANNELS, local and national, play my interview on the news. Over and over, my tearful face says, "I'd tell him I love him."

Internet sites dissect and debate it all. Comments below the articles are not kind. I'm crazy. Trolling for sympathy. Scientists chime in that survival in a whale is impossible. Crackpot Mother believes in fairy tales. Pinocchio's Geppetto and Jonah figure heavily. I'm the laughingstock of the world.

The phone rings. Talk shows call. Radio shows. Podcasts. Everyone wants me for their entertainment. I let the machine get it all. Dan's pretend-friendly-voice tells callers to leave a message. It's been years since we got divorced. Got to change that message.

"Ann? Are you there?" asks Dan's not-pretend-friendly-voice. "I saw the news. I know you're there. You never leave. I know you're there, staring at the phone. I'm coming over."

Shit.

I should put the old chicken carcass away and those groceries. The new milk's probably bad. Should clean the greasy floor. Change my shirt. Rid the carpet of that coffee stain.

I don't.

Dan's standing over the stain in twenty minutes. "This place looks like shit. You look like shit. Are you going nutty?"

"Dan, you saw the news. You heard—"

"I heard you make an ass of yourself."

"I know it sounds crazy but Brian called. He's alive in the whale. He's not dead."

Dan steps into the kitchen, pauses at the carnage, then pulls from the fridge the picture of Brian at graduation. "I'm borrowing this." He slips it into his ironed shirt pocket. "I want a recent one for the funeral."

"You don't hold a funeral for someone who's alive."

"Memorial. Whatever. Give me a list of names of his friends and Kate will organize it."

"If you cared, you'd already know his TWO friends. Toke and Billy."

Dan heads for the door. "I'll let you know when it is."

"Don't bother," I say as bravely as I can.

"You're crazy, Ann. Get help." Dan steps out and slams the door.

A sick feeling comes up from my gut. I haven't heard from Brian since that call. Maybe I made it all up. Maybe he *is* dead and I'll miss his funeral. Maybe I *am* crazy.

— NOT SLEEPING IN THE WHALE —

HOW CAN I ever sleep, if I'm unable to breathe? I'm suffocating! Please get air!

There's a sound of grumble-warble, squeaking wagon-wheel, clicking, and gong, and the whale rises and I go tumbling and he blows out and no light from the hole—so night—and he sucks in and I'm surrounded by fresh cold air. I fill my lungs. It's so good.

The oxygen gets down to the bare minimum before this whale takes a breath. It's fucking scary. If I'm stuck here, I have to learn to hold my breath. I've got to slow everything down and try to make my heartbeat as slow as his. Try to relax. Not panic. The whale doesn't want to die. He always takes a breath.

We tumble a bit, roll, then it gets calm. Maybe the whale will sleep. Do whales sleep? I should have paid attention in school.

—*You didn't study whales, Lard Ass. Only Moby Dickweed.*

—*If I had the internet, I could look up whale sleep.*

—*If you had the internet, you could call Mom, but guess who fucked that up? Besides, when did you ever look anything up on the internet? Apart from porn.*

I should love this. I should love being in a whale. It's dark so I can't see my big blobby body. It's dark like I tried to make my room, breaking off the rod on the blinds and cutting the string. No one's here to ridicule me. No one's inviting me places so there'll be someone to laugh at. Dad isn't calling, pretending there's an unavoidable event he has to go to, or forgetting to call completely. And I don't have to listen to Mom criticizing me or nagging me.

Only thing is—no internet. No TV. No video games. I miss those. I kinda miss Mom. Alone in my whale, I've only got me.

—*And me, Lard Ass.*

—*Fuck you. Can't you shut up? Why are you always at me?*

—*To save you, Duffus. You need me. Without me, you'd be in even worse shape. I say things for your own good, Lard Ass. You have to know what people think of you.*

—*I don't need you! Never talk to me again!*

—*Boo-hoo. Lard Ass got his widdle feelings hurt. You can't shut me up. You'll never shut me up. I'm with you for life.*

My belly jiggles and I can hear him in my head, laughing over my sobs. And sobbing makes me breathe weird—

—*No air again!*

—*Don't panic, Lard Ass! Panic makes it worse. Hold your breath and relax.*

I try. Hold it. Relax. Hold it.

—Listen to this slow, slow heartbeat thumping below us.

I pretend I'm drifting. I pretend I'm fine.

A little longer. Another second. Another.

That annoying sound of grumble-warble, squeaking wagon-wheel, clicking, and gong. The whale is rising and I get fidgeting. I can't hold my breath anymore.

—Just a second longer.

—I need air!

—Hold it, Lard Ass!

We're rushing now and I can't hold it so I blow out hard and suck in, but get nothing to fill my lungs. I'll pass out. I'll die in here —but we're up and blasting out the old hot air and sucking in the new cold life.

I really, really, really need to practice holding my breath. I need to get good at this. What else should I learn so I can live in here? How does someone live in a whale?

—No one does. Only two ever. A guy in the Bible and that woodcutter dad in Pinocchio. And at least one is make-believe.

—I'm not make-believe and I got swallowed by a whale.

—Fine. Three. Three in the entire history of mankind.

—Won't you shut up? Why do you talk all the time? You never did before.

—I always talked, but you were too busy to listen. Computer games. TikTok. Streaming. Jerking off to Vivian in the yearbook.

—I hate you.

—I'm you, so you hate you.

"SHUT UP!" I scream out loud.

My whale sings a low note that vibrates all around me. Maybe he's shushing me. Maybe he wants to sleep. I lie against the moist blackness, the slow thump of his heart under my head, take a deep slow breath, and hold it.

— NIGHT DRIFTING —

THE WHALE SLEEPS, half its brain resting, the other half

38

remembering to rise and breathe. It drifts in the current. Luminescent creatures gather around it, swaying with the water's flow. In the deep fathoms, sounds of other whales calling each other. The whale dreams. It is a restless dream of unseen danger lurking in the distance. The great eye opens and sees nothing in the depths. Clicking sound to find out what is near. All safe for now. Slowly rising to the surface, its back breaks black and slick, and sprays the moon.

— LET THERE BE LIGHT —

IS IT TIME for school? I can't be late again. Maybe I'll see Vivian today. No, wait, we graduated.

It's dark. Can't even see light through the blinds. Or anything. Maybe the power went out. My pillow is wet. I must have been drooling.

The bed is moving. Earthquake—? Why can't I see? Where am I?!

Oh.

Shit.

It's not fair to dream about my home in Burbank and wake in the lungs of a whale. If I close my eyes, maybe I can get back to the dream...

The rush catapults me up and I'm tumbled and flung and the blowhole opens to sunlight! It's day! Yippee!

—*Yippee? What are you, seven?*

—*It's day. Okay? I saw daylight.*

—*Whoop-te-doo! You think that makes a difference?*

—*It does to me. It makes me feel better.*

—*Whatever, Lard Ass.*

I'm sore all over. It isn't bruising, it's muscles. Probably because I'm constantly shifting to stay balanced. I'm using muscles I never knew I had.

The smells from the air outside trigger all sorts of juices in my floppy ol' belly. If this whale is my home for a few days, I need to

39

eat, but water is the first priority. Only there's no chance of anything except seawater. Everyone knows from the movies you're not supposed to drink that. I'll die of thirst.

Can you die of thirst in a sauna? There's moisture everywhere. Maybe it isn't salty like the ocean.

In the darkness, I press on the lung wall and feel a trickle of liquid ooze into my palm. *Should I?*

—*Should you drink whale mucus? Is that the question, Lard Ass?*

—*Will I get a disease?*

—*Will whale mucus kill you? That's what you're worried about?*

—*Or maybe a parasite?*

—*You are going to DIE in here. Maybe whale snot will keep you alive as a liquid source, but all the same, you are GOING TO DIE IN HERE. But go ahead. Drink up. Down the hatch!*

I don't even bother with a tentative lick. The palm-full swallow goes down. It's slimy and a bit salty, but not overly so. Tastes a little sour, like milk that's going bad but isn't chunky and can still be used on Cheerios in a pinch. I drink four palmfuls. If that stays down, I'll try more.

My stomach growls. My whale rumbles a response. I've got to eat. There's the sound of rushing water below me. Feeding time? Squiggling my way, I feel for the flap. My hand finds a fleshy opening and reaches out into—freezing cold water. Bombardment by hundreds of whatevers. I grab and pull a mass of slippery things in.

Light! My wet cave has light! I fling the bright blue squirming creatures from my hand and they glow all the more brightly. Little fish flop among them.

I've got to eat while I can see these things. Pop a small pencil-thin fish in my mouth. I should bite down. I can't. The fish flits about on my tongue. Should swallow it. I try, but my swallower has closed.

—*Chew, Lard Ass. You want it to be alive in your belly? Maybe it'll stop on the way down and slide into your lungs. You want that?*

I chomp down hard and the wriggling stops. It's not like sushi. Crunches and goo—

—*Swallow and catch another. Pretend you're in front of the TV. They're crunchy goldfish, like in the bag. Yum-Yum.*

My brain doesn't want another, but my stomach is reaching up, demanding MORE! I pick up as many as I can find, stuffing them in my mouth like wriggling french fries. Crunch. Crunch.

I grab one large flopper. Something stabs my hand. His back fin is full of spiked needle-like bones. Bastard Needle Fish! I bite hard, separating the needles and swallowing the angry rest.

There are slimy sheets of something scattered around. I kick one of the blue lights over to it. Seaweed. That's on sushi, isn't it? A Japanese chef must have been swallowed by a whale at some point and invented their cuisine.

The seaweed is salty and chewy and tastes like swamp, but I picture dried-fruit-leather and get a lot down.

There are a few torpedo-shaped things with tentacles. Squid? I've never seen Calamari when it wasn't fried. And they always come cut up in rings with the legs separate. Maybe I should pull those off. I grab hold of the torpedo-head in one hand and the tentacles in the other and pull. They separate with a sucking sound. Bite the torpedo. It's got something hard inside like plexiglass. Yank that out and the rest swallows easy.

Load in another wad of seaweed and something cracks under my teeth. Spit it into my palm and hold it near the fading glow. Plastic bottle cap.

The blue light creatures are dying or losing their natural batteries. I need to keep these around so I can see. I tap one to start it up again. Something flies out and stings me between the fingers. Fuck! Damn fucker. Slide my foot on one side of him, and the other on the other side, and I smash hard between my sneakers. Die, you scum!

I need to get these things corralled. I need light.

What can I keep them in? Anything in my pockets? Wallet. Twenty-one dollars. Emergency Visa, ATM card, LA County Library card, driver's license, Cinema Club Popcorn Card. Condom—got a box and practiced putting them on. Pretty good at it now. House key. Toke's Ziploc of weed. Shit. He's going to be pissed.

My hand is getting kinda numb where that thing stung me. Like the dentist was trying to shoot my mouth full of Novocain and I blocked him and he shot the wad into my hand. I pinch my finger. It's an avatar hand. I can make it move but can't feel the skin. Maybe I'm dying. I get swallowed by a whale and a tiny flickering blue light kills me.

The blue flickering things are almost dark now. I don't want to touch any more and get stung. What'll I do?

—*It's like the Alien Showdown game. They're not all gonna be killers. Some can be allies. You gotta learn to differentiate. That sucker you squashed had long tentacles. Maybe a stinging jellyfish. Stay clear of those. Get moving, Lard Ass! Bag those suckers like the angel fish Mom brought home from Kmart.*

—*Dump Toke's weed?*

—*Save it. May need to get stoned later.*

—*And where do I save th—*

—*In the Johnson Jacket. You won't be getting it on with the ladies in here.*

The condom's pretty hard to fill with the marijuana, but I get it done.

Grumble-warble, squeaking wagon-wheel, clicking, and gong. We rise and I'm jostled like usual with the whale breath, fresh air, a flash of sun and then darkness. Only two pale blue squiggling glows are visible. I've got to get more of these wriggling lights while my whale is still feeding.

Pressing both hands through the flap, I open the baggie and let the water and whatevers fill it. I zip it closed and pull it back inside. It's a glowing fish tank!

The glowers are small but all different kinds. Some minuscule dots of light, others like jellyfish dancing among bits of shredded plastic. Little fish and cocktail shrimp swirl with them, my snack for later.

My whale makes a horn sound. Singing low. I should name him. I could name him Moby. Or Dick. They always say *thar she blows* so maybe he's a she. But this whale was way too big and violent, ramming the boat and all. He's a he.

My hand is still numb. Hopefully feeling will come back sometime. I munch more sushi food, lean against the hot, cushiony wall, the Ziploc bag of light shining on my belly. It's like watching TV on the couch. I'm full and watching blue flickering light and, for the first time here, I'm happy.

I'll name my whale Home.

— SHOULD I CRY? —

TOBEY THINKS I'M CRAZY. Dan thinks I'm crazy. The Press, the internet, the entire universe thinks I'm crazy. I guess I am crazy. I must have imagined Brian's voice.

—*What if you didn't, Ann? What if Brian is alive? What if he did call?*

—*What if I'm crazy? I'm talking to myself. Isn't that a sign that a person is crazy?*

—*If they talk out-loud. Everyone talks to themselves in their head. Don't they?*

I don't know what to do. I could call Dan and help Kate organize the funeral. I can't just sit here. I don't even know if I should cry. Should I cry? If my son is dead, I should cry.

—*So why aren't you crying?*

—*I heard him. I think. I can't cry if he's alive.*

— CAVE MAN —

CALL ME A SCHLEMIEL. Ha. Ha. That's got to have been said a thousand times. No doubt that dude Melville isn't laughing anymore. I never finished the book. Guess I'd have time now.

Maybe I wouldn't be in this fix if I'd finished Moby Dick. Maybe I'd be so sick of whales I wouldn't have gone whale watching. Moral is: read books, safer than real life.

How long have I been in Home? I can't keep track of time. The blowhole is light or dark, but I don't always know how long I've slept between his breaths. If I knew, I could carve little lines for each day in my spongy wall. Only that would hurt Home and anything

43

that hurts Home hurts me. All I know is I've been in here long enough to be less terrified and more super bored. I need a computer game. I miss blowing up shit. Having someone's blood get spattered. My avatar wouldn't have been swallowed. My avatar was huge and musclebound and deadly.

Home may be a super big whale, big enough for me to live in him, but he ain't no McMansion. This open part of his lungs isn't even the size of the small upstairs bathroom of our house in Burbank. Not being able to walk is a real drag. Mom was always yelling "get exercise" and now that I can't, I wish I could. I guess I'm using muscles constantly, shifting to stay upright, but it's not like really exercising.

Lying down, I stretch my arms over my head, heave my stomach tight, bend forward, crunching my belly, and reach—can almost touch my knees!

—*Ha! Look at Lard Ass! Whatdya think you're doing?*

—*Sit-ups. Gonna get like my avatar.*

—*No chance in hell.*

I drop back with a thump and try another. My stomach blubber shakes and my arms quiver. This is too hard. I'll never get like my avatar. Not in real life.

—*Told you.*

Now what? If I was home, I'd be on the computer. What did people do before computers? Before television! Before radio! I'm like a Cave Man. What did they do? Sit around and think? What hell!

I can't even reminisce. You got to be old to reminisce. I remember birthdays. I remember Dad and Mom yelling at each other. I'd put on headphones to drown out the fights, volume on maximum, but it doesn't help when you know what you're trying not to hear.

—*You can reminisce that twelfth birthday.*

—*Yeah. The Disneyland visit. Mom and me were singing Old MacDonald had a farm, eee-ii, ee-ii, ohhh. Dad was driving us back and I was singing with Mom.*

—*'Til Dad yelled, "SHUT UP!"*

—*We were having fun.*

—*It's a stupid song to listen to for a long car ride.*

—He didn't like us having fun.

—No one's stopping you now, Lard Ass.

"Old MacDonald had a farm, eee-ii, ee-ii, ohhh," I sing loudly.

Home blasts a sound from low to high. I copy his sound. He sings out another few notes. It's a crazy tune but I'm game. I wonder if he can hear me. A tiny voice below his brain. I hope so.

I sing along to Home and we make good music together.

—— DESTRUCTION ——

THE PEOPLE on the television screen are screaming as they're blown apart, but I can't hear them. I have the sound off in case Brian calls. But he won't. He would have by now. It's been days.

What movie is this? A crowd looks up into the sky with awe as they're obliterated. When was the last time I felt awe? Have I ever? I'm not sure.

Brian must have. That first moment, falling into a mouth the size of a ferry. He might have even said, "awesome."

Why doesn't he call?!

I should shower. I should eat. I should style this mess of hair. I should open the drapes and let the sun in. I should decide what to do next. But all I do is watch television. Stream disaster movies. End of the world movies. Buildings collapse. People fall into burning fissures. Volcanos, ice ages, asteroids, aliens. I fast forward through the talking and watch the destruction over and over, but I feel nothing.

I feel nothing.

Someone's knocking on the door.

I don't care. Brian has a key, so it's not him.

The lock turns.

Could it be him!?

I leap up and stumble, falling to the carpet, my legs asleep from sitting too long.

The front door swings open, Dan steps in and stares down at me. "Holy shit. You look like crap, Ann."

45

I shrug.

"The memorial's this Saturday."

I imagine the soft whispers in a darkened funeral-home hall. People greeting me with sorrowful looks. Flowers and a super-sized picture of super-sized Brian. A spot saved for me in the front. No casket. There wouldn't be a casket because there's no body. There's no body because Brian's alive in a whale.

"I won't be going."

The vein on Dan's forehead asserts itself. He takes a breath, trying to tamp back the frustration. "You have to go." He holds out his hand. "Let's get you up."

I swat his hand and scooch back on the carpet. "I don't have to go and I don't have to get up."

The vein swells. "This is the invitation. It has all the information. When, where…" He pulls a card from his breast pocket. The front has Brian's picture and the words *In Memoriam* on it.

I turn back to my television. A glass skyscraper explodes. In the reflection on the screen, I watch Dan jerk with anger and set the card on the dining room table.

"You have to go. You can't miss the memorial for your only son. Everyone will know."

"Everyone will know?"

"Everyone will *be there*. Okay? Brian's friends, teachers—"

"Your shiny new wife and your shiny new kids—"

Dan kicks one of the dining room chairs. Slats crack as his foot goes through the back. Tangled in it, he flings his leg out and the chair smashes against the wall and a piece flies my way. I flinch as a jolt of something goes through me. This is way better than disaster movies.

I want to see more destruction. "Break the entire set," I say, getting off the floor. "Smash it to bits. I always hated it."

Dan bends to pick up the pieces. "Sorry. I'll—"

"Leave it. I like the new look. Now scram."

I wait for him to have the final word.

He sighs dramatically and walks to the door. "Just—you'll regret it if you don't go to the memorial."

I want him to leave, so I stifle getting the last word.

Dan shifts awkwardly. He's not going.

"What else?" I ask.

He clears his throat and looks at the T.V. Another building explodes. "With the memorial expenses and the cost of living..."

"What?"

"Now that Brian's gone... child support was supposed to stop at graduation anyway, I didn't have to..."

"Stop the fucking child support, asshole, but Brian's alive!"

"You're fucking crazy, Ann."

"If believing he's alive makes me crazy, I'm crazy."

"Believing doesn't make him alive."

"People all over the world believe things that other people don't. I believe Brian's alive and if there's one chance in a billion I'm right, I have to do something!"

"Like what?"

And right like that, it's clear. Relief rushes over me.

"Find Brian," I say. Saying it makes me smile. I have a mission. "Time to go, I've lots to do."

Dan's forehead vein is back. "You should talk to someone."

"I talk to myself all the time."

"You're making me think I need to—intercede."

I know what he means. Send me to a nut house. Can he do that?

"You can't do that. We're not married anymore."

"If you're a danger to yourself or others—"

I pick up a piece of the broken chair and hold it like a bat.

With a *how-in-the-world-did-I-ever-marry-this-nut* look, he darts out, making sure to slam the door.

— WHALE DIET —

REACHING OUT the flap to snag breakfast and a fresh Ziploc full of glowing Wrigglers. Their pale light shows me the catch o' the day. Pencil fish. Seaweed. Calamari torpedo heads. I chomp down. Home rolls and I tumble, my shorts sliding down to my knees. Might as well go naked. No one's gonna see me.

—*You gotta hide your flabby body, Lard Ass.*

—*It's not as flabby as it was. I'm losing weight being on this whale diet.*

—*You'll have to live for years in this whale to lose your jelly rolls.*

—*Maybe I will. Maybe I'll live here for years and you'll have to finally admit it when I get thin.*

—*Keep dreaming, Fat Boy. Go ahead. Strip. Let your clothes tumble and scatter and clog up Home's breathing. Good idea.*

I slip out of my clothes. Everything is sticky and gross and it feels great to be free. Lay the shorts on my T-shirt, place my sneakers next, and the dorky waterproof phone deal, tie the corners of the shirt to make a bundle.

—*Yeah, and how does your hobo pack not get lost next whale move?*

—*I'll tie it to something.*

—*A fence post? A tree?*

I undo the bundle, take off the sneaker laces, tie them together for one long strand, re-do the bundle, loop the shoelace around the knot, and tie it around my ankle.

—*How you gonna walk with that ball and chain, Duffus?*

—*Not exactly walking in here.*

That shut him up.

—*I can hear you, Lard Ass. And it didn't.*

— WRITING ON THE WALL —

I DON'T QUITE KNOW how to start my mission, but know what I want to do.

I swing as hard as I can. Down onto the table comes a chair. It bounces off, unaffected. I raise it again and swing down. It nicks the tabletop but remains intact. Damn it!

I need tools. I slip into the garage via the laundry room. I haven't been in here in forever. Just getting this near the dusty beige Volvo gives me anxiety as if I'm going out. Try to ignore that and find a hammer, but there are no tools where they used to be. When he left, Dan must have taken all that manly stuff figuring a woman and a pudgy-do-nothing-boy wouldn't need them.

On the way back to the dining room, I grab the decorative poker from its station beside the gas fireplace. Aiming for the back slat of a chair, I swing. It hits the chair and bends. What is this made of!?

Grabbing the edge of the table, I lift and do angry superhero move and tip high, farther, and it lands hard, flat, legs skyward, like a belly-up beast. I grab a leg and lean against it. Creaking wood. Lean harder, and wonderful cracking sounds. Now we're getting somewhere. I press down and it bends lower and—the leg breaks free. YES! It's heavy. I swing and a chair flies apart. This is a wonderful weapon. Smashing it into the chairs, slats splinter, legs launch.

All the king's horses and all the king's men couldn't put this set together again.

I pile the pieces in the corner, open a bottle of wine, grab a thick magic marker, and sit on the splintery expanse of dining room carpet to make my plan. Except, how do I make a plan? How do people start?

To-Do List.

Written on the wall because—who cares.

1. Find Brian.

How?

Where do whales go? They have routes, shipping lanes, right? They migrate. I'll map where the whale was, find out how quickly they travel, figure what's the most common route, and pinpoint when the whale will be there. How do I do that?

2. Talk to an expert.

Wherever the expert says Brian's whale is, I'll go.

3. Hire a boat.

I'll need money.

4. Sell the furniture. Except for this dining room set.

That won't be enough money

5. Sell the house.

No escrow. No closings. Cash. I'll take a loss.

6. Pack.

Pack what? I don't want any of this. I'll only pack boxes of Brian's stuff that he'll want when he gets out.

What else do I need to do?

My cell phone. Gotta keep that charged.

7. Buy an extra phone charger and battery.

Where will I go? Could be across borders.

8. Passport.

Before Brian was born, Dan and I dreamed of a trip to Europe. I wanted to go to France or Italy. He wanted to go to London where they speak "regular." We never got further than getting passports and international plug adapters.

9, International plug adapters.

I look at the list on the wall. It feels good to see a plan.

I'm going to find Brian, whatever that takes. I'll find that whale and I'll find my son. I should name Brian's whale. What's a good name for a whale? Moby Dick?. No, he killed everyone. What was the name of the whale in the movie Pinocchio?

10. Watch Pinocchio.

— PLANNING IN HOME —

I'M GETTING USED to this tumbling and rolling. Home blasts hard and gobs of stuff whiz past me out the blowhole. What is all that?

—*It's mucus. We're in lungs. You never had a cold and hacked up phlegm?*

—*Home has a cold?*

—*Why wouldn't he? Look at this place. It's a mess. And stinks. You're killing him, Lard Ass.*

I shake my Ziploc of glowing Wrigglers to get them lit up and look around. This place is like my room. Crap all over. Fishbones. Torpedo Head plexiglass. Shrimp tails and shells. Dead Wrigglers. What am I thinking?

I *am* killing Home. He needs a good cleaning. Scooping up everything that shouldn't be in here, except me, I dump the refuse down the flap. Press all pooled water out as well. The lungs are spic-and-span. Mom wouldn't believe it.

"Hope that makes you feel better, Home."

I've got to make sure I do that more often.

It's time to make a plan. I need to have a To-Do List in my head. Put cleaning at the top of it.

1. Clean Home.

2. Eat food.

3. Catch new glowing Wrigglers, dump out the old.

What else?

4. Learn to hold my breath along with Home.

5. Do push-ups. Sit-ups. Yes, really. I can.

6. Learn Home's songs and teach him mine.

What else?

—Besides change your entire personality, Lard Ass? Besides growing a pair, stopping being a dork, a duffus, a wuss, and a fat slobbery-slob, ugly-as-shit, do-nothing, everybody-hates-you, waste of space?

—Yeah, besides that.

— OUTSIDE —

I LEARN TONS about whales online, but all the internet googling doesn't answer my questions. I need to find an expert. That means I need to go out. Outside. Out of the beige house.

The thought makes me ill. Everyone will recognize me as the crackpot who thinks their son is alive in a whale. I'll be laughed at and whispered about. I should spend another day researching online.

—Brian's in a whale and needs your help and you can't leave the house. You're a wuss, Ann.

Brian was a wuss with his dark room and endless video games and I'm a wuss. Did I make him that way?

—Stop the endless wondering. Take a shower. Get dressed.

I take off my pinecone pajamas. Brian got me these five years ago. I used to like pine trees. Can't remember why. How did he know?

The shower feels unbelievable. How long has it been?

My closet is full of beige clothes. I wish I had something green or red or blue.

Beige bra, beige underwear, beige blouse, beige slacks, beige socks, beige shoes, beige eyeshadow, beige lipstick. Flick on the beige blow-drier but the sound hurts and who the hell cares if my hair curls weirdly.

—*Find the car keys. Start the car. Go.*

The car keys are in my purse which might as well be an Objet d'art, sitting in its place on the entryway table. My heart pounds as I step into the garage. My throat's closing. Pray the car won't start after being idle for so long. It purrs to life—damn it. Of course, Brian uses it. Push the opener button and as the big panel slides up I remember—*Shit, the Press!*—but they've gone. Guess watching an agoraphobe's house isn't interesting.

Put it in reverse and slow out into glare. The sun pummels me and I fish through my purse for dark glasses. Through the windshield, I feel the light boring into my skin. I must have been missing my vitamin D. Will Brian get sick without the sun?

—*Keep moving.*

I can't catch my breath. Everything is too bright. Too big. Too hard. I'll be better tomorrow.

Am I *this* terrified of the world?

Yes.

Fuck that.

Step on the gas.

— BRINGING IN, SENDING OUT TREASURES —

I'VE DONE TEN PUSH-UPS, ten sit-ups, and held my breath three times for a count of sixty. Grumble-warble, squeaking wagon-wheel, clicking, and gong. I hum along. Home blasts his breath. Feeding is more interesting near the surface, so it's time for breakfast. I slip the Ziploc out the flap, dump last night's glowing Wrigglers, and feel around in the stream for food. Something snags my wrist. I yank my arm back. It's caught! I pull hard and my arm comes in with a yellow nylon rope twisted around it and there's more beyond the flap.

—*Lard Ass, pull it in! It could be something!*

I pull on the rope and a mass gets stuck. What is that? Struggling to get it in without flooding the lungs, I heave, and a mound of something lands inside. Glowing Wrigglers flop about with shrimp, seaweed, Bastard Needle Fish, Torpedo Heads, and Pencil Fish. I collect the Wrigglers, stuff them in my Ziploc, and shine their light on the mass—a tangle of yellow rope, a plastic bottle, a rubber corrugated hose-like tube—all intertwined with countless grocery bags. A gold mine!

Munching shrimp, I untangle the rope and bags to reach the bottle. It's Coke-shaped. Red cap on tight. I hold it up to see if there might be a drop of that brown liquid left. I open the top and tilt over my tongue—the drop lands—rancid, sweetness. Yuck!

But the bottle *was* sealed. It didn't leak and sink. I could do a message-in-a-bottle! *Help, I'm trapped in a whale. Get me out.*

—*Don't think that would work, Lard Ass. They may find a bottle, but how would anyone find you?*

—*Radar?*

—*How do they know they found Home and not some other whale?*

I shrug in my mind.

—*And if they found this whale, out of all the others in all the oceans, if they found Home, how do they get you out? They can't very well kill him and tow him to shore and open him up and expect you'll be alive.*

—*I know.*

—*So what's the use of a note?*

—*It's doing something!*

—*Okay.*

—*Only I've nothing to write with.*

—*I have an idea.*

—Your idea is my idea.

—Put something in the bottle. Your license.

—I need my license. What if I get out? I might need picture I.D.

—Library card. It can be traced to you. Someone finds it, they can connect the dots.

—What dots?

—I don't know. Just put it in the bottle.

—I know what dots!

Using the sharp fin bone of a Bastard Needle Fish I poke tiny holes in my dollar, (saving mom's twenty), spelling out letters.

IN WHALE HELP
BRIAN KETCHUM

I add Mom's phone number, roll up the dollar, fold the library card, put them in the bottle, and screw the top on tight, tight, tight.

This feels so cool! I'm doing something and it might get me found!

I want to kiss the bottle but know my inner voice would have a field day with that so—

"Bon voyage, Bottle. Hope you find someone."

Bottle is dropped out the flap and disappears.

—- SEA WORLD —-

THE GIRL SMILES like she's been trained to. "Welcome to Sea World. How many?"

I hope she hasn't been watching all the news about the crazy lady with the boy in the whale. "I need to talk to your whale expert."

"How many in your party, ma'am?"

"I'm not a party. I'm a person wanting to discuss an issue with the whale expert."

"One adult?"

"Miss, I'm not going to Sea World. I want to talk to your expert."

"Ma'am, we can't let you enter Sea World without a pass."

"Okay. One adult."

"One adult day-pass. That's one-o-nine-ninety-nine."

"Excuse me?"

"One hundred and nine dollars and ninety-nine cents."

"WHAT?!"

"Ma'am, other people are waiting. Do you want the pass?"

One hundred and nine dollars and ninety-nine cents would buy me a new set of sheets so I could throw out the ones Dan slept on. One hundred and nine dollars and ninety-nine cents would take me and Brian out to dinner at that great sushi restaurant. One hundred and nine dollars and ninety-nine cents would get me non-beige clothes at Target. I pass the girl my Visa card.

As I sign away the money I ask, "Where do I find the whale expert?"

The girl adjusts her happy-face, "The information booth will be glad to answer all your questions. Have a wonderful visit! Next please."

The information people only direct me to the whale area.

Inside the dark cavernous exhibit, killer whales swim in deep blue. Kids press their noses against the glass as the monstrous beasts glide close. My knees start shaking. There is no air in here. The world is tilting and a huge shape moves toward me. Is this the last thing Brian saw?

"Easy there, let's sit you down." A strong arm has my elbow and guides me to a cement faux-coral-reef in the middle of our underwater cavern. The boy-man is beach blond. Probably a surfer. He's muscular in a way Brian could never be. An Adonis with the Sea World logo is stitched on the pale shirt spanning his too-obvious chest.

"Would you like some water, Ma'am?"

"My son. He's in one."

Adonis adds concern to his look. "Your son is lost?"

"In a whale. I need to find out how to get him out."

Alarm and panic flood his eyes. "Your son was eaten by a whale? Which one—"

"Not here. In the ocean. He is living in a whale."

Laughter burps from the Greek-god lips. "You're that lady? The one on the news."

"I need to talk to a whale expert."

"Why don't we take a walk, get you some air."

He helps me up and leads me out into the blinding light. I see we're heading for a security guy so I pull to get my arm back but Adonis won't let go.

"I need to talk to a whale expert!"

"Ma'am, keep your voice down. We don't want to alarm our guests."

The security officer joins us. He takes my other arm.

"MY SON WAS SWALLOWED BY A WHALE!" I scream to the patrons. "I WANT TO ASK AN EXPERT AND THESE MEN WON'T LET ME!"

Several people lift their cell phones, hoping to capture a scuffle. Shouts of "crazy" and "nutcase" bounce around the crowd. Security talks on his walkie.

A grey-bearded man in a lab coat steps up to me. "I'm Doctor Ziegler—"

I snap at him, "I don't need a Doctor. I need a fucking whale expert."

"I'm a doctor in marine biology. Your fucking whale expert."

Doctor Ziegler takes me to his office. It's a mess. Whale models dangle from the ceiling swimming in the air-conditioner stream, the walls are papered with pictures and posters of whales, and on every horizontal surface are books, files, and whale tchotchkes. Doctor Ziegler moves a big-eyed stuffed whale off a chair and motions for me to sit.

After the first time the doctor watches Toke's video on my phone, he rubs his eyes, slips on his wire-rim glasses, holds a magnifying glass close to the screen, and watches again. The seventh time he has me send it to his computer. He peers it on the bigger screen as I wander the room. Graphs of migration. Posters of whale anatomy. Images of whale varieties. There are a lot more kinds than I thought. Some aren't even so big. There is a silhouette of a man standing next to the biggest whale. I assume the silhouette is of a normal-sized man. If so, a man could definitely fit inside this monster. A hundred times over.

Step to several turn-of-some-century whaling adventure reproductions. Courier and Ives without the sweetness. Whales crashing on top of boats. Whales tipping sailors into the sea. Monstrous whales swallowing terrified men.

Doctor Ziegler coughs. "The video isn't completely clear. From the massive size, it looks like it could be an abnormally large blue whale, but the mouth physiology is not of a baleen species. I've not seen a cetacean like this one."

"Cetacean?"

Dr. Ziegler rubs his beard happily. "Cetaceans are marine mammals. The Odontoceti—toothed whales including dolphins and porpoises and the Mysticeti—the baleen whales. There are approximately ninety species of cetaceans, and more than seventy are Odontoceti. Cetaceans belong to the order Cetartiodactyla with their closest living relatives being hippopotamuses, camels, pigs, and other even-toed ungulates. About fifty-million years ago they diverged—"

"What I need to know is—can a person live in one?"

The doctor opens his mouth to say "no" but stops himself. He takes his glasses off, looking at the lenses in hopes they'll give him something positive to say.

I press two fingers to my lips, trying to keep my rage from escaping.

Looking up from his glasses, Ziegler tries a crooked smile, "It's —unlikely."

Waving my phone as evidence a little frantically in front of his face, I object. "I heard my son. In the whale. He's alive. He called me."

The doctor shakes his head. "I saw you on the internet. You're doing yourself a disservice. Your son would have gone into the first stomach. There are powerful muscles there—"

"—that mash the food to a pulp," I interrupt. "And next the masticated food goes to the second stomach where it is digested. You think this mashing made the phone pocket-dial me but that didn't happen. Brian's alive. In the whale."

Crossing the room, the doctor moves his finger along a poster on the wall, the anatomy of a blue whale, "Mouth goes to stomachs. Stomachs to intestines. Down and out."

Next to him, my finger jabbing, I rhythmically give chest compressions to the illustration, "The lungs. He's in the lungs."

The doctor shakes his head. "If he was in the lungs, he might survive for a bit. He'd have air. But he couldn't get in there from the mouth."

"Couldn't he go 'down the wrong pipe' like when we swallow wrong?"

"You're talking about our anatomy. You're talking about slipping through the piece of cartilage that covers the entrance of the trachea, either diverting air to the larynx, or food to the esophagus, the epiglottis—"

"That's what I said."

"Whales breathe only through the blow hole up top. It's equivalent to our nostrils. They don't have a link to their lungs from their mouth as we do."

"Brian's whale does. He's different."

"Approximately fifty-million years ago, in the Early Eocene epoch, the ancient whales were land mammals." The Doctor returns to his chair, nodding to the colorful chart behind him full of prehistoric beasts. "These first whales, like the Pakicetus here, had long skulls and big sharp teeth. Doesn't look much like a whale, does it? But you study their skulls—"

"So if whales came from land, they had the cartilage flap that made sure food didn't go into the lungs."

"*Then* yes, but they slowly adapted to living in the sea and as their physiology evolved, they lost the back legs, their nostrils shifted up into blow holes, the epiglottis, what you're talking about, disappeared—"

"Except Brian's. His whale has the epiglottis thing leading to the lungs."

"It would be a physical anomaly."

The Doctor's eyes widen. I'm not sure why until I notice I'm looming over him, one hand on either side of his chair, leaning in close. I should back up and smile but I don't. "Did you know my son Brian was born with a cleft palate? You've heard of those?"

The Doctor nods, probably longing for Sea World security.

"My son's cleft palate. Is that normal or is that a physical anomaly?"

"I consider that a fairly common craniofacial anomaly."

As I lean closer, the Doctor's beard recedes into his collar "Aren't there other known anomalies? Like a two-headed calf? Like webbed toes?"

"Certainly, but—"

"Shit happens, Doctor." I jab my finger near his nose and he winces. "Things don't go as planned. Nature screws up."

"You're talking about teratologies, rare occurrences—"

"Brian's whale is a missing link. A missing fucking link that's the bridge between in-water whales and your—" I straighten up to reference the poster of the ancient whales, "—P-whatever land-whales!"

Doctor Ziegler takes the opportunity to dart from his chair and crash into his coat rack, spin, tangle himself in the yellow mackintosh, and tumble to the floor while spilling a whale-shaped hat complete with blowhole and squirter pouch.

"You must be the life of the party," I say stepping to him with my hand out to help him up. He crouches like I'm about to attack.

Maybe I am. When did I turn into such an angry woman? Have I always been this way? Once again I lean too close to the bulging eyes. "My son is alive in that whale."

The Doctor raises his hand to scratch his beard, or maybe to block a slap. "I understand you want to believe that," he says quietly. "I'd like to believe, but based on my knowledge, your son is dead."

His hand blocks my blow.

— WORK IN HOME —

IN THE LIGHT of the pale Wrigglers, I work.

Inspect, place, tie, repeat. Inspect, place, tie, repeat.

Every grocery bag that doesn't disintegrate I add to my contraption. The salvageable bags from the mass of treasure I pulled into my whale get tied to the yellow rope. I tie them so they'll stay open. Tie them on opposite sides, alternating.

The last one secured. Time to test.

I sing along to Home's grumble-warble, squeaking wagon-wheel, clicking, and gong.

Home rises, blasts out, and pulls in fresh air. It smells different. Wonder where we are.

Hearing the rush by the tube, I crawl to the flap with the bag-rope contraption. Tie one end to my wrist and slide my invention out. My Yellow Shopping Cart.

—*Good luck with that, Lard Ass.*

My inner voice almost doesn't sound sarcastic.

—*Thanks.*

The rope tugs at my wrist. Jerks and jumps. The rope yanks tighter. Tighter and heavier.

Hand over hand, I retrieve it, pulling the rope and—one grocery bag after another, full of Torpedo Heads, Pencil Fish, Bastard Needle Fish, Calamari, Shrimp, strands of seaweed, and each a balloon glowing with countless Wrigglers. It's so beautiful!

My Yellow Shopping Cart works!

— OUT TO SEA —

THE GREAT BEAST'S stomachs mashed it, but it remained intact, and now, after traveling the long winding journey through the whale's intestines, Bottle finally slides out with a slurry of sludge. Crusted with the weight of the muck, it descends in the darkness. A brush from the massive tail wipes the clumps free and the plastic container rises.

Breaking the surface, Bottle bobs and bounces. Moonlight gleams over it as huge waves roll underneath. Library Card and Punctured Dollar Bill slide back and forth with each shift. Beyond it, in every direction, nothing but unending ocean. Had Bottle a brain it might be startled at the vastness of the sea and sky and wonder about the infinitesimal chance of ever being found.

— AT HOME IN HOME —

I CHECK MY PHONE every once in a while. It never turns on anymore but I keep trying. When Home is down too long, my ears pop and my joints ache, but I'm getting better at not panicking.

My nails are growing. My beard is growing. Wish I could shave. It's itchy. I bet I look like a psycho.

I have a routine. I sleep on and off. Send out the Yellow Grocery Cart. Pull in food. Eat Japanese. Clean house. Relieve myself down the flap. Re-pack belongings in the hobo-sack tied to my ankle. Do sit-ups. Push-ups. Practice slow breathing. I can hold my breath for a pretty long time when I slow down. Home and I sing campfire songs, pop songs, and his made-up tunes. We sing mostly his tunes. I sing through the rubber corrugated tube to sound more like Home. He sings all the time. Sometimes it sounds sad. Sometimes it is almost like a lullaby rocking me to sleep. There are a few I call his top ten on repeat. Like Grumble-warble, squeaking wagon-wheel, clicking, and gong.

I catch the luminous Wigglers in my Ziploc and watch them. They're my show—*The Blue Light Special. The Blue Light Special* is your usual family Sit-Com. The big ones bully the small ones. Right when the big ones think they're king-of-the-roost, a little one gets the better of them, but in the end, the wimps and wusses always lose. It's pretty funny. I provide the laugh track.

The show's got a fuzzy round Wiggler that has parts dangling off his head. He's a duffus. Comic relief. A big broad triangle one is the muscular guy—the Hero-type with broad shoulders. He's always bumping into Duffus and making him light up bright. Duffus gets mad, but tries to act like he doesn't care. It makes everyone laugh. The little Squigglers are the girls. They circle around Triangle Hero. He shines and they go "oooooo" like he's really special. When they circle around Duffus, they squiggle and giggle.

I watch for a while and try to laugh but I'm not in the mood. This isn't a sitcom, it's real life and that isn't funny. Real life sucks. Duffus is getting harassed like you-know-who. I'm better off in here. No one ridicules me.

—*Almost no one, Lard Ass.*

—*Almost no one.*

When I got out of high school I thought things would get better. I was waiting for the big change. I'd get a girlfriend, maybe Vivian, move on from Billy and Toke, get a good-paying job and leave Mom and Burbank. Move to the beach, or maybe Hollywood Hills.

Only none of that happened. I don't know what I'm supposed to do. I'm supposed to start my life but doing what? How can I choose what I'll be for forever? How am I supposed to meet girls? How do I get a job that pays the big bucks? Mom thinks I should accept anything. McDonald's even. She wants rent. She wants me to do an online course and get a degree. In what? Video games is all I'm good at and I'm not really that good at them. I'm passable.

Duffus has moved to the edge of the Ziploc. He's trying to occupy himself with watching his own feelers float about. His light is dim now. He's a dim bulb. Billy called me that when I didn't know how to use that power drill. So what? He had a dad showing him shit. I had a dad yelling at me and Mom and then making a new family in Thousand Oaks. Maybe he's teaching the new daughters how to use a drill, but he never taught me.

Triangle Hero moves toward Duffus. I don't like the look in his transparent eyes. The silly Squigglers float around behind him, commenting on everything, giving each other snarky looks. Duffus is backed into the corner of the Ziploc bag.

It happens fast. Triangle Hero darts a thing out and Duffus is struck and stuck and reeled in. Triangle Hero does something with the tangly things, wrapping them around Duffus. The laugh track would be howling at the way Duffus is wriggling. He's not gonna make it.

I don't like this show, but it's the only thing on. I shake the bag, hoping that will let Duffus escape from Triangle Hero, but he's knocked closer and his little glow grows dimmer.

If I could pull him out I would. I could pull him out and put him somewhere. Where could he live in peace? If I swallowed him and breathed in hard as he went down, would he get sucked into my lungs and have a place to rest? He could reach out and grab food as I ate. I'd protect him. He could sing and I'd sing along and Home would sing around us both.

Too late. Triangle Hero's eating Duffus.

— BOTTLE BOBBING —

BOTTLE BOBS in the waves.

Sunlight beats down on it. Condensation droplets form inside, dampening Library Card and Punctured Dollar Bill.

Were anyone swimming next to it, Bottle would be noticed. Five feet away, it might still be found. But beyond ten feet, the green-grey waves would obliterate it from view. The vastness of the ocean makes it invisible. Still, it moves with the current. Already 300 miles from where it was first evacuated in the slurry from the whale.

The currents are tricky in this area. Traveling south along the western edge of North America, a slight push and Bottle will join the stream headed for Hawaii. Most likely it would get pulled into the Great Pacific Garbage Patch and there, circle the slow vortex, never to leave the massive continent of trash. If it catches the tug of the more southerly current it might get pulled to Japan, South East Asia, or even Australia. Then again, it may swirl into the northward stream and head for icy waters.

The beacon of Brian's hope rises and falls with the massive swells. Wind pounds in from the west. Rain on the water. Lightning strikes the waves. The storm blows white-caps of foam over Bottle as Library Card and Punctured Dollar Bill slide back and forth in their tiny plastic ship.

The wind shifts and gusts—and Bottle is lifted—tossed—and blown over to the next swell. And this makes the difference. The course is set.

— HOUSE FOR SALE —

ON THE TO-DO LIST scribbled on the wall, I cross off—*2. Talk to an expert.* Next up: *3. Hire a boat.* I'll wait on that.

4. Sell the furniture. Then: *5. Sell the house.*

Kill two birds with one stone. I'll sell the house furnished, complete with beige memories.

I search for that card the neighbor left. There it is, her picture smiling with perfect teeth and perfect hair. Pat the realtor.

Pat is wary when I call. What does the crazy lady want now? But after hearing I want her to sell my house, her voice molds into cheerful greed. She's happy to help.

She trots over and we do a walk-through.

The coffee stains on the carpet are noticed but not mentioned. Likewise, the shattered pile of dining room set, the To-Do List written on the wall, the food decaying in the kitchen, and the mess of Brian's room with its broken blinds.

I suppose I should apologize for the state of things, but I don't want to. I want to own this mess, and the grief, anger, and pain that caused it. I want to honor my—

Pat huffs in a tight noisy inhale. Sound of perturbedness.

"Sorry for the mess," I hurry to say.

"At least you aren't a hoarder with sixteen cats. I'll have a cleaning crew come before showing the house."

I tell her I want the house sold immediately. Furnished. As-is. I'll take a loss if I can get cash asap.

"Closing takes thirty days. Appraisals, inspections,—"

"I want it sold now. Today if possible."

Pat shakes her head. Her curls don't move. "Can't be done. These things take time."

"I'll sell it for $50,000 cash. Someone will pay that today."

"Someone would. But this house is worth twelve, fifteen times that."

"I don't care. I want money now."

Pat's face returns to its wary expression. "At the very least, there has to be a title search, to make sure you're the owner and there are no liens on the house. That alone takes time. Why the rush? What's going on, Ann?"

"I'm going to find—"

—Don't tell her! She'll know you're crazy. She won't help.

"I'm going to find—a new place. Leave Los Angeles. I'm not able to stay here. It's too painful. Every room reminds me of my son and I can't—" I cover my mouth, pretending to cry.

—Nicely done!

Pat puts her hand on my shoulder. "I understand, dear. We'll get this sold as soon as we can."

When I call Tobey about the house selling, he gets big-brother-itis in a big way. He won't let me ruin my life. "You can't make decisions based on a delusion!"

"I'm not deluded, Tobey. I'm doing what a mother must. Find her son."

"If I let you squander your life, I won't be able to forgive myself."

"Living with Dan was squandering my life. You never tried to stop me then."

"Not the same. Chasing a whale is irrational."

I hang up on him, but he calls back.

"I always hated this house, Tobey."

65

"The house is worth money and I'm not letting you give it away for peanuts."

"It's not your decision."

"You want money? I'll give you a loan. You can sell the house, but you sell that house for what it's worth." Tobey talks for twenty minutes about real estate and investments and backs up every point with statistics. I hate him for being so competent.

What have I been doing that makes me so ignorant compared to him? Being a wife? Raising a son? Those might not be excuses.

Big brother wins and I agree to be reasonable about the house.

Tobey insists I drive up and stay with him and Arthur. I know he'll try to talk me out of my plans, but some things can't be talked away.

Counting the $50,000 loan coming from Tobey, with my money market thing and the bank account, I'll have about $86,000. That seems like a lot, but I don't know. Never tried to find a boy living in a whale before.

— DUET —

GRUMBLE-WARBLE, squeaking wagon-wheel, clicking, and gong. Same old song. It's getting redundant.

I sing along to entertain myself. My grumble imitates the one Dad did whenever he walked away from Mom saying things under his breath. I hated that. Come think of it, I did that all the time with Mom as well and I did it because she hated it.

My warble is a mix of that old-timey Tarzan guy and when a wild peacock would sometimes show up on someone's roof in Burbank and screech its weird high scream.

The squeaking wagon wheel is from Gramma. I never heard a squeaking wagon wheel but I think she knew it from old Westerns. I'd play on her monstrous big chair making it recline and go back up with a loud squeak in each direction. Gramma would always pretend to be mad and say, "You sound like a squeaking wagon wheel! Stop riding the BarcaLounger!" and I'd always say, "It's a Squeak-alounger, Gramma, but I'll try to teach it to bark." She'd always laugh. She was funny that way.

The clicking I do is from the alien Predator. The game and the movies.

Gongs used to be majestic and announcing someone grand, but now it's an ironic BOIN-OIN-oin-oin. Guess that's 'cause Billy always made that gong sound whenever I did something stupid. I don't want him in my head. I'm going to do a majestic gong announcing someone grand.

—*Like who? You?*

—*Maybe.*

Home does grumble-warble, squeaking wagon-wheel, clicking, and gong. We're going up again.

Oh.

We're going up again.

I get it. Duh!

Grumble-warble, squeaking wagon-wheel, clicking, and gong is The Rise Song. Home sings it every time. Now I'll be able to know beforehand.

Home sings it again and I sing as loud as I can with him. I do Dad's grumble, Tarzan's peacock warble, Gramma's BarcaLounger, Predator's click, and Majestic Gong. Probably sound like a sick cartoon but it's a duet!

Why is he singing about rising when he rises? Is he talking to himself? Maybe he's lonely. Maybe he's like me. Maybe he's got an inner voice saying, "Get up there and breathe, Blubber Ass!"

—*You think Home talks to himself? Only you'd end up in a whale as nutzo as you.*

The blowhole opens and daylight blasts in and Home blasts out and the walls expand and it's all cold fresh and I'm so happy 'cause I'm a fucking whale singer!

— WHILE BOTTLE JOURNEYS —

AS BOTTLE BOBS in the dark ocean, drifting North into colder waters, lots of small occurrences are taking place.

In Burbank, Ann jerks awake from a nightmare of sea monsters. Now, wide awake in that beige hell, she can't shush the feeling that she's wasted the first half of life and now, about to embark on a futile mission, she'll waste the second half.

Up the coast in San Francisco, her brother Tobey turns away from spooning Arthur and stares out at the glowing streetlight, wondering if his sister will regain her sanity.

Farther up the coast, farther, farther, on a deserted highway, a Native Koyukon Alaska State Trooper swerves his cruiser to avoid a moose and her calf. He honks and flashes his brights, heart angry for almost hitting them. "Damn, deneege," he says, then laughs at remembering a rare word in his grandmother's language.

Seventy miles away, another Koyukon, the market manager, dumps trash from the gas pump receptacles into the dumpster behind the station. His breath glows green in the northern lights as he says a prayer for lost things.

Southeast, in Missouri, Mark creeps into his eight-year-old daughter's bedroom. He lifts Jenny gently, keeping her in dreamland, carries her past the room where her mother sleeps, downstairs, and out to the packed car. Her dog, always one for a ride, hops in the backseat.

In Thousand Oaks, Dan sits in his new beige dining room and cries silently for his dead son, hoping not to wake his new wife and daughters.

As the dolphins circle under the moon in Sea World, across the globe, that same moon has sunk with dawn. The captain of the ship rises, pours himself coffee, and steps on deck to blink himself awake with the grey waves.

Past the cold sea, the kelp beds, and the fjords, to the tidy apartment in Bergen, a mother refuses to let her teenage daughter go out with friends until she's done the chores. The front door slamming is her answer.

Somewhere below the waves, Brian dreams, for the first time, of living in the whale. He's a sushi chef serving sashimi to Mom and a pretty girl with seaweed hair who looks like Vivian and smiles at every dish he presents. As the whale rises, the dream carries Brian and his erection up, and with each smile the girl gives him, he gets nearer and finally is shot through the blowhole as a glorious fountain.

And Bottle keeps bobbing as another day begins.

— LEAVING —

THIS IS THE LAST beige day.

Soon I'll be gone from this house and everything will be different. Everything will be better. Wonderful. Perfect. I'm so happy.

I'm terrified.

I want to tell Pam it's all a mistake. I want to crawl into bed and even if the house is sold I won't leave. I want to spend the rest of my life crying in beige.

The doorbell rings. Throw on a robe and hurry downstairs, praying it's Pam to say she changed her mind and the house won't sell and—

It's Amazon with the packing boxes and tape.

I didn't order many. Just enough to pack Brian's things. I head to his room and try not to judge what's crap and what's treasure. Who knows what he thinks is special. I take out all the drawers and look at the undersides. Look for loose boards or pulled-back bits of the stained carpet for secret compartments. I don't find anything hidden except his sticky yearbook jammed between the mattress and box-spring.

The clothes scattered around the room only take two boxes. One more for the desk contents, model aircraft, play consoles, game discs, etc. One for computer and speakers wrapped in his Star Wars bedding. Four boxes are my son's possessions.

For me, I throw the pinecone pajamas in a suitcase with the few personal artifacts from childhood and I'm done. I dress in my last beige outfit.

When I finish loading the car, I cross off *6. Pack*—from the To-Do List on the dining room wall. I should take a picture of this list only I've never taken a picture with a phone. I want to call Tobey and ask him how to do it, but then he'll know I'm incapable of anything. There's a little icon that looks like a camera. Push and there's the view! It takes me a second, but I get the hang of it. I add *6-a. Leave* and I stare at it with terror and nausea and shakes. When the doorbell rings I cross the new entry off and take another photo.

Open the door to Pam, who reminds me she's Pat. We sign the contracts, shake hands, and I pass her the keys to the house— complete with keychain containing multiple valued-loyal-customer-plastic-reward-cards that I never used.

Walk out the door for the last time. No misty feeling, just a tense vibrating in my chest.

Start the car with the solitary key and pull out into the road, looking in the rearview mirror at Pam shaking her head.

Life has shifted dramatically. I'm homeless.

Home-less. I have no home. But, I do have a mission.

I'm nervous and scared and jittery and nauseous.

It feels good.

Heading to San Francisco via the Pacific Coast Highway. It'll take longer than Interstate 5 up the Central Valley, but I feel better being close to the ocean. Feel like I'm close to Brian.

I'm alone. Adrift. Without an anchor.

Is this what Brian feels like? He's utterly alone. Doesn't know if, or how, he'll get out. I hope he knows I'll try to find him. Would he know that? No. He knows I don't leave the house. Knows me as a dull, lackluster, frustrated person. Knows me as the beige, do-nothing mom. Knows I have no tools for helping him, let alone myself. He'll never expect me to try to find him.

— TOOL —

WE MUST BE TRAVELING in different waters now. Home has new items on the menu. Less green seaweed, more brown and red. One kind has lots of bubbles like the fried noodles at Chinese restaurants. Chinese Bubble Weed. Tastes good. Less Bastard Needle Fish more Torpedo Heads.

I snap-twist the Torpedo Heads, swallow, and dump the plexi-inners out the flap. Something big hits my hand and I grab. Pull a big flopping fish in. I land belly-down on him and stay with a held breath past sixty-count and he stops moving. He's really big. Fat as my arm. Or—fat as my arm used to be. He's a sushi feast! I'll bet he'd cost a hundred dollars in LA. Time to dig in.

My fingernails are long now but these scales are too hard to penetrate. I try biting. No go. How am I gonna get into this fish? I need a knife.

Try the house key. Press it into the white belly. After a lot of pressing, it punctures the scaly skin and goo and blood oozes out, but I can't cut with the key.

My phone. If I can wedge my fingernail into the edge, maybe I can separate the glass screen. I can't get my nail in. I'll break the sucker. I'll bend the phone and crack the glass.

—*You can't bend a phone, Lard Ass.*

—*Watch.*

I press as hard as I can and—

—*You're a wuss! Wusses can't*—

—the phone bends! The glass cracks in half! I've got my knife and—Smart Ass has nothing to say!

— UP THE PACIFIC COAST HIGHWAY —
TO SAN FRANCISCO

THIS WINDING ROAD is exhausting with its twists and turns, and the sun glittering on the waves far below hurts my eyes, and I've never driven this long alone with no one to trade off with, and I'm hungry, and I've had to pee for hours, but I can't stop. After Big Sur, the unending double yellow lines keep me stuck behind a huge RV staring at the airbrushed mountain scene on the back. I flash my headlights but the damn driver never moves to any turn-off, and every time there's a passing zone there's always a car approaching. With nothing to do but think, I get an idea to have Tobey and Arthur set up a website to do that crowd-sourcing thing for brainstorming and funding. Once I figure that out I get antsy again and after Carmel, I can't take it anymore and I move left into the on-coming lane, over the two solid lines, press the gas to the floor and there's no view of what is ahead, no way to know if these are my last moments, and the curve is sharp and the drop-off deadly, and a glance at the old man steering the RV tells me I'm reckless, but that makes me honk hard and long and the curve continues blind and a blue car appears, with the driver wide-eyed as I swerve back into my lane and everyone's horn curses me.

The rest of the trip is done on adrenaline fumes.

When I'm close to the city, I call Tobey. He tells me that Arthur has coerced a neighbor into letting me park in their driveway.

Fifteen minutes later, I'm on the steep hill and there's Tobey smiling from the stoop and Arthur, with his raven-like nose and bulging eyes, waving from the next-door spot. I pull where directed, throw it in park, hop out, rush past Arthur, up the steps yelling, "I have GOT to pee!" Tobey spins aside and I barrel down the slick hardwood hall to the back bathroom.

I close the door, turn the lock, tug down my beige slacks, and as they fall, so do the tears. The Japanese print of orange-and-black carp turns into an abstract blur. What am I doing? I almost killed myself on the road. This is all too much for me. I'm not capable of handling it. Why did all this have to happen? I hate Brian for making everything so hard!

—*No, I didn't mean that. I don't hate Brian! I love him!*

There is a soft tap on the door. "You okay in there?"

I *mmm* a response and flush to make it seem like I'm moving things along. The mirror reflects a person I don't recognize. Sweaty blotched skin, mascara smudged, sunken eyes, hair wild and manic. I'm falling apart. All I can fix right now are the smudges of black.

Tobey's in the living room when I step out. "Get over here," he says, grinning. He slides his arms around and pulls me close.

Arthur comes in and takes both of my hands, looking straight into my eyes without blinking. I'm not used to this kind of intensity. It makes me squirm.

"You are welcome here, Ann. For as long as you need."

I only nod because all words are stuck in my throat with the coagulating tears.

After I'm handed a tall glass of greenish liquid with a sprig of something on top, Tobey commands, "Sit. Stay. Don't think," and my brother and his husband go out to unpack the car.

I sip the green, staring at—color. The room is even more colorful than I remember. Or maybe I'm just so used to beige. This wall is green, this one turquoise, this salmon. Brian called it a party house when he first visited as a boy.

Whatever is in my drink, it's a party. Gin must be the honored guest. The glass is one of those thick "artisan" Mexican deals with the blue rim and all the bubbles and irregularities from Pier 1 or World Market. I sip and gaze out the tall bay windows at the colorful sweep of the city. Tobey enters with a load of boxes and smiles, saying, "Looks like you're finally relaxing."

I think I am. This is the best I've felt since Brian got swallowed. No, since way before that. When was the last time I was happy?

Even if I never find Brian, maybe there is still a chance I'll feel happiness again.

—*You traitor! You haven't even started looking and you're thinking of forgetting him.*

—*I'm not thinking of forgetting him. I'm just—*

Tobey leans in close. "Stop thinking."

— WHAT IS SHRIMP? —

YELLOW SHOPPING CART out the flap. One Pencil fish. One Bastard Needle Fish. Three Torpedo Heads. Brown seaweed. Lots of shrimp.

The shrimp flutters as I pull off the legs and hard coating. It's like they have a container around their body. Like they've got the skeleton on the outside, not the inside. An exo—exo—exo-skeleton! Whoa! Mr. Lesak would shit that I remember this.

Crunch down on the peeled shrimp body. Yum.

—*Surprised you remember anything in biology since you spent the entire class focused on the back of Vivian's head.*

Vivian had great hair. My seat was behind her and I touched it once but Toke saw me and did the tongue-in-the-mouth-blowjob thing and I gave him the finger and got to taking notes real serious. That was when Mr. Lesak was talking about this stuff. There was a group with exoskeletons. Lobsters, crabs, shrimp… What was the name of the exoskeleton group? Fuck it. I'll make my own name. Container food. Fast food. Peel and eat. Peelers.

—*You can't make up names for things, Lard Ass. They have official names in the real world.*

—*This is the real world.*

—*Life in a whale isn't the real world.*

—*This is the real world and this is a PEELER.*

To punctuate my point, I PEEL off the exoskeleton of another PEELER, pop the PEELER in my mouth, and crunch down. Eating PEELERS in THE REAL WORLD is the BEST!

— FLOATING CITY —

DRIFTING ALONG THE SURFACE of the waves, the whale does not feel at its best. The congestion in its lungs is lingering. Like that time years and years ago, back when the sea was emptier and quieter.

A loud churning rumble grows. The whale tilts and rolls an eye to the air. A floating city approaches. A floating mall. A floating amusement park. The dull roar of the engine pounds the water mixed with garbled loudspeaker announcements and thudding music.

The whale blasts out a breath. Another smaller spray shoots up beside the whale.

Screams and shouts spill from the balconies and deck of the massive cruise ship. Passengers crowd along the rails and lean over the edge with their cameras and phones.

Does this pose a threat? Should the whale attack? Could it ram something this huge? Should it warn the other and dive?

The whale sings out into the deep and that weird voice from inside sings back. The whale-song from within is regular now. Could this lung sickness be affecting its mind?

A blast of vapor spouts in the air and beside it an accompanying spray. Curling the barnacled back, with a swish of the massive tail, the troubled beast dives. And is followed.

— SKIN —

I'M ITCHY. I'm in this sauna 24 hours a day. My skin never dries. Something's growing on it. A thin layer of slime that itches.

—*Back of the fridge.*

—*It's sweat.*

—*It's what happens at the back of the fridge. What happens when vegetables are forgotten. You're molding and turning goopy and mushy. Moldy Lard.*

—*It's sweat. Jock itch from sweat.*

—*If it's jock itch, your whole body is your junk.*

—*Maybe I should wipe down.*

—*With salt water? That sounds like a really bright idea.*

—*I could try. A little in one spot.*

—*Give it a go. You're rotting anyway.*

When Home goes up to blow and feed, I tie the rope end of my Yellow Shopping Cart tightly around my Simpsons T-shirt and slide it through the flap into the rush of water. Pulling it back in, I wipe my right foot and calf up to the knee. God, it feels good to have something cold and fresh on my skin. I rub hard and the layer of goo sloughs off. Goo and lots of dead skin. I'll do my whole body. What can it hurt?

I soak the cloth in the tube again and work on the other foot and calf. My toenails are getting long. I'm liable to jab Home if I'm not careful.

I ring out the cloth in the tube and mop up my spills. Don't want to drown my whale by filling his lungs with seawater.

My arms, thighs, stomach. The stomach surprises me. There's a much smaller roll now. Much less to squeeze and beat myself up over.

I wash my chest. It's unbelievable. I've got pecs! The man-titties are almost gone! I'm almost regular now!

"Woo-hooo!" I yell.

Home sings back low and high notes.

—*You'll always be a Lard Ass.*

—*Will you ever shut up?*

—*Never.*

Fuck my inner critic, I'll ignore him.

Back to washing. There really is a lot less fat. I might even get a girl to look at me.

—*Not a chance.*

—*You could be wrong. You could be a mean son-of-a-bitch voice with no basis in reality.*

—*Why would I do that?*

—*To keep me afraid. To keep me quiet and behaved and depressed. You need to stop.*

I wait for the response, but all I hear Home's slow heartbeat. Could my inner voice be gone?

Wait again for the snarky *Not.* It doesn't come. I can't believe it. I should have told him to stop years ago.

Dip the T-shirt out again and wash my face. Get deep in the beard that itches so. Hair and pits and arms and neck and back and butt and move 'round to work on the junk. I'm trying to clean up good and slow and careful, but I get thinking of Vivian in senior year when she smiled at me and the wood appears hard and is easier to clean and fucking great to wash and her smile was white and gleaming and if only—under her sweater—if only—

"FUCK! Oh, God! My fucking god!"

Home blasts me with a low note that trembles over my spasms.

"Sing me to sleep, Home."

Lying against Home's damp hot wall, I feel amazingly good. I'm washed and spent and the voice is gone—

—Not.

— DINNER WITH TOBEY AND ARTHUR —

TOBEY REACHES across the table, refilling my wine glass. I don't even stop eating to thank him. Both he and Arthur laugh at the way I'm shoveling it in. Have I even eaten anything since Day Zero? I remember throwing up, but not eating. Food is good sometimes. As I set down my fork, Tobey gives me the lecture-coming eyes. "Sis, look at you. You're a mess. I think—"

"Wait," I interrupt, "I have a plan. A To-Do List. Numbered even."

My brother's palms out must mean continue. I try to remember the To-Do items on the wall. The picture's on my phone, but I'd have to cross the room. "I won't go through everything right now. Number one is: Find Brian. And there are lots of others. Lots I've crossed off already!"

Tobey glances at Arthur with a secret message that isn't very secret. "Let's go back to the beginning," he suggests. "The police arrive and notify you that Brian is—I'm sorry—dead." He goes on about delusion and auditory hallucinations from stress and certain things being impossible. It's a replay from the other day, but more rehearsed.

I ignore him and smile at his husband. "Arthur, did you know Brian called from the whale? I have proof!"

"You have proof?" Arthur asks.

"Proof," I say with a grin. "Evidence! It was the day after the accident, the next afternoon. Brian called and it's on the log. Incoming calls! 2:16! His name is there." Now I've got a reason to cross the room. I rush to my purse, pull out my phone, and—drop it.

It hits hardwood. Hard.

Black screen looks blankly at me.

Brian's message. Brian's pictures. The call log...

My knees start shaking and that meal begins to creep skyward. Tears rush up and over and the world tilts, and Tobey grabs my arm and guides me back to the table as Arthur lifts the phone, raising it gently like a child being pulled lifeless from the kiddie pool. Is it breathing?

"I had it," I sob. "The incoming call log—proof Brian called."

Arthur looks for signs of life in the phone as he moves back to his chair.

If that log is gone, I've lost everything. It will mean I *am* crazy. My heart counts the seconds.

There's a muffled beep and Arthur hands me the revived device. "It's okay, Ann. Phone's okay."

Pushing aside my dinner plate, I pull up Brian's incoming call from the log, showing the screen to Arthur. "Do you see? 2:16!"

"Pocket dial," Tobey insists.

"No! He called! He's alive and I'm going to find him!"

My brother smiles in a *let's-calm-the-nut-case* way. "Why don't you lie down for a while? You've driven all day. You need rest."

"I don't want rest, Tobey! I want to find my son! I want to be tired and anxious and fucking scared. Because if I'm not, that means I've given up and I *won't* give up. It wasn't a pocket dial. He called! And I don't care if you don't believe me or cetacean experts don't believe me. Whales *were* land mammals. They evolved to live underwater but they used to live on land. Related to hippos! They're odd-toed, or even-toed, can't remember—ingrates—ungrates—undulates—whatever. If Brian'd been swallowed by a hippo that was big enough—he could live in *those* god-damn lungs because hippos have god-damn epi—epi—epiglottis—epigeal—flaps! And—and—and—what do *you* know!? What do *any of us* know!"

Tobey does his calm voice, "We know science. We know the possible and impossible—"

"Science only knows *today's* discovery. What about *tomorrow's*? Or did we discover everything already?"

"We can only go with what we know is true, Ann," Arthur volunteers.

I slam my hand on the table and all the dishes dance. "Bull shit! We can have the belief that things exist we haven't yet learned. The universe is too big to know it all."

Tobey moves the dishes away from my reach. He thinks I'll break something. That makes me want to break something.

I choose the thick artisan glass that's from Pier 1 or World Market. When it shatters on the floor, Arthur's face tells me that I'm wrong.

"Damn it, Ann! That's from our honeymoon!" Tobey yells. "Stop acting nuts! Not acceptable!"

I'm too ashamed to apologize so I double down. "I don't care what's acceptable! I don't care if I'm nuts. There's one thing I care about and that's FINDING BRIAN. If you're not going to help—get outta my way!"

Tobey and Arthur are frozen. Do they think I'll break more things or become violent? Maybe I will. I've been acting strangely, slapping people, throwing coffee mugs and chicken, scaring Sea World experts, destroying furniture, driving recklessly. I don't normally do these things.

Pulling up the picture of my To-Do List, I try to give the impression of sanity. "Take a look at this," I say, passing them the phone.

"You wrote on the wall?" Tobey asks.

"Forget that part. It's a list. A plan. How I'll find Brian. And I was thinking on the drive here that I need help. I need money and solutions, so maybe you can set up a crowdfunding website—"

"You've done enough damage with your Press fiasco," Tobey declares. "I won't let you continue making an idiot of yourself."

I ignore him and turn to Arthur. "I'll need a short film for the website."

Arthur looks interested.

Tobey glares at his husband. "He won't do any such thing."

"And if you want, Arthur, you can make a feature documentary as well. An incredible story of hope and determination, of a woman defying the odds with the impossible search-and-rescue of a boy swallowed by a whale."

Tobey raises an eyebrow, daring me.

"Or a devastating portrait of a despairing woman's descent into madness. Either way the film is bound to be a hit."

I can tell from Arthur's face that he's onboard and I don't want to sit through the inevitable. "I'm going to bed. After you've stopped arguing, maybe start on that short film, Arthur."

Standing, I see the artisan shards on the floor. "I'm sorry about the honeymoon glass."

Tobey sighs dramatically. "Things happen. Glasses get thrown. Sons get swallowed by whales. We mourn and *move on*."

I start toward the stairs for my guest bedroom but can't let him have the last word. "Or we search and search until we find a replacement glass and save the son."

— BURNING —

I WAKE UP to burning feet. And calves. And thighs. My skin is searing me. What have I done!? It feels like I've been skinned alive. I catch a few glowing Wrigglers and hold the dim light up to my legs. There are splotches where there shouldn't be. Splotches of pain. It's excruciating.

Mom's not here to tell me what ointment to put on. Even if she was, there's no ointment. Nothing to kill the pain.

—*Unless...*

—*Don't do it.*

—*I have to kill the pain.*

—*No way. Stupid idea. Jerk off to distract yourself.*

—*My fuckin' Johnson's burning like the rest of me!*

It takes many painful tries with the Ziploc but I manage to collect several of those horrible Stinging Wrigglers. I spill one to the spongy lung surface and slowly lower my foot over it. A tentacle thing spears out and a searing stab jolts me.

Can't hardly breathe from the pain. A sob pops from my mouth. Who cares. No one will hear. Moaning, I step on another of the Stinging Wrigglers. Another hot slice of agony. Please. I can't take it. Maybe these aren't the numbing kind. Maybe they just shoot in poison.

My sobs are unstoppable. Why do I have to have pain? Why do I have to know about Stinging Wrigglers and Chinese Bubble Weed and Bastard Needle Fish?

"I hate this! I don't want to be in this life anymore. I want my old life back," I wail.

My whale wails along with me.

My feet are growing numb. It's working!

I get the Stinging Wrigglers to strike other parts. One on each thigh. One on each forearm. I sit on one and get a whopping shot in the butt.

I crawl over one to have it shoot my chest.

—*Not a good idea, Lard Ass.*

—*Why's that?*

—*The numbness spreads. It may spread inside too. Like deep in. Like to your heart. Something about having a numb heart doesn't sound like a good plan.*

—*Maybe in the shoulder?*

—*Better not do anymore. Could be like bee stings. You can get one or two, but they add up and the venom can kill you.*

I back away from the Stinging Wriggler below me. The pain is leaving. Numbness is dulling it. It's bearable now. But what happens when the numbness wears off?

Pictures of spa ladies pop into my head. Cucumbers on their eyes. Mud-smeared faces. Wasn't there a seaweed wrap?

I figure it can't hurt. Or it can, but it won't hurt *more*. There is no pain number higher than ten.

Send out my Yellow Shopping Cart and keep shopping until I have enough seaweed. Wrap my chest, belly, arms, butt, junk, legs, neck, and face. I'm a seaweed mummy.

— CROWDFUNDING —

I STEP DOWNSTAIRS for coffee and Tobey hands me a mug saying, "It's from Target. You can break it if you want."

"Gee thanks." My brother's still mad at me. Is he also mad at his husband? I wonder who won the argument last night.

Stepping into the living room gives me the answer. In front of the couch, a laptop is open on the coffee table, a video camera sits on a tripod behind it, and Arthur is adjusting a clip-on lamp. He turns to me and bows formally. "Good morning, Ms. Ketchum. Let me know when you're ready for your closeup."

Five minutes later, I'm on the couch, facing the computer, and the camera's red light goes on.

Tobey sulks in the doorway to the kitchen, making it clear he's not participating.

Arthur stands by the computer, calm and confident, careful not block the lens. Definitely a director. "I edited this short intro and it will not go live until you like it. When you do, I'll push the button and your crowdfunding site will be out in the world. Does that work for you?" No wonder my brother loves him. Who wouldn't want a kind, self-assured person in charge?

I jiggle my head and Arthur hits play on the computer.

Nostalgic piano music plays over photos of Brian dissolving one into another, advancing and receding like in those Ken Burns documentaries. It gets me teary right away. A photograph of pudgy smiling Brian dissolves into the image of a massive whale. The music morphs, becoming menacing and anxious. News clippings about Brian swirl past. Fast cuts of whales leaping from the sea. Tails splashing.

I'm getting nauseous. I expected a slide show or PowerPoint. I feel Tobey moving closer, peering at the screen.

Arthur's voiceover plays over the images. "When her son Brian was swallowed by a whale, the last thing Ann Ketchum expected was to hear from him. But she did. Her son is alive in a whale. You can be part of an unprecedented worldwide search-and-rescue operation. Join the campaign today and bring Brian home. Dare to Dream."

"Stop, stop!" I cry.

Arthur pauses the computer playback but not the camera focused on me. I wave for him to cut. He doesn't.

"What is it, Ann?"

"It's so—commercial. So slick."

Tobey is right beside me. "Arthur's an award-winning filmmaker. If you wanted shit, you should have gone somewhere else."

I glare at him, "I thought you were against this!"

"I am but Arthur's an artist—"

"Art or not, it's horrible! The music, the tone of voice, the dissolves—it's manipulative!"

Arthur shrugs. "Films manipulate. So you feel. So you react. We want that. This is about getting people moved enough that they want to help."

"I'm not going to turn Brian into a pop-tart—" I don't know why I said pop-tart. Maybe the word pop. "—a poster boy for kids swallowed by whales. It's exploitative! Next, you'll have Jerry Lewis doing a telethon."

"If we could get him, I'd go for it," says Arthur. "Brian's plight will touch people. People like to believe in miracles. If this can help save him, isn't it worth it?"

Arthur doesn't get any response so continues. "This is not all we'll show. We'll add to it as we go along. An interview with you. The footage of him being swallowed. We'll set up the incentives…"

"What incentives?" I ask. "Incentives beyond saving my son?"

Tobey can't help but explain, "People like to have *things*. Mementos, a signed picture, a T-shirt, something that they can point to and say, 'I got this because I contributed.'"

"A T-shirt?!" There's an edge in my voice I can't stop. "Turn off the camera, Arthur. It was a stupid idea. I have enough money. I'll do it on my own." I stand.

Arthur points for me to sit. Is it because he's a director that I do?

"Ann, you need help with this. Help includes money, support, enthusiasm, hive-mind ideas—"

"You don't have to do this," Tobey says, putting his hand on my shoulder. As I jerk away I remember the camera is still filming and that little moment will be definitely edited into the final film.

"People will help," Arthur says. "They will want to be involved in your worthy quest."

Something jolts me with those words. *Worthy quest.*

I whisper, "I've never been on a worthy quest."

Tobey snorts, "*None* of us have or will—"

"It *is* a worthy quest," I say, turning to Arthur. "Let's exploit the shit out of this and find my son."

Arthur clicks a button on the computer and our crowdfunding campaign goes live.

— TIME IN HOME —

HOW LONG have I been in here? It's hard to keep track of days when you only have a blow-hole. Over a month? Over two? Feels like years.

We spin and Home's heartbeat speeds and something is going on, we're pointed straight up, and there is no Rise Song but we're in a super fast elevator, and I'm pressed flat against the slimy back and we're up—and my stomach flies higher than me and the blowhole opens and we both suck in the same big breath, daylight overhead, cool crisp air—and hover weightless like in space—*he must have leapt out of the water, which means*—we arch—and he dives—face-first—WHAM!—crashes HARD and so do I. He plummets straight down and I slide toward his head—into the breathing tube halfway to the blowhole. *Used to be, I couldn't fit in this tunnel. Better not get stuck.* Home swishes and reverses course and I flop out of the tube

84

and we're shooting up and I tumble backwards, deep into the left lung branch and my hand touches a hard rectangle. I grab it just as we swirl left and another moment we're airborne again and I'm pressed to the top of the lungs and tip and SLAM! Home must be doing exercises or jumping for joy or in an Olympic event.

Another leap and crash and we slow to a lazy drift. What was that all about!? And what did I grab in the back of the lung? I can't see what this rectangle is in the dark. Where's the light?

Where's my light!?

Where's the Ziploc of Wrigglers?!

—*The one thing you shouldn't lose, Lard Ass loses.*

There's a faint glow—or maybe it's the afterimage of the blowhole sky. I crawl in that direction. Squiggle deep into the left branch and the bag is ahead—a few damaged Wrigglers glowing dimly—but it's in too deep to reach. Fuck! Fuck! Fuck!

—*At least now I won't have to see your lardy ass.*

What I need is an arm extension. I could throw the Yellow Shopping Cart in deep, but it's so floppy I can't control it and it could get snagged on all the lung lobes and branches and might hurt Home. What else do I have? I crawl backwards and feel for the bundle tied to my ankle. Feels like everything's still together, T-shirt, shorts, sneakers, broken-phone-screen-knife, dorky waterproof phone deal, rubber corrugated tube, all tied with my Yellow Shopping Cart. Maybe I could get the Wrigglers with this tube. In the darkness, I slide the rectangle thing I grabbed into my bundle, remove the tube and crawl back into the branch. Wait—where's the Ziploc?!

A tiny glow pulses. The Wrigglers are dying! I gotta get that bag now or I'll never find it again! Push the rubber tube toward the small spec of light. The end hits the baggie and maybe the Wrigglers squirm and swirl, but they're so weak, they don't brighten with anger. Now what? How can I use this tube to pull them back? There's no hook. Even if I had one, I don't want to break my bag.

—*Breathe.*

—*Fuck off, I'm trying to think.*

—Seriously, Lard Ass. Breathe. You've been practicing. Your lungs are strong.

Oh. Worth a try.

Squiggle farther, as deep as I can, put the end of the tube against the Wrigglers, exhale completely—put the other end in my mouth and—INHALE!

My breath pulls in the bag tight against the tube.

—It's working! Pull!

I keep up the pressure, take hold of the tube and pull. The baggie slides six inches.

—Yes! Again!

Breathe out through the nose, another inhale. Pull...

Inches, breaths, minutes. The bag, one pinprick of light, gets closer. Another breath. The Wrigglers go dark. I can't see if I'm still attached.

—Keep at it, Lard Ass. You can do it!

Exhale through my nose, inhale, and pull. Feel for the end and my finger touches the smooth, water-filled plastic.

—I did it!

—You did it!

I go shopping for fresh Wrigglers and hold the bright Ziploc over the rectangle I found. It's a little tin box. Worn old writing says *Evans's Menthol and Glycerine Lozenges. George B Evans, Philadelphia.* There's a film of slime and age on it. I pry the lid—

A wristwatch! Cool!

It's clean and dry from being in the box. The band is too small for me. Must have been a woman's watch or a boy's. It's either an antique or retro style.

I put it against my ear and listen. Nothing.

Battery must have died, damn it. Probably the hands wouldn't move anyway.

I turn the little knob to move the hands but it just grinds. It grinds and I remember Granddad's pocket-watch on the chain and Mom yelling, "Don't you wind too much or you'll break it!"

This might be an old-time winding watch. Back before batteries. I grind the little knob a few more times and —it ticks!

"Time! Time! Time!" I sing. "I have all the time in the world!"

Home sings back at me.

The ticking against my ear, I bounce my head to the magnificent beat. It's so fast. Time is whizzing! If I have time, I'm definitely part of the real world. Whatever time I set this watch to, somewhere in the world, it will be within that hour. I'll be *on time* somewhere. Within half an hour at least.

It's great to have a mechanical sound; something other than the massive slow heartbeat of my whale. Each little click is a cheer. One after another. Yay! Yay! Yay! Yay! It's my own pom-pom section. This watch is cheering me. Cheering what I'm doing here. Cheering me surviving.

Air's getting thin again. I should time myself. Wonder how long I can last. I pull a breath in and hold it, watching the golden second-hand circle.

Thirty.

Forty-five.

One minute.

—This is great!

One fifteen.

—Keep going, Lard Ass!

One thirty.

Home sings The Rise Song and is pushing us up and the walls are closing in.

One forty-five.

—Don't take a breath. There's no air anyway. Hold it!

One fifty.

The push as we rise and—

—Two minutes!

Home blasts out and the blow-hole opens and sunlight and I pull in new cold air. The smell of sea and sun and life. A beautiful day. Sun high and bright. I say, "Noon." I have time and it's Noon.

This is the best day of my life.

—Best day of your life, Lard Ass?

—Feels like it. I've got time and my Wriggler light and I can hold my breath for two minutes. You tell me what day was better than this.

No answer, so I know I'm right.

— CROWD MIND —

THE NEW TECHNOLOGY and internet are going to help me find Brian. They already have. I found out Brian is alive because of cell phones. If *I'd* been swallowed by a whale when *I* was nineteen, I'd be lucky if I had a pager. Lotta good that would have done.

I email everyone I know or used to know. They don't appreciate me reaching out for the first time in years only to ask for money. Arthur does a lot on Twitter and Facebook and other sites I never heard of. He knows oodles more people than a beige housewife. Tobey, however, is resolutely uninvolved. I bet it's because he resents Arthur giving me so much attention.

The Kickstarter campaign is going incredibly well. I check constantly and money keeps coming in. Up to $167,045. Amazing. Strangers from all over the world are contributing. People discuss Brian in blogs, social media, podcasts. Many offer best wishes and prayers. Others, not so much.

—Whatever your son did, it provoked God's wrath. He has sinned and must pay. The Lord provided a great fish to swallow up Jonah. Jonah 1:17

—May he find a speedy painless death.

—No way from stomach into lungs, Nitwit.

—Your baby boy is dead. Stop wasting our time.

I want to stop reading but I don't want to miss someone that might help.

—I am psychic with affinity to animal spirits. I can find your son. Guaranteed. Fee negotiable.

—Employed in the space industry and have access to all satellites and can track the whale. Contact me asap.

—Will fund the entire search and rescue of your dear lost boy. My sick father deposited 9 million US dollars in the bank here in Burkina Faso before he dies and I am in search of an honest and reliable person who will stand as my trustee. I compensate you with 30% of the total money for your services and the balance shall be my capital in your establishment. Awaiting your urgent and positive response.

—Professional hunter, done all the Big Five Game: African lion, African elephant, Cape buffalo, African leopard, and rhinoceros. Work in all conditions. Will track and shoot Whale with non-lethal shot to incapacitate, remove trapped person safely, finish whale humanely. 100% reliable. Will work for trophy piece TBD.

—U R cute. Send # 4 good time. M huge. 3=>

I give my middle finger to the screen a lot.

— WHO'S WATCH? —

TIME PASSES and I hear it pass and actually see it pass. The hour hand circles around all the numbers and does it again and again and on day three, I start wondering.

Why would a watch be in here?

A watch wouldn't be swallowed and end up in these lungs. It would take a person like me to bring it in here. Someone was here before me.

I pull with glowing wigglers close. Nothing is odd about the front of the watch. Turn it over and the Wrigglers illuminate engraved script letters: *For Amelia with all my love GP 1935.*

A creepy feeling moves up my back. I only know one Amelia. That pilot lady from the old days, Amelia Earhart. She got lost flying across the ocean. Maybe she crashed and got out of the plane and was swallowed by this whale and she did what I did, scrambled up into the lungs and lived. But how long did she live? How long do whales live? Did she live 'til she was old? What happened to her bones and clothes? Did she slip out when she couldn't take it anymore and get crushed in the stomach?

—Welcome to your fate, Lard Ass. Amelia Earhart died in here or died trying to get out. You'll be the same. Only she was missed. No one will miss you and your pointless life.

I don't want to think about it. I hold the watch to my ear. The ticking sounds like it's counting the seconds of my pointless life.

— MAKING MOVIES —

THE DOCUMENTARY movie is well underway. Arthur helps me unpack all of Brian's boxes and we create a replica of my son's room in the guest room. The only difference is the walls are a beautiful teal and the floors hardwood. No beige anywhere. We set up the computer and PlayStation and hang model spaceships and even throw clothes all over. I get to sleep in the Star Wars sheets and being in his room again feels good. Arthur films everything.

Photos of Brian are scanned. The yearbook photo is scanned. Arthur captures the screen when I do a Zoom call with Dan to tell him about the crowdfunding. He captures the swelling forehead vein and the "crazy bitch" and the middle finger, and when Dan hangs up we slap hands in triumph at the dramatic footage.

The To-Do List photo on my phone is filmed and the lines *Talk to an expert, Sell the furniture, Sell the house, Pack, and Leave* are crossed off with animation.

Toke is interviewed for the film over FaceTime. He pauses slightly each time he's about to say Brian's name, but manages to avoid calling my son Lard Ass. I'm grateful. More interviews with Billy and the girls. They all have awkward smiles and guilty looks but say nice things about my boy.

Arthur processes the video of the whale swallowing Brian, making it even more real and clear, and I can't watch it.

We go to the Aquarium of the Bay to interview their whale expert. This woman has the same opinion as that Dr. Ziegler at Sea World. She insists there is no chance of survival. "Other sea mammals—Narwals, seals, walruses—have links from mouth to lungs. Whales don't. The boy was crushed in the stomach. I'd stake my reputation on him being dead."

Arthur looks like he wants to slap her but instead asks, "*If* there was an anomaly that produced an esophageal flap or epiglottis, would there would be a way to enter the lungs after being swallowed?" The expert has to admit *if* that was the case, Brian could get into the lungs. That's the "sound bite" he'll edit in.

Arthur insists I get new clothes. He says beige doesn't look good on screen. I order online, but buy muted colors. Brown. Dull moss green. Dusty grey. I can't change completely.

I'm interviewed constantly and Arthur gives me pointers so I don't rush my words or move my hands too much or shift my eyes all over. He's definitely a good director. Too bad I'm not a more interesting subject.

While Arthur edits, I research ocean currents and whale migration patterns but don't get any answers as to where to look for Brian. Whale migration patterns flow everywhere on earth. Up around Alaska, into the Arctic Circle, down to southern Baja, around Hawaii. Whales can travel 14,000 miles a year, 1000 miles a month. It's been almost two months. There's no way of knowing where this whale is. My son could be anywhere.

— LESS ICE —

THE GREAT WHALE moves along the edges of the ice. There is much less of it than there used to be. New vistas have opened. Alternative routes. Currents curl in places that were never passable. The whale, curious to find untried feeding grounds, slides along the curve of the underwater formations, weaving below frozen caverns.

Above, a starving polar bear waits on an ice floe for a meal to pass. It watches the shapes in the water. A dark shape rises and the bear swipes splayed claws across the emerging back. The creature jerks and dives and beside it the massive whale rises, crashing into the floating ice. The polar bear stumbles, regains its balance, rears on its hind legs, and roars.

The whale rams the floe, cracking it in two, and sending the bear into the water. Whale mouth widens and—misses the bear as it scrambles onto the broken raft of ice.

The whale tilts and its eye breaks above the surface of the sea to peer at the drenched submissive bear. Satisfied, the whale slowly sinks, watching the bear's distorted image shrink and fade.

— WHAT ANN KNOWS ABOUT WHALES —

ARTHUR'S FILMING me again. "With all the experts saying it's impossible for Brian to be alive in a whale, why do you still believe?"

"I know a whole lot of shit about whales," I tell the camera. "Or should I say Cetacea. Cetacea evolved from Even-toed Ungulates, which include members of the Artiodactyla order such as pigs, hippopotami, camels, llamas, alpacas, deer, giraffes, antelopes, sheep, and goats."

"Goats?"

"Hippos are the closest. What else do I know? Baleen whales filter crustaceans such as krill through hairlike Keratin plates and have a double blowhole. Bowhead, Southern Right Whales—"

"That's plenty."

"I know parts of a whale—the rostrum beak, the dorsal fin and ridge, caudal peduncle, the tail which contains twin flukes articulated by the median notch."

"Thanks, Ann. That's good."

I don't stop. "I know that the sharp beaks of squid don't digest easily and in the stomachs of whales they are coated with a waxy substance produced in the digestive system —"

"There's no reason people will want to hear—"

"—and that is expelled out the rear, or vomited, and this Ambergris is extremely valuable, used by the perfume makers. A small lump can sell for thousands."

"Whale poo wax is in perfume?"

"Isn't that cool?"

"You do know a lot. Thanks," Arthur says. The camera's light goes off.

"Turn it back on. There's a point to this."

He turns the camera on again.

"Whales are very intelligent and can live for hundreds of years. One killed recently had a bit of an ancient harpoon still inside. It had been harpooned before Melville wrote Moby Dick, but survived to tell the tale."

"He *was* old."

"I know whale maneuvers: the Tail Slap, the Peduncle Wave, Spy Hop, Head-Lunge, Logging, Swimming Inverted, and of course the Full Breach—leaping into the air, lifting 100,000 pounds completely out of the water."

"You said there was a point?"

"Getting to it. I know there isn't *supposed* to be an epiglottis that Brian can access the lungs, but there's a whale that blows bubbles out of its mouth, and they can't figure out how it does that, if the lungs *aren't* connected to the mouth. You hear? *THEY CAN'T FIGURE OUT HOW IT DOES THAT.* Shit happens. Things aren't normal. Darwin knew that. Some creature comes out odd. Like the Fifty-two Hertz whale."

"The what?" Arthur asks.

"The Loneliest Whale in the World is a whale that sings at Fifty-two Hertz, looking for a mate but never finding one. He sings at Fifty-two Hertz and no whale *ever* sings that high. No whale would recognize his song. So he's lonely."

"And you think Brian might be in him?"

"No. What I think is, this proves that not every creature follows the rules of how they are supposed to be. This Fifty-two Hertz whale is abnormal. He's an anomaly. Wikipedia says the scientists couldn't identify that species of whale. They think it could be malformed, or a hybrid of a blue whale and another species."

"So you think Brian's whale could be abnormal or a hybrid?"

"Or a new species we haven't encountered. They *do* discover new species, you know. We don't know every creature on earth, especially in the oceans. I looked up how many species are discovered each year. It's thousands."

Arthur looks up from the camera, incredulously.

"The point is, if we don't know shit, then *anything* is possible. Even a boy in a whale. And I'm telling you, we don't know shit."

— LET IT BE FOUND AND SOMETHING IS —

SHIT MUST HAVE GONE out by now. My wonderful message-in-the-bottle would have been shit out for sure.

—*What do you know? Maybe it got stuck in the intestines and is gonna be there forever. And who knows how long a whale takes to digest—*

—*You're me, so you don't know any more about whale digestion than I do and I know nada, so shut up.*

Where is Bottle now? Probably the waves pushed it to shore. Pushed it over to Santa Monica or Pacific Palisades. Maybe a surfer dude will zoom by it as he rides a curl. He'll notice the bottle and all his buddies and the skimpily-dressed tan babes will gather around as the dude shows it. Lots of "cool" and "awesome"s and head bobbing. Someone will call the number on the dollar and Mom will answer and she'll figure a way to find my whale and I'll be out.

—*They'll toss it in the garbage, Lard Ass. They won't even bother to open it.*

—*Shut up! I'm not listening to you anymore!*

—*Good luck with that.*

Any minute the bottle will be found. I can will this to happen. It is happening. The surfer is looking down. Sees it. Scoops it up, and yells to the friends on shore. He's dialing Mom's number now.

—*Not.*

—*You always only see the negative. Never anything positive.*

—*What is positive? I'm stuck in a whale with a Lard Ass.*

I kick the bag of Wrigglers to make them shine and they plop next to my bundle, churning angrily.

*—Great going, Lard Ass. Break the bag while you're at it. I'll be
stuck in a whale with Lard Ass IN THE DARK!! Check that it's not
leaking. NOW!*

I crawl to the baggie by my bundle and inspect it. Looks okay.
Setting it down carefully, I see something in my wadded-up
Simpsons T-shirt. Something weird. A little squiggle of white. Like a
white worm curling or the corkscrew tail of a tiny pig. I hold the
Wrigglers over it. Something's coming out of that damn burr stuck to
my T-shirt. A weird alien tentacle emerging from that prickler. Is this
another creature that lives in the lungs of whales? It could be
dangerous. Like those movies where it gets inside and grows and
bursts from the stomach—

—Dump it out the flap.

Wait. Is this from that burr from that goddamn sticky-sticker
plant I got shoved into?

—Who cares where it's from. Dump it out!

A burr is like a seed. If it's a seed, then—this is—a sprout!

—Whoop-te-doo. You got a vegetable to eat.

—I'm not eating this. It's a wonderful sprout growing in a whale!

This is so cool! This is from that brush in the arroyo that was a
scraggly mess. Ugly, like me. We're not the pretty plants people
want. We aren't sought. We're the ones that no one likes, the ones
that cling to a sock or a dog's butt. We're unlovable but we survive!

—Lard Ass has lost what was left of his tiny mind.

I'm in the middle of a whale, in the middle of the ocean, and I've
got a fuckin' house plant! I've got a living creature that won't say no.
I love this tenacious little squiggle thing.

—Kill me now.

What do people do to make plants grow? When I was a kid, I had
an avocado pit in a glass of water held up with toothpicks but I forgot
to fill the water and the pit got wrinkly and Mom tossed it. I need
some sort of soil. Seaweed? That's the best I can do. And a pot. I'll
grow it in my sneaker. Plants need sun, but things survive, don't
they? Things manage in the worst conditions.

—Lard Ass thinks he has a green thumb now.

—You just keep talking. I've got stuff to do.

I chew and spit. Chew and spit, mashing seaweed into a pulp and filling my sneaker.

The little sprout is only as long as my thumbnail. I transfer it gently to its new home, cover it with the seaweed, and water it with spit.

Little Sprout, don't worry. I'll care for you. I'll protect you. Little Sprout, if I can survive, you can.

—— THE BRIDGE ——

BEEN A MONTH since the Kickstarter campaign was put online. It keeps growing but I don't know what to spend the money on. I pull up the photo on my phone of the To-Do List scribbled on the beige wall.

1. Find Brian. That will be the last to get crossed off—if — WHEN—it happens.

2. Talk to an expert. Done.

3. Hire a boat. Later.

4. Sell the furniture. Done.

5. Sell the house. Done.

6. Pack. Done.

6-a. Leave. Done

7. Buy an extra phone charger and battery. Done.

8. Passport. It came last week. Done.

9. International plug adapters. Done.

10. Watch Pinocchio. I'll watch it with Brian

This is good. I'm definitely making progress. Things are getting crossed off the list.

Arthur knocks on the open door. "Got the video conference with the Greenpeace guy in five."

"Okay, I'll be there." I brush my hair and trot down the hall. Tobey's in his office reading an outdoor magazine. I've never seen him rock climb or hand glide or hike the Sierras. I think he just likes the pictures of rugged guys. I linger at the door but he doesn't turn. He's been sulking for weeks, sure that I'm wasting my time and energy. What else should I do with my time and energy? I ought to go somewhere and give Tobey and Arthur their privacy, but I don't know where to go.

The young guy from Greenpeace is knowledgeable and compassionate and full of fresh-faced dedication. He's thin and bearded and the kind of guy a mother would be proud to call her son. I feel guilty thinking that when he says, "Ma'am, I'd love to help. We at Greenpeace are committed to putting an end to whaling and we'd get a lot of good press finding your son. Japan, Norway, and Iceland are the only countries that still permit whaling. Maybe Greenpeace could stop a whaler from killing your son's whale. We might block them and save that one whale, but we'll never know if it had your boy inside. There's no way to tell. Even if we save whales, we have no way of *finding* your son."

A cold lump forms in my belly. There *is* no way to tell one whale from another and which might hold Brian. Even with this money, even crossing things off my list, if his cell phone is dead, he can't be tracked. Knowing Brian, he used his last bit of battery playing a video game. There is no way to find him. Brian is lost.

I have to get out of here now. I do a finger-walking gesture to Arthur. He looks at me with concern, so I add, "Don't worry, I won't go left. Or two blocks to the right. I won't get in trouble."

Arthur pulls a set of keys off the erect penis of a small copper satyr. "Left, you'll find the all-night soy latte bars. Right, the vegan gastro pubs. Everything's gentrified. Good luck finding trouble." He hands me the keys. "Got your phone?"

I want to yell *My son's in a whale and I'm waiting for his call. You think I don't have my phone!?* But I don't. I smile in what I know must be an overly sarcastic way and step outside.

It's cold and damp. Much colder than L.A. What am I doing outside? I don't go outside.

I walk fast, trying not to think about the Greenpeace guy's horrible truth. The street is steep and I'm quickly out of breath. A bicyclist shoots by, nearly knocking me down. He's on the move. He's got places to go. Not like me. I pass the vegan gastropub. The artisan bakery. The free-trade gift boutique. High-end items that no one needs.

This city makes me angry. Everyone's important here. Everyone's arty. Everyone's liberal and embracing. The bridge is an icon. The colorful houses. The trolly. Sourdough. Alcatraz. The LGBTQ+s. The Dot Coms. The Foodies. The Startups. Why does it all have to be so special? What happened to normal people? Dull people? Where's a place for people like me?

I don't notice where I'm headed until I get here. Golden Gate bridge glows red around me as the sun puts a toe in the ocean for an evening dip. A sign says the walkway closes in half an hour. The expanse stretches ahead and disappears in fog. Normally I'd be scared but I'm too angry and frustrated and also there's a tall cyclone fence keeping me from jumping into the sea and a thick metal pipe barrier keeping me from leaping into traffic. I lean into the cold and march. Every sound is annoying. Whoosh of intermittent cars beside me. Clanging of metal against ship masts. Seagulls crying. Wind moaning through the orange girders and cables.

The sun has drowned as I reach the middle of the bridge. Somewhere along the way the cyclone fencing disappeared and now all that keeps me from jumping is a waist-high railing. I feel the vastness all around me. The movement of the bridge as it's pressed by night winds. No sign of anyone else. No headlights. Am I the only one out here? The only one this alone?

Leaning over the railing, I look down and see nothing through the fog, but I know what's below. Somewhere in that cold, undulating, black ocean, my son lives. I want to join him. Maybe if I was in that water, I'd be close to him.

Are you alive, Brian? Are you somewhere sleeping? It's almost bedtime. But you always stayed up late, hunched over your video games or doing who-knows-what behind that door.

The fog parts and the moon shines in the water, wiggling and squirming, distorted by the waves. It shimmies like it's beckoning me.

My phone chirps and I fumble for it. Maybe it's Brian! Maybe he's right down there, looking up!—I answer, "Brian?"

"There is no problem with your credit card—"

"Fuck you!"

I lean farther over the railing, searching for a sign of the whale. I'll yell right as the blowhole opens and—

Headlights appear and flashing red lights. A spotlight strikes me. Car door slam.

"Ma'am, what are you doing here?"

I hold my phone-hand up to shade my eyes and a badge glints in the darkness beyond the glare. "Just thinking."

"Not thinking something stupid, I hope."

I try to remember what I was thinking to see if it was stupid. The thoughts are gone. "Maybe," I answer.

The officer bends under the pipe separating his car from the walkway and walks into the spotlight. His eyes say that he's had a hard day and I'm his last straw. "You know I have to stop you."

"You do?"

"You have to consider other people. Who it might affect."

"See—my son's down there—"

The officer looks alarmed. "Your son jumped?"

"No, he's in a whale. He got swallowed but he's alive. I'm looking for him and I'm sure he's right below us—"

The officer mumbles into the microphone on his shoulder and steps toward me, palms open. "Ma'am, you can tell me all about it. Now step away from the railing and we'll have a nice talk. Take my hand. I'm Joe."

He smiles like he's a friend and takes another step and a strong grip on my shoulder jerks me from the edge. The phone flies from my hand and lands with a sharp *CRACK* on the pavement.

"NOOOO!"

"Easy, Lady—"

I scramble to get the phone but he grabs my wrist, twisting me 'round, lifting my arm high behind my back. Clawing at his face with my free hand, nails meet stubble and skin, and he jerks in pain. I push backwards hard and he grunts as we hit the railing—maybe we'll fall together—but he bends low to keep us upright and his black shoe taps the phone and it slides on slick asphalt. Slides toward the blackness. Slides to the edge of the world and—falls. Gone. Something in me breaks open and I'm screaming and kicking, trying to retrieve my boy from his fall, fighting for his life, and this man has an arm around my neck and drags me under the metal pipe to his car, bends my thumb and the pain makes me move my arm where he wants it to go and the ratcheting click I've heard on TV tells me I'm cuffed. I scream every curse I know as he tilts me into the back seat.

— ANOTHER NIGHT —

I WONDER WHERE we are now. Maybe we traveled up alongside the Pacific Coast Highway and have finally made it to San Francisco. Maybe right now we're swimming under the Golden Gate Bridge. Uncle Tobey and Uncle Arthur are right above us.

Home blasts out and brings in fresh air. There is no light from the hole. Must be night.

Day, night. Who cares. Time goes by like it always does. Amelia's watch ticks but even though I know the time, it doesn't matter. My beard is growing longer. Today is just like every other day. I exercise and practice holding my breath. I water Sprout and hold him up to the blowhole for a flash of sunlight. The Japanese menu changes. Now I've got—Squeak Weed, which makes lots of noise when you chew it, and Peewee Peelers. Regular Peelers are now called Supersize. I sing along with Home, trying to match his sounds. When I sing through the rubber corrugated tube, the grumble-warble, squeaking wagon-wheel, clicking, and gong Rise Song sounds almost exactly like Home. *The Blue Light Special* changes, regulars disappear, spin-off shows focus on bit characters, but there's always a Duffus and a Hero. The Hero always triumphs.

I don't miss video games. Or the people I knew. Toke. Billy. They weren't really friends. They started the Lard Ass name. I'm glad to be away from them. It's quiet and peaceful here. No one ridicules me or calls me Lard Ass.

—*Except me.*

—*Yeah, except you.*

Home moans out a mournful song. I wonder if he's missing someone. I guess I miss Mom, but I know she's better off. I was so bad at being good. She just yelled and screamed and I never changed. At least she can stop screaming now.

— INTAKE —

I STOP SCREAMING. Officer Joe has left me cuffed in the back of the car and gone into a building. He probably will charge me with scratching him but you don't go to jail for that and I'll be back with Tobey and Arthur in an hour or so. Tomorrow I'll hire a scuba diver to search below the bridge for the phone.

—*That's crazy. That phone is gone. Just like Brian.*

—*Shut up! Brian is alive, and if I have that phone, I have proof!*

The officer exits the building and marches toward the car.

—*You're delusional. And if you don't want to spend the night in jail, start thinking about apologizing.*

The car door opens and Officer Joe looks in. He's got a bloody scratch across his cheek. "Are you gonna behave?" he asks.

"Yes, sir. I'm sorry, sir."

Officer Joe unfurls me from the back seat. The cuffs dig into my wrists as I'm escorted into a bright lobby. This does not look like a police station. The sign says *Admitting*. What should I admit? Joe arranges me in front of a counter where an older woman in a pink smock asks for my ID.

"I didn't bring it, ma'am. I was just taking a walk. My name is Ann Ketchum."

She taps my answer into the computer. "Where do you live?"

"I'm homeless."

She taps that in.

"Not really homeless-homeless, but I don't have a home right now. I sold my house and I'm visiting my brother here in San Francisco."

"What's his name and phone number?"

101

I tell her Tobey's name. "I don't know his number. It's in my phone."

She puts out her palm, moving it in a *get-your-phone-out-pronto* gesture.

"Officer Asshole kicked it off the bridge."

"No-no-no," Officer Asshole barges in. "She was on the bridge lookin' to jump. Fought hard when I tried to help and almost threw me over the railing with her. Look what she done to my face."

"Suicidal and violent." Tight-ass-pink-lady says, typing the diagnosis into her computer.

This is bullshit. "This is bullshit. I'm not fucking suicidal and I only slapped a few people, threw a coffee cup—missed—and a chicken leg, smashed the dining room set, and a honeymoon glass before this fucking cop—"

"YOU are NOT helping your CASE! Now SHUT UP!" She pushes a button and leans into a speaker thing. "Intake Team to Lobby. Intake Team to Lobby."

Two husky men in white stride toward me. The pink bitch turns to the Asshole. "Thank you, Officer. We'll take it from here."

As he fiddles with the keys to un-cuff me, Officer Asshole winks at the pink bitch over the counter. "This lady's the crazy one been on the news. Thinks her boy's alive in a whale."

"I recognize her now. Some people do anything for attention." She squints at me. "You should be ashamed of yourself."

"Fuck you," I reply.

"Gentlemen, put Ms. Ketchum in C-18. Code 6."

The two men clamp their green plastic gloves on my arms. Grips that will leave bruises.

"Watch out, fuckers," I yell. "Hold on tight! I'm CODE 6!"

And the men in white drag me down the hall.

I'm locked alone in a cell after a woman orderly exchanges my clothes for institutional crap that feels very easy to tear. Guess so I can't hang myself. V-neck jumper and pants and slippers. Beige.

This room is the size of our walk-in closet off the Master Bedroom at home. And like that room, the walls are beige. The bedding is beige. Even the washcloth by the mini sink is beige. The toilet is a slightly different tint of beige.

Anxiety swarms over me. I had locked myself in my beige house for years but this is different. I need to get out!

—*Breathe. Stay calm.*

—*Yes. It'll be okay. They'll let me out when Tobey comes.*

—*Tobey thinks you're crazy. He thinks Brian's dead and you're crazy to look for him and how do you know you're not crazy? Brian never called. You imagined his voice. Everyone knows you can't survive in a whale—*

"SHUT UP!" I scream as a nurse enters. She doesn't seem fazed by my outburst. It's what crazy people do.

I smile and try not to look insane. "Sorry. I'm not really like this."

The nurse holds out a gloved hand with two pills and a cup of water. "You need to take these. They'll help you rest."

"Did you reach my brother?"

She doesn't know about my brother. She only knows I need to take these pills like a good girl.

I'll do that under-the-tongue trick. Spit them out when she leaves.

I smile again and take the pills. It's easy to push them under my tongue. This is working. I take a sip of water and swallow but the pills get loose and gag me and fly across the cell when I cough. The nurse has seen it before. She wipes them on the washcloth and hands them back to me.

I drink them down like a good girl. "Please. Tell them I'm not crazy."

The Nurse suggests I get some shut-eye and leaves.

The fluorescents murmur overhead.

—*At least you're back in your natural habitat. The land of beige.*

—*I didn't choose beige! That was Dan!*

—*You've always been beige.*

—*I have not!*

—*Name one way you're not beige! You never had goals. Never had anything you were good at. No hobbies. No interests. No nothing. You're not really a person, just a placeholder for a person. If you were shut in here forever you wouldn't be missed. Dan has forgotten you. Tobey and Arthur can't wait for you to be gone. Brian is lucky to be away, dead or alive! You are so beige that you're invisible. If they look through the peephole in this door, they won't even see you.*

—I did one thing good. I made a little baby boy—

—And you warped him and distorted him and he became fat and sullen and worthless. You know what you made him.

Tears fall as my heart crumples inside. I know.

—– THAT INNER VOICE —–

—LARD ASS!

I shake the Wrigglers again so I can see my toes as I strain to touch them. By my ankle is Sprout, cheering me on. He's poked his little head above the surface of his seaweed soil. If he can push himself skyward, I can do another sit-up. Fifty-two.

—Waste of time.

Fifty-three.

—Ignoring me, Duffus?

Fifty-four. I used to not even be able to do even two.

—Athletes can do hundreds.

Fifty-five.

—Uh—hel-looo—mind to Lard Ass—if you only listened, you might—

—Okay.

—Okay what?

—Okay, you have the floor—or the lung. Take it away.

—Say what?

—I'm listening.

The slow, slow pounding of Home's heartbeat under me is the only sound I hear. I go back to the sit-ups. Fifty-six.

—Okay, Lard Ass, you want it? Here it is. You've been real hell to live with. I'm stuck with a loser and a no-nothing duffus who has

no drive and can't even keep himself from falling in a whale, let alone not use up the phone battery and now I'm here watching you shit out of a flap and jerk off and make up a blue wriggler tv show that doesn't even have interesting characters, just like you, because you have no imagination and no ambition and are bad at everything even all the video games and you are a NOBODY and you're fat and the cleft pallet may have been fixed like mom says but I can see a scar when I look close, and no one likes you and no one ever liked you and Dad didn't want you to go to his new family after the divorce because you would have ruined it and mom hates you and even if you got out, people would see you and wish you were back in here where you don't have to be seen or heard or smelled. The people you think were friends only used you for comic relief and no girl ever liked you and Vivian only smiled 'cause she felt sorry for such a dweeb and you'll die a virgin and... And you're pasty. And squishy... And you have dull hair with no style. And stupid clothes. And... and no skills. And... and... fat ankles. And... and... and... hair growing in weird, not-normal patterns. And...

Fifty-seven.

—*That's all true. Everything you said. Please continue. I want to hear everything you have to say.*

—*Fuck you. Do your stupid sit-ups. Like it matters.*

I bend forward, straining. Fingers webbed behind my head, reaching for my toes. Fifty-eight. Drop back to my spongy floor. This may be a way to shut that inner voice up. Let him talk himself out.

—*I can hear you, Lard Ass.*

I strain again, grinning now. Fifty-nine...

—- BEIGE WAKEUP —-

SOUNDS PULL ME from a deep place. Let me stay. I want to stay here where there is no thought or memory. More sounds. I struggle to remain oblivious, but can't. I open my eyes to a beige wall. Oh. I'm home. Relief brings tears to my eyes. It was all a dream. A long nasty dream. The sounds are Brian in his room. I hear him open the door and turn.

It's not Brian.

A man is white offers me a plastic glass of orange juice. It looks luminous in the sea of beige. I sit up and the world tilts.

"Take it easy. I'll be outside. When you're ready, I'll take you to see the doctor."

In a few minutes, we're outside of an office and an India-looking kid about Brian's age opens the door. He's tall and kind of handsome in a teenage way. He must be an intern—

"Hello, Ann, I'm Doctor Prakash."

He is way too young to be a doctor. Maybe he's a patient, and the doctor is tied up in the closet.

"Please come in."

I step in and there's a bearded man—Tobey! I rush to my brother and he pulls me close.

"Try not to act crazy," he whispers.

Tobey and I sit, holding hands. The faux-doctor smiles like a benevolent waiter waiting for me to decide on my entrée. I glance around the room, looking for any sign of the real doctor. Scanning the requisite framed credentials, they all present the name David Prakash in fine calligraphy. Stanford University. California Board of Psychiatry. Honor this. Certificate of Excellence that.

The handsome imposter-doctor sees me looking. "I'm thinking of growing a beard and getting fake glasses. Do you think it would help?"

Handsome and a sense of humor. "Maybe," I say. "That and a walker."

Tobey's hand jerks in mine.

The boy-doctor laughs at my joke. That's weird. I don't make jokes.

"I'm older than I look," he says.

"So am I," I say.

The doctor laughs again. Why couldn't I have had a son like this?

After a few more pleasantries, he gets down to business, asking several questions about how I'm doing, how I slept, if I'm suicidal... I give him all the right answers.

"If I understand correctly, you're the woman we know from the news. You believe your son is alive in a whale?"

Tobey squeezes my hand as a warning.

I try to keep my voice steady. If I do good, they'll let me out. "I have to admit, I did believe that. The sudden and bizarre nature of Brian's disappearance shocked me. Disoriented me. But experts tell me, science tells me, everyone tells me it is impossible to live in a whale. At a certain point, maybe I'll have to accept that. I just—don't yet."

"Fair enough," the young doctor says. "We Homo Sapiens have a great capacity for self-delusion in the face of unbearable circumstances. I venture to guess that we couldn't exist without this coping mechanism. Life would prove too painful."

He sure talks like he went to all the right schools. Sighing a bit too self-consciously, I admit, "I don't want to be self-deluded. I recognize that I need to face the truth."

Tobey squeezes my hand to let me know I'm doing well.

I see in young Doctor Prakash's eyes that I did great and he smiles and says, "You'll be staying with us for this initial period of 72 hours."

I jerk at these words and Tobey rubs his thumb across my palm to tell me not to react. I take a breath and attempt to remain calm.

"We are going to assess your mental health and well-being to determine the next steps. Because you were suicidal and violent, we need—"

"I wasn't—ow—"

Tobey squeezes my hand like it's one of his stress balls. I blink with the pain.

"You were saying something?" the asshole doctor asks.

Tobey looks at me with a big-brother threat.

"I wasn't—I wasn't—thinking. My phone fell and I got upset."

"People get that way about their devices. One can become attached to them as substitutes for real human connection. It's a form

107

of transference." The holier-than-thou doctor presses a button on his desk and the same orderly enters. "Thank you, Ann. I'm going to speak with your brother for a bit and we'll have another talk soon."

— UNDER WATER —

THE GREAT WHALE curls its back and slides, mouth wide, through the shoal of herring. Swallowing the bounty. Grateful the other is following.

Songs in the distance. Swim toward the sounds. There's a pod out there. Perhaps a group to join. They'll be strangers. Since curling around the great icy pathways, all this territory is unknown.

Yet, the whale can't dive like before. Lungs won't take in enough breath. The mucus never clears. Perhaps it's dying.

— BAD MOMMY —

DOCTOR PRAKASH seems to believe I wanted to die. Yeah, I was on the bridge and looking down and leaning over, but was I going to jump? I remember looking at the moon's reflection and thinking that Brian might be down there...

"Were you thinking that by jumping, you'd be joining him?"

"I'm not sure, Doctor. I can't tell anything anymore. On the one hand, I did think I'd be closer to him if I was down in that water, but on the other hand, am I saying that to make you feel like I'm admitting something and therefore I'm getting better, which will make you feel like you are making progress in healing me and you'll be happy? You're the one with the power, so I feel the need to make you feel good about yourself."

The young doctor nods, like this is progress. "Your overriding motivation is to act like you are getting healthy in order to make me feel good about myself as a healer?"

"Yes."

"We call that codependency. Were you codependent with your son?"

I have no idea what he's asking me. All the diplomas and citations don't mean he can communicate. I shrug.

"Tell me about your relationship with your son."

"My son is in a whale and my relationship with him didn't drive him to get swallowed. He didn't dive into a whale to get away from me."

"Let's forget about the whale for a minute," the doctor says, sounding frustrated.

I won't get out of here if he's frustrated. "My relationship with Brian? Typical mother and teenage son."

"You got along?"

What world does he live in? "I yelled and he snorted."

"That doesn't sound good."

"It's not always easy being a single mom. I did my best, but he was doing nothing, making a mess, being a slob. He had no goals, no interests, I tried to get him to do better."

"How so?"

"The things moms do. I cook healthy meals with vegetables and lean meat but he only wants Pringles and crap food. He's fat. I suggest he get a job, but he only plays video games. I admit, I yell, but that's because he won't listen. He won't react. He just grunts. Does that on purpose to make me mad, like teenagers do."

"Was this always your relationship?"

I remember us laughing. He liked singing with me. He never sings anymore. "We had some good times, but since about four years ago, he stopped trying. He just gave up."

"Did something happen four years ago?"

The divorce. I stare at the young doctor. Who is he to judge me? He knows nothing about life. "I know what you're thinking—I'm a bad mommy and it's my fault Brian has no will, no drive, just plays video games, because I have no will, no drive, and just play homemaker. Like mother, like son. The apple doesn't fall far from the tree and all that shit. You ever think maybe I wasn't doing much with my life BECAUSE I was raising a boy on my own? I'm supposed to have a life, too?"

The doctor's looking at me like I'm a danger to myself and others. He takes a deep breath. "Thank you for telling me what I'm thinking. We call that projection."

"Oh, stop with the psychological mumbo-jumbo." Oops. I shouldn't be talking that way. He'll count that against me. "I'm sorry, doctor. That was rude."

Doctor Prakash smiles slightly. "You're right. You don't need all the psychological terms. I apologize if it felt patronizing."

Is he trying to trick me? I'll wait to see what's next.

"Think about this," the doctor says. "In all our relationships, like you had with your son, like yours with me, we can say things that will bring us closer together or push us further apart. Every comment, reaction, look, can make the relationship positive or negative. This is in *every* relationship, even the ones we have with ourselves. Tell me about your relationship with yourself."

Oh fuck. My brain suddenly gets real foggy. What were we talking about? Relationships. I can't think.

The doctor sees me fidgeting. "Let me ask, are you on speaking terms with yourself?"

"Non-stop."

"Is it on par with what you said about your son? Someone's always giving advice and the other isn't listening or changing?"

Oops.

The doctor pushes a button on his desk. "Think about it. We'll talk again tomorrow."

I'm escorted down the hall and as the orderly unlocks my room. he asks, "Everything alright, Ms. Ketchum?"

Nothing is alright! I yelled at the doctor and I'm a rotten mother and Brian is better off without me because deep down, I'm a horrible person.

My eyes fill with tears.

The orderly steps closer. "It's a tough thing, isn't it?"

I press the tears back and whisper, "What is?"

He sets a warm hand on my shoulder and that feels like a kindness I don't recognize.

"Being human."

—- GLACIER —-

IF IT WERE HUMAN, Brian's message-in-the-bottle might feel a thrill riding the current, rolling with the swells, with Punctured Dollar Bill and Library Card tumbling together.

If Bottle had eyes, it might see itself riding closer to the massive glacier looming over the bay. If Bottle skin it might rise in goose-bumps, feeling the cold gusts bringing white tips to the waves and carrying it next to the glacier. Had Bottle ears they might absorb the tapping as it knocks against the ancient blue ice. Might hear a core-shaking rumble, moaning, creaking, and screeching. The aching song of the glacier splitting. The screaming moment of labor before the shedding that outermost wall. Calving its offspring. Burg birthing.

Those ears might turn to the sounds far across the bay. Sounds of the surf against sand or the barking dog—a long-nosed, scruffy mutt twirling in place, waiting for the toss.

Sneakers backing quickly from the suds rushing up the beach, a young girl flings a stick as far as she can, toward the distant glacier. The dog bounds in after it.

"Get the stick, Pinocchio!"

Had Bottle any notion of irony, it might laugh at the name of the mutt.

An earth-groan pauses all action. Glacier roars and breaks along the massive crack, rumbling, creaking, squealing, thundering, and the calved iceberg tilts in slow motion as huge things do, sliding up and down at the same time, a Titanic but hundreds of times larger, and the green and white and blue rises, tips and lingers—-lingers—and—

—falls—a city falling—

—breaking pieces of itself, scales of ice, pummeling down into thick stewed water, and the newborn iceberg descends, thrusting deep—over Bottle. Over the traveler. Pressing Bottle down lower and lower into the sludge sea. Down into darkness. Down where all is gone and forgotten.

And Bottle, had it lungs, would hold its breath (knowing that to be futile), and wait for the revelation of Nothingness.

Across the bay, the girl and dog stare at the world's unfolding event. The sound is out-of-sync with the image, arriving later. Several patrons rush out of the Petrified Moose Saloon on the bluff, carrying their drinks, startled at the cataclysmic sound. Frantic screams from the drinkers reach the girl on the shore. Screams and she and the dog scramble toward the others as the huge submerged ice mountain heaves up and up and up, out of the sea and the wave starts toward them.

The thick ice-spattered wave rises, rolling, and the water leans forward, speeding across the bay, and with it, carried by its power, is Bottle, pulled from the depths and riding aloft in the chaos.

And the patrons of the bar scream and wave their beers. And the girl's father stands with them, frozen, watching disaster unfold.

And the girl and dog run up the rocky shore to the screamers and the massive wave hurtles across the shrinking distance and chases, chases, and covers the place she had been, covers the place she ran from, covers the sand and the shore and the stick and tries to reach the girl as the dog barks a warning—and rumbles up the rocks, tumbles up the bank and—slows. The girl turns as the wave inches up—a last effort—up to peek over the tip of the parking lot, only yards from her sneakers—drops its ice bounty, and recedes.

The girl stares, imagining what might have been, as her dog barks and snaps at the retreating water.

"Jenny!" her father screams from the petrified crowd outside the Petrified Moose Saloon.

Jenny waves behind, mesmerized by the churning, groaning water.

And as the man downs his drink in relief and patrons clink bottles and cheer their survival, Pinocchio races up the sand and drops Bottle at the girl's feet.

"Not now, Pinocchio," Jenny says, kicking Bottle away.

The dog fetches and drops the traveler at her feet once again. The girl pulls back her foot to kick—when something catches her eye. Bottle is up and in her hand.

Despite that terrifying drama of the calving of the glacier, had Bottle a heart, it would flip with joy. Had it a voice, it would sing, "Found!"

—- LOOK AT ASSHOLE —

TOUCH THE TOES. Ninety-nine.

Touch the toes. Yes! Broke the one hundred mark!

I slide my palm up the spongy wall and drink the liquid.

Sprout is next. Slide palm and sprinkle on my little fella. Wrigglers light held over him. He seems taller.

Home sings the grumble-warble, squeaking wagon-wheel, clicking, and gong Rise Song and I sing along, seconds behind. It's a round. Really sounds good. We tilt up and I hold Sprout ready so he'll get the sun. The blow hole opens and Sprout gets a full dose of the blinding light. In that second of glare, I can see he's got a little leaf unfolding! I have a green thumb!

Set his sneaker bed down carefully. Chew a little more seaweed. Spit it out to spruce up Sprout's soil.

Time to clean up. Lift and shake the Ziploc for more light, search the spongy lung floor for any discarded Peeler shells or Torpedo Head plexi I might have missed. Dump a few scraps out the flap.

Something mumbles in my head.

—*What?*

—*I said, you're doing good, Lard Ass.*

—*Fuck off.*

—*Really. You were swallowed by a whale and you're exercising, cleaning, raising a plant, have a shopping cart, know whale songs…*

—*Where's the zinger?*

—*No zinger. You're surviving in a whale. Not everyone could say that. It's impressive.*

I can't believe it.

—Thanks.

—Don't let it go to your head.

—Not a chance.

He said impressive. That feels good. I'm impressive.

—I can hear you.

—I know.

—Get back to your oh-so-impressive routine, Lard Ass.

Next is Breath Holding. I take a massive lung-full and watch Amelia's second hand do a circuit. One minute. Two minutes. Slow down. Listen to Home's heartbeat. Stare at Sprout. He's holding his breath like I am. Keep holding it, Sprout. We can do it.

Wait.

Wait.

The walls move closer. Home's lungs are closing in on me. He's out of air, too. I gotta hold it now because if I let go there won't be air to suck in anyway.

Wait.

I can't—

—Another ten seconds. I dare you.

Wait.

Shit, this is hard.

—Don't wus out now.

I hold and hold, and Home is rising again.

This is impossible

—You got this, Lard Ass.

Home brings us up, and the blowhole opens and new old air races into the vacuum. I shake the Wrigglers to look at Amelia's watch and pull in a big breath. Two-minutes and fifty-six seconds!

I wonder what the world record is for breath holding. Maybe I'll beat it. Maybe I already have. A world champion! My claim to fame. Only no one will know.

—I'll know.

—Yeah, but no one in the world. Who knows what I could have become. Yeah, yeah, you don't have to say it. I probably wouldn't have become anything. I wasn't good at anything. Mediocre at best. A nobody.

—That's changed now. You're good at things. You're good at staying alive in a whale. If you get out, you can go on TV. Be on a talk show with a famous host.

I turn with a glorious smile, waving humbly at the television audience. "Thank you. Thank you. It's great to be here."

"Welcome to the show, have a seat, so—building a life in a whale—that's quite an accomplishment."

"You know, I guess it is. My first breakthrough came right off the bat when I managed to get into the lungs."

"Quite a lucky break."

"Luck had nothing to do with it. I remembered that when I swallow water too quickly, sometimes it goes down the wrong pipe. That prompted me to search for the flap into the lungs."

"Quick thinking to save your own life. Well done! Still, it must have been quite the ordeal surviving for so long in that place. What did you do for entertainment? How did you pass the time, Brian?"

"I watched a sitcom of glowing Wrigglers—The Blue Light Special. In fact, I'm in talks right now to produce an animated series based on these characters."

"Listen to that crowd. They can't wait to see the show!"

"Thank you. Thank you. In addition to that, I have a thriving houseplant and I broke the world record for holding my breath."

"Amazing feat! And I understand you've become quite a singer."

"Yes, you know whales sing. My whale sang and I sang along. I'd not done much singing before that."

"Really? None?"

"Well, my mom and I used to sing—"

Tears come up as my throat clamps down a sob.

"What are you remembering, Brian?"

"This time right after the divorce Mom and me were visiting Uncle Tobey and Arthur and we got caught in the rain and our clothes and sneakers were soaked and so we got in their kimono-style bathrobes and were standing by the dryer as it jangled and the shoes thumped and it was a cool rhythm and we both got bobbing our heads and Mom started singing an old crooner song and I joined in and we were dancing barefoot and singing 'you can do anything but don't you step on my barefoot toes' and we laughed and laughed and she looked at me like she loved me."

The audience is hushed.

"Doesn't she look at you like that anymore?"

"I don't blame her for hating me. I hated me too."

The famous host pauses for a long moment. "But you don't hate yourself anymore?"

I feel around inside. "Maybe I don't."

The audience is stunned.

I am also.

—*One more thing.*

—*Shit. Here it comes.*

—*You never paid attention to me before. Shut me out with video games and noise. But when you let me talk, spout it all—you listened. I feel you hear me. Now, it's like we're in this together. You rock.*

I wish I had a mirror. I could look at myself and see if I was lying. I could see if this is a trick.

What can I get a reflection from? The broken cell phone glass!

I hold the Wrigglers and the broken glass close to my face. There's something reflecting. Shake the Wrigglers hard to make them super mad. Their light flares. There he is. He's got a thick beard! He's smiling at me. Fuck! Look at him! It feels so good to look in someone's eyes!

"Hey, Asshole! Good to see you!"

"Hello, Lard Ass! Good to see you, too!"

— FOUND OR NOT —

JENNY CLUTCHES her backpack as her father drives them up the long peninsula. Mark wants to yell at the girl for being near the shore when the glacier dropped its iceberg. As she ran with the monstrous wave chasing her, he had a moment of panic. Panic makes him feel out of control and that makes him mad because he's never in control like a Daddy's supposed to be. He needs to set rules. *Stay away from glacier tsunamis! Don't be across the bay from an iceberg!* These

116

rules sound stupid and improbable. Might as well say *don't get hit by an asteroid.*

Rather than scold her, Mark presses down on the accelerator. Speeding again. No one cares in Alaska. Up ahead, the mountains loom, dark and cold, snow covering the peaks. The light is changing. Darker earlier. This was such a dumb idea.

Not that anything he does is a bright idea. They start shiny and lit up on the edges, but they always grow dark and complicated. This one started like a noble gesture. Making amends and that sort of thing. The dog watched each trip to load the car and at 4:29 in the morning he'd finished packing: Cheerios, cookies, juice boxes, backpack, sleeping bags, the tent, and—just to be safe—two loaded convincers—one tucked under the clothes in his suitcase and one below the spare tire in the trunk.

The idea felt right. Felt exciting and cozy at the same time. He was benevolent. Benevolent as he lifted Jenny from her bed and carried her downstairs, wrapped in her thick quilt. Benevolent when the dog jumped in the car's back seat. Benevolent thinking it would be good to have his daughter's pet join their adventure. Mark had felt a tug of something he figured was love as he'd smoothed the quilt around his sleeping daughter and clicked the seatbelt over her. When they pulled out of the drive, the dog curled to join Jenny in sleep and Mark felt new and reborn. He was awake when everyone else was dreaming. A train, also awake, moaned of distant vistas. Mark started for those.

How long ago was that? Two weeks? Three?

"Gimme your phone," Jenny demands. "I want to call Mom. I want to tell her I almost got drowned by that wave."

Mark lifts his steering hand to tousle his daughter's hair. She jerks back. Maybe that's not what you do to eight-year-olds. He's out of touch. "We don't want to bother your mother. She's trying to get well."

"I don't care. I want to call her! NOW!"

"Maybe later, Jenny."

"She'll want to know I almost died."

"She won't. No parent wants to hear that."

The girl squints at Mark. "How would *you* know what a parent wants?" She's got the condescending tone exactly right, emphasizing the *you,* just like her mother would. A miniature version of Beverly.

"I'm here, aren't I?!" Mark says a lot louder than he intended. He thinks about apologizing, but that never works. Only digs the hole deeper.

Jenny glares at him. "I don't know you. You could be anyone. You were never around. First, you had the war as your excuse, but Mommy said you were done with the war. Why didn't you come home then?"

"Beverly—I mean, Mommy didn't tell you?"

"She wouldn't say, but people whispered about it and shut up when I came by. What did you do wrong?"

Mark wonders what to tell her. Probably anything true would be a bad idea. "You know when kids in school do something and they go to detention?"

"I never did."

"Well, your Daddy did. That's where he was."

"What did you do?"

Mark had heard that kids ask a lot of questions, but he isn't ready with answers. He tries to smile at the girl. "I'm here now and that's what matters." Mark points up the road to the scattering of cabins. "And look, here we are. Home sweet home."

"It's not home. It's NOT HOME and I HATE IT THERE and I HATE YOU!"

Ignore her. She's a kid.

They bump down the gravel road to Glacier View Cabins and curl around to number 11, farthest from the others.

Mark slams the car into Park before they're stopped and makes the two in the front jerk against their seat belts and the one in the back yelp and fly to the floor.

Mark steps out and stomps to the cabin. *The dog has to go. The dog is making things a whole lot harder.*

The girl opens the car's back door and coos over her pet on the floor.

Hell, the dog preoccupies Jenny. The dog should stay.

Mark unlocks the door, hurries to the bathroom, opens his Dopp kit, and pops a pill. *Everything's going to be fine.*

When Jenny and the dog enter the cabin, Mark turns to her. "You and Pinocchio stay inside. I've business to take care of."

"You said we were on vacation. You said it was fun time and no homework, no chores, no work. That means no business!"

Mark tries to smile at his daughter. She's much smarter than he'd anticipated. She catches everything. Sooner or later, the secret will come out, and then what?

"Daddy needs to think. He can't think with his daughter talking."

"That's stupid."

"Daddy needs alone time. Adult time."

Distract her. What distracts kids? Parties. Cake.

"Been a while since I celebrated your birthday, Jenny. Let's have it today. With a cake and presents and hats—"

"I had my birthday. I turned eight in March."

"I know, but—I wasn't there to celebrate. Let's celebrate now. I'll buy presents for you."

"And Pinocchio—"

"And Pinocchio. An extra birthday. I'll get all the supplies, but since it's a surprise party, I have to do it in secret. That's why I need to leave you in the cabin for a while."

"You've got a lot of secrets, Daddy."

Mark's heart jumps and blood rushes to his face. Does she know already?

Jenny grins and pulls her backpack to her chest. "I've got a secret, too. It's mine and all mine."

Relief spreads over Mark. "It's good to have secrets. I'll keep mine and you keep yours. We'll never tell."

—- TISSUE THERAPY —-

THE DAYS GO so fast. Here I am again, staring at the diplomas behind the doctor's head. He's waiting for me to answer. What was the question?

He must see my confusion because he repeats the question. "Have you thought about how your relationship with yourself spilled over onto your relationship with your son?"

"I haven't been much of a person," I try. He's going to ask what I mean, so I might as well save him the trouble. "I mean, I haven't done anything. I don't have interests. No skills. No things I'm good at. I'm less than average. I'm almost a nonentity."

"Did you see Brian as less than average? Almost a nonentity?"

I picture my pudgy boy hunched over his computer in the dark bedroom. A wave of revulsion floods me. He disgusted me. Never doing anything. Never trying. Hardly leaving the house. Wasting his life. Just like me.

Shame stings my eyes. I cover my mouth so the truth can't escape.

"Let it out, Ann," the doctor says quietly.

My hand releases my mouth and the horror pours from me. "I made him what he was and—I took it out on him—my anger at myself. I hated him because he was like me. I hated him and let him know it."

"And that's a reason you can't let him go. You feel so guilty for all the criticism and hatred you dumped on him. Think of it this way, if you convince yourself he's alive, then you don't have to face the horror that you'll never be able to make things right."

I'll never be able to make things right. Can that be? Can it be that my son is dead? Can it be that he'll never hear me say anything nice to him? Anything warm or kind. Can it be that it's too late?

The pain of it pounds in my heart. It radiates across my chest, hunches down into my stomach. I cover my mouth to keep from vomiting, but I know I won't throw up. It's not sickness, it's horror at this fact:

It's too late.

My eyes press tight to stem the tears, but they pour out, and sobs overtake me.

I never got to change and never got to see him for himself and not a reflection of me.

Something's on my knee. I open my eyes to a tissue box held by the doctor. Blow and sob. Sob and blow. The spent tissues accumulate around me.

"I feel horrible. How could I have treated Brian like that? I'm sick!"

"You treat yourself like that. It's habit. Maybe time to think about changing."

I nod into another tissue.

"This is your chance now, Ann. Take it. Think of it as a gift. The last thing Brian gave you. A chance to be someone."

Pull another tissue. "But he didn't get a chance. I don't deserve one!"

"Everyone deserves a chance. And another. And another. Throughout their lives."

I grab another tissue and pull out the last one. The box is empty, which makes me cry harder. "Things *do* run out. There *is* an end."

The doctor steps to his file cabinet and lifts a fresh box. "There will always be another box of tissues, just like there are always more chances."

Could I really get a chance?

"Brian's dead. You're not. It's time to rejoin the living."

Pain grows.

It's true. Brian's dead!

The loss of my boy crushes me. My gut folds in and sobs pour out. Finally grieving. There will never be a bottom to this pain. I know that, but I also know something else.

It's time to let Brian go.

— THINKING IT THROUGH —

MAYBE I SHOULD let Home go.

—*Let Home go?*

—*I'm making him sick.*

121

Home blows out a big ragged breath and sucks in new air. How many breaths does Home have left if he's getting sicker with me inside?

—*Don't think about this.*

—*It's time. This can't go on forever.*

—*Let's do sit-ups. You're good at that now. Try for one-fifty.*

—*This is important. Let's think this through.*

How would I find a person in a whale? Maybe someone found my message-in-the-bottle, but what then? They find it and call Mom and she gets excited and what could she do?

—*First you have to find a whale. You find a whale with boats or maybe a drone looking for spray spouts.*

—*You see a spout and then what? How do you know there's a guy inside it?*

—*You don't.*

—*That's what I think. There are probably several thousand whales all over the world, and one of them has a guy inside.*

—*Who knows, maybe a lot of them have guys inside. Amelia got swallowed.*

—*Still, you can't put them through an x-ray machine to check. You can't know. Even if you could have that temperature sensing thing like in the movies, I'm the same temperature as these lungs, so I'd just be part of the lung blob.*

—*So?*

—*So, there is no way to find me.*

—*That's what I thought.*

—*I'm here until I die, or until I decide I've had enough.*

Home sings The Lullaby Song. Maybe he knows I need it now. Still, it doesn't help. When I die, no one will know. If no one knows or cares, it's like I never existed.

—*I know and care.*

Is my inner voice trying to trick me?

—*Thanks, but I still won't ever get out of here. Won't ever be someone.*

—*You are someone, Bri.*

—*What did you call me?*

122

My inner voice doesn't answer, but I heard him.

—- BIRTHDAY PRESENTS —-

THE BARTENDER cards Mark.

"I'm twenty eight."

"Need to see I.D."

Too risky to show his license. Mark offers his middle finger instead and stomps out. Three bars later, he finds a waitress that's less demanding and orders a beer. In a dark corner, he watches the soundless TV. No news about him. Nor in the Anchorage paper. He stays for another drink to kill the shaking. And another.

Now, leaving the bar, he remembers the birthday idea. Another damn idiotic plan.

Mark drives in the darkness. He could just keep driving. He could head north and never be seen again.

A gas station glows up ahead and Mark pulls into the lot. Why'd he have to think of a birthday for Jenny? Silly to spend money on kid presents.

He checks his wallet, passing over the credit card that's sure to have alerts on it. His last twenty. Pocket change?—$1.27. Ashtray holds 59 cents. Shouldn't have gone drinking, but certain things have priority. This cash won't buy but crap presents and won't leave anything for food. Or beer.

The tug-o'-war starts in Mark. The rational versus the extravagant. Jenny hasn't had a birthday with him since she was tiny. This means something. It's important. More important than food. But, if the twenty isn't enough, might have to go another route.

Pulling his ball cap low on his face, he steps out of the car and opens the trunk. He reaches behind the spare tire and pulls the gun from its hiding place. It's cold against the small of his back. Maybe, if he's lucky, he can get by without using it.

The electronic bell sounds as Mark enters. A Middle Eastern clerk nods a greeting. The man looks like all those he fought in the desert. Mark's throat tightens. *Chill out. You aren't there anymore.*

Mark steps to the souvenir section. Alaska shot glasses. Coffee mugs. Gotta be something for a kid. He grabs a stuffed howling wolf, floppy moose antler hat, and Indian bead belt. The presents are crap. She'll know they're from a gas station. Wrapping paper and tape cost too much.

Mark pauses by the beer case. He's got to get at least one. The clerk's watching him in the convex mirror. Can he see the shaking? *Hang in there.*

Making his way past the chips and candies and sodas, he takes the presents to the counter. The man doesn't meet his eyes. That could be a bad sign. Does he recognize Mark?

"Got a restroom?"

The clerk points past the beer.

Mark tries to sound cheerful but manly, saying, "Total it up, I'll be back."

In the mirror, he watches the man scan the items as he walks to the beer case. *I'll just take one.* Reaching in the cooler, he keeps his eyes on the mirror. One in each jacket pocket. One in each pants pocket. Two in his waist, cover with the sweater. Slip the case closed, and he's in the restroom.

Shaking intensifies as Mark locks the men's room and twists open a beer from his pants. Downing it without stopping, he listens for any electronic jingle of another patron entering.

Mark flushes the toilet and slips the empty beer bottle below the used towels in the trash. Deep breath. The metal against the small of his back is still an option if things go south.

Stepping from the men's room, he gets the twenty ready. Don't want to pull back the jacket with its stashed beer.

"What's the total?" Mark asks as he approaches, trying to sound friendly and casual.

"Eighteen dollars, forty-three cents."

Thank god it isn't more. Mark hands over the twenty, tempted to say keep the change just to get the hell out of there, but he needs that money. A trickle of sweat moves down his temple. *Don't notice that!*

The gun resting against his back feels heavy. The clerk pulls out a dollar and slowly scoops out two quarters. *"Let's take care of this!"* the gun whispers to Mark. A nickel. *We need to leave!* Two pennies.

The change jangles on the counter. What does that mean? Does it mean the clerk doesn't want to put it in Mark's hand? Does that mean he knows something? The clerk's hands are not visible behind the counter. Is he holding a gun? Mark swallows as the sweat trickles down to his cheek. The clerk asks, "Receipt?"

Grabbing the bag and change, Mark shakes his head "no" and the door chimes and he's out and the car is way across the lot and a beer bottle in his waist is sliding, about to fall, and he wants to look behind, but doesn't want to because if the man is watching he'll have to do something.

Open the car door, slip in, start it up and he tears out of the lot, screaming a howl of triumph and terror. Take gun from small of back and slip it under the seat. Crack another beer.

Two minutes later, he pulls into the lot of a darkened grocery store, looking for a dumpster. Finds it in the back, at the edge of thick black forest. Mark hops out. The night air is painfully cold. He lifts the freezing metal lid of the dumpster, careful to keep ahold of it so it doesn't clang. He paws through garbage with his free hand, looking for something that could be wrapping paper. Smells of all sorts of foods. His hand feels something mushy. The scent of over-ripe bananas. That could be a birthday dessert.

Seriously?

Take off the brown skin and put it on a plate. It'll be festive.

Mark pushes aside wilted lettuce and retrieves two soft bananas for his jacket pocket. Discarded newspaper. Might work. There's the snap of twigs in the thick trees in front of him. And—a low growl.

Fuck.

Why didn't he take the gun? Adrenaline rushes through Mark but he forces himself to move slowly. Stepping away from the dumpster, he backs toward the car as a bear lumbers out of the trees.

The bear lifts its long nose and sniffs the air.

Get rid of the fucking bananas!

The bear turns its nose toward the dumpster, then toward Mark. Takes a step forward. Mark feels the car against his thigh, moves around to the side. The bear growls, mouth open, teeth glistening with thick saliva. Open the door, and Mark's inside, hands shaking for the keys. He slams the car in reverse, clattering into a stack of wooden pallets. The bear stands upright, roaring as Mark spins the wheel and speeds off.

Twenty minutes later, newspaper covers the presents, twisted closed at each end like large Tootsie Rolls. In Mark's jacket is the last beer.

The lights are on in the cabin and Pinocchio barks when he knocks on the door.

"Who is it?" Jenny asks from inside.

"The big bad wolf."

"You can't come in."

"Then I'll huff and I'll puff and I'll blow the house down!"

"Okay. I'll let you in, Mr. Wolf."

Jenny opens the door and Mark thinks of hugging her but doesn't. "How's my birthday girl?"

"Ready for cake."

Jenny grimaces at the two bananas curled together on the plate, a burning match stuck in the center of each.

"Bananas are what Eskimos use for birthdays," Mark says. "These are real special to Eskimos. Bananas are from the tropics and Alaska is anything but tropical,"

"I don't believe you. And bananas aren't from the tropics, they're from the grocery store." Jenny scrunches her face, takes a deep breath, and blows.

"Happy Birthday!" Mark says, removing the smoking match with trembling fingers.

Jenny squiggles a judging finger at the presents wrapped in newspaper. "That the Eskimo way of wrapping?"

Mark grins. "How'd you guess?"

Jenny smiles and Mark's heart jingles at this triumph.

The newspaper is torn off everything and Jenny coos and oohs over the gifts. Puts on the belt and the moose antlers while hugging the stuffed howling wolf. Mark did good, it seems.

"You promised Pinocchio something."

Mark pauses—and tries—"The moose antlers are for him."

Jenny squeals in a good way and puts the antlers on the dog. She looks happy. The dog doesn't.

"I'm afraid that's the last of it," says Mark.

Jenny shakes her head. "Not the last. One more."

"I don't have anymore, Jenny."

Jenny grabs her backpack, grinning. "Pinocchio got me something."

Pinocchio cocks his ears at his name. The antlers wobble.

"It's our secret, but we'll show you, Daddy."

As Jenny digs in her bag, Mark takes a quick sip of the last beer by his chair leg.

Jenny bounces with excitement. "Look what Pinocchio found!"

Mark looks at the plastic bottle. *Trash? Don't say anything yet. Things are going good now. Smile.*

"What is that?"

Jenny holds the bottle still so he can see the dollar and library card inside. "A bottle with things! From the ocean! Can you get these out, Daddy?"

"Sure. They call this a Message-in-a-Bottle. It's what people do if they are shipwrecked on a deserted island. They send out a message hoping someone will find it and save them."

"We can do that!"

"Let's see what is inside first." Mark takes Bottle and after a few tries, gets the cap off. He shakes and the card and dollar bounce and rattle, but no amount of shaking is going to get these out. "I think we'll have to operate. Hold on. I've got just the thing."

Mark opens his Ka-bar knife and, holding Bottle still, stabs through the top. A few sawing motions splits its belly enough to pull out the contents. Jenny grabs the items.

"Los Angeles Library Card. Do you think this traveled all the way from Los Angeles to Alaska?"

"Could be."

Jenny rolls out the dollar, flattening it. Her fingers feel the bumps. She holds it up to the light, letting the illumination shine through the dots.

"It has writing. Look. Dots like blind people use. But I can't read it."

Mark holds the dollar up, then flips it over and hands it back to Jenny. "It was backwards."

Jenny reads, "*In whale. Help. Brian Ketchum.*"

"Someone's got an imagination."

"There's a phone number. Let's call."

"It's a joke, sweetie. It's not real. Remember before we went on this vacation there was all this news on TV about a crazy lady that thought her son was swallowed by a whale? You know what happens when someone says something like that?"

Jenny shrugs.

"People come out of the woodwork to exploit her. They think she'll do anything to get her son back, so they make up a message-in-the-bottle. It's what they call a scam. To trick her."

"That doesn't make sense, Daddy."

Mark smiles at his daughter. The kid is cute sometimes. "Why doesn't that make sense, baby cakes? Because it's mean?"

"No, silly. Because if someone was going to trick the crazy lady, they would make up a bottle but they wouldn't throw it in the ocean for someone else to find it. They'd keep it and trick the crazy lady, pretending they found it. I found it in the ocean, so it must be real."

Mark twists his face. How did that kid get to be so smart? He isn't smart. Beverly isn't smart.

"Please, Daddy, let's call! We never have any fun. We never talk to anyone. I want to talk to Brian."

"If he's in a whale, you're not going to talk to him."

Jenny screams her high-pitched glass shatter-er. Mark closes his eyes, pretending it doesn't bother him.

Maybe calling is okay. This one call won't hurt. It's not someone they know. With this pre-paid phone, it will not lead back to them. Might as well, just to shut her up.

"Okay, sweetie. It's late now. Let's call in the morning. Maybe you can talk to the guy in the whale."

— DOCTOR AND TOBEY —

MY FRIENDLY ORDERLY takes me down the bright hall to see Doctor Prakash. At the door he whispers, "It's all up to you."

Inside, Tobey is there and he hugs me and whispers, "It's all up to you."

Talk about pressure!

Doctor Prakash looks at me like he's that benevolent waiter again. "How are you feeling, Ann?"

"I feel better and—worse. Worse, because I'm heartbroken. Because Brian isn't in a whale. I wanted him to be alive so there was a chance of me becoming a good mother. But now I'll never get to be kind to him."

The Doctor smiles at me. "Are you saying this as a codependent patient because you want to make me feel good about myself for healing you?"

I keep my mouth shut and try to keep from crying. Deep breath.

"What is it, Ann?"

The tears come again. I squeak out the words over the sobs, "No one can live in a whale,"

Tobey pats my shoulder as if that can help.

"And so—?" the Doctor asks.

The truth drops into me. A block of cold iron sinking into my heart. I have to speak this. There is no choice.

"My son is dead."

— NEW NAME—

I'M GOING to die.
No choice.

I'm going to have to leave Home because I'm making him sick. But it's hard. I love this place. Home's steady heart booms under me. Amelia ticks her seconds. Sprout wriggles up higher in slow motion. This is living. This is contentment. How did I ever manage without it?

—You didn't know any better. They don't teach this in school or on the internet.

Yeah. You have to slow down to be able to hear things. Feel things. Be alive. I wouldn't have known any of this if Home hadn't swallowed me.

—Made you a new person.

—I am a new person. And I have to say—you're a new inner voice.

—Glad you noticed. It's hard to rag someone who's doing so good.

—It's like, I'm so different—I need a new name. Like Ultra-me. Maximum-me.

—Two Point O? Reboot?

—Maybe 'new' something. Neo. Nuevo.

—Actually, you don't need a new name. You already have a new name.

—What?

—You were Lard Ass. Now you're Brian.

I high five myself.

Wow. I'm Brian. This is so cool! I'm Brian.

"Brian!" I yell in the spongy lungs. "BRI-AN. BRIIIIIIII-AAAAAANNNNNN. BRIIIIIIII-AAAAAANNNNNN."

Home does the foghorn-train whistle sound.

I roar my new name. "BRIIIIIIII-AAAAAANNNNNN."

Home makes the train whistle with a vacuum cleaner start and stop.

I repeat, "BRIIIIIIII-AAAAAANNNNNN."

The deep vibrating song comes back—the same length, same two-note tune as my name. Could this be—?

I sing as loud and long as I can, "BRIIIIIIIIIIIIIIIIIIIIIII-AAAAAAAAAAAANNNNNN."

My whale sings back my name.

— BACK WITH TOBEY AND ARTHUR —

TOBEY EYES ME in the back of the taxi. "Was that a sham?"

"What was a sham?"

"What you said to the doctor. That Brian's dead."

I punch him in the shoulder.

"What the hell, Ann!"

"This is the worst feeling in the world, Tobey. You have no idea the horror I'm going through, but you and the doctor want to make sure I'm feeling it. Fuck you!"

"I just want to know you're sane."

"I'm not. I'm fucking crazy with grief. Okay? Brian's dead! I'll never see him again!"

The iron block on my heart presses down.

Why couldn't they leave me with my fantasy? Why couldn't they let me have that? I was happy. Now that I know he's dead, I can't stand the pain.

Tobey pulls me close, an arm around me. I sob, soaking his shirt. As we wind up the steep road toward his house, he says, "You're on probation, you know."

"Fuck you, Tobey! This isn't what to say right now!"

"Not with me, the police. That officer you assaulted isn't pressing charges but if there is *any* incident, or infraction, or whatever, you're heading to jail or the back to the looney bin. Okay?"

I bury my face in his chest. A numbness spreads out from that iron block. Nothing matters.

When Tobey opens the front door, Arthur's video camera points at me. "Okay?" he asks.

I shrug and push past him into the living room. *Is it a living room? Is anything living anymore?*

Tobey shuts the door. "Turn that off, Arthur. Show's over."

131

Arthur peeks out from behind the lens. "Uh, there's still a film to be made."

"No, there isn't. It's not good for Ann. She doesn't need to be reminded of Brian's death. No more film. No more crowdfunding. We'll return the money, right, Ann?"

I look up and see the frustration on Arthur's face. He thought this would be something great. I should make an effort. "Arthur put a lot of work into this," I say. "We won't be searching for a whale, but maybe he can get a film about a mother who finally accepts—that her son—"

The sobs overtake me again. *Please stop the pain. Let me be numb instead.*

Tobey puts his hand in front of the camera lens. "Turn it off, Arthur!"

A phone rings. Tobey paws through his pockets. Pulls out a phone and, with a glance, holds it out to me. "I got you a replacement phone. The same number."

The weight in my chest grows. There is no chance it's Brian, so why answer. "It's a wrong number."

Tobey forces me to take the ringing phone. "You need to start living. That includes interacting with the world."

I sigh and swipe to accept the call. "Hello?"

A little girl's voice says, "Hello? Is Brian Ketchum there?"

The iron weight on my heart jerks. "Who is this?"

"I'm Jenny—" There is muffled whispering for a moment, then the girl asks, "Is he in a whale?"

My knees can't hold me. Tobey rushes to catch me as I crumple to the floor. He's terrified and I hold up a finger to reassure him. Arthur slides across the room to get a better camera angle.

I ask the girl, "What makes you say that?"

"I found a bottle in the ocean. It has a library card and a dollar bill with blind people bumps for letters."

I cover my mouth to stifle the cry. I can't speak.

The girl waits, then, "Hello?"

"I'm here. What did the dollar bill with letters say?"

There's rustling and, "Oops, I'm holding it backwards again. It says *In whale. Help. Brian Ketchum* and this phone number."

—*I wasn't crazy! This is proof he's alive! Brian's alive! He's thinking. He's acting.*

I'm crying and laughing and want to throw up. I've got to pull it together.

"Honey, where are you?" I ask. "Where did you find the bottle?"

"Daddy and me are visiting Alaska."

"Can I talk to your daddy?"

There is more rustling and muffled talking. Finally, a man's voice comes on, "Hello? I'm sure you got a lot of these calls but—"

"My son was swallowed by a whale. It's not a joke. It was in the news."

Tobey reaches for my phone, but I turn away so he can't take it.

The man snorts into my ear. "Yeah, I seen you."

He might be making this up because of seeing me on the news. Fucking jerk. I put on a smile so anger won't show in my voice, "Please. If you could send it. I'll pay you."

Tobey shakes his head vehemently.

Silence on the line.

"I'm sorry, I'm Ann Ketchum. Who are you?"

Silence but for breathing. This guy is definitely a jerk.

"Mark. Strong. Mark Strong."

That's not how people say their names—except James Bond—but I can't worry about that now. "Mark, please. I'm in San Francisco. I'll give you the address. FedEx the bottle to me. I'll pay you one hundred dollars."

Tobey snaps his fingers, trying to make me pay attention to him. I don't.

The man coughs. "Five."

"Five dollars?"

"No, five hundred."

Fuck him. I want to hang up, but I don't. How much is a bottle and a library card and a dollar bill worth? Probably nothing. Probably is a scam. But what if it isn't? "Okay," I say.

"FedEx cash—cash only—to me overnight. Include your address and I'll send you the bottle and what was in it."

Behind his voice, the girl screams in protest. "I found it! It's mine!"

The man tells me to overnight it to Cabin 11 at Glacier View Cabins, Homer, Alaska. "Mark, this is real, right? Please don't let me down."

"Send the money and you'll get your bottle. I gotta go. I've a disappointed little girl on my hands."

The phone clicks off.

I turn to Tobey. "Brian sent a message-in-a-bottle."

Tobey kicks the couch. "You have got to fucking be kidding me. You just got out of the looney bin. Don't do this."

Arthur sets his camera on a tripod and leaves for the kitchen. The camera light is still on, filming the crazy lady. I wave at the lens.

"Tobey, maybe it's true. Brian may have—"

"It's a scam! You're in the news."

"I know but—the dollar bill saying to call my number and his library card. Doesn't it prove it?"

"This proves mankind is full of assholes who don't care who they hurt," Tobey says. "You're sane now, but you're fragile, and this is the absolutely wrong time for this asshole to pull this scam."

"But what if Brian sent it?"

Tobey shakes his head. "People know from the media and your crowdfunding that you believe your son is in the whale. Scammers are looking for suckers! You saw all the nuts out there trying to exploit you. Don't get crazy again!"

Arthur steps back out from the kitchen and hands me a cardboard box. "Here. Open it."

I open the flaps of the box and inside is an empty Kombucha bottle with a dollar bill and a San Francisco library card folded inside.

"It's easy to make, Ann. Took me five minutes," Arthur says.

Tears blur the bottle. This isn't fair. I thought Arthur was on my side! "But he called my number. How did he get my number?"

"People can get phone numbers," Arthur says gently.

"They can't get Brian's library card."

"We don't know it is his library card."

"When I get that card, I can check with the Los Angeles Library and be sure. I need to get it."

Tobey softens his voice, "It's a scam. And you're not crazy anymore. Let it go."

I stifle my sobs with coughing.

When the coughing subsides, I tell them I'm going to take a walk.

I walk until I find a bank, get out five hundred dollars, put it in a package addressed to Alaska, add a prepaid envelope with Tobey's address, and send it off via FedEx. If there is any chance this bottle was sent by Brian, I can't live without it.

—- PACKAGE OF MONEY —-

THE EXPLOSION sends up a fireball and Mark jerks awake—ready to blast the fuckers—ready to charge into the desert and—

Pinocchio barks again. Morning light streams in the window. Someone's knocking. Heart in overdrive, ready for fight or flight, Mark staggers to the door and looks out the peephole. The manager.

Fuck. Get ready.

Where's Jenny? Faint water sound in the bathroom. *Good. Stay there.*

Mark smiles as he opens the door. "Morning."

"Sorry to disturb you. Package came."

Mark takes the FedEx package with a smile, closes the door, and waits. Listens for the footsteps. They grow faint and vanish. Peer through the curtain. No one.

He steps to the table, rips open the package. Five hundred dollars in crisp bills and a return envelope to send the bottle to San Francisco. *Fuck, yes!* Things are looking up. This is the easiest money Mark ever made. They'll be able to hole-up in this cabin for a while. Maybe he could even look for a job. Or not.

Mark collects the split bottle, dollar, and library card by Jenny's antler hat on the bedside table. He pockets the dollar, opens the return envelope, and as Jenny bounces out of the bathroom, she screams, "WHAT ARE YOU DOING WITH MY PRESENT!"

"The lady sent money and we're sending it—"

"THAT'S MINE! I FOUND IT! FINDERS KEEPERS!"

Jenny snatches the package from him, pulls out her treasures, and flings the envelope aside. She stares at the bottle and library card.

"WHERE'S THE DOLLAR!? WHERE'S THE DOLLAR WITH THE DOTS!?"

That's money! Mark thinks, but he pulls the bill from his pocket and hand it over.

"You stay away from my things!" warns the red-faced monster.

—- OUT OF OPTIONS —-

HOME DOESN'T STAY DOWN long anymore. There's slime on the walls around me and a rancid smell that wasn't here before. I'm definitely making him sick.

It doesn't make sense to make Home sicker and sicker if there is no chance of getting out. It's time to think of him instead of me. Time to off myself and give this whale a chance to heal. There is no reason to stay alive and a very good reason not to.

I could slip out the flap, go down the tube and land in the stomach and get crushed. I might be a good meal for Home. A tasty treat, except, not as tasty as when I was loaded with juicy fat. I should do it.

—You still might be rescued, Bri.

—You know I won't be. I'm killing this whale. I need to kill myself so he'll live.

—I don't want to die, right when we're—getting along.

—If the whale dies, I die. If I die, you die.

—But—

—But what? Come up with another solution. Please. I'll be happy to live if there's another idea.

My inner voice has no suggestions.

—There's no choice. It's what I have to do.

—- NEW TO-DO —-

I CHECK Tobey's mailbox for the fifth time today. The package should have been here by now. I included the pre-paid sticker. There is no reason that bottle shouldn't be here. Except. If it was a scam.

Push redial for that incoming call. That man or his daughter needs pickup the phone.

No answer. Not even voicemail. Just "The person you are calling is not available. Please try again later." It *was* a scam.

Brian is really and truly dead.

Now it's over. I've put myself and my brother and Arthur through enough. Time to move on.

"Tobey? Can I get a hug?"

He gives me a tight embrace. When I break away, I whisper, "Do you have a box? I need to take Brian's things to Goodwill."

Sorting through Brian's stuff. I do what everyone does in every movie. I sniff the clothes. There's a whiff of something that might be him, but I can't tell. Baggy jeans. Ragged sneakers. I don't sniff these. Stretched stained t-shirts. Not even worth giving to Goodwill. They'll just throw them away. But I put them in the Goodwill pile anyway. I can't throw them out. I can't imagine them in a landfill.

The dress suit we got him for graduation. Even then it was too tight. Waste of money. Hard leather shoes he only wore once.

Here's his used deodorant. A hairbrush with a few hairs in it. His DNA.

Could he be cloned from this?

This DNA could be inserted into a human egg and make another Brian.

I'd be a better mother now. I'd try harder. I wouldn't yell. I wouldn't ride him so hard.

I don't know where I could find someone to clone him but I'll keep the hairbrush in case. I'll keep the photos. The things with memories attached. Maybe this T-shirt I hated. White skull and crossbones on black.

My son's life is reduced to one cardboard box.

How many Goodwill stores are filled with sorrow? How many dead person's clothes are for sale?

—*Stop thinking, Ann. You need to finish this and start on the next phase. Make a plan.*

—*I made a plan only once before. Nothing came of it.*

—*Make a new plan. Only, don't write on the wall this time.*

I turn on Brian's computer. His old avatar with the monster muscles glares at me from the screen. If I'm going to use this as mine, I can't keep looking at that. Go into preferences and delete. What to put up instead? Not ocean pictures. Screensaver of flowers? No. I go with the grey background. Monotone grey. Like my life. Colorless. A step down from beige.

The weight on my heart is pressing out all my feelings. That's okay. I'll just eat and sleep and exist. Open a blank page. My new To-Do List.

1. Take boxes of Brian's things to Goodwill.

2. Buy dead woman's clothes at Goodwill. Grey.

3. Call ex-husband Dan.

Why? Call Dan to apologize? Call Dan to tell him he was right? To find out how Brian's memorial went?

I don't want to. With Brian dead, I don't have to be in contact with that man anymore. Delete Dan.

3. Return Crowdfunding Money.

4. Find a place to live.

5. Find a job.

No chance I'll find an apartment in San Francisco that I can afford. Maybe I could do house sitting. Watch the pet of a Silicon Valley hipster.

I look up house sitting. After a tedious search, which confirms that everyone has a better life than I do, I find a possibility. Old deaf cat and twelve house plants in the Mission district. This might be okay. Sit in someone else's house and let the world go by. Have food delivered. Keep the shades closed. Withdraw.

—- MEDS —-

MARK DOWNS ANOTHER BEER as Jenny sings a song from a Disney movie he never heard of. For the twentieth time. The noise is unbearable. Rather than yell at his daughter, he sings along. Neither she nor Pinocchio seem to appreciate him making up words or howling when he can't think of any.

"You're not doing it right! This is my favorite song from Frozen and you're spoiling it!" Jenny screams.

"We can't always do things right, Jenny," Mark answers. He knows that's not what a daddy would say.

"You don't even try!" the girl yells.

Fuck. This is all going to hell.

Off the couch and into the bathroom. The door slams much louder than he wanted it to. Things are always more than he meant. More angry. More extreme. Pawing through the Dopp kit. Pop a pill from the small orange bottle. One from the big one. Only three left of the Clozapine. Swallow one. Things will go south when he runs out. Shoulda called Doc Flemming and renewed the prescription before he had this harebrained idea. Gotta get more.

Maybe I could rob a pharmacy.

Then you got one more thing they're after you for. You're always thinking extreme. Call Doc Flemming. He was on your side. He said so.

Mark sits on the edge of the tub, sweat erupting across his skin, waiting for the meds to kick in. If he can figure out all the potential problems, he'll call the doc, only he knows he's not good at guessing consequences.

Jenny pounds on the bathroom door. "OPEN UP!"

Mark stuffs all the prescription bottles back in his Dopp kit and puts it on the top shelf of the cabinet.

"I HAVE TO PEE! OPEN UP!"

Wetting his face to hide the sweat, he flushes the toilet. *Act like a god-damn daddy!*

"You think maybe you could teach me that song?" Mark asks, opening the door.

— FINAL ACTS —

SPROUT LIKES when I slide my hand along the wet wall, get a bit of water and drip, drip down onto his little sprouty body. He slurps it up. I keep looking at him, and every time I check, he seems bigger, but I'm not sure. It's my brain playing tricks. Still, I'm grateful to have a friend. He'll take the trip with me. We'll go together. The trip down the tube.

It's not right to commit suicide, but if there is no real point to surviving and if it helps another creature, maybe it is right. And it's not like I'm an important person like Amelia was.

—*You're important to me, Bri.*

—*Thanks. And you are to me.*

Neither one of us has more to say. This is really tough. I'll even miss myself. Home rises, so I hold my sneaker high. He blows out the old air and fills us with cool new air and as the sunlight pours in, I slide Sprout into that spotlight. He's got four tiny leaves now. "Look, little fella! That's the sun. It should have been part of your life, but isn't and now won't be."

I better clean up really good. Make sure to leave Home just as I found him. I shake the bag of Wrigglers and search the spongy walls. Pick up every little bit of Peeler skins, dead Wrigglers, fish bones and scales. Dump it all out the tube.

I don't know how to say goodbye. I don't want my life to stop like this. But I'm glad it all happened. I'm more me than I ever was. Lot to be proud of. Only wish someone could have noticed besides my own self. At least I got that.

—At least you got that, Brian. You an' me both.

—- DELETE THE PAST —-

I TRY TO SMILE and not seem grey inside. The young hipster gal in the Mission district with the old deaf cat and twelve house plants asks if I'll go out a lot. I tell her I prefer staying in. That seems like the right answer and she gives me the key. She's off to spend three months in Thailand —*This young woman thinks she can manage on her own across the world! I could never do that!*—She leaves tomorrow at 6:00 pm and I'm expected to arrive at 6:05. Fine. I don't want any more interaction than necessary either.

It will be good to be alone. I wonder if the plants will die if the curtains stay closed. Only one way to find out.

It's a long, steep walk back to Tobey and Arthur's and too many people are on the street. I'll take a cab tomorrow.

Tobey greets me at the door. "All settled?"

I wave the hipster's key as evidence.

"Arthur hopes to get a last video. You game?"

I shrug. It's my go-to reaction now that I'm grey inside.

Arthur sets up the video camera and moves me into the light from the window. "The To-Do List. It was a picture on your phone, right?"

I shrug again.

"It would be kind of symbolic, I think, if you were to delete it, now that it's no longer relevant."

"This is a different phone. That one fell off the bridge. I don't have that picture anymore."

"Uh, well, so I kinda recreated it from the footage I shot before. I just sent it to your phone."

My phone jingles. I look at the message to see a photo of my old To-Do List on a wall. "Okay. And you want me to do what?"

"Just show it to the camera and delete it, but wait, I need to test the mic, say something."

"Hello. I'm testing my voice now." It's colorless.

"I'm gonna start rolling."

The little light on the camera comes on and Arthur waits a moment, then asks, "Can you tell us about your plans?"

My throat is dry.

Plans. What a stupid word. It implies a future.

"I don't have plans."

Arthur glances up from the viewer. He's not happy with my performance.

Get it up, Ann. You promised. Arthur needs a conclusion to his film.

"I'm trying to move forward. I'll be house sitting. No plans," I say.

"I understand you once made plans. Months ago."

He sure cut to the chase. Fumbling with my pocket, I pull up my phone. I hold up the photo to the camera.

"I made a To-Do List."

"Read it, please."

I do, starting with *Find Brian*. Ending with *Watch Pinocchio*.

Arthur looks at me behind the red camera light.

I do what I'm supposed to. "My son, Brian, is dead. It's time to delete this list."

Holding up the phone to the camera, I push the garbage can icon. Delete? Yes. The picture disappears. I know Arthur wants tears for his conclusion, but I have none. I'm used up.

After a moment of me blinking dully at the lens, the red light goes out.

—- DOC FLEMMING —-

MARK PARKS in the Safeway lot at the farthest spot from the store. He can clearly see the two entrances from the highway, so hopefully this will go well and he'll get back to Jenny in a little more than an hour. She wasn't happy about spending another afternoon stuck in the cabin.

It's chilly in the car. Winter's coming on and he's not prepared. Why is he never prepared for anything?

Mark lifts the cell phone. Even though no one has the number or knows it's his, his heart does a drum solo the minute he dials 4-1-1. Information connects him to the Kansas City VA hospital. They ask his name so the doctor can get back to him. He hangs up.

Second try, Information connects him to a Doctor Flemming in Kansas City, Missouri. The lady with the answering service is sympathetic when Mark says he's thinking of doing something stupid. She patches him through.

"Yello, Doctor Flemming here." The familiar voice is calm and what the therapists always tell Mark he should aspire to be— Centered.

"Doc, it's Mark."

There's a pause. Static on the line. Should he hang up?

"Mark. Good to hear from you. What can I do for you?"

"I need a refill. A batch of refills. Especially the Clozapine."

"How 'bout you come in and I'll take care of that."

"Can't Doc, outta state. But you can call in a prescription, right? You can call it in if I give you the info."

"That's right, Mark. Only—you're not supposed to leave the state."

"Taking a vacation."

"I know about the situation. How's your daughter?"

"Fine. I need those meds."

"It might be a good idea to—"

"Ain't happening, Doc. Safeway Pharmacy. Homer, Alaska. I'm a little over an hour away, so they'll have time to fill the prescription. Don't let me down."

"Mark, this may feel like the right thing to do, but remember, all feelings aren't—"

Mark hangs up.

Now to watch and wait.

I SHOULD LEAVE a note. Amelia left a watch. Pull from my wallet Mom's twenty-dollar bill. Poke holes like for the message-in-the-bottle.

BRIAN KETCHUM LIVED HERE LONG TIME

—*Write Thrived.*

THRIVED

Too bad Amelia didn't leave a note. Wait, maybe she did!

I paw through my belongings to find the tin box the watch was in. Shake the Wrigglers bright. There is definitely a message scratched in the inside lid. The watch has scraped over a lot, sliding back and forth for years, but I can make out a few words.

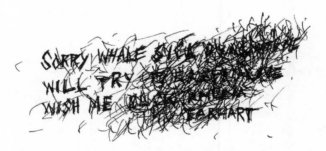

Sorry—whale sick—will try—wish me—Earhart

She left this to be found. I'll leave hers and mine in my waterproof phone case. Maybe someday someone will find these together.

I slide to the flap. Tie the bundle to my ankle. All my belongings will come down with me. It'll be quick. I'll try not to hold my breath so it will be over faster.

"Goodbye, Home."

Tears come up. I never got to see my home from the outside except when I fell in. I stroke the walls and press my face into the wetness. "Thanks for taking care of me."

Sprout is in my sneaker. Maybe he'll stay safe in there and make it out and float up and bounce above the waves and land on a deserted island and grow big and strong.

I want to say one more goodbye. I get out the broken glass from my phone and raise the bag of Wrigglers. There he is, that bearded reflection. He looks a bit scared.

"You're the last face I'll ever see. I'm gonna say it—"

"Don't. I know your thoughts."

"I love you."

The reflection blinks at me, eyes glistening.

"Ditto."

"You can't say it? We're gonna die."

"Fuck you."

"That'll do. Adios, partner. Adios, Home—"

WHAM!

The violent jolt knocks me facedown into the sponge floor. If Home were a ship, he'd be the Titanic and we just met the iceberg. We're spinning, lunging, flying up and crashing down. I hold tight to the piece of glass, the Wrigglers, and my sneaker, cupping the top to keep Sprout from flying out. A bending double-back and arched high and the blow hole opens and voices outside chorus "*ooooh!*" People!

"Hey!" my voice cracks. "I'm in here! HELLOOOO!!!"

The blow hole closes and we bend in the middle, turning right. Home's circling. Another arch and the blow hole fountains—

"I'm here! In the whale!!!"

A voice, "AAa—"

I'm thrown backwards with the jolt. What was that? Did something ram Home? Or did Home ram—

There's a rush of sound below me—the feeding river. A garbled scream.

I scramble to the flap and, taking a deep breath, I slide my head and arms out. Something huge hits me as it tumbles past. I grab and catch part of it. PULL! The current is against me. Fish and *The Blue Light Special* characters batter my face and arms, but I keep pulling. These muscles are working.

Using my new stomach-strength, I YANK. The huge beast tumbles inside, covered with seaweed, sushi, and glowing TV regulars. The beast coughs seawater and screams gibberish. A girl's voice.

"Easy. Easy." I say, pulling one of the tastier seaweeds off her ankle.

Shaking violently, she continues in gibberish, which is probably not gibberish but some other language.

"Hold on. Just a sec." I empty my old TV show, slide my Ziploc out the flap, and pull in a bright new show. Raising the bag close to my face, I smile and wave at the girl. "I'm Brian. Who are you?"

Peering between strands of hair and seaweed, terrified eyes do not look relieved to see me. She whimpers.

I get it. I'm naked and probably look like a creature from a low-budget movie. Unpacking my ankle belongings, I pull on my T-shirt on and slip into my shorts. They are way too loose. It's so weird to have clothes on.

The girl curls up, clutching herself tightly and moaning.

Home moans, too, rumbling throughout us.

The girl wails.

The whale wails back.

I shake the bag to get the television characters riled and bright again. Holding the Ziploc close to my face, I repeat, "You're okay now. You're safe. I'm Brian. You are who?"

The girl peels off a strand of seaweed. She looks about 18. Might be pretty, definitely a 7 or 8, but it's hard to tell with the darkness and seaweed. I smile, pulling my eyes back up to her face after their brief trip to her wet T-shirt.

"You're in a whale," I say.

The girl shakes her head and doesn't stop until Home tilts upward and we drop to the bottom of the lungs and lots of her is touching me as she tries to get righted and we're suffocating and her eyes widen like expecting death and "Wait," I say as the lungs press close and the blowhole rushes slime past us and the sun pours in at the top of our cathedral skylight and she's stunned with the cool air and light and the rush of it is over and we're back in the darkness.

The girl screams.

I've got to act nice. Be sweet.

How?

—*Ask her about herself, Brian. Girls like to talk about themselves. Find out her name.*

I shake the Wrigglers but keep them off to the side. "I'm Brian. What is your name?"

She's coughing and panting and shaking, but manages, "Liesl."

Is that a name? Maybe she doesn't speak English.

"Is Liesl your name?"

The girl seems to nod. Or maybe she's just shaking with fear.

"I'm from Burbank. In the valley. Los Angeles. Where are you from?"

She looks up with a spark of interest. "Hollywood?" Her accent is strong.

"Yeah, Hollywood. You like it?" I ask. "You visiting? Going to school? UCLA?"

Liesl doesn't seem to understand. Maybe she doesn't speak English after all. "What brings you to California?" I can't believe I said that. It's like a line from a movie. I'm like at a suave party doing a cool guy's lines.

She shakes her head. "I not in California. I in Norway."

Cold spreads in me. I knew we were traveling, but I thought we might be around San Francisco or Tijuana. Norway? That's somewhere near Europe.

We're on the other side of the world.

— WAITING AND WATCHING —

SHIVERING IN THE CAR, Mark blinks, staring at the Safeway turnoffs from the road. He's too nervous to listen to music and for sure doesn't want to try the news. Please let this work out. Just another half an hour and he'll know it's safe to go in.

Fuck, it's freezing in here. Would put the heat on but a car idling, exhaust visible in the cold, might be an attention getter.

Why Alaska? Why didn't I think of someplace warmer?

Because I never think, I just do.

Alaska seemed smart on account of being remote and underpopulated.

Nevada coulda worked. Desert might have been better.

No. No more deserts. Two tours was enough.

An Alaska State Trooper cruiser slows on the road, turns into the Safeway lot and circles around to the back, out of sight. A moment later, another cruiser enters the lot and disappears to the back. Two distant uniformed figures emerge from the rear and enter the store.

Damn. Doc gave me away. No meds for me.

Maybe I don't really need them. I'll tough it out. I'll be fine.

Mark starts the car, turns the heat on high, and drives away.

— LIESL —

LIESL CRIES and screams and tries to wake up from her nightmare. I keep telling her that she can't wake up from this but she won't listen. After a while, I give up trying. She'll cry herself to sleep or hoarse or whatever. I did.

When Home rises for a breath, we smash together and she's always shaking and—shit—just vomited on me. I use seaweed to scoop it up and dump the mess out the flap. Yuck.

Must be several hours gone by. I sing whale songs but she doesn't stop shaking. I tell her about the regulars on *The Blue Light Special*, but she doesn't seem interested. She's stuck in terror.

After we sleep, or at least I do, she nudges me.

"We die here?"

"Um, let's not worry about that now."

"People look for you?"

"I don't know. Did you hear anything about people searching for me? Am I in the news?"

She tells me she never heard of me in the news. Maybe somewhere, but not in Norway. "I check," she says.

She shifts and pulls at something beneath her. I shake the Wrigglers to refresh their light.

It's a cool purse made of yellow plastic. Shit. The stuff inside might not be waterlogged. A rush of hope floods me.

She reaches into her purse and the light glows on her face. A phone!

I try to control my voice. "Don't search google—"

The girl taps the screen, says something in her language into the phone.

"Is it working!?"

Liesl holds up her hand to quiet me and keeps talking her gibberish. My heart is banging louder than Home's thunderous beat. After a moment, she stops talking and shrugs.

"A friend. She call when get message."

I want to scream and rip the phone from her hands, but I don't.

Then I think better, and do. She paws at my arm, trying to reach her phone.

I turn away, yelling at her as I dial, "No wasted calls! We need this battery!"

I dial my mom's number. The phone makes weird beeps, but no connection. I press hangup and dial again. More beeps.

"What the fuck! What's the problem with this phone? I dialed my mom. Make it work." I hand the phone back.

"If your mom in Hollywood, no call international."

"FUCK! FUCK! You will make a call to someone that will answer. MAKE IT NOW!"

The girl's eyes are wide. I can't believe I yelled like that.

She's dials another number. Someone answers and she does gibberish again, but now it's mixed with crying and interruptions. We won't get anywhere if she can't get them to listen. "Have them take down a number. Have them call my mom."

Liesl says something to me in her language that's probably something like "shut up, I'm talking on the phone."

I snatch the phone from her.

The woman's voice yells in gibberish. Instantly recognizable as Mom-speak.

"Shut up! You speak English?"

Silence.

Oh no. Did I hang up? Did we lose the connection? "Do you speak En—"

"Yes."

"Copy this number. Call this number. It's my mother. Tell her I am in a whale. This is Brian. Your daughter is here with me. If you don't make this call, you will not see your daughter again."

Silence again. Then angry gibberish.

I yell for her to shut up and listen. She takes the number and reads it back to me, so I know she has it. I can tell she doesn't believe me about the whale. No matter. As long as she calls.

Liesl reaches for the phone but we've got to save that battery so I hang up. She can't have it until she realizes its value. Now I sound like Mom.

Liesl's whimpering again. I show her Sprout. The little plant is already over an inch tall, reaching upward into life. She stares at me like I'm bonkers. I turn away from her, placing my sneaker with Sprout on my side of the lungs. When did there get to be sides? A minute ago, this was all my territory and now I've got less. Like when you're in an elevator alone and it's all yours and then someone comes in and you go to opposite walls. You shift so everyone gets equal space, but this isn't an elevator, this is my Home. Mine. I didn't need to save her.

I hunch over Sprout, my back to the girl. She doesn't know what everything means. She lives in a different world. No idea of ticking Amelia. No idea of sitcoms with blue Wrigglers. No idea that a Sprout can be the dearest friend. And Home.

She may never feel this for as long as she's here. Maybe it's because I was alone. She'll have me as her companion. I had Sprout and Blue Wrigglers and Amelia and Home.

I reach out of the flap and catch a few snacks for her. "It's sushi," I explain. She's not excited. I get her to try a pencil fish but she can't bite down to kill it and coughs it onto our spongy floor and it flops until I slip it out where it came from. She'll learn.

—- RETURN TO THE CABIN —-

IT'S DARK when Mark returns to the Glacier View Cabin. He carries two cases of beer from the car and stashes them under the porch bench in case Jenny's awake. They'll stay plenty cold out here.

Jenny's asleep. She looks so sweet and perfect. Nothing like when she's awake.

Pinocchio whines and Mark lets him out, hoping the dog will run away or get eaten by a polar bear. He unloads his surprise from the car and carries it inside.

Cracking a beer, Mark sets out the real birthday cake with real candles on the table. That'll make up for being away and that lame banana deal.

The dog scratches at the door to come in. Damn.

He lets Pinocchio in and the beast leaps beside Jenny on the bed and curls against her.

Should I let the dog do that? Do I have the rules I should have? I'll let him stay there tonight. Tomorrow I'll figure out the rules.

Mark retrieves his Dopp kit from the bathroom, seven beers from the porch, and settles in at the table. He sets out all his remaining meds and gets to work cutting the pills in half. *I'll make them last and not only that, I'll be on a lower dose so I'll be kinda weening myself off gradual-like. It'll work out fine.*

151

—— READY TO HOUSE-SIT ——

MY SUITCASE is packed and stashed with my purse by the front door. My Uber ride is due any minute. I'm looking forward to house-sitting. Or, rather, being alone. I'm sure Tobey and Arthur are looking forward to my grey face leaving. No one wants to be around lifeless energy.

"You have our key. Come in anytime. Call anytime," Tobey reminds me again.

I try to make a smile. It doesn't work.

Arthur gives me a long hug. The video camera has been retired. "Seriously, don't disappear."

I attempt another smile. Half-assed result.

A tinny jingle sounds near the door.

"That's your phone," Tobey says as if I don't know. "It may be the Uber driver."

The jingle continues.

"You should get that," he adds, back-seat driving my life as usual.

I don't move.

Tobey steps to the entryway and lifts the cell phone from my purse. "Yes?"

He listens for a moment. "I'm sorry, you're not making sense."

Another moment.

Tobey's face changes. "This isn't a joke. Please don't call again." He disconnects the call, shaking his head. "Some crazy woman. I don't think you should keep the same number, Ann. You'll only get hurt with all the kooks out there."

Tobey hands the phone to me. It rings again.

"I'll let it go to voicemail," I say.

Tobey looks frustrated. "If it's the Uber—"

I answer.

A few clicking sounds and a woman's voice says "Hello?"

"Yes?"

"Your son is Brian?"

"Yes, but I can't manage jokes now—"

"He called and—"

"He called!?" My heart somersaults and lands awkwardly.

"I think he has my daughter."

I grab the edge of the couch as my knees collapse.

"What do you mean *has*? Where are you?"

The lady answers, "Norway."

I cover the phone and whisper, "This lady says she talked to Brian. She's in Norway. Says Brian's with her daughter—"

Tobey snatches the phone from me. "This is not funny. My sister has had enough with you cranks and scam artists. Give her peace!" He hangs up.

There's a buzzing vibration in my chest. A humming below the dullness. *Could it be real? What did she mean Brian has her daughter?*

A honk outside.

Tobey steps to the door. "Time to go, Ann. Ride's here."

I look at Arthur. He knows what I'm thinking. He turns to his husband. "Tobey, it might be worth exploring. If nothing else, to explore what Ann's being harassed with."

Another honk.

Tobey picks up my suitcase and purse. "Ann!"

The vibration in my chest says—*Wait.*

The woman sounded worried and scared. That shake in her voice makes this feel possible. The trembling in my chest grows.

Keep calm when talking with your brother. Don't let him see any excitement.

"Tobey, this could be extortion. She could be wacko. But, let's get it on film. The deaf cat and plants won't die if I'm an hour late. If this lady calls again, I'll tell her I can't hear her. We'll get a Skype connection and film it. She won't want to Skype if she's lying."

The car outside honks long and hard and my phone rings.

I pick it up, praying it isn't the Uber driver.

153

Five minutes later, this so-called Norway lady's up on Skype. The side bar window shows her name as Gjesken. She pronounces it for me: Jes-kin. How can I remember that? Southern accent, someone asking—*Tobey and you, y'all related?—We're jus' kin. Jes-kin.* I write the name down so I can use it and sound friendly.

The lady looks like someone from Norway. White-blond hair. Bangs cut too short for an American. She's maybe forty. Behind her, the odd spigot over the sink and the IKEA-like kitchen-ware makes me think she might really be in Norway. I'm shaking because this lady doesn't look like a scammer. Her eyes are red from crying and she's breathless with fear.

"Your son has my daughter. I can pay a—what-do-you-call it?— fee for return?"

I glance at Tobey. "Ransom. I don't need you to pay. I need you to tell me what Brian said."

"He made me call you. He said he was in a whale."

I want to cheer and scream but I ask calmly, "What else did he say?"

"He has my daughter. Said I will not see her again if I don't call you. Where is he? What is he going to do to her!?"

"If he said he's in a whale, he is, and that means your daughter's in the whale."

"Not possible," she says.

"It is possible!" I yell, looking at Tobey.

The woman scrunches her eyes. "I will call the police."

I smile. "You can call anyone you want. But I'm going to need information. Where was your daughter before she called?"

"With friends on the coast."

"Of Norway?"

"Where else!?" she yells. "What is he going to do? Will he hurt her?"

The more scared this woman is, the more happy I become. She can't be lying! She's the real thing. If she's the real thing, then Brian's alive. He's alive and in a whale and I'm not fucking crazy!

I glare at Tobey for a moment to convey all that, then turn to the crying lady on the computer screen.

"My son was swallowed by a whale on June 4th. Over three months ago. I haven't seen him since that day. You talked to him. Did he sound okay?"

"He sounded like an American."

I don't know what that means. "Did he sound insane, or hurt, maybe depressed, or—"

"He sounded like an American."

"What did he sound like!?"

"He yelled at me and sounded like a man that was in charge and wanted things done his way. With an American accent."

That doesn't seem like my son. A horrible thought rises. What if the call wasn't from Brian? What if Brian died and someone is impersonating him, pretending to be in a whale?

"Where is my daughter!?" the lady screams.

"Calm down, um—Just-related—Just-kin."

"Gjesken."

"Gjesken. I want to help. We can do this together. My son will not hurt your girl. He has never hurt anything, except himself. And me occasionally. I'm sending you a link to the crowdfunding site. You'll see it's real."

When she gets the link, she stares at the screen, shaking her head, mumbling in Norwegian.

"See, Gjesken? Now that Brian's whale is in Norway, we can find it and get my son and your daughter—"

"You lie! Fake news! Give my Liesl back!"

She leans forward and the screen goes black.

I try and try but she must have turned off Skype. Fuck! Tobey paces, not sure how to get me back to the place of doubt again. I dial the cell phone, returning her call. Her voice mail is in Norwegian, but probably says something about leaving a message. I tell her to call back.

On-line search: news in Norway, the name Gjesken. Nothing. This can't be the end of it.

Maybe Brian isn't in a whale. Maybe Brian was puked out of the whale and floated and drifted and got picked up by a Norwegian freighter and because he had amnesia, he was taken to Norway, and for some reason he kidnapped a girl.

Kidnapped a girl? My Brian? Much more far-fetched than living in a whale.

Twenty minutes later, Skype rings and it's Gjesken with redder eyes and nose and I'm shaking again.

"Her friends called and told me," Gjesken sobs. She's either lost her daughter or she's a really good actor.

She blows her nose in a way Americans don't and collects herself in a way all people do when they're embarrassed about crying in front of people.

"She was out with a group on a boat watching the ocean life. The whale bang the boat and everybody fall down, only Liesl fall into the water. The whale opens mouth and she's eaten."

Tobey moves to the screen, asking Gjesken, "What about the Norwegian Coast Guard? Are they searching for her?"

"They search but no sign. Too much time in cold water. They say —my girl is dead."

Tobey asks, "Did you try calling your daughter's phone again?"

Gjesken looks like she's about to pull her perfect blond hair out, so I answer for her. "She's tried calling every few minutes. She will not stop trying. That's what mothers do."

We mothers stare at each other.

"Your boy, Brian, he is really in the whale?"

I nod. "Yes. He's alive in the whale with your daughter. Where in Norway are you?"

"Bergen. On the North sea."

"I'll be on the first flight I can get. Can I stay with you?"

Gjesken blinks. "You can have Liesl's room."

Scribble down all her information, hang up, and my shaking stops immediately. I turn to Tobey and Arthur. "I told you."

—- OUR FIRST FIGHT —-

I WISH I didn't have to wear these moldy shorts. I've gotten used to Home's sauna temperature but not with clothes. Liesl fans the air, like that will help. I could suggest she strip, but she might take that the wrong way. Every time Home takes a breath, pulling in cool air, this girl screams. It's getting annoying.

To distract her, I talk about life in Home but she must be sulking. She turns her back to me and empties her yellow purse. Money, a nail file, pen, receipts, two peppermints—

—OH MY GOD! A PEPPERMINT!

I reach out, "Mind if I have a mint?"

Liesl smiles sweetly. "Mind if I have my phone?"

Shaking my head, I remind her that the phone is life or death.

Liesl slides the peppermints back in her purse. "Someday these be life or death. I keep for really need one."

"I really need one now."

"If I be in whale for as long as you, I need also as much as you."

"I'll take one and you take one."

"Not fair. Yours value more because you need more. It be simple peppermint to me and be miracle to you."

"I NEED A MIRACLE NOW!"

She shakes her head. "Not at present unless I get phone."

"I saved your life! If it wasn't for me, we wouldn't be arguing about peppermints!"

"My phone."

I want that peppermint. I want it so bad. But, she'll call someone. I can't let that happen. When did I ever care about consequences before?

She grunts and turns away.

—Don't grunt at me. Have the decency to use words.

Damn. I know where that line came from.

My stomach growls in anger. Dinner time.

Scooping up a Pencil Fish from the Ziploc, I pop it in my mouth, crunching happily. A Torpedo Head is next. With a practiced snap, I twist the tentacles off the body, pull the sharp inner blade out, and slip dinner between my smile. He slides down my throat.

—Let's just see how you manage on your own. I'm not going to lift a finger to put something on the table—

—Did you really just think that?

—Shit. I'm turning into Mom.

—- BIRTHDAY NUMBER TWO —-

PINOCCHIO WHINES as Jenny jumps up and down on the bed singing "Happy Birthday to Me! Happy Birthday to ME! Happy Birthday to MEEEEEE-EEEEEEEE. Happy Birthday to ME!"

Mark wakes, squinting in the glare of the wide picture window.

Don't want people looking in.

"Baby, you wanna close the curtains a little?"

Jenny freezes. "Who are you calling Baby?"

Shit. It's too early for this.

Jenny keeps bouncing. At least she's not on Mark's bed. "If I'm having a birthday, I'm especially not a baby, I'm *older* not *younger*!"

Mark struggles to get out from the chaos of covers. He must have been tossing and turning all night to get this tangled.

"Sorry, Jenny. Daddy missed so many birthdays he's gonna start over at the beginning."

"*I* didn't miss them, *you* missed them. I'm not going backwards!"

The sheet rips as he pulls it from around his leg. He reaches low and finds he's naked. Must have gotten toasted and forgotten everything.

"Do you want cake now? Should we light the candles?"

Jenny leaps off the bed, dancing around the table and grinning at her cake. "Birthday time!" Pinocchio whines again.

"Let your dog out to pee, Jenny."

Jenny opens the door wide. The dog rushes out and cold air rushes in.

"Keep an eye on him." Mark pushes the torn sheet off and slips into his jeans.

Searching the fireplace for matches, he remembers a school-yard joke. How did it go? *Got a match?—Your face and my ass.* He'll do that on his daughter.

"Got a match, Jenny?"

Jenny turns around in the doorway and the morning light halos her hair and she's his little girl waiting to hear from her daddy.

"Your face and an angel."

—- OVER THE OCEAN —

I CAN'T STOP LAUGHING and crying and screaming, "I told you! I told you! He's alive. My boy's alive!!!"

Arthur follows me with his camera, getting all the crazy lady excitement. I don't care if I look crazy. I'm crazy with joy.

Tobey books me the flight leaving for Oslo on Icelandair. It leaves in three hours! Arthur checks my phone's camera and declares its video capabilities are passable. He's dying to come with me to film everything but can't leave his new editing job. "You've got to be the documentarian, Ann. Remember film everything but especially when something interesting's happening. This isn't home movies. Art is life with the boring parts taken out."

We all end up in a taxi and Tobey and Arthur hug me at the airline terminal curb. Arthur reiterates "film everything." I don't tell him I've never shot anything but that one picture of my To-Do list on the beige wall. Just smile and nod.

Next thing I know, I'm passing through security, finding the gate. What a whirlwind. This doesn't feel like me at all. I never was a spontaneous person. Maybe I'm different now. I wonder if I should get another new wardrobe to match this new self. I could change my name. What would be a good name for a world traveler? Sophie? Raquel? Amelia? Not Amelia. She died traveling.

At the gate, the other passengers sit fiddling with their phones. Some look like they're from Norway and are traveling home, wearing garish T-shirts and theme-park ball-caps from their visit to the U.S.A. They look worn out, ready to escape whatever they went through. Some look like they are from the U.S.A. and are heading to Norway, wearing garish T-shirts and theme-park ball-caps.

What do I know about Norway? Not much. People eat fish. There are blond models and reindeer. It's cold. Hopefully, it won't be too cold in September.

We board the plane and I've got a window seat. A very tall young man slides in next to me, nodding a stern hello.

The fight attendants go over the safety protocols, including what to do if we lose pressure and land in water. Maybe we'll land near Brian's whale. I'll be holding my flotation seat and the whale will rise and Brian will wave from its mouth. The plane taxis and waits. Soon we'll be on our way. Airborne. Am I on a crazy wild goose chase? No, a wild whale chase.

When was the last time I was on a plane? Dad's funeral fourteen years ago? Back when I was in college, before I met Dan, I imagined travel would be part of my life. At least once a year. A new place. A new language. Different food, terrain, customs. Of course, I never did. Even before Dan, I had no drive to make anything happen. But now, everything's different. This is exciting. Because my son got swallowed, life's finally interesting.

—*Don't think like that.*

—*It's true. Beneath the fear, I'm actually happy.*

—*You're a bad person.*

The engines roar and we're pressed back in our seats as we speed down the runway. The sound of tires on the tarmac grows and silences as we tilt up, leaving the earth. We curve high around the glowing Golden Gate Bridge.

—*Oops, this would have made a good shot for the film. Sorry, Arthur.*

I take out my phone and, after several tries, figure out how to shoot video. I film the little plane on the screen map on the back of the seat. Try play-back. It works! Maybe I'm not such a clueless nutcase after all. I focus on the bald head in front of me, and manage to zoom in to the shining dome. This close, it looks like the pale arching back of a white whale. Arthur can cut it in as a special effect. I pan to the window and the camera does all the exposure fixing for the darkening view outside.

Tiny lights from boats or ocean liners speck the darkness. Zoom in but the view is too shaky. It's making me seasick. Okay, I'm a proficient enough documentarian. Put the phone away. I stare out at the blackness. Somewhere in that water, creatures live and float and eat and die. Somewhere down there is my son, traveling in a living ship. How will I find his particular whale? The beast must be underwater most of the time. How will I know which one has my boy?

—*You won't.*

—*I will. I'm going to see Brian again.*

—*Think it through. There's no way. You're never going to see him. The girl's phone will die and you'll never hear his voice. Ever. Ever. Ever.*

Panic floods me. I can't breathe. There's no air in here. I need to get up and open the plane's door and stick my head in the cold air.

—*Don't act crazy.*

I unhook my seatbelt.

—*Don't get up.*

If I don't get up, I'll scream.

—*If you scream, you'll be sent back and locked up.*

I squeeze my hands to keep myself from screaming. I swallow over and over, trying to wash down the terror.

—*Don't think. Don't think of anything. You need to get a grip, Ann.*

I keep my eye on the little plane on the seat-back-screen, trying not to think. The plane on the map moves along in tiny increments. I imagine it has little digital passengers flying happily in it. One little digital woman sits in a window seat, trying to remain calm and sane, watching her tiny digital screen. Maybe there'll be little digital whales visible on the map when we fly over them. One will have a digital son inside, waving up at me.

Over Oregon, the flight attendant's trolly squeezes down the aisle. I whip the Icelandair magazine from the seat pocket, flipping to the back for a list of drinks. They show the usual spirits and two Iceland ones: Birkir and Bjork. I order both and a vodka as backup. I will stop thinking.

The Iceland drinks are strong and taste like woods or trees. Both scald going down. They begin to work and my panic eases as I start on the vodka.

The young man beside me turns on his light and opens a book. I glance down. The text is unreadable. Is that because of the drinks or because it's Norwegian? If it's Norwegian, I should ask him how to say 'hello' and 'goodbye' and 'thank you' and 'please.' But, I'm so tired. Maybe later.

The lights go down and the flight attendant hands out pillows.

A jolt wakes me. On the seat-back-screen map, the little plane flies somewhere over Canada. We're heading over the top of the world. My eyes close again.

In and out of sleep. Dark shapes curl through the blackness. A huge mouth spreads and engulfs me. I spin from the beast and into my window seat. The map shows we're over water. Is Brian down there? I move my finger as a wave to him.

—*Go back to sleep.*

Does Brian sleep? He must. How do you sleep in a whale?

—— SLEEPING IN THE WHALE ——

THIS IS THE FIRST TIME I've slept with a girl. And it's not all it's cracked up to be. She keeps crying. I guess I did a batch of blubbering when I first got here. Should give her a break. The problem is, quarters are kinda cramped. Especially right before a breath. When the oxygen gets down to zero, the lungs get tight. We can't help but touch or get mashed up against each other when Home does a curl or dive or blows out the snot. We're both slippery and slidey and when a part of her touches me, I get a woody. I try to hide it, but I bet she notices. The Ziploc Wrigglers have gone dark so she can't see, but with all the tossing and churning in here, I'm sure she's aware. Must think I'm a pervert. Her cell phone is jammed in the front pocket of my shorts. I won't accidentally do any butt-dials 'cause it's off, but if it was powered on, it probably wouldn't have any battery left from all the dick-dialing.

I keep my back to her but this constant wood is making my balls ache. I wish there was a door I could close and relieve things. Maybe I could zap Johnson with a Stinging Blue Wriggler and numb him out.

—*Think about something you hate, Bri. Think about Phys Ed class.*

—*Why did I hate that so much?*

—*The jerks teasing you. Mr. Mansfield teasing you.*

—*They should have a way to do Phys Ed without being ridiculed. Why was everyone so mean?*

—*You know why.*

—*They were scared. Everyone's scared all the time. It makes them mean. What a world it would be if we weren't so scared all the time.*

Liesl whimpers. Her back is against mine and she's shaking. Another one scared. Home does his deep song with the little trills at the end. The Lullaby Song.

"Sleep, Liesl. It'll get better. You're alive. Nothing can hurt you in here. Don't be scared. Sleep."

It makes me feel better to whisper to her. I can help.

Liesl's breathing has slowed. No sounds of crying. Home is quiet as well.

Wish I didn't have to, but—I have *got* to pee. Can't hold another minute. I hope I won't wake her as I slither past. Maybe I can find her purse, slide the zipper silently, get one of those peppermints. My mouth waters with the thought.

Only, I don't want to be that type of person. Not any more.

I bend slowly and move past her, feel in the darkness for the flap, and slip Johnson out. No cold water moves past as I let go. Home isn't feeding. He's not been feeding as regularly. He really is getting sicker. If I had two creatures living in my lungs, I'd be sick. If he stops eating, we die. Not that we won't anyway.

"I visit toilet also," Liesl whispers in the darkness.

I don't know how a girl is going to do this. Butt first, like shitting, I guess.

"Now's a good time. Home isn't feeding. It won't be cold."

I help her over. She grabs my arm tightly and I'm grateful for darkness because my wood returns. I hold her as she squats, rear out the flap.

"Not to let me fall away. No, will let?" her voice quavers. She's terrified.

"Never. I've got you."

After she finishes and I show her how to rinse her hands out in the tube, I give Liesl tips on how to make life in Home. Surprisingly, I have a lot to say. I'm a whale expert. Give a shake of the Ziploc to show how the Wrigglers work. Tell her that some can sting but that can be helpful. Tell her what we'll eat when Home feeds. Tell her about Amelia's watch. She wants to see it, but the Wrigglers are dim.

"Give me my phone and I'll be able to see it," she suggests.

"We can't use the battery as a light. We need it for calling."

"Call now."

"Liesl, we'll call when Home is at the surface, when there's a chance for reception. Only then."

I shake the Ziploc of Wrigglers harder. They anger to a dull blue glow and I hand her the watch and explain how I found it and who Amelia Earhart is. Liesl doesn't believe me. When I show her the back and the inscription, she gets crying. Again.

"Amelia died in here? Years ago? We to die in here, also!" she wails.

I try to distract her. "Let's time my breaths. You hold the watch and time me. I can do over three minutes now."

"I don't believe. Three minutes be crazy long."

I tell her we both need to practice. "It can keep you from panicking. Home doesn't always breathe when I want him to. I have to slow everything down. Don't move. Don't do a thing. Concentrate on making my heart go as slow as his. It works."

164

Liesl lifts Amelia's watch and says, "Now." I inhale as far down and as wide as I can and then pull in even more, stretching my lungs to their busting point. When they are completely full, I close my eyes and drift.

Liesl holds her breath with me. We wait and wait and she puffs out, gasping. I'm still going. I listen to Home's heartbeat. It's so slow, it helps calm mine. I don't need to breathe. I can be still. Still.

After a bit, Liesl nudges me. "You not real doing."

I shake my head. I'm still holding it.

Liesl stares at the watch. "Two minutes."

I'm not even struggling. I've got this down. Nothing phases me. The Wrigglers grow calm and start to dim.

"Three minutes."

Liesl keeps counting. At four, I am feeling it, but I'm thrilled to have a witness, so I will myself to relax and drift. She holds the watch right next to the Ziploc. *The Blue Light Special* is almost out.

"Five minutes."

Dizziness floats in but I'm okay with that. I let myself *be,* without any agenda, without a mission, without distraction. I float and wait.

Finally, I let out the old air and pull in a new one. Liesl shakes the Ziploc and the Wrigglers glare.

"Five minutes and 28 seconds. That so crazy long time. You really good at breath-take."

I smile. It's so much easier when you have an audience to impress.

Liesl hands back Amelia's watch. A long low moan rumbles around us with Home's singing.

"This is the searching song. I call it that because it sounds like wanting to find someone. Missing someone. It has a really nice middle section that is kinda like movie music in a foreign film."

Home's melody vibrates all around us. It's nice to share it with someone.

"Brian?"

"Liesl?"

"How long be you in here?"

"I don't know. I tried to keep track but I got messed up and finally didn't care."

"When be eat?"

"June 4th."

"I be eat the eight day of September."

I do the counting in my head. "Three months in here."

She looks at me and in the glow of the Ziploc, I see tears forming."How we be out?"

"I don't know. I don't know if we can be out. If you get any ideas, let me know."

We're silent for the rest of the night, listening to Home's heartbeat drum and his singing. I hold my breath secretly, so I can replay Liesl saying I'm really good.

—- NORWAY —-

THE PLANE LANDS and the flight attendant says something cheerful in a different language. Most of the passengers laugh. Finally she says in English, "Welcome to Oslo, Norway."

Finding a Wi-Fi spot, I email Tobey and Arthur that I'm here, tired, but fine. I don't know what time it is for them. I've lost track. After a cup of tea and filming the terminal shops and cafes, I board a little plane for the last leg of the trip—Gjesken's town of Bergen. This time I manage to film the takeoff. My eyes close and a second later the thump of descending wheels wakes me and I look out the window as we tilt over a harbor surrounded by orange and red and yellow and green pointy-roofed cookie homes of a gingerbread city. You've got to be kidding. People can't actually live in fairy-tale places like this. It's too perfect.

I make it through the customs saying I'm here for pleasure and will be in the country for two weeks. I don't tell them I'm here to get a boy out of a whale. They probably don't admit crazy people.

Graphic signs point to areas for taxis and busses. Should I take one? But where? I don't know how far from the city the airport is, and how far away Gjesken lives. I should call her. What am I supposed to dial? Am I calling from this country or does my cell phone think I'm still in the USA?

A man in a uniform says something to me and I shrug and mumble, "I don't understand."

In perfect English he asks if I need help. When I explain my dilemma, he calls Gjesken on his cell phone. They talk for a bit, then he leads me outside to a bench by the curb.

"Twenty minutes she'll be here."

I thank him and look at the passengers coming and going. Everything is colorful and different. The sun is low and it's an odd light. A strange kind of brightness. Not the California sun I'm used to. More honest? Or un-compromising? Or sinister?

Voices all around me, conversations, announcements over the loudspeaker. None in English. My heart panics and a tightness rises in my chest. Where am I? What have I done? Who is this Gjesken person? I'm far from everyone and everything I know. Nothing is safe or usual or normal. Everything is wrong. The panic spreads, clamping down my throat. What are they all saying? Do they recognize me from the news? Are they talking about me? Breathe. Breathe. But I can't. Every part of me is shaking. I'll never find Brian. He may be alive but how can I find him? I'm closer, but still without a way to reach him. I *am* crazy. This is hopeless! Tears blur all the unknown travelers.

A tiny green car stops in front of me and through my tears, I watch the lady from the Skype-call exit. Gjesken is in a bright yellow and blue dress. She rushes to me and as I put out my hand, she pulls me into a deep hug whispering, "We will find them and bring them home. Liesl and Brian."

I cry along with her, trembling against this stranger.

— BREATHING IS WORSE —

THE WHALE SLIDES through the thick kelp forest. The sickness in its lungs is much worse. A heaviness presses against the slow booming heart. The inner sounds have grown and nothing feels right.

The great beast moves slowly, singing the come-follow-song, listening to the songs of the others—the humpback, the sperm, the blue—and the tiny voices from deep inside.

There are low areas along here. Fjords. Places to beach and put an end to things. It would be possible to slide up the sand and wait for death. It would be slow, but quicker than this growing illness.

Not yet.

Soon perhaps.

— GJESKEN'S HOME —

GJESKEN MAKES TEA as I look out her window at the city. Everything is clean and fresh and sparking. Nothing is beige.

Gjesken's open-plan apartment has pastel-colored walls of yellow and green and turquoise, with light, light, light everywhere. Beautiful pale-wood floors. *Isn't it good, Norwegian wood?* Photographs cluster in tasteful groupings between the windows. The furniture is all small. It makes sense. Why do we need huge eight-foot couches? Here, everything is modern but cozy and uncluttered. Serene, but with personality.

Gjesken brings the tray of tea to the dining area. She has the whole shebang: teapot, cups *with saucers*, pitcher of cream, miniature silver spoons, and little flat cookies with pretty scalloped edges. I've never encountered such a thing except on Masterpiece Theater. I've only ever microwaved hot water in a beige mug.

As she pours, I study her. Besides her perfect blond hair, she's got perfect skin. Perfect figure. She's perfect, not in a Hollywood model way, but like she's been genetically engineered by an hip IKEA committee. Stylish. Competent. Courteous. Capable.

Everything I'm not.

"Cream?" she asks with a perfect accent to her perfect English.

Of course, I want my tea beige.

She pours and as she lays a little biscuit on my saucer and hands me the teacup, I feel a sudden urge to splash the hot liquid across her perfect self. Knowing jetlag and worry and hunger and whatever might make that happen, I turn away and look at the photographs on the wall.

There's a picture of a rugged outdoor man standing with Gjesken. "Your husband?" I ask.

"Mm. He's on an oil rig now. Not able to leave yet."

She points to a photo of a pretty young girl. "Liesl, a few years ago. I always want to put up newer pictures but years go by and I never do."

"Too bad," I say a bit judgmentally. My pictures of Brian are all back from when he was in high school, but she doesn't need to know that.

—*What's going on? Am I always this snarky?*

I try to make up for it. "Liesl's pretty. How old is she now?"

"Nineteen," Gjesken answers.

"Same age as Brian."

Gjesken glances at me and I know what she's thinking. Two kids, nearly twenty, opposite sexes, tight quarters.

She bursts out laughing.

She can't be imagining it right. Brian won't talk to the girl, let alone try anything sexual. He's curled up in a pudgy ball in the corner of the lungs. Not the kind of guy any pretty girl would even look at. I'm a bad mother for thinking it, but my son's no catch.

Still, Gjesken's laughter tickles my belly and gets me giggling with her. Even without the same visions, we double over with laughter, hardly able to breathe.

Is this my first real laugh in three months? Or has it been longer than that? It feels so good. I want to laugh for the rest of my life.

— CHILD MELTDOWN —

CRYING AGAIN. "You promised I could talk to mommy!" Jenny screams. "It's time to call her!"

Mark pictures himself grabbing the brat by the neck and squeezing. No. That's not what Daddies do. Has he taken half a pill today? Can't remember.

"Jenny, I told you Mommy isn't well and we can't reach her. The doctors said no calls. They said she would call us when she was well."

"You're lying!"

A burst of shame floods Mark's cheeks. How can this girl know? Is it that obvious? He turns away and nearly trips over the damn dog. Mark swings his leg to kick it but the dog leaps aside and scrambles under the cluttered kitchen table. Ripped newspaper wrapping, empty mini-cereal boxes, beer bottles—all sorts of garbage lies strewn across the top. The cabin is a mess. As Jenny chants, "Give me the phone! Give me the phone!" Mark pulls the trash can to the table and scoops everything in.

Jenny screams, "NOOOOOOO!!!!" and races to her father, punching him in the hip.

This kid is really getting on his nerves. "What's the matter now!?"

"You threw away my present! My message-in-the-bottle the boy in the whale sent to me!" She's crying and moaning, her mouth distorted like a red wound.

Mark puts his hand out to comfort her but she slaps it and howls. This child is a monster. He's got to put an end to the noise. *Find the damn treasures, Idiot. Make this right.*

He spills the trash on the floor and the girl dives, pawing through the garbage, flinging aside beer bottles, milk containers, animal cracker box, dog food can, scattering the mess across the cabin floor. Fishing out the split coke bottle and library card and dollar. Jenny places her precious objects on the bed, crawls up beside them and peers close, inspecting them. Mark glares at the girl's thin back. *She's looking for damage. If there is any, it will be my fault. Everything's always my fault.*

"Give me the phone," the girl's back says. She sounds just like her mother.

"You can't bother Mommy—"

Jenny stands up on the bed, scrunches her eyes and waves the punctured dollar at Mark like he's an idiot. "I'm calling the boy in the whale."

This isn't fun anymore. He thought it would be fun and cozy and family-feeling but this is gonna send him over the edge.

"The boy in the whale!" the girl yells, jumping on the bed. "The boy in the whale!"

Fuck it. It will be safe. Mark turns on his phone. "Read me the number."

"It's in your phone. You dialed it before."

Jenny holds out her hand as she jumps. Watching her makes Mark feel sick. He turns his head away, opens the call log, skips the calls to Kansas City, pushes the one for the whale lady, and holds the phone out to the bouncing demon.

— PHONE FIGHT —

MY PHONE RINGS and as I fumble for it, Gjesken races to my side. "If it's Liesl, let me talk to her," she pleads. "I need to hear her voice."

I wave noncommittally and answer the call. The tentative "hello" is not Brian. It's a girl's voice.

"Is this Liesl?" I ask. "Put Brian on."

Gjesken grabs the phone from me! Bitch! She lurches away, hunching over it, whimpering in Norwegian. I pull at her arm. She straightens up, handing me the phone. "It's for you."

Phone to my ear and the girl's voice reaches me again. "Hello, this is Jenny. I found the message-in-the-bottle."

Damn it! That scam! Never even bothered to send the fake. "What do you want? More money? I sent money. You never sent the message-in-the-bottle."

"It's mine."

"So you're saying you still have it?"

"Right here. The dollar bill with the blind-people dots and the library card and the bottle we had to cut it open with Daddy's knife. The library card has dog food on it but—"

"You should have sent it," I interrupt.

"I found it. Finders keepers."

"That's not how it works. Shame on you!"

Silence on the line—or maybe sniffling? *What am I doing? This is a kid.*

"I'm sorry to yell, Jenny. My son is inside a whale and I'm worried about him. Can you understand that?"

"Will Brian get out of the whale or will he live there forever?"

My voice suddenly won't work. I don't know the answer.

The girl fills the silence. She tells me about her dog named Pinocchio and how he has a long nose but it doesn't grow because he doesn't lie and "Pinocchio's daddy lived in a whale and got out and Pinocchio became a real boy, so don't worry."

I should see that movie.

The girl keeps babbling.

—If it's not about getting more money, why did she call me?

"Jenny, why did you call me?"

"I miss Mommy. I wanted to call her but Daddy said no because she's sick. I wish she wasn't because I'm tired of being on an adventure and being away and—"

A muffled sound and the line goes dead.

I must have an odd expression because Gjesken looks at me with concern. I've only met her a few hours ago but she's pretty and has a perfect house and colorful clothes and she grabbed my phone, so I hate her.

I switch the phone to the other ear, pretend to be listening, and laugh heartily. *Take that, Gjesken!*

—- LIESL WANTS TO CALL —-

"IT BE MINE!" Liesl screams. "It time to call and I want call!"

I stick my hand over Liesl's cell phone in my shorts. "You want it? Come and get it."

"You a mean man."

I'm stunned that she used the word *man* about me. I've never been considered a man. It's a thrill. If I'm a man, I've got to stay strong and not give her this phone. "You can't make another call. We need to conserve your battery. It's our only hope."

"I want to talk my Mom!"

"Every time we call, we're less likely to be found. We've got to make a plan."

"You be here three months. You make plan yet?"

"I didn't have a cell phone that had any power."

"Did have power when you be eat?"

I'm not going to tell her I spent my battery taking selfies and calling and playing video games. "I wasted it trying to make calls. We can't make the same mistake."

Liesl slumps. "When we call?"

"Next breath Home takes, we see if it's daylight. No sense calling in the middle of the night when someone might not hear. If it is daylight, we call really fast. We don't chat. We don't let them ask questions. We tell them one thing."

"What thing?"

Now this part I did plan. I've thought about this for three months. "They must set up the most powerful phone tracking system they can. We find out what time it is there and we tell them we have a watch and will call back in an hour."

"How they be ready in one hour?" Liesl asks. "We'll be wasting batteries if we call and they not ready."

—*Suddenly she's the one worried about wasting batteries. I'm the one who's been responsible. I'm the one with a plan. She doesn't know shit about being in a whale.*

"Your phone is our chance and it's risky to wait. We wait three or four hours and we'll be traveling all the time. Maybe out of range. Then we'll be stuck in here and it will be your fault!"

"I not say three or four hour. I ask a question. Hour be short time."

—*"Hour be short time." What does she know about time?*

"You don't know what time is!" I yell. "You don't know an hour or a day or a week or a month! You don't know! *I* know!"

"Have it be hour. I don't care. We never get out any chance. I be stuck also you and you stuck also me. We die here."

173

Is she crying? She better not be crying. I hate when girls cry just to win. I'll ignore her.

"Brian, it be hard breathe. Home up soon, yes? What I say in call?"

She sounds reasonable. Makes me sound like a jerk. Better backtrack. "Say two hours. What would you do to set up tracking a phone? I'd ask Google."

"I tell Mor —mother—go police."

"Police won't believe your mom if she says, 'Please track my daughter's phone. She's in a whale.'"

Liesl is silent. It's too dark to see her face, but I've done enough pouting to recognize this silence.

The air is empty of oxygen.

"I no breathe, Brian."

"Hold your breath, Liesl. Home will rise. Home needs to breathe, too."

I feel Liesl shaking and whisper, "Tell them to go to the police and have them ready to track our call in two hours." I use my last lung-full letting her win so she'll forget we have no air.

A tilt of Home knocks us backward and we're pressed together at the back of the compressing lungs. Her elbow hits my chest and her knee is in my stomach but it feels good. Her phone rises in my shorts.

Liesl's face is against my neck. Silly thought, but I hope the whale breeches slowly.

Home tilts and the blowhole opens to bright sunlight and Liesl's looking up, pretty blue eyes, sand on her lashes. And the moisture and goo is shot from around us out the hole and a blast of cold, cold air rushes in.

I maneuver the phone past my woody and hand it to Liesl. "Call now."

She dials.

174

— CALL FROM LIESL —

A PLEASANT CHIRPING comes from the kitchen. Does Gjesken have a bird?

Gjesken races in and picks up her phone. "Hei." A gasp and she's chattering in Norwegian with love and fear and anger and—it's got to be her daughter.

"What's happening? Is Brian there? I need to talk to Brian!" I reach for the phone but Gjesken pulls away and rushes into the bathroom, slamming the door. The bolt clicks.

I hate this bitch! I kick and pound on the door. "Open the door! It's my turn!"

"Hiljaa! Quiet!"

Gjesken doesn't understand that I haven't heard from my son in three months. I need to talk to him. I need to tell him Mommy's here. Looking for him. He needs me.

The lock clicks and Gjesken opens the door. I reach for the phone and she doesn't move to stop me.

"Hello! Hello!" The line is dead. I want to punch her. "Call back. I need to talk to Brian."

"They won't answer."

"Of course they will—"

"Ann, listen. We've only got two hours. We must go to the police. Get them to track the phone."

"What are you talking about?"

"Liesl will call back in two hours and we have to be ready to track the phone. It's Brian's plan. "

I'm shocked. *Brian's plan?* I pull myself together and exhale all the anger and frustration I feel. Brian's plan. Pride flushes over me. "Okay. Police. What do we say?"

"Brian had an idea for that."

—- POLICE STATION —-

THE OFFICER types in Liesl's name and looks over at me. "Your boy's name?"

I try to pretend to be newly worried. "Brian Ketchum." The minute I say his name, the tears come. "He's nineteen."

"And what kind of boat is it?"

Gjesken looks at me and I look at her. She starts, "Small—"

"—and hard to see," I add. "It's grey. The color of the ocean. That's why we need to track the call."

The officer talks calmly and slowly. He must be used to frantic mothers. "If we get authorization to track the call, we'll do it, get a general area and send out the search."

Gjesken smiles tensely. "We give you authorization. It's my daughter's phone."

The officer shakes his head. "The court gives authorization."

I stifle the urge to slap him.

The officer leads us to a room in the basement. It looks like Mission Control. Several computers and monitors. I should film it for Arthur's documentary but that might get us thrown out. I make a silent apology to him.

The police talk to each other and I can't understand a thing. Heads shake. Emphatic discussions. The clock ticks. It looks like a lot of bureaucracy in this procedure. We have half an hour left. Gjesken argues with the officer, pleading, begging. He makes another call, whispering low into the phone. Hanging up, he gives the go-ahead to someone at the computer. Typing starts and Gjesken hugs me. Authorization seems given but we've only got twenty minutes left. Much tapping into the computer. Other officers join in, giving advice, setting up the system. Or wasting time. This is the longest two hours I've ever spent. At five minutes left, they seem to have everything in place and no worries. I watch the clock.

The time arrives. Two hours.

We wait. No call.

Suddenly panicked, I ask Gjesken, "Will you get reception down here in the basement?"

She says a flurry of words as she pulls me up the stairs. An officer joins us, talking into his own phone.

I pull her outside of the building. Gjesken's phone immediately rings and she answers, "Hei?"

The officer listens to his own phone, gesturing for her to keep talking.

I move next to Gjesken. "Please. Please. Tell her to put Brian on."

Gjesken says something and hands me the phone. I'm shaking. "Hello, Brian?"

A staticky sound. "Mom? Is that you?"

My son's voice! My living son's alive voice! Sobs burst from me.

"Mom, you're in Norway?"

Shoving all the worry and pain and relief down my throat, I force my mouth to work. "Yes. I'm here in Norway. Oh, Brian honey, I'm going to find you. Don't worry."

"I can't talk long. We need to conserve the battery. Is the phone tracked?"

He sounds different. Not whiney. Like he's in charge.

The officer waves at me to keep talking. I have no problem with that. "Are you okay? Are you eating? You must be in the lungs, right?"

"We're in his lungs but—"

"I knew it! Brian, this was your plan. I'm so proud—"

"Mom, let me know when the tracking is—"

The phone goes dead.

"Brian. Brian! Come back." I shake the phone. Gjesken grabs it from me. Dialing. Nothing. We try again and again. No response.

"Tell me you found them!" I yell at the officer.

He hurries us back into the building and down the stairs. There is a blinking spot on a computer screen. A blinking spot in an empty screen.

"Are they near?"

The computer zooms out, until we see the edge of land, zooms out to see the curved coastline of Norway. They're far out in the Norwegian Sea.

Gjesken has the officer write out the latitude and longitude of the tracked phone. He says they will send the Coast Guard out with helicopters and boats. They'll find our children.

"We lied a little," Gjesken admits.

The officer doesn't look pleased.

I spill the beans. "They're not in a boat. They're in a whale."

Silence is followed by a barrage of Norwegian that sounds a lot like threats and curses. Gjesken pulls me out of the room, nodding and apologizing. We run up the stairs and out to the parking lot. When the car doors slam, she bursts into uncontrollable laughter.

"He wants to arrest us! Let's go."

"We have to hide?"

"No, we get a boat. Go to sea."

—- SURPRISED AT MOM —-

IT'S BEEN SO LONG since I talked with Mom. It was good. Not like before. She said she was going to find me. She was proud of my plan. I don't know when she's ever been proud.

Liesl is so happy that we might have the phone tracked, she can't sit still. She turns to me—hungry.

I go fishing out the flap and pull in Peewee and Supersize Peelers, Squeak Weed, Pencil Fish, Chinese Bubble Weed, and Torpedos. She eats like she's starving. I'm the provider. She eats, grinning at me the whole time. She's really pretty in the blue wriggler light.

While she eats, I explain all about Peelers and their exoskeletons, and the Torpedo Heads with their inno-skeletons. She's impressed. After dinner we guess how long 'til they find us. We talk about our moms for a long time. I can't believe Mom is in Norway. I can't imagine her anywhere but our house in Burbank. I don't know how she did it. Dad musta helped. She'd never manage this on her own.

178

— AMBER ALERT —

JENNY TURNS from the TV. "Daddy, what's an Amber Alert?"

Mark flies from the couch, turning off the TV in a flash. "Sweetie, do you want to take Pinocchio out for a walk before bed?"

Jenny's curiosity is up. "What's an Amber Alert?"

"It's when someone's lost. Like a runaway. It's so people can help find them. Let's go out. Maybe the northern lights will be visible."

Jenny groans. "It's cold out there."

"We'll make it cozy. And we can have hot chocolate when we get back in." He bundles Jenny in her sweater. They need to get warmer clothes. She has no winter coat. It'll be really cold soon. People will notice a little girl without the right clothes.

They step out into the brisk air. Pinocchio rushes off to chase something in the darkness. Mark again hopes that the dog won't come back. It'd be hard for Jenny for a few days but the dog is a burden.

Jenny clicks the flashlight on and off. On and off.

"Sweetie, leave it on. Switching it back and forth isn't good for it."

"Pinocchio! Pinocchio, come!"

"Let's not yell. People are resting. We don't want to bother them."

"I hate it here. I want to go home."

They move past other cabins. Lights shine from the windows. Has anyone noticed the father and daughter?

Jenny stops walking. "I'm cold and I want to go home!"

Mark turns around. "We'll go back inside. Get you warm."

"Not the cabin. Home. Home. HOME!" She does her high-pitched screaming again.

Mark picks her up, one hand 'round her waist, the other across her mouth.

A cabin door opens and a man looks out. Mark tries to grin, "Kids. Always having a tantrum, eh?"

The man doesn't react. Mark moves past, hurrying to their cabin. The man watches. Damn it! They'll be caught if he can't keep Jenny in line. "Sweetie, help me find Pinocchio. Let's call him."

Mark sets Jenny down and uncovers her mouth as he calls out, "Pinocchio!"

The girl shines her light into the darkness. "Pinocchio!"

The watching man goes back inside.

Pinocchio bounds up, nearly knocking over Jenny.

"Good dog," Jenny says. "I thought you ran away forever. I was going to do an Amber Alert."

After heating a package of chocolate milk and finally getting Jenny to bed, Mark sits close to the muted TV watching the AMBER Alert complete with a picture of Jenny, one of Pinocchio, and that mugshot of Mark looking startled. The alert mentions the old car he got rid of in Wyoming. Hopefully this car he bought on Craig's list can't be connected to him. He should start calling Jenny by another name. Make it a pretend game. She can pick her own and that'll help her remember it. He'll be Ralph or something. No, he's not smart enough to remember new facts.

Fucking AMBER Alert! Why hasn't this died down!?

— SINGING —

LIESL WATCHES me sing along with my whale. When she tries to imitate Home, I realize how good I've gotten. She sounds like a howling sick dog. I sing The Lullaby Song but Home won't join in. Guess it isn't time for bed.

"Check this out, Liesl. I'm not sure it will work. This is a sound Home makes when he's rising. Maybe he'll rise if I sing it."

I do The Rise Song through the corrugated tube. Grumble-warble, squeaking wagon-wheel, clicking, and gong. It comes out pretty good. But we're still tilted down.

"Again, Brian."

I take a deep breath and sing as loud as I can. Grumble-warble, squeaking wagon-wheel, clicking, and gong.

I sense the shift. Could it be?

Home curls and tilts and—

"He's rising!" I yell.

Liesl screams, "You talk whale!"

I sing, mouth wide like an opera dude, grumble-warble, squeaking wagon-wheel, clicking, and gong.

Home sings, barreling upward, blasting us with his song— grumble-warble, squeaking wagon-wheel, clicking, and gong.

We're knocked back, pressed against the warm wet sponge and the lungs pull us lower and the massive heart thumps right under our bodies and I keep singing and Liesl tries her best to join in and Home arches and—out blasts air and spray and there's the sunlight and I take in Liesl instead of the bright hole and she's glowing, and cool comes in fast and sharp as our room expands and the hole closes tight.

"You did song, Brian! You talk whale and whale listen! It did what you talk!"

"It taught me The Rise Song, but—guess what? I taught it my name!" I scream out, "BRIIIIIIII-AAAAAAANNNNN."

We listen.

"He'll do it," I say. "BRIIIIIIII-AAAAAAANNNNN."

Nothing but Home's thumping heartbeat below us.

"It okay. You make whale go up. You be true hero."

Liesl shifts and part of her grazes my knee in the darkness. "Beklager. Sorry."

I feel her shift and a smell moves close and a soft hand touches my shoulder and moves up to find my face. Her lips press against my cheek.

I'm so glad we're in the dark so she can't see my woody spring to life.

Home sings again. It's a new song. A slow slidey one. Maybe he's singing to me. Maybe he's trying to tell me something. Maybe he's telling me to kiss Liesl.

I turn to find her face but it's no longer there.

I listen to the fast pounding of my heart and the slow pounding of Home's.

—*You're a hero, Bri. A goddamn whale-whisperer hero.*

—- HERO'S JOURNEY —

TURNS OUT if you're from Norway, you know somebody who knows somebody who has a boat. By the time we get back to Gjesken's apartment and she's already got one lined up and I just have to go online to have the crowdfunding pay for it. I call Tobey to tell him the news. The phone rings and rings and finally a groggy, "Ann?"

"I spoke to Brian! He's alive and in the whale's lungs and we're going on a boat to get him!"

"Wait. Wait. Let me wake up."

"Oh, shit. What time is it there?"

"Nearly 4 AM."

"Sorry. I forgot I was across the world. I'll call back later."

But now Arthur's talking to Tobey and he tells me to call back in ten on the computer with Skype.

Ten minutes later I've arranged myself in Gjesken's perfect kitchen with the view of the glowing sunlit buildings behind me. When we connect, Arthur has me move so I'm not silhouetted by the window and when he finally likes the background and lighting, he starts filming and lets me talk.

I tell them all about Brian and how great he sounded and the joy of hearing him after three months. I tell them of Brian's great idea and how we tricked the police into tracking the phone. "Hopefully we can get out to sea before the whale moves too far from that spot."

Arthur moves his face from behind the camera. "Uh, Ann? You know there are easier ways to track a phone. Anyone can do it on the internet."

What?! Is he kidding me? I stare at his image on the screen.

Arthur looks up from the camera. "Damn it, Skype froze."

"No, I'm just not moving," I say. "Arthur, you're telling me we can track the phone without the police? I can do it from my laptop?"

"With an internet connection. Will you have one on the boat? You'll be far from any cell tower or Wi-Fi spot."

Shit! I didn't think of that. We'll have no way to call or Skype or track the phone.

Arthur leans forward. "I've rented portable internet satellite systems when I'm filming at remote locations. These 'footballs' come in plastic cases, no bigger than carryon. And super-clear instructions, Ann. You don't need to be a wiz to use them. I'll search your area and get one delivered to—"

"I'll get together a care package for everything you'll need on a boat." Tobey interrupts, not to be outdone in helping me. "We'll make sure these are delivered right away."

I can't stifle my jet-lag sized yawn. Tobey says, "Get some sleep. I love you, sis," and waves goodbye. I wave at them and reach for the hangup icon.

"Hold on, Ann," Arthur says. "At this momentous start of your journey—your worthy quest—say something for the film."

"You're going to edit out the bit about telling me to say something for the film?"

"Maybe, maybe not. It's sometimes good to break the fourth wall. Show the process."

"You gonna leave *that* in—about the fourth wall?"

"Give me something to move us into act two, the new world, the hero's journey—"

"Who's the Hero in this journey? Brian? Me? He's a schlub kid and I'm a screwed up mom. And act two? This isn't an act, Arthur. This isn't a paint-by-numbers, fill-in-the-blanks, create-a-blockbuster, get-into-Sundance story you can mold. This is my life. I know it's thrilling for you, but I'm not making shit up for your film. I'm scared and tired and excited but what's happening isn't a movie and I can't push pause to make popcorn or pee and I don't know how it ends, so give me a fucking break."

I stare at the screen. No one moves. Is Skype frozen?

"Perfect," Arthur says, grinning.

Tobey reaches forward and I'm left staring at the blank screen.

Gjesken's still on the phone. Lots of talking in Norwegian, list making. I lean back on the IKEA-style couch. I've got to figure out what's happening, but my eyes won't stay open.

In my head, I play back the call with Brian for the millionth time. He sounded so good. He sounded brave and strong.

He was surprised to hear my voice. Never thought I'd leave Burbank. Let alone California. Let alone the USA. I'm surprised, too.

I'm near him. Near my boy. Let's rest now, Brian. You must be sleepy.

Sandpaper rubs across the back of my hand. Over and over. I open my eyes to see a kitten licking me.

"That's Coo-coo, Liesl's kitten," Gjesken says. "I'd better talk to a neighbor about taking care of her."

Oops.

I fumble in my purse. There it is. The hipster's key. How long can a deaf cat live without food and water?

"I've got to Fedex something to San Francisco."

—- IMAGINING —

LIESL AND I talk about what we'll do first when we get rescued. She wants to shower and see her friends and post about her adventure and catch up on the shows she missed. She wants to eat a pizza and have pancakes and soup with a "Raspeball" in it and sweet buns and apple cake. I don't think about food anymore. I stopped long ago. Listening to her, I remember that video games and shows were everything to me, but I can't remember why.

"What you want when first be out?" Liesl asks.

I let myself imagine it. "I want to stand on ground that doesn't move and be in the sun and walk for hours in one direction without stopping. I want to see my Mom and—I don't know, apologize for something. Maybe everything. I want to press my hands into dirt."

"You not sound like normal from Los Angeles."

"I was normal but kinda in an abnormal way. I did nothing. Everything was outside of me. I only watched. Streaming shows, videos, games, people. Here in Home, I have only me and Home. And, I changed. There is no more outside. Home and me are both inside and it's a whole world. And that's enough. Better than enough."

"I be not like you. I no can live without my connections."

I couldn't have either, three months ago. But now it's easy. Maybe if this rescue takes a while, she'll understand.

"When find us, how get us out?" Liesl asks, worried.

The question I've thought about forever. None of my answers will make her happy, so I yawn, hoping it'll spread to her. It does. "Let's sleep now. We'll talk about it later."

Liesl curls up, her purse under her head. I lie back and practice holding my breath.

—*You know there isn't much chance of finding a moving whale, right?*

—*Maybe a* little *chance.*

—*But no chance of getting you out. What are they going to do? Tickle Home's chin trying to get him to open his mouth? Most likely thing would be to kill Home and cut him open as fast as they can to get to the lungs but, oops, it took too long. 'Sorry Mrs. Ketchum, your son suffocated.'*

—*Maybe they could find us and tow Home to land and use a crane to pry open his mouth, we'd crawl out and be free and they'd pull Home back to the ocean and let him go.*

—*Tow him to land, huh? Without the buoyancy of water, guess how much Home weighs. Guess what happens to anything inside when that weight settles. Pancakes.*

—*Maybe they could coat metal tanks with whale-food smells and Home will swallow them and we'll grab them on the way down and bring them in and get in the tanks and go out through the stomach, but won't be pulverized, because we're in the tanks, and we'll go through the intestines and out the butt.*

—*Does that sound like a good idea to you?*

—They'll think of something. Probably have lots of people brainstorming. Scientists and experts.

—No one is more of an expert than you. You're the one who's lived in a whale for three months. Keep thinking. You get any ideas, let me know.

—You, too.

—- SUPPLIES —

GJESKEN WAKES ME with coffee. "Got your key off to San Francisco and many items were delivered while you sleep. Including the Wi-Fi thing. The Football. Very compact." She gestures to a safety-orange hard plastic case.

The Global Satellite Internet Hotspot looks like a spy movie prop. Like it holds a mini nuclear bomb or vials of deadly virus.

When I release the latches, they making satisfying movie sounds. I should film this. Gjesken looks at me oddly when I close the case, pick up my phone, start filming, and open the case.

A white dome fills most of the inside. A few connecting ports. The lid has a quick setup guide. It looks so minimal even I could probably manage.

I pan the camera over the other items piled on the table. Sunscreen. Binoculars. Polarized sunglasses. Wide brim hat with chin strap. Neon purple waterproof phone carrier.

Cut. Putting my precious phone in the waterproof carrier, I slide the cord over my head. Shit. It hangs like a dumb ID badge. Might as well wear a pocket protector. I look like a dork. Brian, I totally understand. Since you had to, and it worked, I'll do it, too.

"Try Liesl's clothes," Gjesken says, pulling items from a bureau and closet. Leggings. Winter coat. Sweater. Gloves. All of them, different colors. I definitely won't be beige anymore.

"We'll be getting cold?" I ask.

Gjesken nods with eyes wide to express that I've never met this kind of cold.

186

Shit. I'm from Burbank. I only get cold when Brian turns the air conditioner down.

"You must be hungry."

My hunger hits the moment the word does.

"We'll have a snack, pack, and pick up more on the way." She pulls a jar from the fridge. A silvery substance in a white sauce. The smell is strong.

"What is it?"

Gjesken laughs, "Probably like serving a hamburger in America and having someone ask what it is. This is pickled mackerel."

I try it, not expecting to manage, but the fish is delicious. I eat several pieces with thick dark bread as Gjesken gathers supplies. We carry everything down to her tiny car and drive off into the dimming light. The hum of the wheels and my full mackerel stomach send me back to dreaming.

—- HOLY MACKEREL —-

LIESL BREATHES SOFTLY. I have to admit it's nice to have another person, besides myself, to talk to. And look at. She's got pretty eyes from what I could tell in the sunlight from Home's blowhole. She's sweet, too.

Uh-oh. Woody is back. I'll turn a bit to take care of things without her knowing. I start out nice and slow, listening hard to see if my strokes make any sound. All I can hear is Home's big thumping heart and his singing.

She's so close. The lungs smell different now that she's here. Better.

Oh, that's good.

If I move my foot, I could touch her.

—*Don't do it, pervert. You're enough of a perv doing this now.*

—*I'm not going to touch her, I'm just thinking. It's a good thought. My foot along that silky thigh.*

Oh, I'd better slow. I'm gonna bark out if I'm not careful.

I slow a bit, but the tension is getting too much to hold.

"What you do?" Liesl asks.

—*FUCK!*

"I—I'm uh, it's—"

There's a long silence and then she whispers, "I know what do, Brian."

—*Fuck, she used my name. I'm gonna burst just from that. Keep still!*

I stutter, keeping my hand still. "I—thought you were asleep."

"No can sleep in whale easy."

"Actually, this helps. It helps me get to sleep."

—*That's great, Brian. You're doing it for medicinal purposes. Purely a sleep device, eh?*

A fucking long silence. My woody waits.

"It's not my fault," I say. "It's not like I can go somewhere and close the door. I'm nineteen. I can't help it."

—*You're grossing her out, Bri. Girls hate this—*

"I do sometimes," Liesl says quietly.

Johnson leaps in my hand. Good thing our blue Wrigglers are dim.

Home's heart is beating slow. Mine is racing.

—*What should I say to that?!*

Liesl whispers, "Can I do with you?"

—*WHAT? What does she mean? Like, on me, or—"With me?" I don't know what Norwegian girls are like. What if they aren't like American girls, not that I know what they're like—*

"At same time. You touch you, and I touch I. Maybe no light—"

She doesn't even finish her sentence and I've emptied the bag of Wrigglers out the flap and we're in darkness. Moist, warm darkness. I move my hand again. Got to go slow.

I can hear her shifting and her breathing changes.

I inhale hard and ask, "Can—can I—do that—what you're doing —for you?"

—*Damn, Brian! I can't believe you said that! You've fucking got balls! She's gonna kick you outta these lungs, but you got some grande cojones!*

She doesn't answer. She's mad. Offended—

Fingers touch my elbow and move down to my hand, lifting it and guiding it to a tangle of hair and a hot, hot, place. My god. I've never—

I shift so I can reach her easier and she's up against me so warm and slippery and slides my finger to some spot, moves my hand until I must be doing it right because she lets go of my hand and I feel her back arching. My Johnson is throbbing and wants everything but I'm so fucking happy to be doing this and she's making kitteny sounds and I speed up and slide my finger on that spot and she's breathing like she's crying only she's whispering something in a different language and it sounds good and I circle that spot and she shakes and presses my hand down to stop it and all of her is pulsing. Throbbing from inside. Her leg goes sliding over me, and her arm moves down and finds Johnson about to pierce the lung ceiling and she strokes it gently and I'm not here but in some place of dark sensation, of urgency and agony and need and want and her hand and skin and everything glows white behind my closed eyes and its GONE—and Gone—and gone.

Holy Mackerel.

"Liesl," I whisper. "Liesl."

She moves away and I think I must have done something wrong but she's fumbling with something and now she's back and something round is in my hand. My fingers explore and it's got a wrapper and I smile and put the peppermint in my mouth, shocked at the colors it sets off in my brain. I roll it all over my tongue and breathe in to get that cool air and it's magical and wonderful and this is *definitely* the best day ever.

Liesl curls her head on my shoulder and my arm moves 'round her, protective and embracing, and it feels like all those movies are happening to me. I'm not watching anymore. I'm doing.

—· NIGHT SKY DANCING —

CURRENTS SWIRL about the whale. For now, the voices inside have gone quiet. The great beast rises and breathes in cool air. It shifts sideways, lifting an eye out of the water. The night sky is vibrant as green curtains of light slowly dance above. The shifting hues and movements create a symphony without sound. The whale watches, knowing beauty when it sees it. But maybe there is more. Maybe this is a sign. Maybe the sickness deep inside will pass and breathing will be easier. Hope rises in Home.

—- THE BOAT —-

WE ARRIVE SOMEWHERE and Gjesken parks. I keep my eyes closed so she won't ask me to do anything. The inside of the car lights as Gjesken steps out. She shuts the door quietly like she doesn't want to wake me, and disappears into thick fog as the overhead lights slowly dim. It's annoying when people are considerate. Makes me feel like they expect the same from me and that makes me want to be bad.

The windows are wet inside. It must be really cold outside. I want to stay curled up under Gjesken's wool blanket, warm in the comfort of her car. I wonder if this little car is the size of the whale's lungs. It would be very close quarters with two people. I hope Gjesken's daughter isn't ridiculing Brian. He doesn't have a way with girls.

—You don't know him anymore. He made a plan, remember? He sounded good on the phone.

I should call him. Maybe I'll get through. I'll call now so I don't have to figure out that football satellite thing. Maybe the whale came close to shore and is right out there in the fog.

Gjesken's purse is beside me on the seat. I unzip it. Is this stealing? Not if it's borrowing. I'm borrowing her phone. I could open the car door for the overhead light, but then I would be seen.

—When you're sneaking into someone's purse and don't want to be seen, it's not borrowing.

—I don't want to open the door so the cold air doesn't come in.

My fingers move through her purse, feeling familiar and unfamiliar objects. There's the slab of a phone. I pull it out and touch

190

the button and—of course it's in Norwegian. At least there is a little head and shoulders icon for contacts. There's Liesl.

The phone rings. Please, answer! Please!

A incomprehensible recording answers in a perky girl voice. Fuck!

Cold air floods in as Gjesken opens the door. "Are you calling them?"

"I thought I should try. We haven't tried in a while."

"Without me? You don't think I want to talk to my daughter? What if you got them and you get to talk and I don't."

"I'm sorry. I'll let you know next time."

"No next time. We can't call whenever we want. They can't waste the battery talking to their mothers. We need it to find them! You know that!"

"I said I was sorry!"

—You sound like Brian.

—With good reason. She doesn't have to treat me like a child.

—You don't have to act like one.

—I'm under stress. Get off my back.

I dump the phone back into Gjesken's purse and step out of the car, about to slam the door—HOLY SHIT! Cold smacks every bit of my exposed skin. This is cold-cold, not Los Angeles air-conditioner cold. This is holy-shit cold. This is penetrating, painful, sea-smelling cold.

A figure emerges from the darkness and lumbers toward us. The open car door doesn't put out enough light to show his face. He extends a hand and growls something in Norwegian.

I shake his offered hand. It feels like tree bark. "Hello. I'm Ann," I say, assuming he'll understand enough English to get that.

The man grunts and moves to the trunk. Gjesken leans toward me. She'll criticize me for something. Did I introduce myself wrong?

"That's Torsten. He's not much of a talker."

Torsten. How am I going to remember that name? Tor— Tourniquet, Torn, Torque. Rhymes with—go through the letters— borsten, corsten, dorsten, forsten,—this isn't going to work. Thor. The god Thor without the H. Tor. Tor is a ten. I didn't get a good look but I bet he's not a ten. He *has* ten. Ten what? Ten fingers. Tor's ten fingers. Tor's ten.

While I'm creating a memory device, the ten-fingers-guy lifts almost all the luggage and provisions we took several trips to load.

Gjesken and I pick up the remaining supplies and follow his foggy form. I can't see anything beyond him. I hope Torsten knows where he's going.

The clomping of boots on ground gives way to the clomping of boots on wood. We're unstable now. On an undulating walkway. If I'm not careful, I may take a long walk off a short pier. Ha-ha. The waves shush me.

Torsten disappears in the fog. I stop, listening for a splash. Maybe he's waiting for me to pass and then a little shove and—

A *scream* to my right and something WHOOSHES past my face. What the hell!? I stumble backwards, heart doing a somersault, and bash into Gjesken.

"Seabird," she says, using a tone she must habitually use on her daughter.

Unable to see, I raise the phone in its waterproof case and turn on the flashlight. It only makes the clear plastic surrounding it glow. Nothing else. Maybe if I take it out—

AH! I stumble on a ragged plank and fall, landing hard on my knees and undoubtedly getting who-knows-what-foreign-disease from splinters. This is why people don't leave home. At least I didn't remove my phone from the dorky case. It would be underwater now.

Back on my feet, I pause to get my bearings. Where is everyone?

Several yards ahead, a lantern comes on, illuminating the edge of what must be the boat at the end of the pier. I step toward the light. At the boat, Torsten relieves us of our supplies and steps onboard, then holds out his calloused palm. Gjesken takes his hand and is pulled across a dark gap onto the boat. I hesitate. I have a bad feeling about this. What am I doing here? I don't do boats. I'm not one for ocean voyages. I'm not one for *any* voyages! What am I doing in Norway about to get on a ship with two strangers? Who are they? Anyone can find out that the Kickstarter campaign brought in a lot of money. What if this is a kidnapping? The panic rises in me. I have to turn around and run back, but what if I trip again and fall into the sea?

"Give!" Torsten yells and he reaches across the black gap and his rough hand finds mine and pulls me onto the boat. "Welcome this Nord Spyd."

My heart is jumping about like crazy. What does Nord Spyd mean? North something. North Spy? We're near Russia. Maybe this is a spy boat and we'll get torpedoed by the counter spies. Probably wouldn't have spy in the name if it was. But still, I'm not going to ask Torsten if he's a spy.

Gjesken pulls me away from the edge. "We'll stay well back so he can do his work."

Who is she? Is she an accomplice? How did she get this man and his boat?

The fog glows. Shimmering wisps curl around the edge of the deck. Dawn is coming. My phone says 6:45.

"Dawn is so late."

Gjesken laughs. "You forget where you are. The top of the world. In winter, we only have a few hours of daylight. Night is most of the day. If we go farther north, the sun won't ever get up over the horizon."

—*I want to go home!*

Torsten lifts the ropes holding us to the pier and heads to the captain's cabin or whatever they call the glass-enclosed control room in the middle of the boat. Helm? Bridge? Lights click on all around us. The ship is big and definitely not for pleasure cruising. No benches. No chairs. I turn on the camera on my phone. If Gjesken stops me from filming, I'll know she is part of the kidnap plan.

She doesn't stop me but carries luggage downstairs. I'll keep filming so I won't get trapped below.

Through the lifting fog, I pan across ropes, buoys, hoses, nets, and poles ending with long barbed spears. Maybe this is a fishing or shrimping boat. As the haze rises, shapes loom overhead. Move the phone up to shoot a massive winch or crane built to lift something large. For hauling in nets? The spot where I was pulled aboard has no railing. It's open, probably to make it easier to pull in the catch.

As the sun inches toward making an appearance, the boat becomes clearer. It's old, made of wood, not metal or fiberglass. Blue and green paint peels along the rails and curved walls. Brownish-red stains the crevices and cracks. Blood?

I move beside the central cabin and turn my phone to film inside the little windowed room where Torsten hunches over dials and instruments, clicking switches. Dim light bounces up from the screens to glow on his face. He's got a bristly salt-and-pepper beard, the prerequisite fisherman sweater and cap, and a face lined by weather more than age. If I googled Scandinavian sea-captain, I'd get his picture.

I move past that cabin-room to the front of the boat. The slippery deck rises, sides converging to a point. At the tip, I film a large object wrapped in canvas with over-sized bolts anchoring it to the floor. Radar?

The engine coughs and sputters to life and we push the waves out of the way, moving into the endless sea. The view on the phone screen looks like the opening of a horror movie. A shiver of dread runs through me. Quickly turn off the camera to hide the scene.

I step again toward the cabin. Torsten, leaning over the controls, looks up and—*I want to get off this boat.* His eyes are like the evil characters in the video games Brian plays. Black, cold, and emotionless. Eyes of a killer.

— ON YOUR MARK, MARK —

SMOKE RISES from the toaster in the small knotty-pine cabin. Pinocchio lifts his scraggly head to sniff the air, as Jenny, eyes shackled to the cartoons on the TV, yells, "DADDY, my waffle's burning! I can't eat it burnt."

At the bathroom sink, Mark pops the last half-pill of Clozapine and swallows it with a slug of beer. If only Doc had come through.

You'll be okay. Didn't need those meds anyway. Beer will do the same thing.

Scratch off the prescription label and toss the orange bottle in the trash. Mark looks at his shaking hand and glares at the man in the mirror.

"Don't you fall apart on me."

"Daddy!"

Mark chugs the beer, puts on a smile, and steps out of the bathroom.

The smoking toaster dings and blackened waffles pop up. *Damn kid couldn't break away from the TV to take care of this?*

"I don't eat burned things, Daddy. Those are yours."

Mark stares at the back of Jenny's head. Cartoon voices scream from the television. Or is that his mind? The buried volcano inside him rumbles. *Remember HALT. Hungry, Angry, Lonely, Tired. Got at least three out of four. Don't act on it. Let that half-pill kick in.* Mark pushes down the rage and tosses the burnt waffles to Pinocchio. The dog sniffs and turns away.

Round two. Last of the waffles in the toaster, turn the dial to low. He'll stand by and keep watch. Breathe in, exhale slow.

"Make sure there aren't any burnt parts!" Jenny adds, her back still to him.

How did Jenny end up such a little snot? She would have been better behaved if he'd been around. He could have taught her manners and discipline and—

Ding! The waffles pop up. Mark brings the breakfast to Jenny with two of the little syrup boxes he swiped from that diner in Vancouver. One of the perks of traveling. Ketchup, mayo, mustard, syrup, jam, cream, saltines. They're stocked up. Even if they run out of the cash that lady sent, they won't starve.

Mark sits behind Jenny so he won't have to watch her eat. The little pink mouth open with mangled waffle churning in it would be the last straw. His fist hurts. It's been clenched for a while. Stretch the fingers. Think of something good. Maybe he can find a job nearby. This is the kind of place to get lost in. Get a job on a pipeline. Clear roads of snow. That would be in demand for sure.

An ad comes on the TV and Jenny turns to him. "When are we going home, Daddy?"

Her eyes look like Beverly's. Accusatory.

Deep breath. "Don't you like our trip, sweetie? We're on a big adventure."

"I miss Mommy. When will she get well?"

Beer bile rises to the back of Mark's throat. He hates that this girl keeps bringing up his lie about Beverly. "Later. We have to be patient. You know what patient means?"

"Patient means not getting what you want!" Jenny snarls. She gives the second waffle to the dog and holds up her dirty plate to Mark. "Bring me milk."

Mark runs through the responses in his head. None of them sound fatherly. He swallows his answers and stands to fulfill her command. Steps past Jenny's precious message-in-the-bottle items on the counter. *I should take that dollar back. See how she likes it. I can be a brat, too.*

Grabbing the milk, he glances out the window. That guy who saw them last night is talking with the manager, gesturing toward Mark's cabin. Maybe he saw the AMBER Alert and put two-and-two together. The volcano in Mark's chest sends up a plume of something to crimp his throat.

"We'll get milk on the road, Jenny. Time to pack."

Mark kicks into high gear, stuffing clothes in suitcases, clearing bathroom of Dopp kit, Jenny's toothbrush, little soaps, towels, dumping food and beers into bags and the cooler, grabbing the stuffed wolf, beaded belt, and moose antler hat, scooping up Pinocchio's bowl, shutting off the TV. He sets everything by the door and looks around. The sink is full of dirty dishes. Counter a mess of garbage. Newspapers all over. Beer bottles. Will that attract attention? Fuck it, there's no time to clean.

"Sweetie, let's play a game. Let's see how fast we can move."

Mark helps Jenny zip up her sweater, puts the leash on the dog, and pauses by the door.

"What are we waiting for, Daddy?"

"It's like when people wait at the starting line of a race. They wait and then get ready and they…"

Jenny grins. "Onyrmark-Getset-Go!"

"That's right. We're gonna go out on *GO*. You take Pinocchio and hop in the car and I'll load the trunk and we'll be off! Think you can do it?"

Jenny grabs the leash and stands ready.

Peeking out the window, Mark holds up a finger for *WAIT*. When the man by the office walks by and enters his own cabin, Mark loads up with suitcases, coolers, and tote bags, gets the trunk key ready, and whispers, "You say it and open the door."

"Onyrmark.... Getset.... Go!"

Jenny yanks the door wide and races out with Pinocchio. Mark opens the trunk, kid and dog hop in car, everything loaded, SLAM— and slide behind wheel and key and engine starts and drive scattering gravel as they swerve around the cabin and race up toward the paved road. In the rearview mirror, the man and the manager both run behind, waving for them to stop. Good thing he threw mud on the license plate. The manager will probably call the police.

"I beat you, Daddy," Jenny teases.

Mark grips the wheel, shaking with adrenalin, pulls onto Alaska Route 1 and, in the mirror, the Glacier View Cabins slowly recede.

"You packed my presents and the message-in-the-bottle from the boy in the whale?"

Fuck. He left the bottle and library card and dollar. It looked like garbage. Oh well.

"Pretty sure I did, Jenny."

—- I KNOW MORE THAN TORSTEN —-

THE FOG IS GONE and sun glints off everything: the railing, the deck, the waves, the coastline. The cliffs and islands are beautiful. Small colorful houses dot the shore. This may be the most beautiful place I've ever been. And if not for Brian, I'd never have come here. Norway wasn't on my radar. Of course, neither was anywhere else.

After a while, there's nothing but sea. No land. No gulls. Nothing but monotonous grey waves. It's breezy, and even with a blanket around me, I'm cold. But I don't want to go down below into the eating/sleeping area that I haven't even seen yet. I want to keep watch. Maybe the whale will rise and I'll yell something. *Brian, your Mom's here!*

Seems like the sea is getting choppier. I move to the railing to look down at the heaving swells. A wave hits, sending up a splash of spray. It's freezing!

Behind me, a gravely voice says something. I swivel. Torsten continues growling something I can't understand so I give him the international *I don't know what the hell you're talking about* palms up shrug.

"Come bridge," he says, nodding me to the control-room-cabin. I guess I should call it the bridge.

Inside, Gjesken stands over a large nautical map. I move beside her and Torsten leans past me to point at a spot in the vast blue. His arm brushes mine. Was that on purpose? Is he hitting on me? He doesn't have a wedding ring. Do Norwegian men wear them?

I glance at his mouth. A clenched line of lip surrounded by roughly clipped beard. Porcupine quills. That'd hurt to kiss.

—*What are you thinking? Are you starved for affection?*

—*You know the answer to that.*

I've not been a wife, a lover, a friend, a woman, a student, a worker—anything—for a long time. I've been nothing but a mother.

The porcupine quills move. Did he say something? I play it back in my head: "See?"

I nod at his finger on the map. "That's where we are?"

Gjesken corrects me. "Where Liesl's phone was when the police tracked it."

Torsten points to a place below the phone spot. "Nord Spyd. Boat us." He points to an area above both spots. "Whale." The points are several inches apart. How far that is, I don't know. He moves the boat finger across the map to the whale finger. "High five."

His hand isn't up to slap mine. He doesn't even know what high five means and he's going to find this whale?

Trying to remain calm, I ask, "How does he know that's where the whale is?"

Gjesken explains how Torsten guessed based on where and when Liesl was swallowed, where and when the call was tracked, calculating speed and direction, patterns of migration—

I interrupt her, "But what if he's wrong?"

"Ann, we need to leave it to him. He's a professional."

"Professionals can be wrong. I've met lots of them."

Torsten turns to me slowly. "I wrong, you make funeral."

Is it too early in this trip to tell him to go fuck himself?

—*You've had no sleep, you're stressed, your son's in a whale with a girl. Yes, it is too early to tell him to go fuck himself.*

I jab the map with my finger so I don't jab him. "We need to get a new reading on the phone. We need to call those kids and get a reading. We can't go on hunches about patterns of migration—"

"Torsten knows all about whale migration—"

"So do I!" I say

—*What are you, twelve?*

—*Now's not the time.*

—*Put on the mature voice.*

I put on the mature voice. "I know about Cetacean behavior, echolocation, physiognomy—including that a whale *shouldn't* have an epiglottis but this one does—social structures, diet, and MIGRATION. I know that normally a whale off the coast of California does *not* go up around Alaska's Bering strait, skirt the shrinking Arctic ice along the top of Canada or Russia, and end up in the Norway Sea. It's *never* done. But the thing is, this isn't a normal whale! This whale doesn't follow migration rules! So, I don't care what kind of professional you are, Thor-silent-whatever, we need to call our kids and get a new fucking reading for their location!"

Torsten's cold eyes fill with anger and he hisses something that doesn't need translation.

I do my own killer-eyes. "Yeah? Well, same to you."

Gjesken pulls me out of the cabin. "Let's go downstairs."

I clomp loudly on the narrow, slippery stairs, trying to make sure Torsten knows I'm a force to be reckoned with.

Below deck, my heart races from my magnificent tirade upstairs, as we pinball our way along a dark, thin hallway. Gjesken, taller than me, has to scrunch to not hit the ceiling. She opens a small door, "Our bedroom, you and me," and steps in.

I follow. There's a bunk bed and one bare lightbulb. It's not a walk-in closet, it's a closet, and we're face-to-face with no space to move.

Gjesken takes a breath like she's a yoga instructor and I'm supposed to follow her lead. "Ann, you're upset. I'm upset. But we can't take it out on Torsten. We need him. You must show respect. "

"He must show me respect!" I yell, hoping it's loud enough to hear in the captain's cabin or—PARDON ME, THE BRIDGE.

Gjesken tilts her head. "You're acting like a child."

I bet she says this to her daughter with that same superior, patient demeanor. My revenge is to present her with an overly artificial smile, hopefully indicating that her diagnosis might be dangerously underestimating me.

Gjesken points that she wants me to move so she can leave. I back out of the closet and she marches down the hall, calmly reporting that she'll "be in the galley."

I'm certainly not going back on deck, and there is nothing to do in this closet, so I casually wander into said *galley*. Looks like a kitchen to me. A table in the center, cupboards, a rudimentary stove. Gjesken busily unpacks our provisions.

I can be busy, too. I pick up the heavy orange case and put it on the table. Set up my laptop beside it.

Opening the lid to the satellite "football," I read the guide. It's simple. Push the power button. Waiting the required 60 seconds, I turn on my laptop. The network connection is made instantly. The phone in its dorky waterproof case around my neck bings as well.

"What's Liesl's number?" I ask, as if everything's hunky-dory.

Gjesken doesn't look at me. "Liesl's phone won't be on."

"We need to call to get their current location. We'll use the internet to track them."

Gjesken crinkles her nose. "They won't have the phone on. They won't leave it on wasting the battery. We can only wait for them to call."

The crinkled-nose bitch is right. But I don't fucking care.

"What's Liesl's number?"

Gjesken relents and tells me the number a bit breathlessly. She's hiding her hope poorly. I get the first few numbers in but it's hard to dial through the thick waterproof plastic.

"Easier if you take the phone from that ugly package," Gjesken suggests. She's got an idea for everything.

"This is what people wear in California. It's the latest fashion." That shuts her up, except I forgot the number and have to ask again.

I dial through the clear plastic as if it's natural. Hold it to my ear, trying to look California-chic. It smells like fresh rubber.

The ringing is muffled. I should take the phone out of this so I can hear.

"Put it on speaker," Gjesken says, waving her hands at me.

I do, just as Liesl's voicemail comes on.

Gjesken immediately cries hearing her daughter's voice.

—*This lady's really pissing me off.*

—*She's missing her daughter.*

—*Brian was swallowed way before her daughter was. I'm the one who's suffered. I'm the one in pain.*

The voicemail girl stops jabbering and a tone beeps.

"Hi Liesl, this is Ann, Brian's mom—"

Gjesken yells over me with desperate Norwegian chatter.

I get louder. "Tell Brian I'm in the Norwegian Sea and I'm going to find him—find you both."

Gjesken won't stop yelling her gobbledygook so I switch the phone off speaker and turn my back to her. "Tell him to call anytime. I want to hear from him. Tell Brian I love him and—"

Gjesken pulls the phone from my hand, the cord yanking my neck. She bends to it, whispering tearful words—

"GIVE ME MY PHONE!" I scream, pulling on the cord.

"Let me talk!"

We struggle, tug-o'-waring.

"It's my phone, you bitch!" I yell, yanking hard.

The cord breaks and we both jerk backwards. I've got the cord. She's got the phone. The hangup beep is audible. Fuck. Did that fight get recorded? If Brian hears that, he won't want to be found. It'll remind him of what he escaped from. Shit!

Gjesken hands me my phone, turning away.

I stare at the cord. The ends are frayed where it ripped.

—*This was sent by my brother and she destroyed it!*

—*Oh, please.*

Gjesken has her back to me, her shoulders shaking. Crying again.

—*She broke my fucking phone thing.*

—*You going to act like a jerk the whole trip? Say you're sorry.*

—*I'm not saying I'm sorry. She started it.*

—*Just say something.*

The waves rock the boat. The swishing mingles with Gjesken's sniffling.

"Shall we make lunch?" I offer, trying to sound friendly.

Gjesken doesn't look up but puts a knife and two onions on the table. I see her plan. She wants me crying.

—- NATE, ALASKA STATE TROOPER —-

ACROSS THE WORLD, up over the North Pole, around the Bering Strait, down in Homer Alaska, the manager of the Glacier View Cabins dials his phone.

When the State Trooper arrives, the manager greets him with *Dzaanh nezoonh*, recognizing a fellow Koyukon Alaska Native. Not part of the elder generation, neither man can speak more than a few words of Athabaskan, their ancestral tongue.

The manager tells of what he suspects about the man and girl, the car's description, last known direction, and—"I started cleaning the mess and found this." He gives the trooper the message-in-the-bottle with the pin-pricked dollar.

The trooper dials the number on the bill.

A woman's voice answers.

Nate puts on his official voice. "This is Nate Pike, Alaska State Trooper. Who am I speaking with?"

"It's Ann Ketchum."

"I'm calling about something I found. Your number pricked on a dollar."

"Yes, I know what you're talking about. My son sent that. You have it?"

"The manager of the Glacier View Cabins found it and called me. A man and his daughter were staying here but they skipped out."

"Please, Officer, you have the bottle and library card? I need those. My son—"

The woman sounds desperate. Nate slips into his calm voice.

"I'm only calling because I think the man might be the one from that AMBER Alert."

There's a pause on the line. Nate waits.

"He took a child?" the woman asks.

"It's been in the news." Nate explains, but it comes out annoyed. *Don't people pay attention to anything?*

"Sorry, I've been away, haven't seen the news."

Nate feels his distant memory-fear rise as he tells the woman about the eight-year-old girl, Jenny, and the man who absconded with her. He tells of Jenny's mother, Beverly, and her pleas for the girl's return. Nate knows the tone in his voice is wrong. He's taking it too personally.

"I don't know about this, I'm sorry," the woman says.

"I'm sorry if I sounded—perturbed. Didn't mean to spread that on you."

"That's okay. I spread things on people all the time."

This makes Nate laugh and the feelings from his past dissolve. "Thanks for that—" He looks down at the punctured dollar bill to get the name. "—Ms. Ketchum. Sorry, to bother you. I thought it might be a clue."

"Please, I need to have that message-in-the-bottle. It means everything to me. The man said he would send them to me but didn't."

"You talked with him?"

"And the girl. They called me."

Nate breathes out slow, his heart ballooning with hope. "Check your phone and give me the number he called from. If he uses that phone again, we'll track him and we'll catch him."

There's a rustling sound and the woman gives Nate the number.

A flood of excitement rushes over him. "I'm very grateful. You may help save this girl."

The voice on the line gets small. "Please. All I ask is that you send me the bottle, library card, and dollar. Please. If things don't work out, I'll really need them."

"I'll need to keep them for now, but I'll make sure they aren't disposed of. I've got to go. Thanks for your help." Nate hangs up. Keeping the dollar with the number is a no-brainer, but the other stuff—pointless.

He tosses them on the mess on the counter, looks through drawers, the fridge, side table, under the bed, checks the bathroom. Finds the empty prescription bottle in the trash. The label has been scratched away. No telling what it held.

"All yours. Thanks, brother." Waving at the manager, Nate steps out of the cabin to his cruiser.

—- LOST AGAIN —-

HAD BOTTLE A HEART, it would be sinking. Lying on top of the stained paper plates and empty syrup containers, it is discarded. Library Card lies inside, but without its traveling companion Punctured Dollar Bill.

The Glacier View Motel manager pulls the garbage bin inside the cabin and begins cleaning. Had Bottle emotions, it might feel despair. This is the end of the line. The leftover birthday cake lands in the trash first. The cereal boxes. Countless empty beers. The newspapers used to wrap presents. Takeout food containers. All thrown in the trash. Heaping on each other.

As the manager grasps Bottle, light spreads across the dark room from the opening door. The trooper is back. "Said I would, so I will," the man explains, holding out his hand. And Bottle is transferred from one person to another. Bottle and Library Card are re-united with Punctured Dollar Bill and slid into a clear evidence Ziploc. They lie on the front seat of the trooper's cruiser, gently rocking with the movement of the road. Had Bottle a voice, it might cheer, "Saved!"

— MISSING —

MARK DRIVES just a touch above the speed limit. He figures anyone in Alaska doing the speed limit has got to have done something wrong. They pass through the first traffic in weeks, slogging their way through Anchorage. Jenny's happy enough, singing songs Mark doesn't know or want to know.

North of the bridge over the Knik River, they split off onto Route 3 and pass through Wasilla and keep driving until there's nothing but endless road with pine tree sides. Radio can't pick up a thing. There'd better be a town somewhere with something to eat. A gas station up ahead. Who knows when the next one will be.

Mark peels off into the parking lot. "I'll gas up and you can go to the bathroom."

"Don't have to go."

"You better, Jenny. We don't know when the next stop will be."

"Don't have to."

Mark stops himself from saying more. "I'm going in. Stay in the car."

After putting a hundred-dollar bill down for fill-up, a bottle of milk, and a twelve-pack of beer, Mark steps out to the pumps.

Jenny's out of the car, messing with stuff in the back seat, but she's not visible from the mini-mart, so it's probably fine.

Mark gets the gas flowing. It's one of those damn nozzles that doesn't stay on, so he has to squeeze the handle tightly.

Now that they'll have gas and he's got beer, they can go for another long while. It's good to be far away from where they were gonna be caught, but the drive is really dull. Maybe he can drink a bit if he keeps the bottle hidden between his legs. He glances through

205

the car at Jenny. She's pawing through her backpack, shaking out the sleeping bag, dumping tote-bags of food onto the back seat. Let her make a mess if she wants to.

The girl moves to the driver's side and bends. The trunk pops open.

"What the hell, Jenny?"

"WHERE'S MY BOTTLE FROM THE WHALE BOY?"

Mark glances to see if anyone from the mart is watching. "Get back in the car."

"Not 'til I find my bottle present!"

She's bending into the trunk and, behind the open lid, Mark can't see what she's getting into.

There's a click.

"DO NOT TOUCH THAT!" Mark yells, slamming the gas nozzle back in its holder and darting to his daughter.

Jenny stands frozen, hands in his suitcase, her mouth quivering.

"Take your hands out slowly."

Jenny slides her hands from the suitcase. Mark WHAMS the trunk shut, lifts Jenny and tosses her into the back seat beside the cowering dog.

"Don't ever go in my things!"

He slams her door and stares at the gas pump readout. $37.16. Shit. Too dangerous to go back and get the change. He curses as he starts the engine and drives them back onto Route 3.

Don't look in the rear-view mirror. Don't do it. Damn. The girl is looking scared. Fuck.

"Jenny, we were in a hurry and your bottle was left behind."

"We can go back," Jenny whispers.

"No, we can't."

In the mirror, he sees she's trying not to cry.

"You've got to learn. Things people love, always disappear."

— LUNCH IDEA —

AS OUR NORWEGIAN LUNCH COOKS, I sew the cord back onto the waterproof phone case with thick fishing line. It will look more hobo chic than California chic, but it will never fall apart.

I finish just as Gjesken calls Torsten down to eat.

Over dark rye bread, potatoes, salad, and little meatballs, Gjesken talks with Torsten. Who knows what they're saying. Probably something about the crazy American bitch. I'm not sorry.

The phone call from that trooper was disturbing. An AMBER Alert. I had a creepy feeling about that guy wanting money for Brian's bottle. He sounded dangerous. Hopefully, his phone will be tracked. Why do children have to be taken?

Gjesken clears her throat and gives a little head shift toward Torsten. I suspect I'm supposed to say something.

"Torsten, I'm sorry. I didn't mean to be rude. Please accept my apology."

Torsten nods benevolent forgiveness. Gjesken blinks at me.

"And, you too, Gjesken. I'm sorry."

Gjesken crinkles her nose in approval. No wonder her husband's away on an oil platform. That nose crinkle would do it for me.

A roll of the ship sends little meatballs tumbling across my plate. I wait for them to reverse and try to stab one on the move. *Take that!* Damn! Missed it.

Torsten and Gjesken mumble in their cockamamy language.

The meatballs roll again. *I'll get you yet!* Stab. Miss.

Another swell, we tip, the meatballs roll, and I stab—*YES!*— impaled the sucker. Does Brian use a spear to get his food? No. He must pull food in by reaching out the whale's epiglottis. I pop the meatball in my mouth. Something is tickling my brain.

—*Brian is eating. That means something.*

My meatballs make another journey across my plate. I stare at them.

—*Brian's reaching out the flap and bringing food into the lungs.*

My meatballs roll again.

—Brian's bringing in whatever the whale swallows.

I point at my plate. "These don't have to be meatballs. They don't have to be food. They could be anything."

Torsten and Gjesken stare at me.

"I'm going to make a list. We'll need to have things delivered to this boat right away."

Gjesken and Torsten blink at me.

"Brian and Liesl are in the whale's lungs, which means there's an epiglottis. I don't care if it is a birth defect or a new species or an old throwback to the Ice Age. Our children are in the lungs of a whale because of that flap."

Torsten and Gjesken look at each other. They don't get it.

I hold up a meatball. "Whatever can travel down the whale's throat—can get pulled into the lungs. It doesn't have to be a meatball."

Torsten grunts. "Make list. But money big."

I shrug that money is no problem and he hurries up onto the deck.

"A list of what?" Gjesken asks.

"What we dump into the sea."

—- MORNING AFTER —-

LIESL'S HAIR is in my face. Her head is hurting my shoulder, but in a good way. I don't want to move. I want to keep this moment forever.

—Don't expect her to wake all lovey-dovey, Brian.

—She was into it. I didn't force her.

—Your wacking off embarrassed her. Why did you do that!? You couldn't wait?

—Wait 'til what? Getting rescued? Dying of old age?

—When she wakes up, she'll remember and jerk away.

—Maybe not. Maybe she likes me.

—Get ready to hide your head and stick to the edge of the lungs, outta her way.

Liesl groans and stretches against me. The predictable happens as her skin moves across mine. Luckily there are no glowers to light this pole.

Sitting up, Liesl is quiet. I want to see her face to know what she's thinking.

—*No you don't.*

"Everything okay?" I ask quietly.

"Except be in whale?" she answers.

I can't tell from her accent if she's sarcastic or not.

"Yeah, 'cept for being in a whale."

"Mmm," is her answer.

That's not much of an answer. It's not yes or no. She doesn't want to say yes but she's too kind to say no. She thinks she'll hurt my feelings. I'm used to that. I should let her know. We'll pretend it never happened. I can go back to being the schlub dork.

Liesl quietly asks, "You think I tøs now?"

"What?"

"Tøs—ludder—low, bad girl."

I want to hug her. She's scared of what I think! No one *ever* worries about what I think. "No. I don't think you're a Toss."

I put my arm around her and she relaxes a little, but seems like she's crying. Little kisses on her cheeks taste of salt, but then again, everything in here tastes of salt. Her neck tastes like salt. Her chin tastes like salt. Her lips. Her tongue. This is nowhere I've ever been. The dark moist pinkness, her tongue swimming alongside mine, diving and gliding, curling and sliding. We're doing a dance of whales in our mouths.

—- PLATFORM TROUBLES —-

THE WHALE GLIDES around the deep-sea oil platform. Sliding against the massive pipes, it tries to scrape off barnacles. An alarm sounds up above. Rising slowly to the surface, spraying out for breath, it hears shouts from the platform and a sharp crack. The whale turns, eye rising above the waves. Another crack and a bullet

209

stings the massive jaw. Submerging, the whale slaps the water with its tail. More gunshots, and the whale dives, small rivulets of red trailing behind.

—- LETTER WRITING —-

WE THOUGHT to bring the laptop and the "football" satellite internet thing, but we didn't think of bringing a printer or paper. And didn't think to put these on the list of items to be delivered. Now we're ripping up one of Torsten's nautical maps into fifty little pieces. He's not happy.

Put my pen to the scrap of paper. When was the last time I hand-wrote anything? With online shopping and bill-paying, I don't write checks or lists. Oh, I did do two lists. One all about giving up and Goodwill. One was a worthy quest plan on that beige wall. I wonder what I could cross off now.

—*Number 1: Find Brian.*

—*Incomplete.*

—*Talk to an expert.*

—*Now I am one.*

"I'm not writing in English," Gjesken states emphatically. "Not twenty-five of them."

—*Hire a boat.*

—*Check.*

"Ann, are you listening?" Gjesken stares at me. "If it's one of mine swallowed, Liesl will translate it to Brian. English will be too slow for me."

"Fine. I'll do twenty-five in English, you do twenty-five in Norwegian and we'll both sign all fifty, okay?"

Gjesken doesn't answer. She's already writing.

I get to writing super fast. I want to beat her. I'll finish my twenty-five before she does.

She pushes her first one aside. I've still got another sentence to go. Damn!

I finish one and start the next. My handwriting is worse as I ramp up the speed. Gjesken writes like she's a secretary doing shorthand. How can she write so fast? She's probably cheating. She's probably cutting several sentences. I'm not going to cheat. I'm not going to cut one sentence and I'll still win. Oops, that word's illegible, but I can't correct it or Gjesken's going to know. Ow! My hand is cramping!

—- REMOTE MARKET —-

TWO HUNDRED MILES north on Alaska Route 3, as he pulls into a gas station lot, Mark wonders at the chance of making a duplicate message-in-the-bottle. Not only could he make one for Jenny and she might speak to him again, but he could make another to get more cash from that lady. He could buy a coke bottle and poke holes in a dollar bill. Jenny might remember the words, the number is still on his phone, but the Los Angeles Library Card is another matter. He doesn't know anyone in LA.

"You must be hungry, eh, Jenny? I'll get you some chips."

Mark knows he shouldn't keep letting Jenny have chips and cookies and chocolate milk and soda, but it keeps her from screaming. *I have no idea how Beverly managed on her own.* She'd smirk at him if she was here. *Of course* he had no idea. Beverly said as much, "You don't even know how to pack her school lunch or wash her clothes."

Come to think of it, he hasn't washed their clothes once yet.

What made him want to do this anyway? He'd only been discharged and home for a few weeks. Now he's hiding in Alaska, running from the law, AMBER Alerts all across the country. It might have worked if Jenny was a baby, but this demanding creature is a pain in the ass. And what was he thinking bringing the dog!?

"Take Pinocchio out to do pee-pee and I'll get you snacks."

"Nobody says pee-pee except to babies."

She's speaking again!

"Then take him out to do do-do."

211

Jenny tries not to smile. He's got her.

"Pinocchio can wait. I have to go badly."

Mark can't go into the market with Jenny. Man and girl. It's too obvious. He's got to get her to go in later, after he's bought everything.

"Jenny, Pinocchio can't complain like you do. You're going to make him sit while you take your time? He may have to go *really* badly."

"I have to go really, *really* badly."

"He may have to go really, really, *really* badly."

Jenny reluctantly gets out of the car holding the leash. Pinocchio bounds toward a strip of grass, dragging the girl after him. She laughs, "He has to go really, really, really, *really* badly!"

Mark watches her run. He does feel something for her. This trip may be making that feeling grow, but also shrink. Being a parent is hard.

Pinocchio pulls Jenny to the grassy area where he pees and she reads the historic marker sign: *Getting the Gold.* All about the different methods of obtaining that precious metal.

Inside the station market, Mark picks up a coke bottle that matches the one from the ocean. It's not as cloudy and scratched, but maybe there's something he can do to make it look like it's been in the water for a while. He could drag it behind the car from a string, letting it bounce and tumble on asphalt, but that might call attention to them.

Animal crackers. Oreos. Potato chips. Chocolate milk. And a twelve-pack for him. Should add something healthy. String cheese and beef jerky.

Mark scans the front pages of the papers. *Car Crash kills Seven, Domestic Abuse Sparks Condo Fire. Early Cold Snap Freezes Drunk. Bear Mauls Hiker.* The rest is about wars and the usual disasters. He grabs the only non-local paper—USA Today. It's the most likely candidate for news of a kidnapped girl. Scanning the paper, he finds them in the Missouri section. *Missing girl taken by father. Traveling with large dog.* That does it. Pinocchio can't stay with them.

Mark notices the Alaska Native clerk watching him from behind the counter. The man keeps glancing at the portable television by the register. Don't know what's on that TV but the way the man is looking at him, it might be the AMBER Alert. Maybe a picture of him and Jenny and that damn dog on the screen right now.

He can't run now or it'll be obvious. Mark's heart does jumping-jacks as he sets the items on the counter and smiles wide. The picture on the AMBER Alert was his mug shot. He had that dazed look. A smile will make him look different.

Mark's face stiffens as the man rings the groceries with no reciprocal smile. Does it mean he knows? Pay with the cash. The Eskimo man says nothing when Mark exits. Hopefully, the drama of white people holds no interest for him.

Mark carries the groceries to the car. "Hurry, get in the car, Jenny."

"My turn to pee." Jenny hand the leash to Mark and runs into the market.

What if the Eskimo man talks to her? What if he asks her name? What if she tells him?

Mark pops the trunk and reaches into his suitcase. Should he take the gun out now? Should he have it handy, just in case? What if the man tries to stop Jenny from coming back to the car?

Mark tucks the gun into his pants behind his back.

First things first. Get rid of the dog, Mark.

Keeping an eye on the front door, Mark removes the tag from the dog's collar and slips it in his pocket.

He leads Pinocchio to the rear of the market and ties him to the propane tank.

Damn it, Jenny's going to be furious. She won't forgive me. But the dog is so recognizable. I've got to leave him.

"Sorry, Pinocchio. Stay here. Give me a few minutes and you can start barking. No, give me half an hour, okay?"

The dog cocks his head.

Mark scratches Pinocchio behind the ears and backs away.

Around to the front of the building. Now the moment of truth. Will the clerk try to stop him?

Mark takes a deep breath and steps into the store. The clerk looks up from behind the counter. No sign of Jenny. Mark forces himself to smile wide again and taps on the woman's room door. "Sweetie, hurry. Pinocchio saw a deer and took off and we need to go find him."

Jenny is out instantly and they both race to the car. "Which way did he go, Daddy?"

Mark points north, where the forest skirts the road. A perfect place to lose a dog. "Buckle up."

As he pulls the car out of the lot, Mark glances in the rear-view mirror. The clerk stands in the market doorway, watching them leave.

Jenny's eyes are wide, scanning the trees that whip past by the side of the road. "We're going too fast. Pinocchio can't run that fast."

"You didn't see him. That deer was racing and he was right behind it."

Jenny screams her ear-piercer. Mark better do something to make it look like he cares. He swerves the car onto a dirt road leading into the forest and turns off the motor.

"Let's call for Pinocchio."

They step out of the car and, scanning the dense trees, Jenny calls and Mark calls.

Boo-hoo, no luck.

Jenny's crying. Mark knows it's his fault but there was no choice.

"We need to go back to that market, Daddy. He may be looking for us."

"Honey, Pinocchio's in a strange place. He won't be able to make his way back. But he has his tag. Someone will find him and call and he'll be okay."

Mark puts an arm around her tiny shoulders and leads her to the car. While she buckles herself in, he returns the gun to his suitcase, then back down the dirt road to the highway and head north.

Jenny keeps her face against the window, crying as she watches trees swish past. Mark stares at the line of asphalt stretching off to a single point.

I'm turning into quite a bad man.

—- FIRST TIME —-

THE DANCE OF THE WHALES in our mouths is blowing my mind. I never knew kissing was such an incredible thing. It's like sparklers going off all over my brain and body.

I feel her move. It seems like she's pulling her T-shirt off. She keeps moving, so that must be her bra. I bet I'm turning red. Unless I'm pale because all the blood has gone to my woody.

—Do something! She's inviting you!

In darkness, I move a hand up—reaching out—Skin! That's her waist, I think. Slide up slowly. Slide over her slipperiness—okay, her ribs—slide toward her breast—

She stops me.

—Stupid. She doesn't want to—

"I no to get baby inside. You have something?"

—Oh my god! Does that mean she's—She's saying she's willing! This is going to happen!

I do a silent scream in the darkness and, trying to sound suave, I reply, "Yes, as a matter of fact, I do."

Collect fresh Wrigglers for the Ziploc. When their blue light shines over us, I sneak a peek at her. SHE'S GOT NO CLOTHES ON! I can't pull my eyes away.

Liesl smiles shyly and whispers, "You have something?"

Do I ever!

It's difficult to get the condom full of Toke's weed from my shorts pocket with the woody taking up so much space, but I finally manage.

"What in that?"

"Pot. Marijuana. I thought I should keep it, in case. Who knows, it might come in handy. Can you put it in your purse?"

She unfolds what looks like a takeout menu and makes a little origami container and I dump the weed inside.

Liesl zips up her purse and looks away. She's probably changed her mind. The moment is gone.

"You believe that item be safe?" she asks shyly.

I blow into the condom and fill it like a little balloon. Clamp tight the end and give the middle a squeeze. No deflation or hissing air. "It's safe," I say, slipping it on like I'm a pro.

"I do the sex only two time, Brian. I no special good do it."

"I'm not an expert either."

Liesl lies back. In the blue glow of the wriggler light, her eyes look wide and scared. Mine probably do, too. My heart is pounding so much it feels like it might give out. Don't give out before I do this, please!

—*You're supposed to move in now, Bri. Do it right or she'll know. We've all seen how it looks in the movies*—

—*I can't have you talking through*—

—*Dude, you've never done this. You gonna wing it?*

—*You're going to have to shut up now.*

—*Screw it up and*—

—*I'm kicking you out of this party.*

"Liesl," I mumble. "I—uh,—this is my first time—"

—*No! No! Don't tell her*—

"They always say it's like riding a bicycle, you never forget, but, when I was first learning to ride a bike, I fell down a lot. If this is like that—I may not be so good."

—*Shut up! You're blowing it!*

Liesl doesn't look like she's judging me or laughing at me.

"Brian, it hurt first time and I afraid it hurt again and I scared I not be make the sex noise or what-be. Maybe we makeup as do. Like you make up live in whale—you hold breath, sing whale song, grow plant, time watch, and sushi every day. I try be good at make up as you."

A massive joy spreads over me and fills every corner, pushing that voice down, down, far away.

I lie beside Liesl and our hands move over everything, skin leaping up to feel skin, lapping it up, and reaching for more. My hips do a slow dance against her side that I never learned. Turning to move over her, I move between her legs and can't really tell what is where. She reaches down and guides me. Pressing at the spot, with a slide, I'm there, and there is all-enveloping hot and swelling, surrounded, and in, and this becomes that and the same, and pulsing and sounds, heart red slippery beating pain of good and more good and the ache builds to our dance and red fills all rising over, almost over the top to get to the reason and we're there and there and there and there and sinking into the warm dark place of no need.

Parting only enough to breathe. Everything vibrating in tune.

Wow.

—*You did it, Bri!*

Wow.

Liesl pulls in a sharp breath, shaking. Is she crying? Was I that bad?

"Are you okay?" I whisper.

"Hmm."

Shit. I was bad.

Liesl shakes against me and since I'm still inside, I'm hard instantly and I want to do it again but don't know if I should, so I make a little move and she doesn't stop me and I press again. Oh my God, this feels so good! I could do this for the rest of—

"Vent," Liesl whispers in my ear.

Oh! Her voice and breath so close does something—oh! I press in and—

"Vent. That mean *Wait*. I—it hurt a little. I guess is normal but, vent."

I pull out and even though I'm sad, I'm happy at the same time. Bri did it! With a real live girl!

I can't think about anything else. I can't think of anything but being inside Liesl.

"Liesl, uh, was that okay for you?"

"Yes, okay. Was okay for you?"

I run through the incredible responses in my head. *Phenomenal. Mind-blowing. The best thing ever. When can we do it again?*... "Uh, yeah. It was cool. Better than cool. Great. Sorry if I hurt you."

Liesl sighs. "I guess be normal to it, the more you do."

—*Please, please, please...*

"I'm okay to do it anytime," I volunteer.

Liesl curls into my shoulder and I put my arms around her and pet her as she shakes.

Home sings a new song, one I've never heard before. This'll be our song.

—- HELICOPTER OVERHEAD —-

I REALIZE I haven't filmed very much and Arthur will be pissed. We're waiting for the supplies from my meatball idea, so better get to work. Film the bunk beds. My suitcase. The Football again. Stumble down the hall to the galley. The shot is shaky but I can always say it was a choppy sea. Pan around the cupboards, coffee pot. Up on deck. Torsten is fishing. I film him. Go to the bridge, film that. Film the sea. Film the sky. I've run out of subject matter. Hope that will do.

Phone put away in its case, Torsten waves me over. He hands me a fishing pole, helps me bait the hook, and casts the line into the waves. He catches my smile. "You face picture happy."

Happy? I feel around inside and find it's true. For the first time in years, I'm happy.

Torsten moves his head, gesturing to something far off. "Husman?"

Husband? Is that what he's asking? Is he asking because he's interested? What should I feel about that? Does he have a fling with every distraught mother that gets aboard his ship? Would I want a fling? I don't even know what a fling is anymore. "Divorced," I answer, watching his face for clues. "Split up." No clues yet.

"Husman pappa of boy in whale?"

I nod.

"Why no he on boat?"

Good question. "Dan doesn't believe Brian is alive. He doesn't think anyone can survive in a whale."

Torsten opens his mouth to say something but stops himself. Probably about to say he doesn't think Brian's alive either. Probably about to say I'm a fool for being out here. It's only the money that

218

keeps him from saying what he thinks. He wants me out here as long as I can pay for it. When the money runs out, *adios!* or however you say it in Norwegian.

"I don't care what everyone thinks. I can't sit home and cry. I know Brian's alive, so I have to try." I squint at the fishing line piercing the sea.

"Brave lady," Torsten says.

Brave? No one has ever called me brave before. Is he saying that to ridicule me?

"You adventurer. Brave," he says seriously, as if relaying something to go on my permanent record.

A flush spreads over me. Whoa. Adventurer. Brave. It feels good to have a compliment. Good enough to make those salt-pepper quills attract my attention again. How would they feel to kiss? Maybe I should have a fling—

Torsten shrugs. "Brave, even if fail."

The quills return to sharp pricks, probably dipped in arsenic. No way I'd kiss that. "We won't fail. We'll find that whale. We'll get them out."

"How get out?"

I don't know how the fuck we'll get them out! Luckily, a jolt hits the line and I reel in as fast as I can. It's a big, beautiful thrashing fish. Torsten nets it when I lift high enough. Grabbing the thick tail, he slams its head brutally against the deck. Blood spatters onto my coat and the waterproof phone case around my neck. I expect to feel horror but this isn't that. It's a surge of my adventurer spirit. Here I am, halfway around the world, getting splattered with blood while fishing in the Norwegian Sea. Since Brian got swallowed, I'm not the same person. I like this me better.

Down in the galley, Gjesken makes breakfast with the fish. We three sit silently, enjoying the delicious meal. Nothing could drag me away from this incredible food—except the sound of a helicopter.

We rush on deck. Here's a helicopter, over the Nord Spyd, in the Norwegian sea, all because of me! *I am an adventurer!* Whatever happens, however this ends, I have created an ENTIRELY NEW FUTURE from the beige one I was going to have.

I hold up the waterproof phone case and take a selfie with the helicopter behind my head. The wind whips my hair but nothing can hide this grin. It may look like shit, shot though the plastic, but I send it to Tobey and Arthur with a text: *See what your Kickstarter has wrought! Thank you!!!*

Torsten grabs the line lowered by the helicopter and two large duffle bags are fed down to his arms. A wave, the line retracts, and the helicopter roars off.

A text comes in from Arthur: *You getting on film, right?*

Shit. He's gonna kill me.

Below deck, Gjesken, Torsten, and I unpack the duffle bags. It's everything we requested.

"How soon 'til we reach the area, Torsten?" Gjesken asks, in English for my benefit.

"I make hour or small. We do put in sea and later in sea again, again. Each five minute. Again. Five minute moving with boat. Again. One be eaten, then High Five. You make with batteries and all much. No let drop in sea fast, only slow."

Gjesken puts the first battery in place and flicks the switch. The siren blasts, making us all jump. It's really loud. This might just work.

We prepare everything and bring the fifty packages on deck. Torsten uses the overhead winch to haul up a net from the waves. The ropes creak and groan, pulling the catch toward the open back of the boat. Inside boils a shimmering mass of flopping creatures. Bait.

The tying of live shrimp and squid and fish is much harder than I expected. I kill the first dozen I try to knot a line to. Sorry, fellas.

The boat slows. Torsten yells that we're over the spot he's predicted the whale would be near. "Set computer for tracker. Call phone for where Liesl be new time."

I rush to get the orange football and look like a real pro turning it on. Wi-Fi connection—*almost—-almost—Go!* Open the tracking site

Tobey and Arthur sent me. Gjesken types in Liesl's phone number and dials her phone. She puts the call on speaker. Liesl's voice mail again. Damn it! Children! Turn on your phone! What can you be doing that's more important than getting rescued?!

—- ANOTHER TIME —

IT'S THE THIRD TIME and I'm sure you're not supposed to use the same condom over and over but we don't have a choice. Things have definitely taken a turn for the better since she arrived. This feels really good. I'm inside Liesl again and it feels like Home. Inside Liesl is hot and slippery like Home where I've been living for the last three months, but also like Home where I belong. My world is blurring into itself, like mirrors reflecting each other.

"I take a picture with you? Us together?" Liesl asks.

I try not to turn into one big grin at the idea someone wants to be in a picture with me. "Sure. But we have to turn off the phone fast so we don't waste the battery."

Liesl pushes her power button on and the glow lights her face. She's pretty with her hair all messed up and her eyes shining. Ping. Ping. Ping…messages coming in. We must have a signal!

"Dial your mom, Liesl!"

I sing The Rise Song and Home tilts upward. Yes!

The phone answers! They get gabbing in Norwegian.

"Ask your mom if my Mom's there."

More babbling.

Liesl hands me the phone. The battery symbol is red. Could cut out any minute. I hold it to my ear, hearing a muffled sob. "Mom?"

"Brian! We're at sea! We must be near you. Can you see us?"

"Mom, I can't see anything. Can you track us?"

"If we have Liesl's phone password."

"Put Liesl's mom on."

"No, let me talk to you—"

"PUT LIESL'S MOM ON NOW!"

221

I hand Liesl the phone and tell her to give her mom the password. There is a moment, in her eyes, that tells me she's opposed to the idea.

"Do it, or we can't get out."

Liesl says something in Norwegian. She calls her mom cuckoo. My mom wouldn't appreciate that.

"Mor?" she asks into the phone. "Mor?"

The call is disconnected.

"Did she get the password?" I ask.

Liesl shrugs. "I said it."

"We have to leave the phone on so they can track it if they got the password."

"No! It's almost out of battery!"

"We'll be out of battery soon no matter what. Now is the time they will be trying to track us. Leave it on, but turn off anything that takes power. Any apps that go on automatically."

Liesl closes various programs and we wait. Somehow everything's changed. Our glow is gone. I peel off the condom and slide it into the pocket of my discarded shorts, trying not to be too obvious that I'm saving it for future use.

—- PLEASE SWALLOW —

DOWN IN THE GALLEY where it's warmer, we stand over the computer, staring at the screen. The engine drones. The swells rock the boat. The internet icon spins. We refresh the page. I film the screen for Arthur, but nothing is happening, so I stop.

"Are you sure you got the right password, Gjesken?" I try to sound casual. "Should we try another?"

"It's the right password. I should have guessed. Coo-coo— Liesl's kitten."

It occurs to me if I'd let Brian have a pet, I might know all his passwords. He only asked for a dog right after the divorce and I said something like "maybe later." He never asked again. If we'd have gotten one, he wouldn't have gone whale-watching. Maybe

222

he wouldn't have been swallowed. Maybe I wouldn't be looking for him. Maybe I'd be in the beige house now, vacuuming while he plays video games. *Thank God I didn't get that dog!* A horrifying lump of shame rises. I've got to put it somewhere and look at Gjesken—

"Gjesken, you were talking for too long with Liesl. You shouldn't have done that. They may have no more battery. We won't be able to track them if the battery's dead."

"You were the one who wouldn't give up the phone!"

She is really annoying me. Why couldn't someone else's daughter get swallowed? I pull in a breath and try to explain things. "This is our last chance. If the battery is dead, we can't find them. If this can't locate them, they'll be lost forever."

Gjesken glares at me. "I know that! You aren't helping things!"

She's right. I'm making things worse. We both have children in the whale. I should be kind.

"I'm just saying—" The kind words don't come out. I try again. "—it'll be your fault if we lose them!"

Gjesken slaps my cheek. I deserved that.

I slap her back.

We both strike out and she grabs my left wrist and I get hers— arms up, struggling to pull away and lash out—"You aren't running things!" I scream, my cheek stinging. "I paid for this boat, the food, this satellite thing—"

"Money means you run things? Americans always think that!"

"How dare you! You're here because of me! If it wasn't for me, you wouldn't even be looking for your girl! She'd be dead. My boy saved her!"

Since our arms are locked, she kicks me in the shin. *Ow!*

"My daughter is the only reason you're here! You wouldn't have a chance without her. She's the one saving *your* boy."

She scoots back as I kick at her. The boat tilts and I fall, pulling her, she lands on me and—

Ding.

We freeze, wrists still clamped by fists.

Ding.

Rising to peer over the top of the table, we stare at the computer screen. A little spot blinks on the expanse of blue sea.

We give the coordinates to Torsten, Nord Spyd revs, and we speed off. Only ten minutes later, we've reached the spot. Torsten orders us to drop one of the fifty packages. He steers the boat in a wide spiral, calling out "Drop now!" every five minutes. For each one, we click the power button and the siren blares, seal up the plastic, attach the bait, and lower it overboard. The sound muffles instantly. This is going to work!

Siren after siren turned on. Package after package lowered into the sea. After the first ten, our hopefulness fades. This is ridiculous. Worse than a needle in a haystack. This is an exercise in futility.

After thirty, Torsten steers the Nord Spyd to widen the circle. It's pointless crap-shoot. No reason it could work. And a siren? Why would a whale even approach something blaring like that? The whole idea is stupid.

It's cold out and I want a jacket but Gjesken doesn't look cold. She's got an apron on. Who wears an apron? Fuck her. I take another package from the pile, seal it and hand it to my companion. She glares at me.

I glare back. "What's your problem?"

"Do you hear anything? You didn't turn on the siren! This would be wasted!"

"Fine, let's trade. I'll put the bait on!"

We switch places and Gjesken peels open the plastic, turns on the siren and passes it to me.

Hands in the bucket and—*Shit, these squirming fish are slimy and cold!* I struggle to tie the suckers to the blaring package. I can tell Gjesken's dying to hop in and fix things, but I get the bait attached. "Thirty-one," I shout over the siren.

"Thirty-two," she yells back.

"It's thirty-one!"

Torsten yells at us, "Stop baby fight!"

I lower the package into the water and the shrimp and fish attached pull it down under the dark waves, muting the piercing noise.

We work without looking at each other. I wish we hadn't switched jobs. This really is horrible, trying to wrestle live creatures.

We drop number thirty-eight and a geyser shoots up from the sea, a momentary rainbow in the spray. A whale! Gjesken and I rush to the side of the boat. The whale circles, opens its wide mouth, and in goes our package!

"The whale swallowed it!" Gjesken screams.

I've seen Toke's video enough times to know Brian's whale and this isn't it. Much too small, too smooth a head, wrong color... The whale blasts again and dives. Its left fluke is torn. Another clue it's not the whale that swallowed Brian.

"It's not the right whale, Gjesken."

"It might be! Anyway, it proves that a whale will eat our package."

"It proves *this* whale will. Maybe this whale has been following us and eaten every package we've dropped!

"I don't believe that."

"Who cares what you believe! It doesn't help if it's eaten by a whale with no children inside! This is hopeless!"

Torsten yells again from the bridge, "No time! Drop now!"

We prepare number thirty-nine.

I'm miserable. My nose is dripping from the cold wind. I wipe a finger across and—*Yuck! It stinks!* My hands are freezing and slimy with fish muck. I hate this!

Siren on. Bait attached. Lower into sea. Siren on. Bait attached. Lower into sea. One after another. Forty-seven. Forty-eight.

"Last one," Gjesken says, turning on the siren. I guess she was right about the count. I attach the bait and she moves next to me, her hands out. I understand. Together, we hold the package for a moment, then lower it down, watching as it's pulled into the depths. I close my eyes and think a silent prayer.

—*Please let Brian's whale find this and not be bothered by the siren and let it swallow the package and let Brian and the girl hear the siren and let them reach out of the epiglottis flap and pull the package in. Please let each of those dominoes fall into the next. Please.*

I open my eyes to see Gjesken with her eyes closed.

—*We're both praying over each package. Either that or she's tired of looking at me. I don't blame her. I've become a bitch, a monster. What is wrong with me? Where is the beige, placid creature I used to be?*

Gjesken open her eyes and calls to the bridge, "Torsten, that's the last one. Number *fifty.*"

She had to do it. "You had to do it, didn't you?"

"What is your problem, Ann? We set out all fifty. This was your idea. We need to watch for the beacon now." She smiles like she knows everything.

I'm sick of this and—"I'm sick of this! I'm sick of worrying and watching and waiting. What if the whale isn't even near here!? What if he goes away from all this noise and sirens? I would! What if all the packages are swallowed by whales *without* children inside!? What if the right whale does swallow one and Brian can't catch it and pull it in? This is a waste of everything! We'll never find them!"

Torsten's rough hands grip my arms. He bends close, eyes skewering mine, breath of tobacco and fish. "You not help. Next now. Down and look computer. Look signal. Go."

Gjesken wipes her slimy hands on her apron. Now I see why she has that on. I'm covered in fish goo.

I start toward the stairs and Gjesken calls after me, "Ann, as *you* know migration, feeding patterns, and all information, tell us, which way does the whale expert suggest Torsten steer the Nord Spyd?"

I show her my teeth, yelling over the waves, "I defer to the captain of the ship."

Torsten grunts and sets a course for wherever as I step below.

After washing and changing into Liesl's clothes, still smelling of fish, I sit in front of the computer and stare, watching for the beacon. It's hard to focus on nothing happening. I can hardly keep my eyes still. I want to look at the sea, not this boring radar thing. Why is it my turn first? Where's Gjesken?

—- INTERRUPTUS —-

LIESL HOLDS UP THE PHONE for me to see. A blinking red battery icon fills the screen and then—black. Dead. Done. Just like us?

"Now what!?" she yells. "You tell me leave on and now we have nothing! We never found!"

"They may have tracked the signal. They may have—"

"How long we wait? Hour? Day? Week? I no live here that long!"

"If I can do it, you can, Liesl."

"I not you! I need things! I need friend and television and internet and Mor and food and bath—"

"It's not my fault you got swallowed. I saved you! You would be dead if it wasn't for me!"

"I want be dead if stuck here with you!"

"Fine! Jump out! I was much happier before you came along and spoiled things. I had room! I could stretch out. I could do what I wanted when I wanted!"

"I hate you!" Liesl screams.

"I hate YOU!" I scream back.

In the darkness of one glowing wriggler, I see her reach for something. There's a tug on my ankle. She's at my bundle and lifts a pale shape—my sneaker!

"Don't you dare! Put Sprout down! You'll kill him!"

"You kill us anyway!" Liesl screams and lifts her hand to throw the shoe far back into the depth of the lung branches where I can't fit.

I leap and land hard, my elbow in her stomach. She gasps and I've got her arm and squeeze to make her drop the sneaker. It lands sideways and I jerk away and grab Sprout.

"If Sprout's hurt, I'll never forgive you! I grew him! I protected him!"

"Vent," Liesl whispers.

Shaking the Wrigglers, blue glows. Sprout is leaning—bits of his roots show out of the seaweed! Damn her! A howl escapes me. "Look what you've done!"

"VENT!" Liesl yells.

Her tone scares me and I catch my next howl before it escapes. "What?"

"Vent—wait," she hisses.

"What is it—?"

"VENT!" she screams.

I repeat the word to myself several times, trying to distract myself from wanting to strangle her.

"Vent, what is sound?" Liesl whispers.

I force myself to pay attention. There *is* something—a siren or horn. Something definitely not whale sound. I set Sprout far from Liesl and slide to the flap and send the Yellow Shopping Cart out into a bombardment of things flying past. The siren sound gets louder and stays loud. It's right outside the flap like a mini police car has pulled over to investigate speeding fish.

I haul the net inside. The sound is unbearable. Liesl shakes the bag of Wrigglers again, forcing them bright with anger. In the net are flopping fish and Peelers attached with wires to a thick plastic bag.

"Turn it off!" I yell.

Liesl fumbles with the bag and pulls out a siren. She finds a switch—silence.

She reaches into the bag and screams.

She hands something to me—What is it? A ball?—and I smell and tears form so fast. The incredible intoxicating magic smell of an orange.

"One again!" she holds up another.

I paw through the sack. A plastic bottle.

I un-screw the top and smell. No smell. Tip it back for a tentative taste. My God! I take a huge gulp and sobbing, I whisper out the word of the precious liquid, "Water!" passing it to Liesl. She drinks and hands it back. We share it all.

Another item in a plastic container.

I open it and Liesl holds up the Wriggler Ziploc. A note in my mother's handwriting, but super sloppy.

Dear Brian and Liesl,

We, your mothers, are looking for you. We hope this message will find you. Inside is a beacon. It only works to 300 feet below sea level and we don't know if it will work inside a whale, but—(something unintelligible). We're in a boat on the Norwegian sea. We tracked your call and hope—(something unintelligible). If you are reading this, turn on the beacon. We will be looking for you. Know we love you more than anything.

Mom and Äiti

Liesl and I grab each other, laughing and crying. They're close! They're going to find us! We'll be found and saved!

We pull the beacon out and below it there's a cell phone. We turn it on and it's got a full battery! But there's no service. We must be deep.

It's a bright screen and I turn the light to Liesl. She doesn't look exactly like I thought. I've only seen her in the dim light of the Wrigglers and I must have morphed parts I couldn't see well with memory stuff. I thought she looked like Vivian in High School. Liesl is pretty, but nothing like Vivian. My brain really twisted what I saw. I wonder who Liesl imagined me as.

Behind Liesl is wet, quivering whale lung. The light shows too much, the veins, and grayish pink, and slime we shouldn't see. I need to see Home only as I've imagined him. I quickly lower the light.

We read the directions for the beacon, and when we figure it out, click it on. Hopefully, it will work from inside Home.

"I'm sorry, Liesl. I'm sorry about getting mad."

"I'm sorry if Sprout hurt. Is okay?"

"He's gonna be fine. We all are. Now, to the oranges! Let's only eat a segment at a time to make them last and last."

Pressing a thumbnail into the dimpled flesh, a squirt of citrus fills the air and I get to crying again. Back home, we had a big orange tree in the backyard and it made so many oranges. I used to throw them really hard against the fence to watch them splatter. The yard was full of rotting residue and fruit flies. Mom was furious but I didn't care. I was a crappy son. I'll never waste another.

—- BOTTLE'S JOURNEY —

IT SEEMS AS THOUGH Bottle's journey is nearing its end. As evidence in a possible crime, it lies in the clear bag in the front seat of the Alaska State Trooper's vehicle. Sunlight sparkles down through the windshield, warming the scratched plastic. On Punctured Dollar Bill, George Washington is scarified with the letter T from KETCHUM poked in his face. He does not look happy. Library Card, bent from being inserted into the bottle top, is slowly regaining its shape, stretching out, presumably happy to be off the tossing waves.

Were Bottle able, it might pat itself on the cap for its mission accomplished. Were it anthropomorphized further, it might feel a sense of dread. Dread that it could end up pushed to the back of a dusty shelf in the evidence-storage room of a law enforcement agency—forgotten.

Or perhaps it would not be forgotten. Would Bottle be introduced as Exhibit B in a courtroom? Would the prosecutor expound on its perilous oceanic journey? Would the jury methodically scrutinize Bottle and find it instrumental in bringing the alleged kidnapper to justice? What would happen to Exhibit B after the trial? What happens to evidence when it is no longer needed? After the verdict, would Bottle be reunited with Brian or Ann, or would it be put in a recycling bin to become reincarnated as a post-consumer-content item and enjoy a new purpose? Perhaps it could become part of a traffic cone or sleeping bag insulation. And what of the stippled dollar bill? Would it circulate for years, each temporary-owner always calling Brian's mother, pulling her from sleep, causing more tears and heartache until the woman finally gave up all contact with the world? Or would Bottle and its contents be un-ceremoniously tossed in a trash can, dumped in a dumpster, tumbled in a truck, hauled up a sloping road to the top of a massive landfill to be poured out—falling, bouncing, clattering—to the bottom of the odorous pit and there, to be covered with shredded tax receipts, packing peanuts, and liquified lettuce while hungry gulls bark overhead?

Such is the stuff of speculation. For the present, had Bottle an existential notion of a future, it might yet bask unconcerned, relishing the NOW of the warm vinyl seat in the trooper's cruiser.

—- PINOCCHIO OUT BACK —-

THE MANAGER of the gas station lifts the trash bags from the containers beside the fuel pumps, still thinking about the man and girl who were in the market. Could they be the same two from the abduction story in the news? Should he call the police? What if he's wrong? It's never right to call just because someone *might* be someone that *looks* like someone who did something bad. What if they are simply a father-daughter on a road trip? *Stay out of the Qallunaat's affairs,* Queequeg hears his mother warn in his head. *Koyukon have no business with whites.*

Carrying the garbage behind the market, Queequeg hears a whimper. A dog, tied to the propane tank, crouches low, afraid and shaking.

"How long have you been here? Do you want water and a biscuit?"

Pinocchio's ears rise at the word biscuit. His tail wags.

Queequeg steps to the dog, trying to look fearless and kind. It must work because Pinocchio lays his ears back and keeps his tail wagging. Queequeg offers his hand for a long sniff and after being judged acceptable, he searches the collar for a tag.

"No I.D.? I've been there. I'll call you Togo. You okay with that?"

Pinocchio looks okay with that.

Queequeg leads the dog into the market, gives him water and the promised biscuit, bought from his own store. Behind the counter, he turns on the electric heater and puts his jacket on the floor.

"I know you, Togo. I've seen your picture. You are famous from the news."

As the dog curls in front of the warming air, Queequeg calls the Alaska State Troopers.

—- NATE AND TOGO —-

AFTER NATE GAVE DISPATCH the abductor's phone number that the message-in-the-bottle woman told him, everything felt hopeful. They would track it, he'd catch the man and save the girl. But now, hours later, the hollow pit in the Alaska Trooper's stomach is growing. Anxiety that he's doing it all wrong again, even though he knows this isn't his fault.

When she was eleven, his sister went missing. Nate was thirteen and the hell of those few days is written with permanent marker on his psyche. The yelling, the accusations, the second guessing, the chaos of everyone trying to help. His mother and father both accused Nate of not looking after his sister. It was his fault she'd been kidnapped. If she was killed, that would be his fault.

When his sister turned up in Seattle, visiting a boy she'd gotten a crush on, all the relief didn't erase the horrible visions Nate's imagination had created. Terror, even if unwarranted, doesn't vanish.

This girl hadn't run off to visit a boy. Jenny Hollender, age 8, was abducted from her mother's home by her father Mark Hollender, age 28, a veteran, two tours in the desert, diagnosed with PTSD, and incarcerated for assault. Not the kind of man you want around a girl. This was one of those cases where you don't approach if the child is in close proximity to the man.

Nate had seen the pleas the mother made on TV. She had that same exhausted tension around her eyes that Nate's mother had all those years—

Dispatch blasting through the radio jolts his heart.

232

"You get the phone tracked?"

"No, but you'll want to check out a dog."

"I don't have time for a—"

"It looks like the dog in the AMBER Alert. Guy at a gas station found him."

Nate swerves the car to the shoulder, kicking up gravel, slams it in Park, and grabs his notebook. "Where?"

He gets the specs, flicks on the roof light-bar, and speeds onto the highway. *Please let it be the right dog. Let it be a clue that will solve this.* If Nate doesn't screw up, he could catch the abductor and save the girl. The glory would go to him and all Alaska State Troopers. And—might erase a bit of that shame from his past.

At the gas station market, Nate introduces himself to the clerk, guessing the man will speak as much Koyukon Athabaskan as he does.

"Dzaanh nezoonh, brother, I'm Officer Nate."

"Dzaanh nezoonh, I'm Queequeg." The man stares at Nate, waiting to see how much the officer knows.

"Moby Dick?"

"You got it. Mom was a fan of the story, saw the old movie once, but she wasn't a big reader. She thought Queequeg was the one who survived to tell the tale."

"Oops. That was—"

"Call me Ishmael."

"Right. Ishmael. Suppose that coulda be worse."

"Yep, I'll stick with Queequeg. You want to see the dog? He's down here." Queequeg motions for Nate to look around the counter.

Nate peers at the wagging dog and shows Queequeg pictures of Mark and Jenny.

"They're the ones alright. The man paid for everything in cash and rushed the girl out, telling her the dog had run away."

Queequeg tells Nate what the father bought and gives him a copy of the cash register receipt.

233

Nate stares at the dog. "I guess I'll take him to Fairbanks Animal Control. I'd keep him at my place, but my condo doesn't allow pets, and the trooper station will lock him in the storeroom."

Queequeg smiles. "Leave him with me. I'll bring him home and keep him happy until the girl is found and can take Togo back."

Excitement prickles over Nate's skin. "Togo's the dog's name? There's a tag?"

"No, that's just a name I call him. Togo was a famous sled dog."

Nate takes down Queequeg's information, thanks the man, pats Pinocchio, and heads out. As Nate gets into his cruiser, he wonders about all the good people in the world versus the bad. Still seems like there are more good. He touches the warm evidence bag containing the message-in-the-bottle on the seat beside him. Like that lady he called, the one that gave him the abductor's phone number, seems like she's one of the good ones.

Before he has time to think it, he pulls the dollar bill from the evidence bag and dials.

The phone rings and rings and a lady finally answers. When Nate reintroduces himself as the Alaska State Trooper, she sounds happy to hear from him. His heart gives a little jig and he wonders about it. What can he possibly feel for someone he doesn't know?

"Did you save that girl?" the woman asks, sounding genuinely concerned.

"Not yet. But because of you—we're closer."

"I'll be sure to let you know if there are any more calls from that man, but, please, tell me you have the bottle and library card—"

"They're right beside me. I'm holding them for evidence now but I'll make sure they get back to you when we're done with them. If you don't mind me asking, what's the importance of the bottle and all?"

"I'm also on the case of an abduction. My son."

Nate chokes back the lump that bubbles up his throat. "I'm so—sorry."

"I'll find him," she says cheerfully. "I'm close now."

Nate listens to the static, waiting for more.

She adds, "I'm in the sea of Norway. I'll find him. He's living in a whale. I'll get him out."

The Boy in the Whale. The crazy lady was all over the news several months ago. She doesn't sound insane. She sounds resolute.

Nate smiles to himself. They're on similar missions. "Yes, you'll get him out," he says. "You'll do just that."

The phone static rises in the pause—then she says, "And you'll find yours."

Something in her voice makes Nate blush. This is absurd. His phone hand sweats and he switches to the right ear. Nat knows about projection. All troopers have to take the mandatory psychology course. Who is he projecting onto this voice? Why does he feel so excited and jumpy?

"Are you there?" she asks.

"I'm here," he answers. He looks up at the sky. This makes him feel like they're close. Both using the same big sky. Half a world away—or less, if you go over the top.

More static, only Nate can't hear much over his incessant heart. She's a mother. She has a boy in a whale. Most likely married. But wouldn't her husband be fielding these calls? No. Nate remembers his mother didn't even let Dad talk when the police came to ask about his missing sister. Mom wanted to be in control. If Dad screwed up, her baby might be lost. Maybe that's happening with this lady.

"I'm Nate."

"I'm Ann."

Another flush moves through him. Fuck it. Make a move.

"Look me up anytime you're in Alaska," he says, really hoping that might happen.

"In the past I would have said I'd never be in Alaska, but now—I'm in Norway, so anything's possible. I promise I'll call if I hear anything."

"Thanks, Ann."

"Bye for now, Nate."

Nate hangs up and types *Ann* next to the number on his phone. Why not?

— POSSIBLE PING —

TORSTEN STEERS the boat, cruising at what he insists is whale wandering speed, about 12 mph.

It's been hours. Are we circling? Heading somewhere? The screen is a rectangle scorched on the back of my eyes. Even when I close them, I can see there is no change. Eyes open, eyes closed, all the same. Just a vast expanse of nothingness. This is futile. Pointless. An exercise in despair and—

Ping.

I open my eyes and there it is.

A little green cursor and a high *Ping.*

"It's on! They put the beacon on!" I yell.

Torsten and Gjesken rush to join me in the galley. They stare at the blank laptop screen. I will it to happen again. Was I dreaming? Nothing shows on the screen. I can't believe this! I close my eyes for one minute and—

"Brain mistake," Torsten mumbles and heads back upstairs.

"You need sleep, Ann," Gjesken suggests. "Sleep is essential in times of stress."

Sleep is essential in times of stress, I mimic in my head. Who made this woman official mother figure? Shit. If she's a mother figure, is this what I sound like to Brian? Some self-important know-it-all who's full of benevolent advice? Yuck—

"I'll watch the screen. You take a nap," the parody of motherhood continues. "You're dreaming and we need someone alert monitoring the screen."

She's becoming a real asshole. But maybe she's right. When did I open my eyes? Before or after? Did I really dream it? Damn!

The *ping* sounds again and Gjesken screams and hugs me and all of a sudden I need her to do just that. We hold each other, staring at the little green flashing spot. She really isn't that bad. She's just worried about her girl, like I'm worried about Brian.

236

Torsten stomps back down, sees us hugging and the blinking flash and shouts, "High Five!" He scribbles numbers from off the screen, and races upstairs, yelling, "Computer up deck!" As we carry the equipment up, the Nord Spyd revs and curls to the right, racing toward the low-hanging sun. The pinging from the computer speeds up. We're already getting closer to it.

Torsten yells, "Gjesken, hold wheel and I make ready!"

She does as she's told as Torsten races to the front of the ship. I should film this. Lift the phone hanging from my neck and push the video button. I'm framing it, trying to hold the view steady. Torsten is unwrapping the object bolted to the deck. Untying the ropes, pulling the canvas back, revealing—-what is that? Is that a massive fucking gun?

I run to him, camera jiggling the scene. "Torsten, what is—"

"Harpoon cannon."

My gut leaps. Harpoon? Is this a whaling boat? Bile bubbles up my throat. Norway is one of three countries that still allows whaling. Japan and Iceland are the others.

Fuck!

"We can't use a harpoon, Torsten."

"Stay back, Ann."

"You can't shoot the whale. We need to keep that whale alive."

"I know what do," he growls.

"Let Torsten work, Ann!" Gjesken screams over the pinging computer.

"He wants to kill the whale! He'll kill our children!"

I grab Torsten's arm but he pulls from my grasp, so I swing to punch him, he dodges and my fist whooshes past his face. He grabs both my wrists and shakes me. "I do work."

I'll break his nose the minute he lets go of my wrists. "My child is in that whale. You cannot harpoon it!"

Torsten glares at me. "I harpoon yes." He yells something foreign to Gjesken like—*keep this bitch away from me, I need to kill the whale*—and shoves me hard. I land on my rear, sliding across the slippery deck. Gjesken rushes to grab me as I stand but I'm in no mood to dance. "Let go! He's trying to kill Brian!" I get one arm free and try to pry her fingers from my other wrist. Beyond her shoulder, Torsten loads the harpoon into the swiveling cannon.

Gjesken screams at me in Norwegian. Probably a Norway excuse why killing whales is necessary.

A large military-like shell is loaded into the back part of the cannon. No! This can't be! Now that we found them—"PLEASE!" I scream as the pinging gets more insistent and becomes an unbroken accompaniment to my pleading.

A salty water blast to the left, spray rising high—the smell of it —sick phlegm—and the monstrous black back glides beside us. This is him at last! This is Brian's whale! Brian's in there!

The beast is massive. Much larger than anything I've ever seen. He's unfathomable in size.

In the corner of my eye I catch the movement as Torsten spins the harpoon and I bite Gjesken's hand and when she lets go, I leap at the whale-killer, knocking him against the railing, holding him back with all my might. The whale curls its back, the dorsal fin slices the water and I scream "Brian, RUN!" as the enormous flukes rise—like a wave goodbye—and slide underwater.

"HA!" I scream. "He's gone!"

Torsten spits out angry gibberish, flinging me across the slippery deck. I land again and slide again but I don't care, because the pings are getting further apart. The whale's gone. I've saved my boy. I'll call and tell him to dump that beacon. I'll tell him I saw what a beautiful monster he's in.

The pinging grows faster again. Damn it!

"He come return," Torsten says as he takes hold of the harpoon cannon.

Scrambling to my feet, I yell at the sea, "Stay down! Stay down!"

Pinging's constant now and another geyser blast, right by me. Spray hits my face and I yell, "BRIAN! GET AWAY!" toward the open blowhole as Gjesken calls out, "LIESL!"

The scarred, barnacle-studded back goes on forever and I see all the features I've learned—dorsal fin, dorsal ridge—

A massive explosion makes me duck. The harpoon flies and the monster jerks and dives, tail slapping the water angrily.

"High Five! I nail!" Torsten grins.

The pinging stops. Not a sound. Did the harpoon go all the way inside and destroy the beacon? Did it skewer my son? Is that whale falling like a mountain, spewing rivers of blood? He'll never rise again. Brian is lost. Maybe he wasn't hurt in the lungs, but if my son is still alive, he'll feel the whale fall. My boy's terrified. Brian...

My knees buckle. A rush of horror swarms every cell.

As I turn to him, Torsten sees something in my eyes and takes a step back.

"You mother fucking—" I start toward my victim—

Ping. And another. Faster now. A rush of pings and then one long whine and WHAM!—I'm slammed to the rail as the boat lurches. We've been struck! The whale's doing what he did before! He's doing what he did to Brian's boat and Liesl's boat!

I slide on slick wood and the water parts with the rising beak and a monstrous black shape emerges from the sea, a beast of muscle and rage, leaping higher and higher, flying impossibly into the air, and a massive eye turns sideways and sets on me. I want to wave but the eye vanishes as, fins outstretched, the mountain rolls against sky, and then drops, sending a tsunami cascading over us. Soaked with the arctic water, we feel the beast rub along the underside of the ship, pressing us up, we tip and, damnit—I've worn the wrong shoes, I always wear the wrong shoes—I slip, heading for the part of the boat with no railing, and the wood is slick and the boat tips farther and there is nothing to grab and there is no stopping this and I'm at the edge—and off—and take a breath and—-drop into stunning, overwhelming cold.

Under down deep. Bubbles and fear and murky darkness.

The freezing water envelops me. Pain everywhere. Eyes sting from salt and cold but I keep them open. The massive creature spreads past in the dark gloom, filling all edges of my vision and as he passes I reach my hands out, feel the rough rubber, barnacles scraping my skin. He goes on and on and on. He lasts forever. Then he moves over me, and passing, the sides converge in the thick caudal peduncle leading to the tail's median notch and both flukes curl, rising and descending, swirling the current, sending me deeper, before disappearing into murky darkness.

There's a muffled ringing in my ears. I look down—the phone in the waterproof case is lit! What if Brian's calling right now! Fuck!!! I need to get to the surface. I need to answer but the clothes are so heavy. Kick off the shoes. Slide out of the coat.

Out of the darkness, fast now, the whale appears, heading straight for me. Nearer and I brace for him to take me in as the phone rings on and on.

Swallow me. Let me join Brian. I'm ready. Yes...

—- HOME IS MAD —-

I GOTTA FIND OUT what happened. The new phone has reception but it just rings and rings and no one answers. I know Mom would answer if it rang. Something's wrong.

Home's really mad. We heard a loud explosion and Home jerked and thrashed and dove. Liesl vomited her orange segments. That made her cry but she cried more when the whale rose and blew and through the blowhole she heard her mom call her name. I heard Mom yell something like "get away." We listened for more but then Home did what he does. He rammed. Probably rammed the boat. Sounded like Mom screamed. What if Home knocked her into the sea? Maybe she was swallowed. Maybe she's on the way down and I can pull her in. I crawl to listen at the flap. How would that be having Liesl and me and Mom all here in Home's lungs? It would be tight. Would cut back on the entertainment around here. Please don't swallow Mom.

—- IN THE SEA —-

BRIAN'S WHALE doesn't swallow me and passes like I'm not worth the trouble. Thanks for the ego boost.

I need to get to the surface or I'll drown. I kick toward the light, still holding my breath.

I'm rammed from behind—sending bubbles exploding from my clamped mouth—a bus-sized creature passes by, smaller than the huge whale. A shark? Fear jolts my body and I scramble upward. Bursting to the surface. Coughing for air.

Torsten throws a life preserver as another spray shoots up and the black back bends and the tail rises to slap the sea. I grab the floating circle and hold on, trying to tread water but my legs aren't working. They're too cold. Is this how someone dies? Is this how I die? I thought it would happen on the Santa Monica freeway.

Torsten and Gjesken are yelling from the deck. What are they yelling? The water hurts only my shoulders now. The rest of me is numb. Why didn't the whale swallow me? I want to see Brian. Please come back and swallow me!

Torsten and Gjesken won't stop yelling. I better make an effort for their sake. I pull at the life-preserver to bring it over my head, but it's much heavier than it looks. Not a good idea to duck my head underwater to get it inside. I'll never come back up.

—*Would that be so bad?*

—*You have to live for Brian!*

—*I'm tired. I want to be swallowed and see Brian.*

—*Get moving or you'll be dead and then he's dead!*

Straining frozen muscles, I heave the lifesaver over my head and struggle my arms through and I'm hauled through dark water and nothing matters anymore as they lift me onboard. All is blurry and painful and hurrying and somehow I'm naked and under blankets and the lady is rubbing me all over and mumbling words that don't make any sense. Maybe if I ever get warm, my tears will thaw.

— NATE CONTRIBUTES —

NATE PULLS HIS CRUISER to the side of the road. He can't stop thinking about that whale-lady Ann. It's absurd. He doesn't know her.

A quick search brings up the crowdfunding website. There's a picture of a pudgy boy. The video explaining the situation sends Nate typing in his credit card number. He'll be part of the cause.

Nate watches the video six times. Or, rather, the part with Ann talking to the camera. She's got a bit of the drab housewife to her, but something else pulls Nate in. He knows that feeling a connection to her might be just about when his sister went missing, but so what. Feelings can sometimes be right.

As he watches, an update posts on the page. Pictures from a boat. A map showing the coordinates. Out in the Norwegian Sea. A new picture of Ann with a helicopter over her.

She's not a drab housewife. She looks wild. Unabashedly grinning. Her hair flies. Her eyes shine. Nate thinks—*She's blossomed.*

— FROM HIS POCKET —

MARK UNCLAMPS HIS HAND from the steering wheel and tries to shake blood back into it. These miles are endless with Jenny giving him the silent treatment. Been like that for hours, since Pinocchio was left behind.

The road stretches forever and nothing changes. Pines along the sides. Heavy flat sky overhead. No traffic. No billboards. Nothing to look at but the dotted yellow line off into infinity. But the yellow's been glowing blue for the last hour. Not a good sign. Gotta dial down the stress. Breathe. Find a distraction.

Mark turns on the radio and searches until he finds a music station. Can't risk news.

The grey clouds look like waves. If this keeps up, he'll drown. Alaska was a dumb idea. It's already too cold and next comes winter and darkness. He's not going to manage darkness.

Jenny shifts and Mark glances at her. She's looking at the dashboard. Shit, he's going over ninety again. Slow down. Should use cruise control but less control'd be bad right now, what with the yellow line turning blue and the waves in the sky.

The radio makes a weird sound, like an alarm at a nuclear facility when someone gets contaminated with radiation. "This is an AMBER Alert—" Mark fumbles for the button, switching it off.

Damn it. If the radio's putting out the alert, do they know his car? He'll be caught soon. It must have been easy to stay hidden in the days before cell phones, internet, and TV. Now everyone gets the news at the same time. They'd be tracking him if they knew this new phone number. Luckily, he hasn't made any calls to anyone who knows him and it's always off.

Mark glances at Jenny to see if she's reacted to the radio announcement. She stares out the passenger window, expressionless.

Up ahead, a sign. Exit 3 miles. The next sign shows the logos of places to eat. All the usual chains except one: Fisherman's Catch. Food will make Jenny forget the dog. Kids forget quickly, right? Besides, he needs a beer to keep the bad stuff at bay.

He signals well ahead. Even though they're the only one on the road, he wants to get in the habit of good driving. Don't want to do anything that might bring attention.

"What'll it be, Jenny? You like Taco Bell?"

"I hate Taco Bell. Mom knows. You don't know anything."

She's right, I don't know anything about her.

"Which then? Denny's? McDonald's? KFC?"

Silence. She's not going to cooperate. As they pull onto the exit, Jenny points a demanding finger to the dismal blue cement-block building: Fisherman's Catch.

"It looks closed, sweetie. Let's try Denny's."

Her finger doesn't waver.

I've got to fold this hand if I'm gonna win later.

He steers the car over the rough gravel, avoiding the massive potholes and puddles dotting the parking lot. The place has one filthy car out front. Not promising.

"Let's look inside. We can leave if it doesn't suit you," Mark suggests, hoping it won't.

Mark watches Jenny purposely step in the puddles on the way to the front door. He guesses this isn't the time to tell her not to.

Inside the glass-enclosed vestibule, he passes the gum-ball, fake-tattoo-decal, plastic-egg-with-worthless-jewel machines when Jenny tugs his sleeve.

"I need coins."

Jenny presses her face against the glass case full of stuffed animals. A mechanical claw hovers over colorful teddies and alligators and penguins.

"These things are rigged. The claws are hard enough for an adult. You'll never—"

"I NEED COINS!"

Mark scoops the contents from his pocket and hands it to Jenny. "I'll order us something. Burger okay?"

Jenny grunts.

Mark enters the restaurant. It's a relief to be in a place that isn't lined with TVs. Maybe it's good she chose this joint.

The sign says *Please wait to be seated*. A lanky teenage boy with bad skin approaches him with a menu. "Only one?"

Since when is one, _only_ one? Mark holds up two fingers, nodding to Jenny in the vestibule.

The kid cocks his head, squinting at Mark. Could it be that he knows? A man and young girl traveling alone. He might have heard about them on the news.

Mark adds, "My wife is feeling sick and taking a nap in the car. I'll order her something to go."

The teenager leads him to a booth.

Settled by the window, Mark orders a beer and ginger ale. The menu has illustrations of sting rays, swordfish, and whales. The prices are steep. He'll call that lady who wanted the message-in-the-bottle again. Force her to send more money for the bottle he no longer has.

Mark watches his daughter in the glass vestibule as she bends and twists, trying to control the crane with her body.

I told her the game is rigged. All games are rigged.

The drinks arrive and as there are no burgers on the menu, Mark orders the fisherman platter and a bowl of clam chowder. Hopefully, Jenny isn't allergic to any of it.

"What does your wife want?"

"Fish sandwich."

The guy leaves, puts the order on the chef's wheel, goes into the kitchen, and takes it off the chef's wheel.

Mark watches Jenny. How did she get so big? He missed all of her growing up. As he watches, the glass separating them flows with liquid rainbows. A tightness forms in Mark's chest. *Not now. Not now.* The jagged lines start in the corners of his vision. Everything becomes swirling patterns like the paintings done by that Vincent guy with the cut-off ear. Mark presses his fingers hard on the side of his head, pleading the bad to retreat. *Not now.*

Go to the car. The meds are in the Dopp kit in the trunk.

No, the last one was taken at the Glacier cabin.

I can ride this out.

Images return of the last time. The unstoppable rage taking over. Broken chairs, shattered mirror behind the bar, bloodied faces, arms trying to hold him. None could. The blinding light of the taser.

Don't let it happen again.

His heart stomps in his chest. Swirling patterns bend the room. Tremors tickle his fingers.

Please, not now.

His daughter selects more change from her hand and freezes. Her head snaps up and she glares at Mark through the glass. Can she tell what is going on with him? Does she see what's bubbling under the surface?

Jenny marches in from the vestibule and heads across the restaurant toward her father. The spots on the carpet where her feet hit glow orange. Mark wills himself to smile.

At twelve feet, he knows something's wrong. At six feet, he wonders if they'll be caught because of it. At three feet, she raises her little fist and SLAPS down hard on the table.

"You left him! You left Pinocchio on purpose!"

He wants to remind her that the dog ran but his mouth has disappeared.

"You lied, you scummy, scum-loser, doo-doo-bag!" Jenny lifts her hand, uncovering the dog-tag.

Mark turns his head and the jagged lines follow, blurring his vision. He tries *Jenny, not now,* but it doesn't come out like words, more like underwater sounds.

His daughter blends into the booth. A colorful smear.

The beer might push the jaggeds down for a while. His hand can hardly find it, but then cold shocks his mouth with fizz and lights pop in his eyes and gulp and gulp and gulp to wash it all down, press it all down, clear it all away, and the jaggeds recede to the edges.

A horrible amplified squeaking approaches.

A thought forms. *The dog tag proves who you are. Pick it up NOW.*

Mark's shaking fingers fumble to raise the silver circle from the tabletop. With it in his grasp, he can't remember if it goes in his mouth or somewhere else. Clattering scraping plates appear and a to-go Styrofoam spacecraft lands with way too much squeaking.

The colorful blur in the swirling booth across from Mark coalesces into a little girl. "What's wrong with you?" she hisses as she grabs a fried shrimp and chomps down hard.

"Oh! Hot. Hot!" She spits it out and the teenage boy laughs and Jenny gives him the finger. "Don't laugh at me! I'm stolen! I'm Amber and he's stolen me! He got rid of my dog and I hate him!"

The boy blinks.

Get it together. You can do it.

Mark pulls all the jangling jaggeds in and wills himself to stand. He slips the dog tag in his pocket, throws two twenties on the table, scoops up Jenny in one arm, the to-go styrofoam spaceship in the other, and marches toward the door.

"Hold on. Hold on…" the boy mumbles.

Mark spins, glaring at the jerk. "WHAT?!"

This kid better keep quiet or I'll keep him quiet.

The boy looks terrified. "Nothing."

Jenny kicks and screams as Mark carries her out.

Dumping the girl in the passenger seat, Mark moves to the trunk. He needs that thing hidden there. What was it? Something to do with keeping someone quiet. The jaggeds tickle the edge of his vision. He'll need more beer. Open the trunk. What's he looking for? Meds?

Why won't that girl keep quiet!? Glance up to see that teenager staring at him from the diner window. That's what it was, Mark's got to take care of that jerk. Paw through his suitcase, feeling for that thing hard and cold.

A motorhome angles off the highway ramp and slows. Faces press toward Mark. Is everyone watching? Can't do shit with everyone watching. Mark slams the trunk, hops behind the wheel, and pulls out of the parking lot way too fast. He waves at the staring family in the motorhome as the jaggeds close in and Jenny wails.

He is so fucked.

— ON THE DECK —

WHERE AM I? It's dark and I'm in a strange, unbalanced place. I'm rocking. Oh. On a ship in the Norwegian sea. I sit up and my balance gets worse. Am I drunk? Did I drink something? They fed me pine-tasting liquid. Norwegian liquor? I remember. I was frozen. I was in the ocean and that mean whale passed me by. Why didn't he swallow me!? I want to see Brian and his pudgy little face.

I pull on clothes and wrap a blanket around me. Sliding the phone cord over my neck—I should call Brian! What time is it? I wonder how hard it is to sleep in a whale. Maybe I shouldn't call until it's light. I dial anyway.

It rings. And rings. And rings. If it's ringing, doesn't that mean there's a connection? If there's a connection, why doesn't he answer? Is he hurt? Is that girl keeping the phone from him?

I can't sleep. I'll never be able to sleep again.

Holding on to anything in the darkness, I feel my way out of my bunk to the stairs and crawl on my hands up to the deck.

Blue light everywhere. This isn't the Northern Lights, it's from below. The ocean is lit up like a vast cell phone. Undulating fluorescent glows in the water. It's magical. A fairy world.

I bend over the railing to get a better look. The wind pushes my hair in front of my face. It dances across the blue.

An arm comes around me and Torsten's voice rumbles, "One time in water only."

He turns me from the rail and I'm face to face with him. Torsten's eyes are lit by the blue glow but they're un-readable.

"You go bed. No feet. Many whiskey."

It all comes back to me. The harpoon. This asshole. I raise my arm to slap him—he catches it. I spit at him but it lands on my chin, bringing to mind something about spitting into the wind. "I remember what you did. You tried to kill the whale. I hate you. I'll never forgive you."

Torsten keeps hold of my wrist. "I shoot harpoon and it stick. Now have good long time track possible. Old beacon inside only down thirty meter but now good much better."

"The harpoon wasn't to kill the whale?"

"Harpoon deliver good beacon stay. We see on computer all time now."

Shit. I almost made that not happen. "I'm sorry, Torsten. I didn't know."

He releases my wrist warily. "You worry, mad like whale."

I don't understand this, but I let it go. "So—high five?" I ask, raising my palm—he flinches, ready again to catch the blow. I must consider not striking people anymore. It's getting to be expected. Keeping a smile on my face and my palm still, I repeat, "High five."

Torsten stares at my hovering hand.

I count the fingers aloud as I move each and raise them higher. "High five?"

A grin spreads his salt and pepper quills. "Okay. High Five!" He puts his hand up and I slap it with mine.

He smiles wider. The quills look soft.

—*What would happen?*

—*You're drunk, Ann.*

—*What would happen?*

I take a step forward and move to place a kiss on his porcupine quills. Only I stop inches from him. It was going to be a dare-type kiss. A peck and retreat. Now, lingering here, his breath clouds merge with my breath clouds.

248

He's considering it. I don't know what I'm doing.

—*Bullshit. You know what you're doing. Question is, what the fuck are you doing?!*

He bends closer. His grey eyes dance as the air between us shrinks and heat rises in my throat. The tips of those prickly hairs brush my lips and my knees weaken. When was the last time I was kissed? It's been years. Please do.

The beard tingles against me and travels over my cheek and chin. My breath is quick and I need to sit or be held, or I'll fall. I put a hand on him to steady myself. He pulls me close and the lips touch in a tentative hello. Tapping and retreating. Tapping and retreating. Like the surf on the shore.

Ringing, my phone lights, illuminating our chins. I fumble for it —"Hello?"

Muffled and breaking up but "Mom" is clear. Brian!

"Honey, honey, oh, Brian!" I miss him so much! I want to hug him, pull him close—

Forgotten, Torsten backs away, giving me space.

"I tried to call you earlier, Brian—"

"I was busy—what happened? Home, my whale, jerked. I heard you scream. Did Home ram your boat?"

I tell him of getting rammed, but don't tell him of getting knocked in the water. I don't tell him that I wanted to be swallowed. He'd probably think I was trying to check up on him. He always says I never give him any privacy.

Brian interrupts me, "Home rammed boats at least three times that we know of. Me, Liesl, and you. There must be others."

This beast means to kill. It will make getting Brian out harder. "The whale is violent. Crazy. Can whales get rabies?" I ask.

Brian makes the half-laugh he does when I'm being thick. "Mom, did you see any other whales around when you saw my whale?"

I look up at Torsten and get it. Every creature goes after sex at some point. I turn my back on Torsten, angry that I'm blushing. "There was a bus-sized thing, but too small for, uh,—mating. A shark or something, Stupid whale goes around ramming boats, swallowing people—"

"Home, my whale, is wild and irrational, like someone who'll do anything. Like someone who'll fly to a foreign country, get on a boat, put sirens and oranges in the sea…"

"Are you saying I'm crazy? Damn it, Brian! If you had a child, you'd understand. I don't have a choice. I'm a mother!"

Oh.

The whale is a mother. That bus-sized creature that rammed me wasn't a shark or a mate, it was a little whale. She's a mother trying to protect her baby.

I turn to Torsten. "The whale's a mother."

"Yes." He raises his fist like he's going to punch someone, "Mad like you."

Brian's voice pulls me back, "I guessed it from her songs, The Lullaby Song, The Rise Song… She's singing to her bab—"

Silence.

"Brian?"

He's gone. Damn it! Damn, damn, DAMN! I WANT MY BOY!

Rage fills me. A mother's rage. Of course that whale's mad! She blows her top just like me. I'd ram a boat, too. A flood of whale-sized mother-power surges through me. I turn to Torsten and he backs away—looking at me like he's about to yell *Thar She Blows!*

Got to channel this energy. "Torsten, show me on the radar that thing you harpooned into that poor whale."

"You sleep now—"

"Fuck sleep. I'm a mother."

—- MOTHER AND CHILD AND TROUBLE —

HOME DIVES. Not far, because it's harder for her to breathe. The world has become so much more dangerous. Down below, there is less danger, but air always forces her up. With the problem in her lungs, she can only hold her breath a bit longer than Baby.

The calf curls under Home's belly and nurses on hot fatty milk.

Home sings as Baby feeds. The Lullaby Song.

On Home's back, the small harpoon protrudes from thick blubber, blinking its message to the world.

On the Nord Spyd, Ann sits below in the galley, watching the blinking dot on the computer screen. In the bridge, Torsten follows the whale's course and turns on a shortwave. He whispers into the mic in Norwegian. Reading off numbers from the whale beacon.

Fifty miles away, a knock on a door wakes the captain of a very large ship. The man hurries to the radar room where the screen shows a blinking transmitter. The captain smiles. Torsten came through. He'll get a fat commission for this.

The order is given and new coordinates are set. The great ship turns, setting a course for the whale and her calf.

—- PINOCCHIO IS LOVED —

PINOCCHIO LIES on the inherited bear-hide rug by the wood stove, his feet jerking and twitching.

"Togo's dreaming of chasing rabbits," Queequeg explains to his son and daughter.

The man is wrong. Pinocchio is dreaming of chasing Jenny. The dog spent most of its life in the fenced yard in Kansas City. Never chased a rabbit. Wouldn't know how to dream of one.

"Can we keep him, Papa?" the boy asks.

Queequeg shakes his head in the warm firelight. "The whites believe that animals belong to people. They believe you can own a creature, and they make the rules. If the *Qallunaat* want this dog back, the dog'll have to go with them."

"We would love him more."

"Someone might love more, but it doesn't mean they win. If only we *could* go with the ones that would love us more. That would be a blessing." Queequeg bends his face to the two precious foreheads and presses a kiss on each. "You can love Togo and give to him and still he may leave. But how happy he'll be to have known you and gotten your love."

—- SWIRLING PATTERNS IN THE BEDSPREAD —-

JENNY LIES on the motel bed, her head buried in the pillow. No amount of explanation or cajoling or bribery is turning her. Mark cracks open another can and pours the beer down his throat. It's keeping the hell at bay. Only a few flashes of light on the edges— little rainbow jaggeds, but not bad.

No doubt that teenage jerk at Fisherman's Catch called the police. This is much harder than he expected. He'd like to check out the news but doesn't want to get Jenny riled any more than she is. She sees her father as the enemy and there is nothing he can do.

Or maybe there is.

He could go get Pinocchio. It will take several hours to get there and back, but if he can bring her the dog, he'll be forgiven. But will the dog be there? It's very cold out. Will the dog have frozen to death? Didn't he read a headline about someone dying in the cold snap? And the other headline about the bear mauling a hiker. Maybe Pinocchio got eaten!

Jenny mumbles something.

"Jenny, I can't hear you through the pillow. What are you saying?"

"You lied to me. You kidnapped me. You're a kidnapper and a liar and you made me lose my dog!"

"Sweetie, I didn't kidnap you. We're on an adventure. A vacation. Father and daughter."

"I know what's real! I've seen me on TV!"

The wave patterns in the bedspread swirl around his daughter's head. Mark turns away to stop the motion he knows isn't real.

This dome-shaped motel room is claustrophobic. Blue walls. Stupid Eskimo drawings of seals and walruses and fish. The same patterns swirl in the curtains. The television on the wall is growing, a giant black mouth. *Why did she pick this place!? Damn Igloo Motel. It's going to turn on me.* The carpet writhes with blue icy swirls. Mark feels the tendrils twisting up his ankles.

That's not real. It's imagination. Like a movie. You can feel it but it's not real.

Only—he can't breathe. Jenny's staring at him. Why did they get married? What? He's not married to her. She's too small. But look at the anger in her eyes. She's a miniature version of Beverly.

His chest is hurting. *Gonna die.* It's panic. *Breathe.*

Jenny stares at Mark. She looks scared. He tries to talk but his mouth is made of mud.

"Daddy, are you sick?"

Mark pulls in but nothing fills his lungs. He's underwater.

"Daddy, should I call someone?"

The carpet's icy swirls inch nearer and the television grows—a wide black hole sucking in everything. The curved walls bend closer. Jagged rainbows come in from all sides. Sounds are crushing Mark. The beer didn't stop it. He's been off the meds for too long. There's no turning this one back. It's coming. He knows. He's been here. He's got to get out before he's dragged under all the way.

Jenny pulls Mark's phone from his coat on the chair. The screen lights as she pushes the power on. "Should I call emergency?"

She's going to get me caught. She's got to be stopped. Get the thing in the suitcase.

Mark drops to his knees and crawls across the foaming swirls to his suitcase. Hands deep into cloth, he feels the smooth metal and pulls the gun out. It shakes his whole arm and a jolt of fear punches his stomach as he raises the barrel.

The girl in front of the gun-sight freezes.

"Put down that phone, little girl."

As the girl puts the phone down on the bed, her face turns into a mask of that famous painting with the man screaming. Open mouth, panicked eyes. Grotesque terror.

No, it isn't the screaming man mask, it's a laughter mask. The mask is making fun of him.

Mark tries to hold his gun steady but it wobbles too much to get good aim.

"DADDY!"

The mask drips and turns into a girl and the girl drips and turns into Jenny. His daughter crouches in the bed, sobbing behind his shaking gun barrel.

What are you doing?!

Mark lowers his arm and bites his pistol hand hard. The pain gets his mind sharp enough so he can see what might be reality. *Hold on.*

Place the gun on the side table beside the bed. Jenny shrinks back from it. Mark watches the barrel curve toward him. He wills himself to ignore the vision, picks up the cell phone and turns it off, putting it in his pocket.

What was he doing?

Mark bites his hand again, drawing blood. The pain zaps his mouth into working. "Jenny. Don't let anyone in. Use this gun if you need to. Only if you need to. Only if someone's trying to get in the door."

Jenny stares, terrified.

"That person at the door might be me. I might try to get in and if I don't sound nice, don't let me in. If I try to break in, shoot me."

Tears slip from the girl's eyes. The igloo is curving, disappearing into the television's black hole.

"You've seen it on TV. Just point and shoot."

Mark puts the plastic room key on the swirling ocean of the bed. "Lock the door with the bolt after I go."

Jenny's no longer angry. Only scared. He should comfort her. A father does that, but he can't trust himself. The painting of a white whale on the wall bubbles and squirms, threatening to destroy him. Time to move.

Mark whips on his coat and waves. His hand strobes jagged light. "Crap. It's all fucked. Lock the door."

He bursts out into the cold black and hears Jenny slam the door, snapping the lock.

The cold sends the jaggeds underground for a moment.

If I can drink enough, I'll pass out and there'll be no chance of making trouble. Got to find a liquor store or bar. Pass out in the car. Too late to look for Pinocchio. He's a frozen dog that's likely a bear-picnic anyway.

— PERP'S PHONE TRACKED —

THE PERP FINALLY TURNED ON the phone. Not for long but long enough.

Thank god. Now to capture the man and save the girl.

With the destination programed into his GPS, Trooper Nate steers his cruiser north. It's growing dark. Another month of relative normal and then the long season of hell. The winter darkness brings a surge to his work. Domestic abuse. Drunkenness. Assaults. No one handles the never-ending-nights well.

Nate wonders about the abandoned dog at the gas station. It was left on purpose. That might mean the father doesn't care if the girl is sad. He might be disassociating from her. Not a good development. Nate presses down on the gas. As long as a moose isn't crossing the highway, he'll be okay. Damn deneege can destroy a car if they're hit.

Forty minutes later, Nate arrives at the Igloo Motor Court. Of course, no one with a kid could pass this. A kid would insist on staying here. Hell, Nate'd always wanted to stay here himself. Each cabin, a little igloo. He pictures that message-in-the-bottle-lady here with him on their honeymoon, toasting with Champagne.

What? Focus, man!

No cars out front but that doesn't mean anything. The father would park in back if he were hiding.

Nate curves his cruiser past the blue vacancy sign over the office, out of sight of the igloos, in case someone's on the lookout.

Setting his stiff trooper's hat on his head, Nate steps to the office, jingling the bell as he enters. With the igloo motif, he half expects to be greeted by a fellow Koyukon complete with caribou-fur coat and fishing spear. A white man ambles in from the back—looks like a Vietnam Vet. Seventy something. Long grey hair, walrus mustache, tattooed arms. Lots of his type came to Alaska after that war, determined to escape the world.

Seeing Nate's uniform, the man's eyes dart to the back room. Everyone gets nervous around a trooper.

"What can I do you for, brother?" the man asks.

"You have guests? A man and girl. She'd be around eight."

"A man came in few hours ago. He didn't come in the office with anyone and I didn't look out at the car. Don't know if there's a girl."

"He still here?"

"Sorry, Brother, don't got your gig. Don't keep tabs on people. Just take the money and give 'em the key."

"What room?"

The man lifts the reading glasses hanging on his chest. "Igloo Eight."

Nate taps the counter twice, saying he's grateful.

All the igloos are dark except one. Number eight. Nate creeps close to the door. Hears the sound of a television. He moves to the circular window. A curtain covers most of it, but there's a little slit he can peek through. On the edge of the bed is a girl's foot. Sneaker. Striped sock. Bare ankle. Could be the girl. Can't tell if she's alive or dead. Is the father with her?

Nate circles the igloo but can't see through the other port-hole windows, so he returns to the door and listens for clues. Only the television sounds. He pulls his Glock from its holster. *Don't let the man be in there. Don't let him hear me.*

Hand on the doorknob. *Slowly turn, be silent.* It's locked. He could knock, but if the man's there—could be dangerous. A well-placed kick to the left of the knob should do it. If Nate's wrong, he'll have to justify the busted door. If he's right, he'll be a hero.

Don't shake. You're a professional. Gun ready. You'll scan the room and if the man is there, you'll plant your feet and warn him not to move.

Nate has done it in training and seen it done in movies, but when he kicks, this door flies back instantly and crashes against the wall. The girl looks up, eyes blue, reflecting the television. As Nate scans for the abductor, she reaches to the bedside and BLAM!

Nate flies backwards, lands flat on the asphalt outside the doorway. The girl screams and the television laughs and *this isn't how it's supposed to go.* He's not supposed to die here.

He blinks up at the sky which turns into a face. The girl looks down at him. "I'm sorry," her mouth says and she's gone.

The blue neon vacancy sign shines upside-down and beyond that the northern lights dance, curtains of yellow and green shifting and curling. The great theater in the sky, if only he'd let go and fly up to it.

Another shape blocks the view, a silhouette leaning over him saying something about *alright, brother* and *hang in there.* But it needs to move out of the way of the dancing sky curtains. *I'm required on stage,* Nate thinks. *They're waiting for me.*

— JENNY ON THE RUN —

JENNY RUNS. She may not know as much as a grownup, but she knows when she's in trouble. You don't shoot someone and not get in trouble.

It's dark except for the greenish swirls in the sky. The air is cold. Colder than she's ever felt and she didn't grab her coat after she shot that man. Now her life is ruined. Maybe she'll freeze to death. Maybe she'll be eaten by a polar bear.

Her sneakers slap the road with no direction other than AWAY.

The green curtains overhead hardly light the blackness below. Jenny has no idea of what's ahead. They say the world is round but they may be wrong. Tonight she may run off the edge. *It doesn't matter,* she thinks between ragged breaths. *I'm not important anyway. I'll just be one of those lost people that never got found.*

THE MOTHER AND CALF glide through the sea. There are songs of others ahead. Home clicks her sonar to learn more. A gathering of Minke whales, their long sleek forms dart about, sifting krill. A teenage male moves close. At twenty-five feet long, he's no threat to Home's massive body, just curious. She meets his eye. Clicks bounce between them. Baby peeks out from under its mother's belly. The Minke rolls and dives, circles and flips, performing a dance for them.

Above, a dark shape shadows the surface. The teenage minke rises, blasts out, pulls in air, dives—a sharp boom, a piercing of the water, bubbles trailing as a barbed harpoon flies and collides with the back of the Minke. An explosion rips a gaping hole in the whale. Blood plumes from the wound—a Medusa's head of red snakes writhing in the water.

Home dives, pressing down on her calf to shield it and send it into the dark depths.

Above them, the Minke swirls and twists in pain. It tries to swim away but the rope reels it upward to the whaler's shadow.

Home sings out The Lullaby Song for Baby but also for the thrashing terrified Minke. A song that might be a comfort or a sorrowful goodbye.

Blood clouds the water, obscuring the screaming teenager as he is hauled up to the boat.

Home presses her sweet one farther down, but she knows Baby witnessed it all.

—- MARK'S FEELING BETTER —-

SNOW FALLS as Mark stumbles out of the bar. The flakes light up in the neon beer signs. Pretty red and orange swirling diamonds. Looks almost like the jaggeds returning, but this seems real.

No one follows him out of the bar. That could be a good thing or a bad thing.

He looks down at his knuckles. No blood. Good. Probably means no battered bodies inside. No cops or tasers. He didn't slip under. He didn't shatter. It felt possible, but he made it through.

Better get back to Jenny. She'll be worried. Shouldn't have given her the gun. Probably made her more scared.

Mark walks stiffly toward the snow-covered car. The white layer is pristine. Untouched by life. He'd like to be that way again. Pure. Undamaged.

You can stop all this. It's simple. Don't go back to the igloo motel. Get in the car and drive into new snow. Jenny'll be safe. She'll go home. Leave her now. It's the right thing to do.

Tears move across his vision and he knows that's what he needs to do. Let her go. Drive into virgin territory. Disappear. Make amends by leaving her behind.

At the car, Mark leans over the hood, licking the fresh powder. It tastes like mountain water or metal. His tears make little holes in the white landscape. Jenny's like snow. Fresh and new. Even when she's a brat. She's the only thing he ever made that was good. Her smile hurts him when she sends it his way. Makes him feel something like —being liked. If he takes good care, he might even get her to love him. If he could make that happen, things could be wonderful. They could start a new life. Make plans even.

That's settled. He won't leave her. Not now. She'll get over the dog. They'll get more money from that lady with the kid in the whale. Everything will work out. Mark drives, singing a made-up song about hope and love. The white flakes fly into his windshield in a mesmerizing headlight dance.

Mark slows as he nears the motel. The Igloo Motor Court is lit with flashing lights. Trooper cars. Someone ratted on him. Maybe the hippy manager. Jenny's probably in the back of a cop car telling them all about her daddy stealing her away. Mark feels a pang of grief simultaneously as an internal weight lifts. Sorrow and relief spread over him. Jenny is safe-and-sound now. He can't hurt her. No more worries. This is a good thing. Soon Jenny'll be back with

Beverly. No one will care what he did, when she's back. No one will look for him. No one will find him. He'll disappear forever.

Keeping the car at the same speed, Mark continues past the motel. As the lights grow small in his rear-view mirror, tears bend and stretch the beams. Jenny. Jenny. Jenny. She was a good girl. She was sweet. He was her Daddy. Did he ever say he loved her? Does he? One way or the other, he should have said he loved her. A daughter needs that, doesn't she?

He steers the car north as the sobs shake his chest.

—- JENNY'S LOST —

JENNY'S FACE is wet with tears and snowflakes and her runny nose. It's really cold out. She'll end up frozen in a snow drift. The sky curtains swirl above but don't light the ground. Green overhead and dark white below. No sounds from her sneakers. Is she on the road anymore? The snow is too thick to tell. Only thing for sure. She's lost.

She wipes her nose with her hand and the sharp smell startles her. Gun powder? That's evidence of her crime. The tears come harder now. Maybe they'll freeze and make little icicles under each eye. That would look funny.

Questions fill her. Did she kill that man? How long will she be in jail? Will she ever see her dad again? Will she ever see her dog again?

"Where are you, Pinocchio?" Jenny asks out loud.

A dog barks.

Could it be that easy?!

"Here Pinocchio! Come, boy!"

A scraggly grey dog bounds out of the pale darkness and puts two snowy paws on Jenny's freezing legs. "You're not Pinocchio. Who are you?"

The dog has a tag but it's too dark to read.

"Are you lost, too? Do you want to stay with me? We can find a place to spend the night. Maybe there's a cave with no bears. You can keep me warm and I'll keep you warm."

Jenny takes off the beaded Indian belt present her Dad gave her and slides it through the dog's collar for a leash.

They trot in the snow together. She's not alone. She's got a companion.

"Can I call you Pinocchio?" she asks the dog.

Far off, a young voice yells, "Rascal!"

"Are you Rascal?"

Jenny walks toward the distant voice and a cluster of lights becomes visible. The person keeps calling and Jenny heads for the wandering beam of a flashlight in the falling snow. The dog tries to run forward. "Hold on, Rascal," Jenny says. "I'm not letting you go until we know for sure. Don't want you getting more lost."

The beam of light gets closer. Jenny calls out, "Hello. Are you looking for a dog?"

A voice in the darkness calls back, "Yes. Did you see one?"

"I have a dog here."

Snow-muffled sounds of running and the flashlight bobs and bounces over the whiteness. A dim figure of a short kid stops, shining the light on the dog.

"That's Rascal alright. Thanks for finding him."

"You live over by the lights?"

"Yep. Wanna see?"

Jenny hands her belt to the kid. "You can use my belt 'til you get Rascal home."

The kid walks ahead, leading Rascal, and making sure to shine the flashlight so Jenny can see the ground.

They come to a grouping of mobile homes. In the light shining over a door, Jenny gets a look at her companion. He's a pudgy kid around her age. *Thick dark hair. Squinty eyes. Maybe he's an Eskimo.* Jenny thinks. *He should be living in an igloo and not this trailer home.*

"Come in. I'm Ray."

"Jenny," she answers before she realizes she shouldn't say her real name. Now it's too late to change it. She'll have to get smarter if she's going to not get caught.

She mimics Ray's action of kicking the side of the door to knock the snow from her sneakers. Hope there's heat inside!

There's an old-fashioned style fat television on. The walls are full of velvet tapestries with polar bears and moose. A string of laundry hangs over a radiator. Jenny moves close.

"Hungry, Jenny?" Ray asks, handing her the belt off Rascal's collar.

She's starving. When did she eat last? Not since that one bite of super-hot shrimp at the stupid fish place.

Ray opens a can of Spaghetti O's, dumps it in a blackened pot, and lights the stove.

Surprised a kid is allowed to use the gas stove, she asks, "Where's your mom? Or dad?"

"They're away 'til late. Down at the council meeting." Ray clears off a spot on the coffee table in front of the TV as Jenny huddles over the clicking radiator. When the food is boiling, Ray sets out their dinner.

The Spaghetti O's are great. Jenny's never had them before. Sweet and satisfying. Like thick, candy soup.

Rascal hops next to Jenny on the couch and puts his head on her lap.

"My dog is lost, too," Jenny says. "Only he doesn't have his tag on, so I don't know if I'll find him."

"Where'd you lose him?"

Jenny tells Ray of the market, but she doesn't know the name or the road or the town. There's no way to find Pinocchio. "He's lost forever," Jenny says, trying to keep the tears in.

"You can't remember anything about the market?"

"All I remember was there was a sign about getting gold out of the ground."

"Like one of those history signs?"

Jenny nods. The exhaustion of the day is getting to her. "Is it okay if I stay here?" Jenny asks. "I can sleep on the couch."

"Mom sometimes doesn't make it to the bed and collapses on the couch. She'll squish you. But—if you don't snore, you can sleep in my bed with me. You'll have to share that side with Rascal."

Jenny thanks him and helps pile the pan and bowls in the sink and they turn off the television and go to bed. It's cozy with Ray and Rascal tucked next to her. She feels warm and tired, only when she closes her eyes, the gun goes off and that man collapses in the doorway. Replaying the vision, she sees the uniform and the badge. He was a police officer. They get super mad when you kill one.

—- BRAINSTORMING —-

THE WAVES KEEP ROCKING. The hours keep drifting. Gjesken and I both stare at the radar screen showing the blinking beacon on Home. Torsten's turning the wheel lazily, keeping the Nord Spyd well back from the whale, now that we know that she's a mother and fierce about protecting her calf.

I'm so bored. I should film something. Or go fishing. Or call someone. Maybe that Alaska State Trooper Nate. Except he's busy saving that kidnapped girl. I'll call Tobey and Arthur!

I stand up and stretch. "I'm going to try to reach my brother." I step out and after I get everything setup, I text Tobey and Arthur: *Can we talk?*

Minutes later, Skype rings. My brother and his husband lean together smiling at me. It's so good to see them!

"I thought you'd be filming this, Arthur," I say.

"I'm recording the screen through the computer."

I tell them everything, except about almost drowning. They are amazed at my plan with the siren and oranges and overjoyed that I've found Brian's whale. I tell them about the whale being a mother and that we have a beacon on her and the Nord Spyd is following.

"Nord Spyd," Tobey repeats. "What does that mean?"

When I say I figure it's about spies, he gets to typing.

"Norwegian for *North Spear*."

North Spear. That's not a good thing.

Arthur asks, "Now that you found them, how do you get two kids out of the lungs of a whale?"

I shrug. I've been too busy thinking of how to find Brian, to think about how to get him out.

Tobey and Arthur brainstorming ideas. They suggest dropping scuba gear in for Brian and Liesl to go out through the intestines. I remind them about the bone crushing muscles of the stomach. They suggest capturing the whale in a net and using a helicopter to hold it up while a hydraulic lift opens the mouth and the kids walk out. I tell them that this whale probably weighs more than 200 tons. Its tongue alone weighs more than an elephant. They suggest capturing the baby by net and towing the child to shore so the mama will get beached and the hydraulics open the mouth and the kids walk out. I nix the idea for lots of reasons, the first of which, I'm not kidnapping her baby.

My brother and his husband stare at me. We're all thinking. There has to be a solution. Only maybe there isn't. Maybe there isn't a way to get someone out of the lungs of a whale. Arthur asks, "What about a superhero?"

I should laugh 'cause he's filming. "Ha, ha. Do you know any?"

Arthur turns a bit red and answers, "I do."

—- NATE IN THE HOSPITAL —-

THE BULLET-PROOF VEST did its job, Nate is alive, but last night when the girl shot him, the violent blow to his chest spoke to him of death. Now bored and aching, he shifts in the hospital bed. Pain stabs his side. Broken rib? Sucking in a breath to squash the hurt, he leans to the bedside table and finds his phone. The weather app opens first. Snow continuing. He doesn't remember snow. It didn't snow. The white glare from the window tells him otherwise.

Should check emails but something pulls him to that bookmarked site. Crowdfunding for the Boy in the Whale. The updates show new coordinates of the ship Nord Spyd in the Norwegian sea. The boat is closer to shore. Are they turning back?

Have they found the boy or are they giving up? He wants to call Ann and get word. Tell her he's thinking of her—

Robbie and Massak tap on the door as they open it. Nate slips the phone under his sheet. The shame-feeling pulls him back to high school and his crush on the girl in Math class. Why must we always hide what we are attracted to? Why can't we love without losing strength? Nate retrieves the phone from beside his thigh and lays it on his soft bulge.

"Auditioning for a superhero role, Nate?" Massak asks, grinning.

"What the fuck were you thinking, busting in without backup?" Robbie asks, playing bad-cop, as usual.

Nate puts his hand out to shake theirs. The pain from the ribs almost makes him cry. Stifling a grunt, he asks, "What happened to the girl?"

Robbie and Massak look at each other. Clearly, they have no clue what he's talking about.

That means the girl is still lost and the father is still out there.

Nate lets the two officers chat and chide him for a while longer, then pretends to get sleepy. "The drugs are kicking in, fellas. Gotta get my beauty rest."

When he's alone, Nate calls a cab company and puts on his uniform. It's stained. Did he pee his pants when he got shot? Damn. And where's his gun? Maybe the nurses' station has it.

Holding his jacket over the stain in his trousers, Nate steps up to the nurse on duty.

"I'll be heading out now. Know where I might find my service revolver?"

After several exchanges and intercessions with doctors and security, Nate leaves fully armed.

A long cab ride through pristine snow brings him to his cruiser at the station. More chiding and praise, and back in the cruiser, his chest aches. Is it just the gunshot? At his apartment, fresh change of clothes, phone charger, and he's ready to go. He's going to help that girl if it's the last thing he does.

—- WAKING WITH RAY AND RASCAL —-

THE GUN GOES OFF and the man falls and Jenny jerks awake. She lies shaking beside the boy. Who is he? The dog between them reminds her. She ran and saw the dog and then the boy. Rascal and Ray. She ran from the policeman she killed.

The dog thumps the bed with his tail as Jenny tries not to cry. Ray wakes, gets up and waves for her to follow. They slip past the living room where he makes the two-handed sleep gesture about the snoring lump on the couch. Tiptoe into the kitchen. Pop-Tarts from the cabinet.

A groan in the living room and the large woman stumbles into the kitchen. She blinks down at Jenny, "Who's this?"

Ray pops breakfast into the toaster. "She just stayed the night, Mom."

Ray's mother squints at Jenny, peering close. "I seen you. I know you from the TV. You're that girl that's wanted."

Found out, Jenny darts to the door, bursts into brightness—and collapses face-first in a thick snowdrift.

Ray rushes to pull her up. "Are you really wanted?"

"Please don't tell. Please."

"By the police?"

Jenny sobs. "I didn't mean to. I was scared."

Ray's mother fills the doorway. "Come on in, girl. We'll take you to the troopers."

Jenny lurches over the drift and high-steps through the snow as fast as she can. Heading anywhere that's *away*.

"Come back!" Ray yells.

Jenny keeps running.

"Fire up the snowmobile and get her back before she freezes, Ray," the mother says, yawning. She hands Ray two coats and the keys and closes the trailer door.

The roar of the snowmobile grows and Jenny, huffing out billowing clouds of breath, stops running. Ray slows and hands her a coat. "What'd you do?"

"Shot a policeman."

"No wonder you ran. Where you headed?"

Jenny shivers a shrug.

"Everyone has to go somewhere. Pick a place."

"I want my dog."

"Then that's the place. Get on. We'll visit Lightfoot Rose."

Jenny climbs behind Ray on the snowmobile. They take off and she's freezing and the wind hurts and the noise is horrible but they're going fast, flying almost, and this is the most fun she's had in forever!

—- ORANGES —-

WE DON'T KNOW what's happening with our rescue. Not knowing feels worse than when we were drifting with no hope. Liesl wants to call her Mom with the new phone, but we can't waste the battery every time we have a whim.

We open the second orange. Home's lungs fill with the wonderful scent. We pull each segment apart and eat them one at a time, relishing the juice and zing and sweetness.

Liesl and I squeeze the skins of the orange after we finish eating the fruit. Little explosions of citrus oil fill the air. We rub the bruised peel against our flesh, each other's flesh. That leads to our favorite pastime.

A sudden rise by Home sends me deeper into Liesl and she screams and grabs me tighter, pressing me in and Home blasts out the air and pulls in a cold breath, blasts the air again. It jolts us in the most fantastic way, like we're screwing on a rollercoaster and when I go deep, the rollercoaster drops and I go deeper and Liesl screams with what sounds like it must be a great feeling and I'm going to pop and Home rises and blasts and grabs air and blasts again and again and jerks around with each blast and it's not so good anymore because we've separated and are banging into each other and *what's wrong with Home?* This constant blasting of air. It's not normal.

Liesl screams, "Home sneeze. It be oranges."

Home sneezes over and over and we're jolted and jostled and Liesl smashes me in the neck and the Wrigglers shake up angry bright and we tumble and I hold Sprout safe against my chest as we search for orange rinds and my ankle bundle hits my balls and we keep searching and gathering orange and the Yellow Shopping Cart unwinds tangling in Liesl's hair and find more rinds and dump them out the flap and hold onto each other so we'll stop crashing and the blowing and blasting continues. Maybe Home isn't sneezing, maybe she's trying to breathe. Maybe she can't and she's dying.

Liesl must think the same thing because she whispers in my ear, "We eat marijuana."

She wants to get stoned so we won't notice while we die.

Might as well.

She pulls her purse from my bundle, unwraps the folded origami menu and we both start munching marijuana. The taste reminds me of when Dad made me clean out the bottom of the lawn mower of the cut grass clog that had dried and molded and fermented into something tart and pungently earthy. The pot doesn't taste really good, but it's a nice change from fish and seaweed. We chew and swallow as Home continues to lurch violently.

I've never eaten pot. Hardly smoked. I know people put it in brownies, but how much? What if we eat too much?

"Do you think we should keep eating or stop?" I ask Liesl.

"We eat all. After, whatever happen, we not care."

We keep munching and swallowing until it's gone. But nothing happens. Maybe it doesn't work if you don't smoke it.

Home lurches again and my sneaker hits me in the face. I scramble to illuminate it with the Wrigglers. It's empty.

"Sprout's missing. We've got to find him."

We search with the phone and Wrigglers and find a lump of seaweed tucked in a spongy lung fold. Sprout's little tendril still reaches out. Still looking for sun. I lift him and squiggle as far as I

268

dare up the channel to the blowhole and raise him to get sun each time it opens with a violent lurch.

"Soak in the rays, Sprout. You're alive."

"Sprout say not place to live," Liesl says.

I can't believe she's saying that. This is Home. "We're in a place. It's home. And it's still Life."

Liesl twists her mouth to the side like she's not so sure.

This is important. I need her to understand. "Here, it's the same as outside. We talk, we eat, we look for entertainment, we—you know—"

"—do sex." Liesl smiles. "I know. Sprout plant we have. A house plant or yard tree. We water him, clean house, want things we don't have—it *is* life."

"Someone's in a whale, someone's in a house, someone's in a cave, someone's in prison—"

"Someone in city. Someone in pastoral."

"Someone's in Burbank. I sent a message-in-the-bottle from this whale. I should have done that when I was in Burbank."

"Sent a message?"

"Put a message in a bottle—'Help! I'm trapped in a suburb and can't escape.'"

Liesl cracks up. She's so pretty with her teeth in a row. "Help! I'm trapped in Norway and can't escape!"

"Help! I'm trapped in front of the computer and can't escape!"

"Help! I'm trapped on cell phone and can't escape!"

It's hilarious. We're rolling on spongy lung with laughter.

"I'm trapped in a worthless life!" Liesl blurts out.

"I'm trapped in meaninglessness."

"We're trapped wherever we are!"

Everything becomes very clear and profound. I understand. This is what I want to say. "We got saved! Home saved us. We could live here forever. What do you want to do? Pick anything."

Liesl scrunches her mouth, thinking hard. "I teach yoga and Norwegian."

"I'll teach weight-loss exercises, top-forty whale songs, and create the world's first glowing-wriggler sitcom."

We make plans for what to do with our lives in Home. Maybe stop re-using the condom and have a baby. Start a family in the whale. Home-school our kids. Have birthdays. Graduations. Somewhere after our fourth child, we notice our whale has stopped sneezing.

— SEAL MAN AND ARTHUR —

I KNOW ENOUGH to film this. The helicopter hovers over us, whipping the waves and battering everyone with sharp wind. A rope drops from above and Torsten holds it as steady as a man wearing a harness is lowered, pointing a camera at me. I point my phone at him. Zoom in. Birdlike nose. Bulging eyes. My brother's husband, Arthur.

The idea of seeing someone that knows me sends tears blurring the view. The moment Arthur's feet touch the deck, I throw my arms around him. He holds the camera at arm's length to document the hug.

I introduce Arthur to Torsten and Gjesken and when he's unhooked from the harness, it's pulled back to the helicopter.

Arthur points his video camera up as a man gracefully slides down the rope onto our deck. Crewcut. Wide shoulders. Thick neck. This must be our superhero.

The man sends back the harness and signals in a brusk military way. Several camouflage-duffel bags are lowered and the helicopter flies away. The loss of the wind and noise is a relief.

The man scrutinizes Gjesken and me. He steps toward me, his gloved hand extended. "You're Ms. Ann Ketchum, initiator of this mission."

I blink my hello.

"I'm Garret. Here to find and rescue your boy, and—" He turns to Gjesken. "You must be the local."

"Gjesken."

"Here to find and rescue your girl." Garret lifts all the duffel bags. "Let's meet at mess at eighteen-hundred to discuss tomorrow's operation."

My heart jolts at the word tomorrow. Does he mean I'll be holding Brian tomorrow? Could this be?

"Who can show me to my bunk?" the superhero asks.

I turn to Gjesken, "Do you mind? I'd like to talk with Arthur."

Gjesken formally extends her hand toward the stairs.

"After you, Ma'am," and he follows her down.

When he's out of sight, I whisper to Arthur, "Where did you find him?"

"Don't ask, and I won't tell."

"Okay, but who is he?"

"Ex-Navy SEAL."

I want to ask what makes him an ex-Navy SEAL as opposed to current-Navy SEAL but Arthur grabs my arms and stares at me, a look of bewildered shock on his face.

"You look—" Arthur pauses.

What? Have I aged from stress? Am I a bedraggled mess?

"You look fucking fantastic, Ann. I didn't really grasp it on the Skype screen. I've never seen you look more alive and beautiful and —shit, you found your mojo!"

Relief and pride spread over me. "Really?"

"No matter what happens, this documentary will be about the fucking awakening of Ann Ketchum."

—- HISTORIC MARKER SEARCH —

RAY INTRODUCES JENNY to Lightfoot Rose, saying she's a cousin from down state. Something in the woman's wrinkled face shows she knows this to be a lie, but she welcomes them in.

After hot chocolate near of the stove, Ray and Jenny huddle in-front of an old computer, looking up the historic markers in the Yukon area. With each one they find, they go on Google street view.

One is near a log cabin. One is near a cemetery. One is near several mounds in a field. One is near a gas station market.

"That's it!" Jenny screams. "How can I get there, Ray? Is there a bus that goes there? I don't have any money."

Ray turns to the old woman watering the herbs in her window garden. "Lightfoot Rose, who's heading down past the Junction?"

The woman doesn't look up. "That'd be Jarvis. He does that run three times a week."

They take the snowmobile past several mobile homes and a cinderblock library/town hall and pull to a stop in front of a tarp-covered cabin. A propane truck is parked in the driveway. The two children crunch across the packed snow to the door, but Jenny stops Ray before he knocks. "What are you going to ask him?"

"If he can give you a ride to the junction."

"Why would he?"

"Why wouldn't he?"

"Because I'm a kid. I'm not supposed to travel alone."

Ray looks at Jenny like she's crazy. "That may be something not allowed somewhere else, but not here."

He knocks.

— NEW MORNING —

MARK WAKES, shivering in the back-seat of the car. Pinocchio's quilt and the sleeping bag probably kept him from freezing to death. *Where am I?* He remembers parking off in the woods. The windows are covered with snow. Mark rolls one down, pushes the wall of white, and jerks back, as a distorted face blinks at him. A baby moose with velvety horns. Reaching out to feel the softness, Mark smiles. The baby is nudged aside and a massive mother presses its head through the window and into the car, taking up all the space. Mark scrunches away from the monster. *Is this real?*

The nostrils send out jets of steam. The lips peel back on yellow teeth the size of dominoes. Hot breath hisses over the cowering man with the thick smell of acrid wildness.

Real or not, don't attack, please.

The moose snorts, spattering Mark in the face, and pulls away. The back of its head catches on the window edge and the beast panics, jerks wildly, lifting the car. It lunges to reach Mark, dominoes gnashing inches from his face, stopped by shoulders against the door frame. Another jerk and twist and it pulls out, free of the car. The mother and child spin and gallop into the forest.

Mark rolls up the window and dives over the seat to the front, roars the engine to life. Blast the heat. Wipers strain against snow.

Where's Jenny?! Oh yeah.

The night rewinds with flashing lights and police cars outside of the motel. The police found Jenny and she's probably flying to Missouri now or Beverly's flying to Alaska to pick her up.

Mark realizes he can relax now. Get a little shut-eye and have something to eat other than fast-food, animal crackers, and cereal. A steak would do nicely. A soft bed and a steak. Hopefully, he can get this car out of the snow and back on the road.

Checking for angry moose, he steps outside, wipes the windows clear, kicks the tires as if that will help, then he puts the car in drive. The wheels spin a bit but catch, and he angles the car out of the trees and onto the freshly plowed road. He'll stop at the first place that's got a restaurant and a vacancy.

—- OPERATIONS ORDER —-

AFTER DINNER, Garret signals for Arthur to start filming. Once the red light is on, Garret clears his throat. "Warno. Ma'ams, Sirs, thought it best to convey the OPORD to all concerned. First our Situation; We have two friendlies, Brian and Lisa—"

"Liesl," Gjesken corrects.

"—Leesul held captive in what we believe to be the lungs of this Moby Dick. Said Dick has been identified and tracked. 2. Mission;

We intend to extricate said friendlies from Dick. 3. Equipment; We have three state-of-the-art scuba outfits, knives, pistol, underwater explosives—"

"We can't hurt the whale," I say, looking for agreement.

"Ma'am, let me finish the OPORD. We can discuss once everything is on the table. Number 4. Support; None to speak of. Civilians with no military or medical training. Correcto?"

We all nod and Garret continues. "5. Commo; We have two cell phones held by the friendlies within Dick. From my briefing, these offer spotty com at best. 6. Command; I'm in charge of the operation. I will determine the best course of action based on field intel. Should something happen to me, next in command is the ship's captain."

I bite my lip to keep from speaking. Glance up at Arthur and he's smiling behind the camera. Undoubtedly got the shot of my silent disagreement.

"The plan is to move out at 0900, making our way to the Dick and open up that cocksucker like a God damned tin can." He holds up a hand to stop my interference. "Of course, collateral damage to the Dick will depend on him, ma'am. Our sole objective is to retrieve your kids and we will do just that, irre-motherfuckin-gardless."

"You're going to retrieve Brian and Liesl from the whale? You mean get them out, but how?" I ask.

"Whatever means necessary. I'll establish contact with the friendlies—your children—and extract them from the Dick. We'll rendezvous with this ship for pickup."

Garrett looks at us like *Mission Accomplished*.

Is he crazy? This sounds more insane than a boy living in a whale.

I dial my cell to the new phone in the whale to tell Brian of the plan. The phone doesn't connect. They must be out of range. They wouldn't keep that new phone off, would they?

—- HOUSTON —-

LIESL HOLDS the bag of Wrigglers in front of her face, staring at me through *The Blue Light Special*, acting out the characters. She keeps slipping into Norwegian. I don't know what the hell she's saying but it's hilarious.

I start talking gibberish to show her how it feels and that becomes so funny. "Mori camrick goof-minkle orbee boolah," I say like a politician.

Liesl says something in a high squeaky voice and I don't know if it's real words or made-up but it cracks me up bad. My stomach is gonna get even more buff at the rate I'm bustin' a gut. "Bust a gut. Bust a gut."

"Is when people has sex?" Liesl asks.

That cracks me up even more and woody rises and I shout out, "You want to bust a gut with me? I want to bust a gut with you."

"Bust a gut, yes."

I reach inside the ankle bundle for my shorts. There's my T-shirt. Liesl's purse. Got the shorts and feel in the pocket—Yes!—pull the condom out—it rips. Shit!

—*Pretend to put it on and don't tell her.*

"Houston, we have a problem."

"What Useton?"

—*Don't tell her about the condom!!*

"Houston is someone who listens to problems. Ours is—the condom broke," I say before I can change my mind.

"Can you do—where you get out before—?"

"Sure," I say happily, very unsure.

She rolls on her back, placing the bag of Wrigglers on her breasts. Good thing they can't sting through the plastic!

I move in and watch my hands on her nipples through the blue baggie. It's like a porno video but feels super hot and not creepy and no one is gonna interrupt by calling me to dinner.

Sliding into her and—a ringing.

We both part and paw for the sound. The new phone. Liesl picks it up.

"Hallo?—I can't hear you.—Hallo?—Hallo?"

She covers her mouth to keep from laughing and puts the phone on speaker.

Snippets of mom's voice and what must be Liesl's mom. Overlapping. Interrupting. All broken up. "—tell you about—start—betw—worry—seal—should—extra—because—careful—important—don't—again—"

Liesl moves close to me and whispers, "This be way hear Mor all time."

"Me, too. I only pay attention to every tenth word."

This is the way moms always sound! We cover our mouths so our laughter won't be heard.

They go on for another few minutes but we get engaged with other things and don't even notice whenever they stop talking.

—- FOOTAGE REVIEW —-

SCROLL BACK all the way to the beginning. First shaky footage is the little digital plane on the map-screen on the airplane seat. That seems years ago. I was petrified.

Arthur slaps my shoulder happily at the shot of the bald shining head on the plane. The circling landing over Bergen garners me an excited, raised thumb. "Great stuff!"

He looks a bit disappointed when we jump to the footage of the boat. "Didn't you go to the police station for tracking?"

"They wouldn't let me film there," I lie.

Arthur does a half-smile like he understands but that a *real filmmaker* would have shot surreptitiously.

The boat shots continue. Hallway to the galley, very unsteady shot.

"It was a choppy sea," I explain.

Upstairs shots of Torsten fishing. The deck. The bridge. The sea. The sky. The arrival of supplies, blinking icon, the unveiling of the harpoon cannon, Arthur descending from the helicopter and—The End.

Arthur is silent.

"I'm sorry. I know I should have been filming everything. I just —life was so new and I was worried about Brian and—"

He shakes his head. "This is the most ragged and sloppy and un-focused with swish-pans galore and losing the subject and I've never seen anything as incredibly, engagingly visceral in my life!" Arthur kisses my cheek. "You're fucking fantastic!"

— THE WHITE BEAR HOTEL —

MARK SLOWS THE CAR across the road from the White Bear Hotel. A tall totem pole juts from the snow in front. The pink neon sign says *Vacancy*. Got to be old. Four stories of wood isn't something someone builds nowadays. Big porch. Tall windows. Probably from the gold rush times when it provided rooms for trappers and miners and whores and people running from something. Now one more guy on the run.

Mark splurges on a top-floor room with a bathroom attached. The check-in clerk warns that the hotel has no elevator. "You okay with four flights?"

Mark assures the man that the climb is fine, knowing that everything he owned was left at the igloo motel so there's no luggage to haul upstairs.

After pointing out the saloon and restaurant off the lobby, the clerk hands over the key and Mark starts the journey up. On each floor, he peeks down the hall and sees no one. It's good to have a quiet place all to himself. Out of breath by the fourth floor, he unlocks his room. It's very old-timey. Iron bed-frame. Mirror with black spots where the silver has fallen off. Lace doilies under antique lanterns. The patterns in the curtains and bedspread aren't that bad. Only moving a little. He goes to the window and pushes and pulls and whacks until it slides up and open. Fresh cold air. Far below, his car looks like a toy on a white blanket. The snow-covered mountains glow cotton-candy pink.

Cold wind whistles over him. He shivers and shoves his hands deep into his pant pockets. The metallic dog-tag jolts him with memory and sadness and shame. He runs the tip of his finger over the surface, imagining the engraved letters. Pinocchio. The address in

Missouri. Thank God he picked it up from that fish-place table. Not only so he wouldn't get caught, but so he has something. It's the only thing he has. The only thing related to Jenny.

Time to rest and breathe. Time to forget everything. You're done.

But Mark doesn't feel done. He's alone and lost and never will see his little girl again.

It feels like the sound of the iron door clanging shut. Caging him again. Cutting him off from everything.

Mark sobs, staring out at the sea of white, clutching the precious dog tag.

—- EVIDENCE —-

NATE PULLS into the Igloo Motor Court parking lot. He gets out of the car and stomps through the snow. Although it's daylight and he knows there is no danger, he's shaking when he approaches number 8. Duct tape seals the door where he broke the lock.

The long-haired manager wanders over. "Worried about you. Glad to see you're still walking the earth."

"Thanks for your help. Can I look around?"

The manager pulls off the tape and flicks on the light in the small curved room. Looks like nothing's been touched. "What happened to the girl?" Nate asks.

The manager shrugs. "Didn't see no girl. Your cohorts took the weapon but nothing else. They said to seal it but I got a business. You can see it's a mess, plus with the food—don't want varmints wandering in. Think I can get to cleaning?"

"I'll check, but probably's okay."

The manager leaves him and Nate steps into the room.

Cookies, juice boxes, beer cans, dumb Alaska souvenirs. Man's clothes and girl's clothes. Bottom of the man's suitcase—a newspaper article about the abduction. Picture of the kidnapped girl. That's proof.

He lifts his phone to call about cleaning the room, but he pushes re-dial instead.

She answers on the second ring.

"Hi, Ann, Nate Pike here. The Alaska State Trooper."

She whispers for him to wait. He hears shuffling and footsteps and then her voice saying hello. She sounds glad to hear from him, but maybe he's just imagining that.

"I'm just checking in. Wondered if you heard any more from that man or his daughter."

Damn, now she'll think that's the only reason I called her.

"No, but I'll certainly let you know if I do."

Ask her about herself.

"How's your search for your son going?"

Ann tells Nate of finding the whale and setting the beacon and the Navy SEAL arriving and the plan. It sounds crazy, but he doesn't tell her that.

"I wish you the very best. I'll be rooting for you. By the way, I'm a Koyukon. Alaska Native. What people used to call Eskimo."

Why did you tell her that?

Silence. Maybe that's a deal breaker.

She answers with a smile in her voice. "Well, I've never met a Koyukon before. That's new. But—everything I do now is new, so I'm glad to know you. What's happening with the kidnapped girl?"

Nate tells her of finding the Igloo Motor Court where Jenny was, but not about getting shot. "This's a cute place. Each cabin is like an igloo. I'll send you a picture. Maybe you can send a picture of the boat you're on."

"I'll have to do it later. It's too dark now."

Nate realizes it's the middle of the night in Norway and after apologizing too much and being assured it's alright, he hangs up. There's a warmth in his chest that isn't from the gunshot bruise. It feels good.

Back to work. Nate's going to save Jenny and when he does, the girl is going to need her clothes, pajamas, coat, and toys. He collects the scattered items around the room and pops into the bathroom. Pink kitty toothbrush for girl. Man's Dopp kit has several orange prescription bottles. All empty. With his phone, Nate googles the drugs. Anti-psychosis meds. *Fuck.* Not good. The perps's off his meds and that means the girl's in big trouble. How's he going to find them?

Nate loads everything into the suitcases and carries them to the cruiser's trunk. Waves at the manager, "All yours," then raises his phone toward the igloo.

—- IMAGE SEARCH —-

CREEPING BACK into the closet bedroom, I slide into my bunk and stare at Gjesken's mattress above me. Her slow breathing and the waves creaking the boat form a soothing lullaby, but I'm wide awake.

—*I wonder what my state trooper looks like.*
—*Go to sleep!*
—*He sounds like he really cares about my success.*
—*You have a big day tomorrow! Go to sleep!*

I slip out again and feel my way down to the galley. The glow from the porthole is enough to see. Turn on the football. Turn on laptop. Connection made. Image search: Alaska State Trooper Nate Pike.

There he is.

Something in my chest jingles.

He's handsome in a kind-man way. Younger than me, looks like. Would that be a problem? His eyes glow and it feels as if he's in the dark room with me. My face prickles warm.

I make the picture bigger. Long eyelashes. A hint of something funny in his dark eyes. Hair that's thick and black and would be so great to run my fingers through.

—*Go to sleep.*

His cappuccino skin looks delicious.

—*What is with you?!*

I'll call him back.

—*He's a police officer and working and called only to see if that kidnap-man had been in touch.*

—*He asked about Brian—*

280

—He's not interested in a beige woman!

I touch his screen lips and shut the laptop.

—I'm not beige anymore.

My phone makes a ding and there's a photo of an igloo and my Koyukon trooper smiling in front of it. He's smiling right at me. For me. Now I'll never get to sleep.

— ALASKA TO MISSOURI —

MARK LIES IN HIS HOTEL ROOM watching paisleys swirl on the ceiling. Several morph into birds and others into sea monsters, but the terror doesn't fill him. Even seeing shit that isn't there, he feels okay. Jenny's safe. The AMBER Alert must have been cancelled. The cops will back off. He'll call that message-in-the-bottle lady and get more money. Things are good. A crow dances with a penguin in the corner of the room and they merge into a sparkly blur of light. Maybe he can find a doctor to prescribe meds and send the visions back underwater.

Not much to do except watch visions. It's lonely without the girl. Could he have made it work? Could he have made it work with Beverly if he had stayed?

Mark pictures Jenny reuniting with her mother. They hug at the airport. Is Beverly in Alaska or is Jenny back in Missouri? Beverly will be kissing the girl. Did Mark ever kiss Jenny? He can't remember. Beverly will take the girl to an ice-cream shop, not knowing that crap food's all Jenny's eaten since being with him. Maybe the joy Beverly feels will spread all the way to him?

He dials the hotel phone.

The phone rings and rings and Mark is just about to give up when that familiar voice picks up. Scared and angry and tired. She never sounds any different.

"Hey Beverly. It's me."

"You cocksucker! I can't believe—" Beverly cuts herself off, collects herself, and begins again with a calm voice. "Mark. Excuse me. I've been under a lot of stress. You might imagine."

"Yeah. Me, too."

Beverly does her fake sympathetic sound and asks what he wants.

Mark is suddenly back there—weeks ago—she was asking what he wanted. He didn't know how to say it and she didn't know how to listen and they got nowhere and when they went to bed, he got everything gathered and crept in Jenny's room and and took her. All he wanted was to give his daughter a little vacation. Now Beverly's asking again. "What do you want, Mark?"

"Just checking that everything's cool now."

"In what sense?"

"Did Jenny fly down or did you fly up?"

There is a pause and Beverly whispers, "What are you saying? Did you let her go?"

"Let her go?" A glob of something hot spins in Mark's chest. Several giant crows appear on the iron footboard, bobbing their heads at him. "Didn't you hear from her? From the police?"

"Mark, please. What's going on? Jenny's not with you?"

The blob churns in Mark's chest. The crows dance and chuckle. He throws a pillow but it passes through them and knocks a beer off the TV. What's happening? It's about the girl. She's really missing now. Did she run away? Was she taken? Something might happen to her. Someone might take advantage.

"I'll find her, Bev. Don't worry. I'll find her and bring her back to you."

A sob escapes Beverly and Mark hangs up. Shaking overtakes him. Where is his baby?! He'll go to the police. They'll help.

If you go to the police, they'll only arrest you. That won't help find Jenny. Think, Mark! What would Jenny do? You need to think like she would.

She doesn't know anyone in Alaska. The only person she knows is me and she won't know where to find me. What about my cell phone? Does she have this new number? No, I never gave it to her.

She's lost. She's out in the wilderness. It was cold last night. She froze. And the bears got her. She got frozen and eaten like Pinocchio.

Mark fingers the round dog tag in his pocket.

Jenny'll go to where she last saw Pinocchio. She'll try to find that gas station.

— REUNION —

SEVERAL HOURS LATER, the propane truck shudders to a stop in front of the market. Jenny looks at the gold rush sign. It has little caps of snow roofing each letter. So different from yesterday. Was that just yesterday? She was standing right there with Pinocchio and Dad was smiling and life was different, not bad like now after killing that man.

Jenny thanks the driver, Jarvis, and jumps down from the truck.

The bell jingles in the market like it did last time. At the counter, the Eskimo-looking man's eyebrows raise. "I think I know why you're here, Jenny."

Jenny steps slowly to him. "I'm looking for—"

Boom, boom, boom. Behind the counter, a thumping sound, like a bass drum in the marching band.

The man looks down at the sound by his feet. Pinocchio whines. "Pinocchio!"

The dog puts his paws on the counter and barks.

Jenny rushes to hug her dog. Flesh and fur reunite with words and licks.

Queequeg smiles at Jenny's joy. "The lost is found."

There, behind the counter, on the blanket set down for the dog, Jenny curls next to Pinocchio and buries her face in his fur. Eyes closing, both breathe easier. A synchronized rising and lowering of their chests.

Queequeg knows this is good. Whatever happens, this dog is going home with this girl. Time to call that Koyukon trooper.

— WHY TOBEY ISN'T HERE —

I SLIDE MY FINGERS into that thick black hair and his cappuccino skin moves closer and closer and his breath is sweet and warm on my lips and—

Arthur's face hovers over me. "Come on, Ann, breakfast is ready."

Damn. Just a few seconds longer would have been nice. I grumble up and join everyone in the galley. Arthur films us between taking bites of herring. I learn he's already interviewed the Navy SEAL, Gjesken, and Torsten this morning. I must have really slept late.

After we eat, the Navy SEAL gets to prepping his equipment and Arthur and I sit on deck. He can't get enough of the sea.

"I'm really glad you're here, Arthur. It's so nice to have a friend to talk to. It's such a great surprise 'cause I thought that editing job was going to last a long time."

"It was. I quit."

My face must betray my horror—*this is all my fault! I've destroyed his career!*—because he squeezes my hand, saying, "I quit because this is important. You and Brian, you're important."

Tears spring up and his words feel so good to hear, but make me mad at my brother for never being like his husband. "I guess Tobey had to stay and hold down the fort," I say a little too sarcastically.

"No fort to hold down. I suggested he come."

—*The self-centered Prick Asshole.* "So, he didn't want to come. He didn't want to come and support his sister and nephew—"

"That's not it. Since you've been gone, he kept watching the footage, the Skype calls, and all the clandestine filming I did while you were staying with us. Watching it, over and over. He asked me, 'Am I this controlling all the time?'"

"Bullshit."

Arthur laughs. "Unbelievable, but true. We talked about how he treats you, me, everyone. How he stifles people by being supremely capable, expert-in-all-things, opinionated, critical, and always right."

"Why do you put up with him?"

Arthur shrugs. "Maybe I need that. Maybe it allows me to be the irresponsible one. Gotta look at my part. It takes two to tango."

"Did Tobey accept all that, about being a controlling—"

"—jerk? He's going to therapy and support groups. Gonna try to live-and-let-live. That's why he's not here."

"So he can do therapy?"

"No. Because he didn't want to come here and start running the show."

I'm stunned.

Arthur gives me a warm hug. "Tobey's not here because he loves you."

— DREAMING UNDER THE COUNTER —

PINOCCHIO'S FEET TWITCH. He dreams of running with Jenny in the surf, chasing hundreds of floating bottles.

Jenny's eyes jitter under their lids. She dreams of blowing out birthday candles and having her mom and dad cheer and clap. She hadn't dreamed about Mark before, but she hadn't known him before.

In her dream, her daddy hands her a present. Could it be that Jenny's missing him? Jenny's father's voice rumbles in her dream.

Jenny opens her eyes and the dream-sounds continue. Her father's voice is there, asking about her dog. Asking about her.

From the floor below the counter, Jenny looks up. Queequeg isn't talking but his hand moves to feel for a baseball bat below the register. Jenny can see his hand shaking. Is he afraid of her daddy? She has been.

Jenny taps the man's leg. Without looking down, he moves his palm flat, like a *STAY* signal.

"I just want to know if you've seen the dog or the girl. It's a yes or no answer."

"I don't want any trouble."

"I'm not talking about trouble! I'm talking about a girl and a dog."

Queequeg slides his fingers around the neck of the baseball bat. "Mister, I think you should leave now."

"I tied the dog here and you must have found it."

Jenny wants to scream—but there's a clicking sound and Queequeg lets go of the bat and raises his hands like he's being robbed.

Pinocchio does his high whine.

"Do you have my dog back there?"

"He's not your dog," says Jenny as she stands. "Pinocchio's my dog!" A rush of blood colors her cheeks on seeing her father. His eyes are dark and sunken, he hasn't shaved, a rash has spread up his neck, and in his hand, a gun shakes, pointed at Queequeg. *Another gun? How many does he have?*

"Jenny! Thank god. Come here."

Queequeg gently puts an arm around Jenny's shoulders. "She's not going with you."

"Get out of the way or you'll be sorry," Mark demands. It doesn't sound as threatening as it does on TV.

Jenny's eyes shine big. "Don't shoot him, Daddy."

Mark smiles in a fake way, making his voice sing-song like people do with babies. "It's okay, sweetie. Tell the nice man I'm your daddy and you want to go with me."

Jenny wants to say he stole her and he's scary. She wants to get him back for abandoning Pinocchio. She wants him to suffer. But most of all, she doesn't want to go with Daddy.

Queequeg looks at Jenny. "The police are looking for you, Jenny. They were here."

Fear floods over her.

Queequeg smiles. "If she wants to stay, you'll let her, won't you, Mister?"

Mark nods slowly. "Yes. You can stay. He'll call the police and they'll come get you."

Jenny knows what that means. After all, she shot a policeman.

She looks up at Queequeg. "I want to go with my dad. Thank you for taking care of my dog."

Jenny leads Pinocchio around the counter and stares at Mark until he lowers the gun. He puts his arm around her but she squirms away and heads for the door. As it rings open, she turns to Queequeg and waves. He waves back, his face twitching.

Mark stops. "You got a phone?"

Queequeg doesn't answer.

"Hand it over."

Queequeg slips it from his pocket and holds it out.

Mark grabs it. "Landline?"

A glance to the old push-button receiver behind the counter. It's collected as well. "Car keys?"

They're tossed to Mark.

Mark feels strangely proud. He's been able to think ahead and anticipate everything. Maybe they'll be fine.

As Mark, Jenny, and Pinocchio walk across the snowy lot, Mark tries to sound cheerful. "I've got a hotel room up a ways. They have a totem pole."

Jenny doesn't react.

At the car, Mark dumps Queequeg's phones and keys in the trunk, then realizes the next customer who drives up will be told everything. He's got to finish things.

"Sit tight, Jenny. I'm going to hop back inside and get snacks for the road."

He slouches toward the market. Jenny calls out, "You go in there and I'll never ever, ever talk to you or like you again. I'll hate you forever."

Mark stops, keeping his back to his daughter. His legs twitch. When he finally turns, he's smiling strangely. "Sure thing. Let's get this show on the road."

He comes back to the car, opens the door, slides the gun under the seat, and hops behind the wheel. Jenny and Pinocchio climb in the back.

"Good to see you safe-and-sound, sweetie. You too, Pinocchio."

Jenny doesn't feel safe-and-sound, whatever that means.

— ON THE WAY —

NATE KEEPS THE SIREN OFF except to pass slow-moving tourists. He is only an hour away from the gas station. Thanks to Queequeg, the girl is finally safe. His phone dings. Check it and it's a picture of Ann on the boat, her hair swirling. Shit, she looks good. He wants to call her. He could pretend it is just to give her the good news about the kidnapped girl. *Maybe after. Focus on the job, she can wait.*

Who he should call is dispatch. Maybe there's another trooper nearer. But that would mean he wouldn't be the one arriving. The one opening the door. The one seeing Jenny and telling her everything is alright.

She's safe with Queequeg. No reason to bring in others.

— COMING DOWN FROM ON HIGH —

DOESN'T DO MUCH GOOD to have the munchies in a whale. I scoop up Peelers and pencil fish and seaweed, but what we want are Fritos and potato chips and Cheez Whiz. We don't manage but a few nibbles of the ol' standbys. Nothing tastes good. I'm tired of being slimy. I'm tired of not getting to walk. A glimpse through a hole to the sky a few times a day isn't enough. The pot high is over and Liesl and I are both in rotten moods. She's getting on my nerves with her sighs and the way she smacks her mouth when she's about to say something.

—*You think you don't get on her nerves, Bri? You're not a joy to live with. Remember how you were with Mom? You never talked. Mom would ask a question and you'd grunt or sigh like she was stupid.*

—*Do I still do that? Shit. If I do, Liesl must think I'm a jerk.*

I turn to Liesl. "Could I ask you a question and have you tell the complete truth?"

Liesl agrees.

I'm scared, but I ask, "How would you describe me to someone else? If I wasn't here, what would you say about me?"

Liesl squirms. It must be bad. Embarrassing to say in front of me. I try to ease her mind. "Hey, I already know a lot of it. I'm kinda a dork..."

"I not know what is dork."

"Forget it," I mumble, like a teenager talking to Mom.

"I say—I meet man. Amazing man who live in whale. He look like a tømmerhugger. The man cut trees?"

"Lumberjack."

"He is handsome lumberjack with lots muscles and he funny and sweet and kind and he know all how live whale and catch fish and take care of Home and me. He hero man."

Damn! This is the best gift I've ever gotten. She sees me as a hero. I get a hero-sized woody.

Liesl and I make our tongues do the whale dance and I try to do it slow and hero-like and it feels good and Home jerks and we turn sideways and roll and Home is darting around, attacking or evading.

Something's going on. I slide from Liesl and move to the flap and stick my hand out to see if Home is feeding and bits of fish and things hit me and—something chomps onto my wrist! Fuck! What is that?

"Something's got my arm!"

I yank but it has a super-tight hold on me. Could Home have swallowed a shark? It'll drag me out! After all this, I'll be dragged out and eaten by a fucking shark!

"Get it off me!"

I pull hard and it pulls back, it must be a shark! I jerk my arm but can't break free. I may lose my arm but I've got to stay inside!

"Pull me!"

Liesl grabs and pulls with me and we get my arm inside and—there's a hand grabbing my wrist! A gloved man's hand! I want to kick him off, we don't need another roommate, particularly a guy, but I see the edge of a wet suit and realize this might not be another tenant and we pull on the arm and then a shoulder and finally all of him flops in.

The head-lamp shines over us, its glare stinging our eyes.

"Too much light!" I yell. He slips the lamp off and tilts it up to his own face. His head is covered with wetsuit rubber, goggles, and a scuba mask. He pulls the mouthpiece out and takes a tentative breath.

"Un-fucking-believable. Brian and Liesl, I presume."

The man's eyes glance down at Liesl's breasts. *Hey!* I scramble to hand her a T-shirt. It's mine but who cares. Get it on!

Liesl dresses as the man pretends not to watch. I keep my hands over my faded woody.

"Name's Garret. Ex-Navy SEAL. Here to get you out. The whale inflicted a bit of equipment damage on the way in. The supplementary tanks I was packing are gone. I can take one of you now, sharing this oxygen. I'll come back for the other after we get number one safely aboard the boat. Who's first?"

I'm the hero, so I know the answer. "Liesl."

Garret looks at me like—*right answer.*

Liesl doesn't argue.

The man unhooks a black sheath from his belt, flashes a glimpse of the monster knife inside, and holds it out to me. "In case."

"In case of what?" I ask.

"Might need it to cut your way out."

"I'm never going to hurt Home."

"Still, might need it."

I take it. It fits okay with my new-hero image.

The man has Liesl practice sharing the mouthpiece. I don't like her mixing saliva with another dude but I don't have a choice. When she has it down, Garret slides a harness around her and clips it to his belt. They're tight together, face to face. This is making me angry.

"How are you getting out? The stomach will mash you," I suggest.

He gives a tug to a thick line tied to his waist. "Out the mouth. Attached a hook with rappelling rope on the way in."

"You hooked Home?"

"Stabbed the barbed trident in. Should hold."

I feel sick. And mad. "So you're going to climb up and what, wait for Home to open her mouth?"

"I'll convince her to spread 'em with this." The asshole holds up a short spear-like weapon.

Who is this jerk!? "Don't you dare hurt this whale. She's my home."

The man ignores me and pulls Liesl to the flap. "Let's go," he orders.

Liesl turns to me, terrified. "Brian—"

"No time. Vamanos," the jerk says.

"Liesl—"

The man pulls her out and they're gone.

Home squirms and bends. That man better not be hurting her.

I picture him as a mountain climber, using a pick to jam into the side of Home, pulling himself and Liesl upward.

More twisting and rolling by Home. What's he doing to her!? She's bucking like a wild horse, trying to dislodge them. Will they get out? Will they even make it to the top? I want Liesl to be okay but I hope that man slips and gets smashed in the stomach.

If Home doesn't open her mouth, they'll run out of air. Will they come back and try to get in? Can we live together? He's more the hero type than me. Liesl'll want to be with him.

Will I ever know if they get out? If no one comes back for me, I'll know.

I can't do anything but wait. What did I do before Liesl came? Watch *The Blue Light Special*. Catch dinner. Practice holding my breath. Jerk off.

I'll jerk off 'til the jerk comes back, if he comes back. If I hear him coming down, I can always—what was it Liesl said?—*Vent. Wait.*

Only, I can't. I'm too scared. The lungs feel huge and empty and I'm so alone.

— LIESL AND THE SEAL —

THE SEAL HOLDS HIS BREATH as Liesl sucks oxygen from the tank. He pulls them both up the rope, lighting the way to the mouth with his head-lamp. Garrett stabs with his spear and the massive jaws open. They hurry out and Liesl turns to look. The whale is enormous. Beside it, the calf seems minuscule but that baby must be ten meters long.

Garrett kicks his flippers to get them rising. He's in a thermal wetsuit but the girl is in shorts and a T-shirt. She's going to get hypothermia soon. Light grows above them, with the silhouette of the ship becoming clearer. Garrett takes the mouthpiece for a breath, then passes it back to Liesl. Just a bit farther.

Liesl's panicking, shaking against him. She won't last much longer.

He taps her to hand over the oxygen. She shakes her head. He has to take command of the situation. She won't make it if he doesn't. He pulls the mouthpiece from her and inhales deeply. The girl thrashes about. He takes another few breaths and passes the mouthpiece back, but the girl is convulsing. *Don't you die on me.* She's limp now. *Damn it, girlie, You have to hold on.* At least the cold will help keep her from going brain-dead.

The Navy SEAL breaks the surface and blows his air horn. Behind him, Torsten revs the Nord Spyd close as Arthur hands Ann his camera and heaves the life preserver as far as he can. It lands near Garret, and Torsten and Arthur pull them to the boat. Gjesken is screaming with joy but seeing her daughter's pale head listing, the scream turns to agony.

As Torsten helps the Navy SEAL on board, Arthur and Gjesken haul up Liesl and lay her on the deck. Garret dives into superhero mode. Palm to the girl's chest. Pump. Pump. Pump.

Ann looks over the railing, searching the water. "What about my son!? Where's Brian?"

The Navy SEAL tilts Liesl's head back, jaw up, nose pinched, and breathes into her mouth. Pump. Pump. Breathe. Pump. Pump.

Torsten stares helplessly as Gjesken cries, Ann screams for Brian, Garrett does CPR, and Arthur films.

The SEAL lifts his mouth from Liesl's lips and turns to Ann. "Your son is in the whale. I'll go back for him, but right now, shut the fuck up!"

Ann obeys orders, shaking with adrenaline. Arthur moves beside her and puts a hand on her shoulder as he films the others.

The SEAL yells to Torsten, "You, get on the fucking radio and get a helicopter ambulance here!"

Torsten rushes off as the SEAL continues compressions. Pump. Pump. Breathe. Pump. Pump. Breathe. Nothing. The girl is lifeless. Pump. Pump. A burp of vomit flies from Liesl's mouth. Garret turns her and seawater and bile trickle out. A powerful slap on her back and she coughs and sucks in air. Gjesken screams, kissing her daughter, and babbling incomprehensibly.

— DISASTER —

AS NATE PULLS HIS CRUISER into the gas station parking lot, he can't help but grin. In a few seconds—

Queequeg is at the market door, not looking happy. Something's wrong.

Nate gets all the disastrous news. Mark and Jenny're long gone and there's no way of knowing where they are. He's back to square-one, but things are even worse. The man has a second gun and seemed willing to use it.

Queequeg borrows Nate's phone to call his wife. The poor man was threatened and now he's without a phone and no car keys and it's all because Nate didn't follow procedure.

Why didn't he call dispatch!? It's his fault what happened to Queequeg. It'll be his fault if Jenny is hurt.

Nate keeps blinking to drive the tears inside as panic and fear and shame burn through him. He will never be forgiven.

— AMELIA AND SPROUT SAFE —

THE NAVY SEAL MAN said he'd be back, but he's not back. That means that he and Liesl didn't make it out of Home. Or it means they didn't make it to the surface. Or one of them didn't make it and they're trying to save the other. Or it means—

—They made it, Bri. Dude's on his way back.

I need to get ready. I need to be on the move the instant that Navy man returns. When I leave I've got to make sure Home has clean lungs. That means packing and cleaning.

I put Amelia's watch in the waterproof cellphone case and turn to Little Sprout. Carefully working my fingers around in the seaweed, I loosen Sprout from my sneaker. Capillaries of white spread through the chewed mush.

—Look at all your roots, Sprout! You've been busy!

—Sprout ain't the only one that put down roots, Bri.

—Yeah. Guess that's right. Maybe everything has to put roots out. Grab on to something. Make it feel like we're not drifting in a void. Gotta feel attached to life.

—You've done that. You built roots. More than you ever had before.

—I feel them. Roots with Sprout and Amelia's watch and glowing Wrigglers and Liesl and Home.

—and?

—Myself.

I put Sprout in with Amelia and the new phone and slip the cord around my neck, tighten the strap so it can't fall off. I thought this was so dorky. Might have been dorky but it saved me. Thanks, Mom.

Now to cleaning.

I shake the bag of blue Wrigglers and look around the lungs. A bit of orange peel. A rotten Peeler. Decaying jellyfish. Everything is pushed out the flap. I put on my shorts. They don't fit at all. Should send them out the flap into the stomach.

—You gonna go up to the surface without shorts?

—They won't stay on, and will weigh me down.

I half expect a comment about how no one wants to see me naked. It doesn't come. I'm still getting used to this new inner voice.

Lay the shorts down. Sneakers on top. Tie shoelaces together. Stick the broken phone pieces in a sneaker and stuff Liesl's T-shirt in to keep them contained. Liesl's purse. Her bra and panties. I smell and wood comes.

Take a break from cleaning.

After, I use my socks to gently rub down the lung surface and stuff them in the rubber corrugated tube, put that on the clothes pile and the Navy SEAL's knife, and wrap my Yellow Shopping Cart tight around it all.

—*That Navy dude might want his knife back.*

I retrieve the knife and even though I want to keep the bra and panties, I send the bundle out the flap. Down to the garbage compactor.

"Hope this doesn't give you a stomach ache, Home, but that'd be better than letting stuff fester in your lungs."

I'm naked with a world traveler's watch and an unlikely sprout growing over my heart. The Wriggler Ziploc will stay until the last minute. The knife will go back to the SEAL man. Now. Slow. Down. Breathe in. Hold. Count to five hundred. Breathe out.

"Thank you, Home, for hosting me."

I sing a bit to her, waiting for the SEAL man. He'll be here soon.

— WHAT ABOUT BRIAN? —

ARTHUR FILMS behind as Gjesken follows the SEAL carrying Liesl below deck.

—*It's not fair! Gjesken gets her daughter but I don't have my son. Why not me!? Brian should have gone first. He's been in there longer!*

—*Liesl here is good. You should be happy. This means the plan works.*

—*But I want Brian!*

—Suck it up and go down there and see if you can be of help. Those two are freezing. Do something constructive. Make coffee.

I go down and pause at the bedroom. Liesl on my bed and Gjesken is stripping off her freezing clothes. Always the gentleman, Arthur's got his camera turn away, focused on the Navy SEAL as he barks, "Mama, get in beside her and warm her up."

Liesl's mom curls close, holding her shaking daughter. Garrett covers them with the thick quilt. I'm so jealous I can't watch. I leave to make coffee.

Tears fall as I spoon out the grounds.

—I have to be nicer. I have to try.

Garret steps into the galley. "Good. I need that. As soon as I warm up, replenish my equipment, and we get new coordinates, I'll go down for your son."

I pour him a coffee and carry two cups into the bedroom.

"She okay?" I ask Gjesken.

Gjesken smiles and her eyes gleam. She's much prettier now. A face flooded with joy and relief. She takes a cup of coffee. "Thank you, Ann. For everything. For my daughter."

A recognition hits me. I saved her daughter. Without me, the girl wouldn't be alive.

Liesl opens her eyes and looks at me. "You Brian mother?"

"Yes."

"He amazing. Most amazing man ever know."

Amazing? My boy? No one ever called my son amazing. I never even thought that.

Gjesken smiles and stage-whispers to Liesl, "He must get that from his mother. *She's* amazing."

I'm too stunned to react.

— SNEAKING INTO THE HOTEL —

THE GIRL AND DOG are asleep as Mark slows by the wooden totem pole in front of the White Bear Hotel. He hadn't noticed before that it's a carving of a polar bear. *Why call it a white bear when you could call it a polar bear? Some things make no sense.* He pulls the car into the parking lot behind the hotel. The lot is empty of everything but snow. That's good.

When Mark turns off the engine, Jenny groans and she and Pinocchio yawn.

Mark wonders if the hotel allows dogs. "We might have to leave Pinocchio in the car if they don't let dogs—"

"If he stays in the car, I stay in the car. I'm not leaving him anywhere. I don't trust you."

Mark understands. He never has been trusted and with good reason. He's not consistent. Not reliable. Not ever looking out for anyone but himself.

"If he stays in the car and you can stay in the car, I stay in the car. I need to know you're safe." Mark leans over the seat to his daughter, "But let's sneak him in rather than stay in the car, okay?"

Jenny tries to hide it, but it's clear—sneaking a dog into a hotel is the height of fun. Mark decides to make it more so.

"You lead Pinocchio to the back door and wait there. I'll go in the front and scope out the scene. Then, if the coast is clear, I'll tap on the back door like this."

On the dashboard he taps two times and pauses and taps once.

"I'll answer like this." Jenny taps out the rhythm in reverse.

"Good thinking. If there is no tapping, the coast isn't clear and we'll figure out another plan. We'll be going up to room four-oh-two."

Jenny repeats, "Four-oh-two."

"Take Pinocchio out and wait near the door," Mark says. As his daughter leads the dog out of the car, Mark retrieves the gun from under the seat and tucks it in his jacket.

Mark opens the hotel front door and tracks in snow. The clerk looks up and recognizing Mark, returns to his phone scrolling. Mark sends him a tight smile and heads for the stairs then stops, hits his palm against his forehead as if *Oh my, I just remembered something!* and heads for the back hallway.

Tap, tap, pause, tap.

Tap, pause, tap, tap reply.

— AFTER THE HELICOPTER —

ARTHUR FILMS as the helicopter carrying Liesl and Gjesken flies away. Now on to the next step. Getting Brian!

Garrett's with Torsten inside the bridge. Arthur and I join them.

"When do we get Brian?" I ask.

"We're checking," the Navy SEAL answers. "We got off course with the rescue and everything."

I dial the phone to let Brian know he's got a wait. No service.

"Are we far from the whale now?" Arthur asks.

Torsten points to the blip on the radar screen. "Whale. Some far."

"Gotta go prep. Lemme know when we're over the whale," the SEAL says, leaving.

Arthur films the radar screen. Then points to a second blip blinking on the screen.

"What's this?" Arthur asks.

Torsten curses in Norwegian and gets on the shortwave radio.

An angry barrage of Norwegian words. Torsten is furious about something, and it has to do with the second blip on the radar screen he keeps pointing to.

"What's wrong?" I ask.

"Fine, all fine." He waves us out of the bridge and slams the door.

I don't believe him for a minute.

— JENNY'S GUILTY —

MARK STARES at his daughter as she lies on the bed, kicking the iron headboard. She's bored and frustrated and there's no TV. What hotel doesn't have a TV?

The jaggeds swirl at the edge of his vision. This is getting really hard. If he gets rid of Jenny and the dog, things will be easier. He felt so much relief when he thought she was safe and away from him. He's got to get Jenny back to Beverly. He turns to his daughter. "Sweetie, we'll stay here for the night but in the morning I'm going to have to leave. You'll call the police and they'll take care of you."

"I can't, Daddy."

Mark hopes that means she wants to be with him. Not that it would work out, but it would feel good to be wanted.

"You have to, Jenny. It's not safe for you to be on the road like this. The Police will tell Mom and you'll—"

"—go to jail."

Mark almost bursts out laughing but suppresses it. "You won't go to jail. You'll be sent home."

"The police are after me."

Mark remembers she said she'd seen herself on TV and knows the AMBER alerts are about her. Poor kid thinks that's bad.

"The police *are* after you, but they'll be glad to find you."

Jenny kicks the headboard. "They'll put me in jail because I shot that man. When you left. He busted in and I shot him. That's why I ran away."

Blood rushes to Mark's face, his heart staggers, and the jaggeds push in from the edges of his vision. He touches the glass of the window to feel something cold on his palm. "Tell me what happened."

"He kicked in the door and I shot him like you said. He flew backward and I ran away. I didn't know what else to do."

The jaggeds creep farther into Mark's vision. Where are his meds? In that igloo motel room. No, none left. There were flashing lights around the motel when he drove past. Something did happen.

Jenny's eyes fill with tears. "They'll put me in jail forever."

The iron cell-door clangs in Mark's ears. She didn't destroy a bar, put eight people in the hospital, but she shot someone.

"Where's the gun, Jenny?"

"I dropped it when it went off."

"Do you know who busted in the door?"

"He had a uniform and a hat with a gold badge and I killed him."

Jenny buries her face in Pinocchio's coat and sobs.

You're an idiot, Mark. You took your girl away from home and now she's killed a cop.

— WHALING FOOTAGE —

I TEST A SMILE in the ship's tiny bathroom mirror and a woman I don't recognize smiles back. Who is this person? I've changed so much. My hair is wild compared to when Brian slouched out of our house. My skin has color to it. My clothes aren't beige. Will I look okay to Brian? Maybe I should do something to make myself look more like a mom. I wonder if Torsten has a blow-drier.

Taps on the door. "You okay in there?" Arthur's voice.

I open the door, still staring at the stranger in the mirror. "Do you think Brian will—I don't know—will he think I'm—"

"Brian is going to be just as happy to see the new you as I am."

Arthur steers me out of the room. "We've got a bit of time before the boat reaches the whale. You want to see any footage?"

"Yes, anything."

Arthur sets up his laptop and opens a folder with a long list of scenes. *Brian Swallowed. Ann Interview. Aquarium of the Bay Expert. Dan Skype. Greenpeace Skype. Ann Skype. Whaling Footage. Gjesken Skype...*

I point at *Whaling Footage.*

Arthur shakes his head. "You don't want to see that."

"I do."

"I won't show you."

"You will because I'll let you film —what do you call it?— reaction shots."

That gets him. He sets up the camera on a tripod behind the laptop, focused on me. "I compiled these from many different sources. Obviously, it's not original footage." The red light goes on and Arthur pushes play on the computer.

Shots of whaling ships. At the bows are huge harpoon cannons bolted to the deck like the one on this boat. Arthur's voice narrates. "The barbed harpoon tip, designed to secure a rope, carries explosives as well. When hit just below the last rib, the barb penetrates deep into the blubber, the hooks deploy, releasing the firing pin and triggering an internal explosion that kills the whale instantly. Only that doesn't happen. The harpoon shoots, the barb hits bone and explodes outside of the body, causing pain and suffering."

Videos of the massive whaling cannons firing, ropes uncoiling on deck, a whale is shot, the charge explodes, blood flies. Images of the traumatic wounds. Ripped blubber. An expert talking. "The whales don't die quickly. They're hauled aboard to be cut apart while still alive."

Footage of Norwegian tourist shops lined with tins of whale meat. Japanese restaurants serving whale meat to customers. Arthur's voiceover—"The Japanese eat the meat, but because whales live so long, it's high in pesticides, mercury, and other carcinogens. It's not healthy to eat."

Thick blubber being sliced from the sides with massive saws. "There really is no reason for whaling. They're selling whale meat in Norway to feed animals raised for their pelts. Minks feed on whale deaths." Pictures of fashion models wearing fur coats, hats.

Shots from aboard a whaling ship. The crew loads the explosive harpoons. A whale breeches. The harpoon fires, an explosion of blood across the back of the whale. It dives and is pulled up with the rope. Blood spouts from its blowhole. Men on the deck fire rifles down onto the writhing beast. It turns, fins rising, belly up.

I slam the laptop shut as trembling spreads over me.

"Shit, I just thought of something." Arthur opens the computer and flips through the files. "Call Gjesken and put it on speaker."

I dial. It rings and Gjesken answers. "I'm so grateful, Ann. You'll never know—"

Arthur interrupts her. "Gjesken, we need you to listen and translate."

He presses PLAY on a file. The film of Torsten in the bridge yelling into the shortwave, pointing at the second radar blip.

Arthur hits PAUSE. "What did Torsten say?"

We both lean closer to the phone.

"It's hard to hear," Gjesken says, "but it sounded something like, 'You promised you'd stay far back until after. Don't get closer. They can't know you're here.'"

We hang up and Arthur turns to me. "Don't jump to any conclusions yet. Doesn't mean there's a problem. Let's focus on getting Brian out."

But I know we're both thinking the same thing.

— WHAT'S THE HOLDUP? —

THAT NAVY SEAL GUY should have been down to get me by now. I've called but no service. If that dude doesn't come, I'm gonna be screwed. Since I dumped my Yellow Shopping Cart and everything else, it won't be easy to catch dinner.

At least I kept the Wriggler Ziploc. I shake them and hold their light up to open the waterproof phone thing around my neck.

Sprout doesn't look happy without his sneaker. His top is smushed.

Shit.

"Hey, little Sprout. You doing okay?"

I slide my hand along Home's spongy wall and get a palmful of water.

"Sorry to up-root you. Have a drink and get your strength up."

Trickle water over the little plant.

I don't want to say anything but he's not looking good. Maybe he'll die. Maybe the SEAL man won't come and maybe I won't be able to go shopping anymore and Sprout and I will die in Home. Maybe Home will die with me rotting in her lungs.

—*You won't let that happen, Bri. I know you. Anyway, that Navy guy is on the way. You'll see.*

—*Yeah. Everything will be fine.*

Me and my inner voice both suspect that's not true.

— CALL TO ANN —

THE JAGGEDS rim Mark's vision and a buzzing's growing louder. It's getting late. They should eat something but he can't go downstairs now. He's too fucked up. What did the girl say? *Uniform, hat, gold badge, killed.* He can't have her thrown in juvie jail. He has to keep her. But they lost all their belongings, so he'll buy clothes, a different clunker car, dog food... He needs a lot more cash..

"Jenny, remember the message-in-the-bottle you found?"

"The one YOU LEFT IN THE CABIN!"

This kid is a brat.

"I'm need talk to that lady again. She can help. Do you remember the number?"

"It's in your phone,—"

Mark hears the word she leaves out. *Idiot.*

All his life. All his fucking life. "I know that! You think I don't know that!? I'm trying NOT TO USE THAT PHONE! DO YOU REMEMBER THE NUMBER OR DON'T YOU?!"

The girl's face crumples. She's no help.

He needs a piece of paper. From the bedside table, he pulls a sheet of stationery for The White Bear Hotel with an illustration of the polar bear totem pole. *Idiots. It should be The Polar Bear Hotel.* He powers on the cell, pulls up the last call, scribbles the number on the paper, turns the phone off, sits on the bed, and dials the hotel phone. It rings several times and then Ann's voice says, "Hello?"

"This is the fella that found the message-in-the-bottle."

Jenny's face un-crumples as she grabs Mark's shirt. "Me. Me!"

Silence on the other end.

"Listen, Lady," Mark growls, while pushing Jenny away. "That money you sent wasn't enough. I need you to—"

The woman cuts in, "This is really fucked up for you to call now. Things are crazy here and—and—you didn't send the bottle!"

Jenny keeps tugging and screaming, "ME!"

The buzzing grows and Mark's eye is twitching. Something's bubbling inside him. "Lady, lady—" *What was I talking about?* "Lady, my daughter wants to speak to you." He hands Jenny the receiver. *Fuck. I need a drink.*

"Hello?" Jenny whispers, suddenly shy. "I found the bottle. Is your son still in the whale?"

"Yes, he is. You doing okay with your daddy?" the lady asks.

"Will you be able to get the boy out?"

"We're trying."

Mark pulls the receiver from his daughter. "Sweetie, you can talk again but first me and her have to talk." He turns away. "Lady? I'll send the bottle this time. I promise."

Jenny tugs at him. "Daddy, we left it—"

Mark covers the girl's mouth with his free hand, pressing her head on the bedspread.

"You have the bottle?" the lady asks.

"Sure. Right here."

"And the dollar and library card?"

"All safe-and-sound. Right beside me." Mark jerks his head as if the lady might get the gesture over the phone. Jenny squirms under his hand, sending green rivers swirling up his arm, so he leans his body across her to keep her still. Is she suffocating? Would that be bad?

"I can send you the same amount."

Tears fill Mark's eyes. If only everyone could be like this lady, he might have a chance. "That's really nice of you," he says, his voice breaking.

"Where should I send it? I can FedEx it today."

Mark pauses. Paisleys dance across the buzzing walls. There's no reason this lady knows about him and the kidnapping and AMBER Alert. He's just a guy that found the bottle, right?

He lifts his body off the girl. Her eyes are wide above his hand. Jaggeds swirl in and distort the face. *Who is this?*

"Hello? Are you there?" the phone asks.

Mark tries to remember what they were saying. "Yes. What did you want?"

The phone asks for his address.

There's a piece of paper with squiggles.

Make the squiggles into letters. Make the letters into words.

The phone repeats about *where* in his ear.

Mark bites his tongue hard. The pain jolts him but his vision doesn't clear. Where is he?

"I'm at the hotel. It's a polar bear. A polar bear and everyone knows they are white, so why call it that? Send it here."

Mark hangs up and lets go of Jenny.

She punches him over and over. "You smothered me! I hate you!"

Mark stands and wants to say, *that goes double for me*, but the swirls spin the room and the carpet rushes up and he can't catch air and the ceiling is on the wrong side and the dog's tongue burns his cheek.

A mass of orange lava bubbles in Mark's chest. The eruption is coming.

— CALL FROM ANN —

IN HIS FAVORITE CORNER BOOTH, Nate takes a bite of his elk burger as he gazes at the picture of Ann on the boat. He wants an excuse to call her again. Last time, he screwed up. What time is it in Norway if it's dinner-time here? He searches for the answer online when his phone rings—*Ann*—and his heart jumps. How can he be so excited about someone he doesn't know?

"Nate here."

Ann tells Nate of the call from Mark. How he asked for more money. How he sounded confused and not all there. How she spoke to Jenny for a moment.

"Did they say where they were?"

"I asked for his address to send the money but he seemed really out of it. He talked of a hotel that's a polar bear and everyone knows they're white, so why call it that. I looked on Google and there's The White Bear Hotel near Healy, Alaska."

Nate wants to kiss her. Not only because of the information about the abductor, but because of her voice. The strength and confidence and warmth in it. She's got a resolve he doesn't see in people.

Nate hurries to the register as he talks. "You're a god-send, Ann. I can't tell you how grateful I am." Money to the cashier and "Two large coffees to-go." Grab them and out the door, "That man has psychosis and may be a danger to his daughter. You're helping save her."

"Then I'd better let you get to saving," Ann says and hangs up.

Nate hops in the cruiser, punches the hotel into the GPS and roars off. He's got to hurry. It's a haul. The longer without those drugs, the sicker that dude is gonna be.

— TORSTEN PREPARES —

I HOLD THE PHONE to my chest. I wish we could have talked longer but he's got to save that girl. Still, it would have been so nice to confide in Nate how scared I am. What if Brian is brought up like Liesl was and isn't revived? What if that second radar blip is a whaling ship?

My hair whips in front of my eyes. It's growing so long. I had the housewife-hair forever and it never danced in the wind. I was never even in wind.

I turn and Arthur's filming me. Beyond him, Torsten's doing something by the tripod-mounted harpoon gun. He lifts a large metal canister and loads it into the rear tube of the cannon. A two foot long arrow-like spear slides into the front. From the videos Arthur showed me, I know it contains explosives. Torsten hooks a thick rope to the slot in the spear, with the rest neatly coiled below. "What are you doing, Torsten?"

Torsten jerks. I surprised him. Good.

"Harpoon in all time. Safety."

"Why would we ever need to use it? If we see my son's whale, we aren't going to shoot it."

306

"Safety. No leave empty. Seawater bad in gun."

He's lying.

— SPEEDING ON ALASKAN HIGHWAY —

NATE'S GOT THE SIREN BLARING and lights flashing. Safer in case anyone pulls onto the road. At one hundred miles an hour, he needs this path kept clear. High-beams light the way. If he hits a patch of uncleared snow, he's gone. *God, damn it, why can't this be daytime! Why can't this be summer and midnight sun!* Please keep the road clear. No moose. No traffic. No ice. No wrecks.

The lump in his throat makes it hard to breathe. The lump he can't forget. The missing-sister memory lump. "It's your fault!" his mother screamed.

Please, let him save this Jenny girl. Let this work out. Something has to make up for dropping the ball back then. Even though it wasn't the horror they'd all imagined, he was never trusted again. Never could live that down.

He roars the cruiser toward the lit portion of road but the pavement keeps replacing itself, stretching on forever. GPS says twenty more miles. That's less than ten minutes at this speed.

Please let him make it in time.

— SECOND RADAR BLIP —

ARTHUR GESTURES FOR ME to follow him into the bridge and points at the second blip on the radar. "It's on the same course as we are. I think it's a ship. It's much larger than this one. And, you already know, in Norway—"

"—it may be a whaling ship."

I step out onto the deck and dial. As the phone rings, Arthur moves in front of me to get a closeup.

Please pick up, Brian. Please—

Brian answers. "Mom, what's going on? Is that Navy man coming back to get me?"

"Brian, we're trying to get to you but the whale swam fast."

"Okay. I can wait. I'm used to it."

"There's a problem. There is a beacon that was shot into your whale. It's how we're tracking you, but another ship got ahold of the beacon coordinates. They are also tracking you. I think it might be a whaling ship."

There's silence on the phone. Did I lose him? "Brian?"

"I hear you. Thanks for letting me know. I'll hang up now to save the battery. Bye, Mom, I love you."

The call ends before I can say I love you. Why did he say that? Does Brian think the whaling ship will kill his whale and he'll die? Does he know something I don't? Maybe Torsten is going to kill the whale the minute Brian is rescued. That's why he has the harpoon ready.

I step to the bow to study the harpoon cannon. How can I disable this thing? How do I open it?

Grabbing the harpoon spear, I yank hard to pull it out, but it must be engaged by a latch. If I can open the back, maybe I can remove whatever launches the harpoon, but it's not clear how it opens. This looks like the trigger—

Torsten yells from behind me, "Not for use!"

I turn to him. "Better fucking not be."

— A WHALER? —

HOME CURVES and I roll with her. My muscles are all tense and my eyebrows hurt and breaths come too fast. It's been a while since I had this feeling.

—*You recognize it, Bri?*

—*Helpless anger.*

—*'cept you're not helpless.*

I breathe to let out the feeling. Breathe to relax my brow. Breathe to loosen my shoulders. Breathe to think clearly.

—Mom said the whaler has the beacon coordinates.
—Yep.
—Then we've got a plan.

— SCREECHING CREATURE —

"DADDY, ARE YOU OKAY? What should I do?"

The voice pulls at him. It's familiar but annoying.

"Me and Pinocchio are worried."

Mark tries to turn his head to the sound. Where is he? On his back. Is he on the ocean? Everything is undulating. A little creature lowers over him. A wolf-mask moves in beside it.

"Daddy?"

A wolf-mask pushes close and runs wet slime over Mark's mouth. The green jaggeds zig in from all sides. Something is going to happen and he can't control it. If he could move, he might be able to get a drink. A drink might drown the monsters crabbing up his gut. Why didn't he get a refill on those meds? Too late.

Where did he put that thing? He left it somewhere.

"Daddy?"

It was in the car and he picked it up. Cold metal. It's somewhere near.

A movement swirls, color and light, and a face jiggles over him. The face carries the box that lights up with a sound. Beeping. *No!* That isn't supposed to happen. *Turn off!*

The creature bobs and bounces in front of him. A riddle. What was the question? Too late. Mark rolls and pushes himself up to reach the beeping box. The creature darts back with a scream and the wolf-mask moves close, making a rumble, showing teeth. This beast needs to go.

Mark staggers to his feet, lifts the chair, and flings it at the growling thing. The rumble cuts off with a high squeal and the beast shrinks. Good. One down.

Tremors move from Mark's hands up his arms. Jaggeds and paisleys circle in, creating a tunnel in his vision.

At the end of the tunnel, the creature stares at him, rays of light swirling out of it, a black message dangling from its tentacle. A hole in the throbbing head opens to blackness and a screech claws at him. This thing is causing him pain. This creature with the open hole.

Mark lunges at the taunting monster and it darts back. More screeches from the hole. Growling sounds from beast under the table. Jaggeds push in from all sides. Mark's vision smears as he turns his head to coolness tickling his face. The square dark hole in the wall is open. Cold rushes at him from the portal. If he can get the monster out into the cold dark, he'll have peace.

Arms snatch and he almost grabs the screaming creature, but it twists and vanishes behind a door that wasn't there before. Rhymes and sing-song words spill around, ridiculing him. "Baddy! Baddy!"

Heart spasming with fear, there is still a part of Mark that's trying to think. He knows the visions aren't real. He's been told countless times. This screaming monster behind the door isn't real. But if he can rid himself of it, he'll rid himself of the visions. All his problems will disappear if he can erase this vision.

Turn the knob but the door won't open. "Kick it in! Kick it in!" chants the crowd. Mark feels on display. This is his moment to shine.

The toothy-thing hiding under the table won't stop howling. But it's not the beast he wants. He wants the creature behind the door.

He kicks the door and fire shoots up his leg. The entrance is enveloped with flames, as if that will scare him. Nothing can stop him now. He has a mission. Kick again. Fire scorches him, but a panel of the door shatters. He'll be at the screaming creature soon.

"BADDY!"

This barrier is breaking. A few more kicks and he'll be through. Kick.

— EMERGENCY —

JENNY KNOWS she shouldn't use Daddy's phone unless it's an emergency but the door is breaking apart with each kick and this looks like an emergency. If she calls 9-1-1 the police will come. The police will throw her in jail for shooting one of them. She has to call someone else. Daddy said the whale lady would help.

She pushes the green button. A list of numbers comes up. Jenny pushes the first one.

"Hello?" the lady answers.

"Hello, this is Jenny. I'm in trouble."

— JENNY'S CALL —

THE GIRL'S SCARED VOICE jolts me. I turn my back to the wind and cup the phone, staring at the choppy wake. "Jenny? The one that found the message-in-the-bottle?"

"Daddy's breaking down the door. He's real mad."

There's the sound of a thump and the girl whispers, "Please."

Fuck. I'm thousands of miles away. What can I do?

"Okay, Jenny. You need to stay away from your daddy. Where are you?"

"In the bathroom."

"Good girl. In the hotel? What room?"

"Four-oh-two."

"Look for anything under the sink or in a cabinet. A spray, cleanser, anything."

"There's Lysol spray and toilet paper."

Another crash.

"He's almost here."

"Take the spray and get down behind the toilet. You can get there. Squeeze as far in as you can. If your daddy tries to reach you, spray him in the eyes."

"I can't get under."

"You can. Do it and I'll be right back."

My fingers hardly work, but I put the girl on hold and push the next number.

My Alaskan trooper answers on the first ring.

"Nate, that abducted girl is on the phone right now. She's in trouble. Her father is breaking down the bathroom door. Room four-oh-two."

"Got it." And he's gone.

I switch back to Jenny. "Jenny, are you there?"

There's a loud crash and the girl's scream and the line goes dead.

— BATHROOM —

THE DOOR SHATTERS and passage is open. White hard cold with sharp smells.

A high scream taunts him again, "BADDY!"

He pushes into the chamber. The squiggling creature wriggles under the round bowl of rainbow neon. He'll catch the thing and break it open. Let the light get in.

Can't reach it. Thing swirls and kicks and jerks, disappearing parts.

A hiss and poison stings his face. Clouds of stinging bees crawl into his eyes, up his nose, down his throat. Cough and gag and reach through the attack. Reach past the toxic gas. Grab the twig and pull. The thing screams and its teeth gouge his hand but he's got the twig tight and won't let go.

— FOUR FLIGHTS UP —

VACANCY NEON HALOED in darkness. Break too hard. Spinning in snow. Out the door before the cruiser comes to a stop. The shame from the past mingles with the dread of the present. Nate runs for the entrance—busts through the door—"STAIRS!"—the shocked clerk points—and the trooper races—

Make it in time.

Round the landing and up.

Make it in time.

Round the landing and up.

It's your fault if she dies!

Round another landing and down the hall, gun drawn, if he gets there too late he will not let that man live, boots shaking the building, *four-oh-two*—heel lands shy of the knob and the door flies open. Entryway closets—can't see into room, mirror—*that's me*—ahead under table—dog—cowering. *Stay.*

Grunt from around corner, unable to see—

Gun leading, Nate spins out of the entranceway and—*there at the window*—points his pistol at the man's back. The girl screams—unseen. *Where is she?* Thin arms flail from behind the man as he lifts her out the open window. *Can't shoot—he'll drop the girl.*

"Mark?"

The man freezes.

"Jenny, hold tight to your daddy," Nate calls out. "Mark, I'm here to help. Will you let me help?"

Slurs come from Mark.

"It's okay, Mark. I've got your back. We'll solve this together."

Nate moves closer. If he can reach around and grab the girl's wrist, he will hold on, no matter what.

Get across the room.

"Mark. I'm here to help."

A gurgle comes from the man as Nate takes another step.

"Your daughter Jenny's in trouble. Can you help me, Mark?"

The man holds the girl away from his body—*she's hanging out the window! Don't drop her!*—The girl struggles to cling to her father's arm.

Another step. "Can I hold Jenny, Mark? Can I help?"

The man makes a choking sound.

"What you're feeling isn't real, Mark. You know that. Your daughter needs help. Your Jenny needs you."

The man's arms shake. He's losing strength.

Another step. Three more feet.

"I'll help, Mark." *One more step.* Nate's got to put the gun away if he's going to get a good grip. Slide it back in the holster, slip close, get there before he drops her—the man shifts and—*Reach!*—

Nate grabs the little wrist and side-slams the man. Mark falls backward and the full weight of the dropping girl torques Nate's arm —she dangles screaming, dancing groundless over dark air—but he holds on. Puts a second hand around her and pulls up and she's in his arms.

"You're safe, Jenny. You're safe."

He holds her close, her body trembling against him. Or is it Nate's body trembling against hers? He's vibrating with adrenaline.

"Save Daddy. Please," whispers the little voice in his neck.

Nate looks at the man writhing on the carpet. Eyes rolling. Mouth foaming.

Nate puts Jenny down and cuffs Mark. "This is just so he can't hurt himself or anyone else. Hand me that pillow and blanket."

The girl rushes to help. They cover Mark with the blanket and raise his feet with the pillow. Nate calls for an ambulance as he kneels beside the man. Frothy spit dribbles from the man's mouth.

"Stroke his head, Jenny. Make him know it's okay."

Jenny strokes her father's head. His panicked breathing slows.

"Good job, Jenny. I'm Nate. We met before. At the Igloo Motor Court."

Jenny's eyes widen. "Are you who I shot?"

"Yes, but you didn't hurt me." Nate smiles and opens the top of his shirt to show the thick vest. "This is bulletproof."

The girl's mouth quivers. "Am I going to jail?"

"No, Jenny. Nothing bad is going to happen to you. You're safe now."

— SPACE WALK —

I CAN'T LET HOME be killed by whalers. That means one thing.

—*Um, Bri, you thinking what I think you're thinking?*

—*You know what I'm thinking.*

—*We'll die. We go out there and we die.*

—*You want to let Home die? Home dies, we die.*

My inner voice can't argue with that.

"Listen, Home. I'm gonna go out. I'm gonna try to get the beacon off you. You know we have—like, a friendship, right? You and me. We're buddies."

Home doesn't sing or say anything.

I call out my name. "Briiiii-annnnn."

Repeat it back, Home. So I'll know we got a rapport going. No sound from Home except the slow heart thumping below me.

Calling as loud as I can. "BRIIIIII—-AAAAAAA—NNNNNNNN."

Nothing.

Well, shit. Gotta go anyway. Gotta assume Home and I look out for each other.

Might need the knife the Navy man gave me. Don't know how a beacon is attached. Slide the phone cord through the knife sheath belt loop. This is some monster necklace.

Next breath Home takes, Spacewalk, here I come.

I sing a bit of The Lullaby Song to make Home know I'm safe and she's going to be okay.

—Either really stupid move or pretty brave move, Bri. You get out, no reason you get back in. Sure you want to risk this?

—If I can't get back in, I die. I stay in here and Home is killed by a whaler, I die. I've got to keep Home alive.

—Taking off the beacon might mean you get lost for good.

—Might. Okay with you?

My inner voice takes a long pause.

—Yep. It's the right thing to do.

Okay. My heart is racing and that's not gonna make my long-breath-holding any easier. I sing The Rise Song to Home.

Home rises gently. Does she know what I'm going to do? I feel for the flap and slip two fingers under. When the blow hole opens, I'll go. She might open her mouth to catch Peelers or Torpedo Heads on the surface.

We do the curl and Home blasts out and daylight shines and I pull in my breath with the whale and slip out into the tube. Is this the last of me?

Feeling slick walls, there's the rope the Navy hero left. Pull hard, scrambling up, muscles straining, much quicker than I thought I'm in the massive mouth. Open now, Home. Let me out. Got to make you gag. I flop and squirm and wriggle on the tongue. It arches and jerks like a wild bull for a bronc rider. Every part of me is moving every which way. Please gag!

A convulsive heave and a rush of hot vomit knocks me from behind. I'm caught in the tide of goop and the gigantic jaws open and spew us out. Tumbling in grey and—I'm in a dancing forest! Tall waving plants all around me—it's seaweed-world!—and FUCKING COLD!—get UP!—light above, freezing everywhere. Push and wriggle to the light—tangled on a sea-strand—rip it and—bursting up into air. Air! AIR!!!! I scream!

—*Stop joy. Have Mission. Go.*

I spin and beside me is Home, curling down. Monstrous black flesh moves past—scars, barnacles. Near her tail, there's a red blinking light. Got to be the beacon. I pull in a breath and dive, kicking through seaweed tangles. I'll never get to Home in time. She'll pass by and leave and I'll be out and alone. I'm working too hard swimming—my breath won't last. The fin is by my arm and I reach out—but miss. It glides past. The tail is almost here. Kick and pull at water but, I know I'll miss it. I'll miss it and that will be the last of Brian. Last of me and maybe Home. The tail passes gracefully in the deep green space. Curtains of seaweed wave at the disappearing form and she's gone.

Kick to the surface. Breathe cold air. It's so bright. Can't see with so much sun.

—*You did good, Bri. It's all good. You got out. You lived in a whale for a long time.*

—*I learned about myself.*

—*You and me both.*

—*Sorry I couldn't save you, Home.*

It's cold. I'll get that hypotherm-whatever and die. Maybe in a few minutes.

—*Sorry I didn't get to say goodbye, Mom.*

A BLAST of water shoots beside me and Home rises, lifting me with her!

You came back!

She's so slick and firm and I slide, trying to grab on to anything —sharp barnacles scrape my skin as I kick for the center of her back, tumbling, a massive gritty water-slide of flesh and there's the fin— *grab hold.* I get a grip and will not let go. Blood swirls from barnacle slices in my skin. Hope sharks aren't nearby.

The beacon is level with my chest. I'll take it off, disable it, and when I need to, re-able it. I grab it with one hand and pull. It's stuck tight, barbs into the blubber. Another pull, hard.

We're buffeted by the waves, skimming just below the surface.

—Damn it! This will not beat me!

Both hands on the beacon, feet placed beside it and PULL!

—It won't come out!

The Navy guy's knife. I hate to do it but I slide it from the sheath and push the tip into Home's thick flesh—*I'm sorry, Home!*—under the barb and cut around it and push up with the knife blade—the beacon flips out—I grab for it!—Yes!—the knife falls—*sorry, Mr. Navy SEAL*—feel around the blinking device and a switch under my finger clicks and the red light turns off. Yay! Now Home is safe and —BAM! Something large hits my back. A shark?! Turn and it's a smaller whale poking me! Baby! Someone wants to play—BAM!— another poke and the beacon drops, disappearing into the depths, and Baby dives after it. Don't eat that! FUCK! Fuck fuckity fuck fuck and more fuck.

Okay. Beacon is gone. Would have been nice to have it for me, but I'm glad Home is free of it. This is good. And I got to see Baby!

I'm shivering. How the hell do I get back in Home?

Hanging onto her fin, far ahead is Home's mouth. Looks forever away. Damn. My arms are really cut from the sharp barnacles—

I feel the ridge of one. It's like a circular shell embedded in the skin. Pull on it. It doesn't shift. Years ago, Mom took me to an indoor cliff-climbing place but I wasn't strong enough to do it. Too much flab to muscle. Not anymore. I pull and step and reach and pull and hoist and step and each barnacle cuts my hands and feet but I make my way along her expanse of back. Make my way to her mouth. Home drifts along at the water's surface. Does she know? Is she staying up so I can breathe? Pull and step and reach and fuck that hurts and pull and hoist and that took the skin off my knee and step and I'm at the blow-hole now. It opens and the scent of home sprays out, warm and inviting. Can I climb this blowhole? No. Only space for my head, not my shoulders.

I wish I could look in Home's eye. I could climb down—

—*Head for the mouth, Bri. You need to get inside or you'll freeze to death.*

I pull myself over the landscape of Home's head and lower myself in front. Pressing against the sealed crack, I caress the edges of her mouth, fingers wide, palms flat. I learned that from Liesl, only with her I used the tips of my fingers. It feels good. Makes you want to open—

The crack breaks apart and I breathe a lungful and dive into the blackness. Riding the water over and down and warm and dark and there's the flap and I slide in and land shivering. Breathe—a warm wet welcome breath in my Home.

"You're safe now, Home. I saved you and you saved me."

— ON THE HORIZON —

CURSING FROM THE BRIDGE. Arthur and I turn to see Torsten peering through binoculars at a dark shape in the distance. A ship. It's much bigger than the Nord Spyd.

"TORSTEN!" I yell. "You get talking to that ship. You tell them to get out of this area. You tell them about my son and you make them leave!"

Something about the way he doesn't react makes me think my orders will not be followed. I join him inside the bridge, trying to remember something about—*does it bring you closer together or further apart?*—as Torsten pushes the lever and the motor growls at a higher pitch.

"What's going on, Torsten?"

Arthur, filming the radar screen, nudges me to look at it.

One blip on the screen. The ship. Where's the whale? Where's Brian's whale!

"The whale beacon is gone!"

We speed toward the other ship. Its grey shape grows larger and I rush outside to see it, but I can't make out much detail.

Arthur zooms in with his camera and hands it to me. The view wobbles but I can see. There are many men on deck moving about—and the shape at the tip of the boat—the shape silhouetted against the sky is unmistakable. A harpoon cannon. This *is* a whaler.

— NO BEACON —

WITHOUT THE BEACON, we won't be found by the whaler and—we're not going to be found at all. What should I do now?

Home blasts out spray and pulls in cold sharp air. I take a deep long breath, catching a glimpse of the bright sky. Live, I guess.

There's a muffled sound and a second later, a powerful jolt hits us with a deafening BOOM. A painfully loud tone howls all around me. Home screaming? We're twisting and turning, tumbling 'round and up, and Home's heartbeat is ramming below me, fast and thunderous. What's happening to us!?

— ANN IN FRONT —

I SCREAM, "My son is down there! You assholes!"

The Nord Spyd moves closer to the massive whaling ship as the murderous crew scrambles to fire another harpoon. I keep screaming but they don't care.

Torsten yells into the short-wave in Norwegian as Arthur films everything.

The water is red. Blood and bubbles swirl. I rush to the Navy SEAL. "Do something! Brian's down there!"

319

The man shakes his head. "Not my op."

"You must go down. You must save my son. He's in there and he'll die if he doesn't get out."

"Not in the cards, lady. That whale is mad with pain. It'll kill me and your son."

I scream to Torsten. "Ram that boat! Ram the fucking bastards!"

"Will sink. They steel, we wood."

"Get close! If they reel in the whale, maybe we can save my son."

I picture them cutting open the side of the whale and my boy walking out. Dripping with blood but alive.

Only I know that's not how it happens. Things happen slowly. I've seen the footage. Docking a whale is a slow process, and by the time the cut is made, Brian will be dead.

I want to dive in to join him. Please, don't let my boy die alone.

The whaler winds the rope with a massive crank. The whale is straining against it, trying to stay under, but it's pulled toward the ship.

I've got to be bigger than I've ever been. I've got to do it now.

Five steps and I'm at the bow.

There's the trigger.

"No touch!"

And I spin toward Torsten.

I spin, turning the harpoon with me. It's definitely the right thing to do when I see Torsten's face whiten and his hands rise.

Arthur pans his camera back and forth, trying to film both me and Torsten. I'm sure he's furious that he doesn't have a second camera now. The Navy SEAL also lifts his palms to me. Not his fight.

Now that I've got the power, I don't quite know what to do.

"You gave that whaler the beacon coordinates, didn't you?"

"I give, but tell kill after boy out. Big whale. Big money."

My finger twitches on the harpoon trigger. I want to shoot this fucking traitor.

— HEARTBEAT —

WE'RE BEING PULLED. A harpoon? Home opens the blowhole and gasps in cold air. I hear yelling outside. If we're pulled up, will I be able to crawl out?

Why would someone kill a whale? Are they thinking that killing Home will save me?

It probably doesn't have to do with me. Another of life's arbitrary actions. One day a boy is swallowed by a whale. One day a whale is killed. One day Amelia Earhart is flying. One day she's living in a whale.

I'll sing to Home. Tell her I'm here. It's got to be scary for her. I sing The Lullaby Song. For her and her baby.

The booming of Home's heart is slowing. That's not a good thing. She sings a low note and the high note. It sounds like *Hello/Goodbye*. She knows I'm talking to her.

"Goodbye, Home," I sing, "Thank you for being my mother. Thank you for caring for me. Keeping me warm. Feeding me. Giving me comfort."

I'm crying now. Maybe Home is crying.

The heartbeat below me slows even more. The gaps between the thumps get longer and longer. Each. Time. I. Wait. And.

One.

More.

Comes.

And.

Then no more. No more heart. No more song. I'm inside a dead whale. The lungs only have this much and then that's it. I'm dead, only not quite yet. Soon.

This is what death is like. It's a slow silence. A coldness. And nothing.

I'm glad I got to do this. It was better than any video game.

Sorry about everything before, Mom.

Sorry for making you sick, Home.

—*Sorry for being a dick and calling you Lard Ass, Bri. You're a cool—*

—*Not now.*

I stand, trying to stay stable and—jump, lifting my knees high to drop, butt first—a cannonball—landing hard on the bottom of the lungs. Scramble to my feet—leap and cannonball down. Back up—leap. Cannonball. Up and down. Up and down.

—*You've gone crazy, Bri. Chill the fuck out.*

Up and cannonball again.

—*Come on, Bri, this is stupid. You trying to bust a hole in the lungs?*

Scramble up and again.

—*The last thing this dead whale needs is you jumping—Oh.*

Cannonball. Scramble.

Cannonball. Scramble.

"Don't die, Home!"

Cannonball. Scramble.

Cannonball. Scramble.

Home jerks and I fall.

Back to my feet. Cannonball.

A thump response.

Cannonball.

Another thump. Yes.

Cannonball.

Another thump. Home's heart answers. Slow beats, but she's alive.

—*Whoa, dude. You are beyond cool, Bri. Shit. Whale CPR.*

Home blasts a spray and breathes in. Sounds of yelling. They better not think hauling this whale out of the water is a way to save me.

I have to find out what's going on.

I've got to get to the blowhole. Pulling my way up the tube. It's super tight.

—I won't fit.

—You're not fat anymore. Get in there, Skinny Ass!

I squiggle up the tight walls to the blowhole. Guess I am Skinny Ass! At the top, I press hard. This hole is sealed tight. I tickle all around it. Maybe I can get Home to breathe by irritating her.

Tickle. Blow on her skin. Pinch bits of flesh.

The blow hole opens wide and I jam an arm up and—Shit, it's cold air! Okay, keep it out there. If I can hold this open, Home won't dive.

More yelling outside.

Pressing up, I slide my head up and ram it through the tight hole into—blinding light. Painful freezer-sharp air.

My eyes can't adjust. Only whiteness with something nearby. Looming. A ship? The whaler? The brightness is too much. Someone yells something.

Above me, I make out a railing on a ship. Figures. The edges get sharper. A rifle points down at us.

I scream, "Stop. I'm here! Don't shoot!"

Several yells in another language.

What was it Liesl taught me? "VENT!" I yell.

The rifle is knocked upwards right as its sharp CRACK sounds.

Home flinches and I pull in a breath, expecting her to dive, but we're pulled closer to the side of the boat.

"Don't you dare!" A voice screams. A familiar voice.

I twist and crane my neck. There's another boat and at the front a woman aims a harpoon gun at the whaling ship screaming, "Get the fuck away from my son!"

Mom found me.

— SHOWDOWN —

IS THAT BRIAN down there? It doesn't look like him, but who else would be in a whale? Maybe there is a whole sub-culture of—

The phone rings around my neck. That's Brian—I have to answer.

"Hello?"

"Hey, Ann. Nate, the Alaska State Trooper, here. Just wanted to let you know I got that girl safely rescued. Jenny wants to say—"

"Nate, the whaling ship harpooned my son's whale and if they pull it up, Brian'll die. Can't talk—" I hang up.

Keeping the harpoon cannon on the killers, I scream at the scruffy head sticking from the blowhole of the whale. "Brian!"

The head grins, his raised arm gives a thumbs up. This man looks nothing like my son. This man is bearded and long-haired and the arm is—muscular. The man yells, "Make them cut the line, Mom! Free Home."

Good god, it is Brian. The voice is his, but so strong. I want to burst into tears but somehow I don't. "Brian, we need to keep the line so we don't lose you!"

"No. I'll get out only when Home is cut free. Tell them!"

"Torsten, tell them to cut the line."

Torsten gets on the megaphone, screaming to the ship as Arthur films.

The men on the whaler argue with each other. I may have a few allies there. I scream to those ones. "My son is in the whale. You can't kill him. If you kill the whale, you murder my son!"

Torsten moves closer to me—I spin the harpoon back to him. He can see I want nothing more than to shoot him.

"They get boy out," Torsten says. "Promise, professional. Lift whale and cut and boy pull out hole."

— LONGITUDE AND LATITUDE —

NATE STEERS with his knee, his headlights sharp against the back of the ambulance carrying Mark. He searches on his phone, the glow lighting his face, then looks to Jenny beside him in the front seat. "Promise you won't ever do what I'm doing. This is an emergency."

"I can hold the steering wheel," Jenny says. "Dad let me sometimes. But only in Alaska because the roads are straight with no traffic."

Nate agrees and Jenny slides close to the trooper and holds the wheel.

Nate opens the Boy-in-the-Whale crowdfunding site. The latest coordinates update the longitude and latitude of the ship. The Nord Spyd is in the kelp forests off the Norwegian Coast.

"Hold this wheel steady, Jenny. Stay right behind your daddy's ambulance. Someone's in trouble far away."

— GOTTA GO —

HOME THRASHES and makes wheezing sounds. This can't be how this ends.

Mom yells across the waves, "Brian, stay there! They'll cut you out from the blowhole."

"That will kill Home, Mom. I won't let it happen."

"These people won't let the whale go. She's already wounded. Please, let them cut you out."

"I'm going back in. If they kill Home, they kill me."

I hear her scream as I pull my arm back inside and drop to the dark, familiar sponge. Home pulls in a great breath. I was clogging her breathing.

"I'm sorry, Home," I say, stroking her lung wall.

I can't let them hurt her. If I stay inside her, will it keep her alive?

— BATTLE —

MY SON SMILED before he pulled himself down, through the blowhole, back into his whale. Is that the last I'll see of him?

The men on the whaling ship seem to be discussing things.

"I'll give you money!" I yell across the waves.

Torsten shakes his head. "Whale more money."

A man on the whaler ship rotates the harpoon toward the thrashing whale.

325

I spin my harpoon cannon to aim at the whaling ship. "You shoot and I'll shoot you!"

The men on the boat freeze. I'll keep this aimed and—

Torsten pulls my arm from the harpoon gun. God damn him! "Arthur! He's trying to stop me!"

Arthur moves closer, filming it all. "Torsten, you interfere and everyone will know. It's all gonna be in the documentary. You want to be the bad guy in the movie?"

Torsten drops his hands from me and I aim the harpoon back at the whaling ship.

"Tell them I'll shoot."

I glare at Torsten and he grabs a megaphone and calls out to the ship, yelling in Norwegian.

I look across the waves. The men on the whaling boat are having a discussion while my son's whale trashes against the harpoon rope.

One of them points at us. Counting? Surely they aren't calculating something like profit-versus-murder. The crazy woman with the harpoon, the documentary filmmaker, and the Navy SEAL. Likely Torsten would side with the whalers. Do they count the boy in the whale? Probably not. To them, he's already dead.

Across the waves, another harpoon gun is brought on the deck of the whaling ship. And rifles.

The Navy SEAL mumbles "shit" and disappears downstairs. He's abandoning us.

The harpoon cannons and rifles turn away from the thrashing whale and point at the Nord Spyd. A sharp blast and a harpoon flies and—BAM!—explosion rocks the side of our boat!

I drop to my knees. Should I fire my harpoon? How long does it take to reload? Will we have time—

WHAM! Another harpoon explosion hits us, blasting a hole in the back of the bridge. Fuck!

I aim the harpoon. I've no idea how this works, but might as well try. Pull the trigger. The harpoon flies from the cannon and explodes against the side of their ship. It leaves a black mark, but no damage.

Torsten dives next to me and empties the spent shell from the harpoon cannon. He reaches down to a case and so I can learn, I bend to watch him and—PING—a sharp ring hits the metal where my head was! They're shooting at us! Arthur, Torsten, and I dive flat on the deck as bullets fly over us. This can't be happening!

— NOISES OUTSIDE —

SOUNDS OF EXPLOSIONS. But it doesn't feel like Home was hit again. If they're not shooting at Home, what would that explosion be? Are the ships firing at each other? Did Mom just start an international war?

I could try to crawl up and look, but they may read that as me being okay with getting cut out. Maybe I could swim out of Home's mouth and pull the harpoon from her. Probably not. Home would have pulled it from herself if that was possible. I can't do anything. I can't help.

All I can do is sing to comfort her. Tell her I'm here and I'm not going to leave her.

I start with The Lullaby Song.

— OUT OF THE MIST —

ARTHUR STOMACH-CRAWLS across the deck to get a better shot of me being terrified. Another harpoon explodes against the Nord Spyd. There must be water getting in somewhere because we're tilting severely. Unfortunately, we're tilting toward the whaler, making us easier targets. Bullets hit the wood railing sheltering us. We'll sink or get shot or both!

A buffeting noise grows. What now!? Wind pulls my hair as a roaring military helicopter zooms low over us, a loudspeaker broadcasting commands in Norwegian. The shooting stops as a two more helicopters roar in to hover over the whaling ship.

Peeking up, I see the whalers waving papers at the helicopter. Permits? Do they have permits to kill people?

A blue inflatable boat speeds in front of our ship. Greenpeace? Where the hell did they come from? The newcomers in orange jackets yell at the whaler. Another smaller helicopter arrives, news logo on the side. And another. And three more inflatables.

A racing boat circles us. Beyond it, several more boats converging on us. Small, large, even a sailboat. Still filming, Arthur moves his eye from his camera and smiles at me. "Someone called the cavalry!"

Every person in every boat is yelling and filming with their phones. The whalers lower their rifles and turn away the harpoons. Cheers rise above the waves.

I know what Brian wants me to do. I know I have to do it even if it means I won't see him again. I swallow a sob and yell to the whaler ship. "Cut the rope. Let the whale free!"

Chants start in Norwegian. I guess they're screaming, "Cut the rope. Let the whale free!" or something like it. The whalers confer and then—they cut the line.

The gathering of ships and boats honk, ring bells, and cheer.

And the whale sinks out of sight.

The whale sinks, taking Brian with her.

All that's left are the red waves.

— GOODBYE —

WHATEVER HAPPENED, Home isn't attached anymore and we're going down. We may be going down to die.

If we are going down, I've got to get out before we swim far from the ship. I grab the Ziploc—*Goodbye, Wrigglers!*—dump them out the flap and reach far into the tube—feel around—there it is!—the Navy SEAL rope.

Deep, deep breath and I glance at Amelia nestled with Sprout in the waterproof phone-case around my neck. Suck in a bit more air and there's no time to think or get misty as I slide out of my home, pull on the rope, up through blackness, hand over hand, up into the wide mouth. I feel up to the barb holding the rope, yank it out, and slide around on the massive tongue. Home heaves and the mouth opens as a mass of hot stomach mess hurls up and carries me out with it.

Out into freezing water. The cold is a shock but I don't let myself breathe. Drop the barb and the rope. Above is light, but it's a long way off. Maybe I'll make it. I won't think about breathing. I'm a non-breather. My feet flap calmly and carry me up. Red swirls spiral around me. I look down and see blood trails coming from that massive dark form dropping into the blackness and then—nothing. Home is gone. Grief hits me as hard as when the whale-watching boat got rammed off Catalina. Home is gone. The one home I really had. Where I became me. Goodbye. If I'm crying, it's blending with the sea.

Kick toward the light, but now that Home is gone I'm not sure it matters. Anyway, I'm too far down. I won't make it. No matter how much breathing practice I've had. I might as well give up and let the cold and water take me, like it took Home.

— NO MORE —

THE BOATS AND SHIPS and helicopters are circling and swirling, people film the horrible whaler as it turns away from the scene. They cheer and honk and ring bells but what are they celebrating? There's nothing happy here. Brian is lost.

That little smile he gave before sliding back into the blowhole was the last I'll see of him. The last of Brian. His whale is sinking to the bottom.

Arthur films the ships and boats and protestors, but there's a slope to his shoulders that wasn't there. He glances up from the lens at me, tears overflowing. He's thinking the same thoughts. This will be a sad—not happy—ending movie.

I dial the whale cellphone number. The one we sent in with the oranges. It rings. That means there is a signal. It's ringing in the whale's lungs. Can I actually say goodbye to my son? Will I be able to stand it, knowing we'll never see each other again?

The phone rings and rings. What does that mean? Did the whale already die and stop filling its lungs with air? If the whale is dead, then is Brian dead? Maybe he's suffocating right now. Can't even manage to whisper goodbye.

I stare at the waves, churned by all these boats and motors.

The cheers and horns and bells stop. The truth is dawning on everyone. This is a tragedy and they all know it. It's been too long for any positive outcome. The waves rock us and I stare and stare as my knees weaken and my heart shatters.

As the tears form salty seas in my eyes, I whisper to the depths, "Goodbye."

— MY RECORD BREAKING BREATH —

THE LAST OF MY AIR. I look down at Amelia in my phone container. Six minutes, forty-eight seconds. This is my personal best. A record breaker, but no one will know.

There are shadows of things above me, all sorts of shapes and sizes. Ships? Sharks? No matter, I won't make it up that far. This is it. Can't hold my breath any longer. I wonder if it will hurt to pull in cold water into my lungs. Even if it does, it shouldn't last long.

Goodbye life. I'm glad I got to know me—

I'm nudged hard from below.

Is that Home?

I turn and the calf is there, pushing me upward.

I grab hold of a fin and cling on, and we're speeding up and moving between all these shadows and the light is brighter and sunlight makes cathedral rays in the green water and closer and up and—bursting out, a fountain of vapor and breath of stinging air! I'm alive! Home's baby blasts a geyser beside me. In the dazzling brightness, there are boats everywhere. What party have I interrupted?

A motor revs beside me and Baby jerks and disappears. Did the motor get it?! Someone's yelling in another language as the boats swirl closer. They need to get back! Where is Baby?!

"BRIAN!"

I turn toward the sound—still too bright to see but I know that voice. "MOM!"

There's a scream and splashing and arms clutch me, stinging my freezing skin, kisses all over my face. A hissing-whir from above as two scuba men zip down lines from a helicopter and swim toward us. One grabs me and says something in Norwegian and he's got me in a life saver and another has Mom and we're pulled through the waves to a boat. Cheers erupt and bells clang and horns blast all around. They're going to scare Baby and that infant may not come up to breathe!

Up and on the deck, wrapped in blankets. Rubbing and shaking. Someone hugs me as he sticks a camera in my face. Uncle Arthur!

A scuba man adjusts the blanket so it's tucked between my legs and with a few practiced moves, clicks a harness up near Johnson and around my waist. "We take you up," he says, pointing to the hovering helicopter.

I un-click the harness with shaking hands. "I need to check on Baby."

"We take you now. Hospital."

He works to click the harness on me again but Mom steps between us. "He needs to check on Baby. Let him."

I smile at Mom because she isn't acting like Mom at all, and I lie down on the deck close to the waves and sing The Rise Song.

"Torsten, give him your megaphone!" Mom yells at a crusty bearded man that looks like a cliché of a sea captain. He hands me a megaphone. I don't know how it works but I give it a try. I sing The Rise Song to the sea. Grumble-warble, squeaking wagon-wheel, clicking, and gong. I sing it over and over but nothing happens. Maybe Baby got hurt by the motor. Is the blood in the water Baby's?

Everyone in the boats is filming me with their phones and moving closer.

"Move back!" I yell to them with the megaphone. "Be still!"

And they do. The circle around us grows wide and calm and silent. I sing again.

Nothing.

Tremors shake my body. I'm freezing. Sing again.

"Let's go." The scuba man says, pulling on my shoulder. "Nothing here."

Mom grabs the man's hand. "My son will be ready when he's ready." She sounds like she means it. He lets go of me.

Grumble-warble, squeaking wagon-wheel, clicking, and gong.

The sea rolls. The ships in the wide circle bob gently. No sign of any whale.

Maybe Baby dove down to be with Home at the bottom of the sea.

Grumble-warble, squeaking wagon-wheel, clicking, and gong. Please, Baby. Please.

A blast of spray shoots into the air. A small-curling back. It's Baby! I need to tell it things are okay so I sing The Lullaby Song. It moves close and I reach out. Baby slides its long body against my hand.

"Are you alright, Baby?"

I don't see any torn flesh. Baby looks fine.

A massive geyser of spray explodes in front of Baby, showering us all. Home! The barnacled back curls and arches, going on forever. Baby slides beside, under the long fin. The back continues and continues. The wound from the harpoon in its side is ragged, but the bleeding has stopped. Maybe Home will be okay.

I sing the new Hello/Goodbye Song. Home circles our boat slowly, staying on the surface, and when she returns to where I lie, she rolls to her side. Her eye emerges from the water and looks at me. A huge mournful, loving eye. Ancient. It must have seen everything there is to life.

"Thank you, Home. Thank you."

Home sings a mix of The Rise Song and something else and then "riiiiiii-aaaaaannnnnn." The two-note song I know is my name.

She rolls and blasts another geyser. She arches away from the boat and dives, her tail rising as if to wave, before slicing into the water and disappearing.

Baby echoes the movement and vanishes after its mother.

Maybe they'll be okay. I'm going to believe they will be.

As I get up, Mom puts her arms around me and the scuba man gets busy with my harness.

"Brian!" Uncle Arthur yells and I turn to see Home leaping from the waves, a mountain of grey—rising into the air and spinning—an exuberant salute. To me? I want to say yes. It's to us, to joy and life and love and friendship. The great beast flies—a weightless miracle spinning over the sea—curls—and smashes into the water, sending a tsunami—bobbing all the boats—and—with a flamboyant flip of her tail—disappears into the depths.

— CIRCLE OF SHIPS —

NONE OF THE BOATS or news helicopters or ships want to leave. They all keep honking and ringing bells.

The scuba man insists now, re-clipping the harness around Brian.

"You'll take me with him as well," I say.

"Don't worry, Mom. If they try to fly without you, I'll jump."

They raise my son toward the hovering helicopter. I'm not even nervous about him dangling overhead. He's survived living in a whale!

Brian grins down at me. I can't get over how he's changed. There is no panic or shame in his eyes. His voice and stance and gaze are unbelievable. He's a man.

Arthur grins as he films. Like me, he got the ending he wanted.

My phone rings and I leap to answer, still weirdly hoping it will be my son. It's Nate.

"Are you okay? Did the Norwegian Coast Guard come?"

"*You* sent in the cavalry!"

"Did it work?"

"Yes. Brian's out and safe and the whale and her baby are and—thank you!"

"So glad. I'll let you get back to him." And he hangs up.

I file away his consideration to think about later. The second scuba man fits a harness on me and I give Torsten a final glare as I'm pulled into the air. Rising, the Nord Spyd looks so small and the ocean so big.

In the helicopter, I move next to Brian, so our legs are touching. Making it real.

"You don't look like you, Brian."

"I'm not him anymore," he says. "And you don't look like you either, Mom."

"Guess we're going to have to get to know each other."

This man, my son, smiles at me through his scraggly beard. "I'm not going back to Burbank, Mom."

"Neither am I. I sold the house. Besides, it never was a home."

Brian chuckles. I don't know how much to say, but maybe saying things doesn't matter. He's alive. I squeeze the top of his strong hand, even though I know he hates that. He doesn't pull away but turns his hand belly-up to squeeze mine. I want to hug him and kiss him and eat him and pinch him and shake him and yet below that, there's something else. Something I know. He's not mine anymore. And, really, I'm not his. I'm mine. Unbelievably.

The helicopter tilts, heading for the coastline. Brian closes his eyes. Probably too much to take in. I don't know what he'll do next. Don't know that he does either. Don't know what I'll do next, but maybe, since I'm in traveler mode, and acclimated to cold weather, I'll head to Alaska.

— SPEAKING —

SPROUT is in the open crack of the hotel curtains, soaking up the sights of Oslo. He loves the sun! I can't handle it like he can. I've got him in a coffee mug that Mom filled with dirt. He's five inches tall. Shot up the minute he saw light. Turned on Mom's laptop to find out what Sprout is, but I couldn't take it, the pull of it, the sickness it leaves, so she looked him up for me. Found out he's a Medicago polymorpha or Bur Clover. He may not be a four-leaf-clover but I'm lucky to have him.

Thought Mom wouldn't spring for a private hotel room for me. She did. Mom's been very cool about giving me space and not hovering. She's really different.

Everything is so weird. I can't take being around a lot of people. There's too much noise and chaos. I miss the one constant sound of Home's drumming heart below me. My first meal, after lots of water, didn't go as expected. The smell of the hamburger and fries sent me to the bathroom. The pizza came but looked like a thick round newspaper with wood-chips and grease and stains. I had to order sashimi. It went down like usual, only not as fresh.

My skin is super dry. I need to stay in the bathroom with the shower running and the lights off. I don't know how to be comfortable. Clothes and furniture and carpet and floor and sheets and walls and switches and knobs are all so artificial. Everything smells like cleaner or disinfectant or car exhaust. It's hard to breathe the fumes.

I feel sad and want to see Home, but I know that isn't going to happen. We're apart now.

Liesl and her mom and dad came by my room. The dad thanked me but you could see he was suspicious about what I did alone in a whale with his daughter. Liesl was all clean and chirpy and had her hair done and didn't look like the Liesl in Home. I didn't even get wood. We hugged but it was weird and not like it was. That's okay. Nothing ever is like it was.

Uncle Tobey flew over right away. He was really apologetic about something. Wouldn't stop saying he was sorry and so glad Mom didn't listen to him. I told him it was okay.

Uncle Arthur is ecstatic about the distribution bidding war for his not-even-finished film. Dad called and was nervous-sounding and said he was happy and all, but couldn't fly to Norway right now, and I knew the score and so I said something like *see-ya-'round* and *gotta go* and put him out of his misery. That's over.

My uncles shopped for clothes for today's event. Uncle Tobey suggested a suit jacket with the collared and cuffed shirt. Mom talked him out of that, so I'm in jeans and a T-shirt and sweatshirt. Even these are uncomfortable. Stiff and scratchy.

Put on Amelia. Listen to her tick. I don't want to shave or do some hair thing. This is who they get. Me.

Staring at Sprout, I can almost see him growing. He's got scraggly leaves. Then he'll make little yellow flowers and more burs.

—*You're growing, too, Brian.*

—*Yeah, but I'm scared.*

—*Scared is okay.*

Someone's at the door. Look at Amelia, who says it's time. I open it to Mom.

"Brian, you don't have to do this if you don't want to."

"I want to. It's important."

I give a glance to Sprout and step out into the carpet tunnel with Mom. Lights hum. Smells of purple and yellow. Reach for Mom's hand. She jerks—surprised—and squeezes. It's good to touch.

We push the button in the elevator and as we drop sharply, Mom sucks in air.

"That was nothing," I whisper.

She bursts out laughing and it spills over me and I'm part of it and the doors open to cameras and people and it's time for a show.

Flashes pop all over me as I sit down at the table in front of several microphones. In the front row, Mom smiles big and Uncle Tobey beams beside her. I scan the packed room and find Uncle Arthur. He waves from behind his lens, filming along with the multitude of Press cameras. I shift and the crowd gets quiet.

"I—"

—*Shit that's loud! Back away.*

My heart is really doing a dance. Will it give out now? It can't. I've got things to say.

—*Go ahead, Brian. You can do it. You survived me. You've got this.*

Deep breath. Hold for twenty as the cameras click away. Amelia's on my wrist. Home is blasting air somewhere. Let it out slow and start…

"I—I'm going to speak English. I've learned a few words in Norwegian, but not enough for a Press conference."

I give a little smile and hundreds of cameras click and flash.

—*Breathe.*

"I know you have a lot of questions. You wanna know what happened in the whale's lungs. How I survived. What Liesl and I did to pass the time."

The audience laughs. More flashing. Shit, this is too much. Pull in another breath and hold it. I pretend to rub my ear with my wrist so I can hear Amelia's ticking. Let out the breath…

"What did I do? We do? It was where I lived. I did the same stuff you all do. Ate. Slept. Worried. Hatched plans. Cleaned house. Fought. Made up. Exercised. Got food. Watered the plant. Learned. Sang. Changed."

"Details may come later, but right now, no questions. Sorry. I'm just gonna make a statement."

I can feel they want more. Makes me feel guilty but, fuck that, it's not gonna happen.

"First, thank you—to all the people that contributed to me getting out. I don't call it saving me, because actually Home, my whale, saved me. But thank you. You helped bring me back into this world. Really, it wasn't me you helped. You helped that one person, who never gave up on me, find my whale and see both whale and me, safe. My mom. Thank you, Mom."

Look at her. She's such a different person, but I've got her crying.

"I want to say another thing. I lived in a whale and it was my whole world, my home. I even named her Home. If I didn't treat Home well, she would die—and if she died, I died. But Home nurtured me and protected me and—I love her."

Oh shit. Now it's happening to me. Mom and me both.

—*It's what people do, Bri. Keep going.*

"This place—this little spec in the stars—nurtures us and protects us. We need to love it. It's the only home we have, and if we destroy it, we're committing suicide."

I sound like a professor or talking head.

—You sound like you. You sound great. This is super important.

"Okay, listen. This is super important. There are *no* reasons to kill whales. None. They are magnificent, intelligent, loving beings and killing them is murder. Stop killing whales! These are my friends. I'll get in front of any harpoon that's aimed at one of my friends. You want to know what is next for me? I'm going to devote my life to making sure *not one more* of my friends is killed."

Everyone claps and cheers. Do Press people do that?

—They're listening, Bri. You tell them.

I put my hands up and the crowd becomes silent, just like in the movies.

"We aren't alone in the world. We're all connected. Even when we're—disconnected."

Mom nods. She gets that one.

Silence. They're waiting. Waiting for me.

"We all need saving and we can all save each other. It's up to each of us—to save each other—and everything on this earth—every single day. Thank you."

—Great fucking job, Bri!

— BALANCE —

BOTTLE, ITS BELLY COMPLETE with Library Card and Punctured Dollar Bill, jiggles in the Alaska State Trooper's cruiser.

Had Bottle ears, it might hear Nate tell Ann that Mark is on his meds and getting care in a Missouri facility and that Jenny sent her father a dog tag with his name and her home address etched on it, "In case you get lost."

Bottle might hear Ann ask about Jenny's desire to be a veterinarian and Nate ask about Brian's whale protection foundation.

Beside them, in the front seat of the cruiser, had Bottle a way of judging temperature it might notice the heat flowing from these two tingling bodies.

Had Bottle eyes it might notice these people blatantly looking at each other—with *yes*.

Had Bottle skin and blood it might blush as the cruiser comes to a stop in the parking lot of the Igloo Motor Court.

And, as Bottle and Library Card and Punctured Dollar Bill are cradled into the Igloo, as they are placed on the low bureau next to the plastic ice bucket below the television, and are promptly forgotten, they might feel something approximating peace. They might feel as if a conclusion has been reached. Closure or balance.

And as Ann and Nate find each other, as they laugh and are awakened, if Bottle could wonder, it might imagine the whale far across the seas.

Might imagine those great lungs clearing and the wound in Home's side healing.

Might imagine the whale mother and child, curling and dancing in the deep, singing to each other.

And here in the Igloo Motor Court, as love blossoms on the bed, Bottle might cheer all we fearful, brave beings who stumble face-first into the wonder of life.

THE END

Made in the USA
Las Vegas, NV
06 October 2023

78663810R00203